The Tier

Josh Berg

PRODUCTIONS

The Tier

Copyright © 2015 by Josh Berg

Cover art by Daniel Tyka

Edited by Eva Whitmore

Published in Canada by

Lonely Titan Productions

http://www.LonelyTitan.com

ISBN: 978-0-9949794-1-4

Acknowledgements

For my dear sweet mother, whose patience, generosity and kindness transformed me into a gentle monster, and for my good friend Chris Spence who had to deal with that monster's neurosis while making this book happen.

Table of Contents

Errant Realms

The world of Errant Realms is a discordant futuristic place dotted with fantastical mega-cities that seethe with diverse and enigmatic beings, road-warrior brigands, powerful magics, volatile deities, ravenous monsters and even more ravenous corporations. Banding together in vast cultural stews, the more civilized races, including Humans, Elves, Dwarves, Halflings, Gnomes, Orcs, Goblins, Ogres and Minotaurs, create sprawling and exciting urban centers filled with unique religions, styles, perceptions, conflicts and intrigues. On the fringes of these settlements, the wilderness is overwrought with strange tribal cultures, deadly mutants, horrendous spirits and nearly invincible dragons. Meanwhile thousands of bewildering denizens constantly seep in from foreign and often hostile dimensions. In the unseen corners of the world, the billions of semi-sentient nanobots that inhabit the planet seek to emulate the animals, monsters and peoples that surround them. The resulting panoply of automatons range from packs of metallic wolves to giant automaton ants to sleek composite robotic businessmen. These merciless constructs re-create the natural habits of the creatures they resemble, often resulting in unfortunately bloody encounters and particularly heartless business meetings. In urban centers powerful and influential gangs vie for control of the slums while the stalwart forces of good and order fight against the tide of a seemingly unwinnable war.

Interlaced amongst the base construction of most urban centers, the electronic node-way of the internet weave creates a digital landscape overlay that can be accessed by those with the proper technology. In this electronic virtual space everything from street directions to the star rating of a nearby restaurant to a giant glowing pink whale can be rendered and set within the virtual geography, allowing it to appear in the physical world where the creator desires. Second cities and towns spring up in these places not constrained by the usual laws of physics and reality, making for many profoundly interesting digital locales. Surging through this dynamic alter-world, skilled hackers create software monsters and hardware strongholds, constantly surrounded by all of the extraneous visualized oddness of this collectively created electronic consciousness.

In stark contrast to the dangers of the slums, corporate enclaves which house countless wage-slaves are shining miracles of form and function offering both security and servitude to those who crave such things. These fortified corporate arcologies are often formed into massive multi-tiered pyramids that contain all of the goods and services that the residents could ever need. Every nook and cranny of these cutting-edge living spaces is filled with ultra high-end technologies and hyper-stylized cultural accoutrements while private corporate armies await to swat down all those who would dare to threaten their lifestyles.

The Six Alternate Realms

While most average citizens of the world are only familiar with the Material realm that they see and interact with, Errant Realms borders with six other known alternate dimensions or "realms". While five of these realms are actual alternate dimensions with unique geographical properties and even more unique inhabitants, the sixth is known as the spirit realm. This bewildering surreal place overlaps the material realm and can be seen and interacted with by any creature who has the power to do so. The other dimensions are usually accessed through the use of powerful spells, but at times a traveler can find and access a naturally occurring gate or portal that leads to one of these alternate dimensions.

Tirileth City

This colossal patchwork hive city is surrounded by a sprawling shadow-shrouded neighborhood. A wondrous construction, "The Tier", is twenty-eight miles across at its base. It rises more than two miles into the sky and it's one mile across at its pinnacle. The lower stretches of the city burrow thousands of feet beneath ground level. A reinforced amalgamation consisting of forty different levels interspersed with world renowned constructions and locations, "The Tier", as it's known by the locals,

2

is literally stacked with exclusive culture. The hyper-expensive Koshikawa skymall hovers as a shining globe that floats just above the top level, while the ominous solid obsidian walls of the black tower sit as a symbol of the punishment that awaits any corporate transgressor. In the city's core, the impossible temple of Zool remains to this day as an infamous puzzle, while "Dante's Inferno" nightclub offers nine levels of depravity for the corporate zombie and street creeper alike. Further down, deep beneath the streets, the chambers of the forgotten dead teem with wretched shambling monsters, while the mighty war dragon Grognoraxoth looms in the murk of his great lair, a dread reminder of how the city could erupt into violence at any moment.

Tunneling up through the core of this great city is the most notorious of areas known simply as "the Warrens". Subject of hundreds (if not thousands) of holo-vids, songs and VR games, the very mention of the Warrens of "The Tier" elicits images of fierce close-quarters combat, high intensity free running, and dark sunless ruins filled with strange and dangerous monstrosities. This infamous area occupies hundreds of blocks through an estimated ten to fifteen levels; some of the lowest portions of the Warrens remain unexplored and aren't officially mapped or documented. This part of "The Tier" is by far the most dangerous area in the city and more than four hundred gangs and countless other underworld operators occupy the hotly contested regions therein. Marshalls and enforcement officers only travel to some parts of the Warrens if they are in force, and even then only if it's a serious emergency. Local murders are rarely if ever investigated. Most sections of the Warrens are made from a mixture of ancient structures, new construction, modified buildings and bracing pieces designed to hold the entire mess together. Convenience stores built in old castle walls, and apartment blocks springing up around medieval turrets, are commonplace, as stairs, ladders and bridges serve as connecting points. The passages of this place can be profoundly confusing and disorienting to the uninitiated, as at times even the internet weave within the Warrens is hacked and altered to mislead anyone not intimately familiar with the terrain. Native predators (both humanoid and monstrous) will use this fact to their advantage, striking at their intended mark and vanishing before reprisal. Murders, muggings and assaults are common in the Warrens, and in many neighborhoods gun fights won't even slow down commerce. It's widely believed that anything at all can be bought in the Warrens. From automaton slaves to micro-nukes and everything in between, often found within the great crime mall and the black markets that litter the lower levels.

Eric Gibson

I think there might be two things in the world that I like more than Jenny Miller's breasts, but I can't for the life of me remember what they are at the moment. Breathing? Yeah, that's one of them. That's good enough for now. Damn it man, be discreet. I think she almost saw me looking that time. No wait, you'd have to notice that someone exists in order to see them. In that case I'm lamentably safe. Though knowing my brand of luck she'll end up noticing me for that reason and that reason alone, like Murphy's razor or whatever. What did Mr. Jansen say? Something about cells and cellular processes … I'd like to have a cellular process with Jenny. Introduce her nucleus to my mitochondria, or something. I quickly glance at the clock, still two torturous hours to go. My slow countdown to freedom. Of course "freedom" is a relative term when you're trapped in butt-fuck nowhere, small town Canada. The choices of life condensed into a series of uninspiring channels: fucking, drinking, fighting, hockey. I shudder at the various prospects, tinged respectively by anxiety, apathy, indifference and horror, in turn. Matt's having a party tonight; it may grant an opportunity for the first three activities anyway. Maybe someone will bring some pot. That would be a nice change of pace.

"Hey man. Check this out." Jordan leans over and angles his phone towards me. I look over just in time to see a tiny video of some kid trying a rail slide with his skateboard and failing, badly. Jordan laughs. "That was Mike," he says knowingly.

"Mike Friesen?" I ask.

"Yup, you notice that he's not in school today?" Jordan tilts back to his spot, herded there by the venomous glares of Mr. Jansen.

I wait a half-beat then whisper, "When was this, last night?"

"Yeah, we went to the bank and tried the rails there," Jordan says. He skates, he's not bad either. With help from his brother he even made a ply-wood half-pipe that now occupies a place of honour beside their parents' garage. "I sent you an email last night with the video attached, didn't you see it?" Jordan whispers back. Somewhere in the background, Mr. Jansen is trying in vain to describe the process of cellular mitosis; a sea of vapid stares greets his efforts.

I look towards Jordan and say, "I must have missed it. Are you going to Matt's tonight? His parents are going out of town."

"Yeah, for sure, stole a bottle of wine from my folks," Jordan says. He grins and looks back at his phone. I'll have to get some booze for tonight too. I might be able to grab a beer or three if dad just opened a new two-four, otherwise I'll have to see if Jordan's brother would be willing to pick up a twelve for me.

"Would your brother be able to buy me booze?" I ask during the next interval in Mr. Jansen's attention.

"No, sorry, he's in the city this weekend," Jordan retorts, eyes glued to his phone. Well there goes plan B. I could ask Lisa if her sister could pick it up but …

"What about Lisa's sister?" Jordan says, sensing my thoughts.

"Lisa's been acting weird lately," I whisper back.

"Mr. Gibson, I would appreciate if you could pay attention," Mr. Jansen announces, his standard first warning. It's still a little while before he actually gets pissed off though.

"Yeah," I mumble. Jordan just looks back to his phone. I pick up my mechanical pencil and pretend to take notes while I actually sketch. The first challenge of the night is before me then, the finding of booze or some type of individual who could facilitate the acquisition of the same. Second (and very distant) challenge of tonight: talk to Jenny in a manner that doesn't result in me wanting to hurl myself bodily into a wood chipper. I truly believe that this is possible. I just have to find the right combination of intoxication, bravado and semi-delusional thought. A new brain would help too. Previous conversations have nearly caused me to march off despairingly into the wilderness to be feasted upon by wild animals. Tonight will be different though, I can feel it.

The rest of the school day crawls by. I decide not to ask Lisa if her sister will buy me booze, instead hoping that I can grab something from my house. Matt, Jordan, Colin White and I flee from the building as though it were on fire when the final bell rings. We exit into the parking lot and pile into Jordan's shitty Sunfire. I call shotgun so Matt and Colin are forced into the anemic confines of the back seat.

"So looks like Mike's arm is busted in two places," announces Colin as we get under way. Being the only one who owns a digital video camera of any quality, I assume that Colin was the film's author.

"Is he home now?" Jordan asks while turning out of the parking lot and accelerating in the process.

"Yeah he got a cast and went home," Colin replies.

"Fucking idiot," Matt opines. Jordan laughs and continues to accelerate, taking the familiar streets that lead to Matt's house.

"When do your parents leave?" I ask. The car jostles, slows perceptibly, then makes a hard right.

"They're already gone, they left this morning. I wouldn't have gone to school today but if I miss again I'm suspended," Matt replies before lighting a smoke with his Zippo.

Jordan turns up Matt's street and asks, "So is Mike coming out tonight?"

"Don't think so. He says he's got some codeine and he's just going to get zapped and stay in," Colin replies.

Jordan mulls on that for a moment that says, "I could pick him up if he wants, think I should text him?"

"For sure, see what he thinks," Colin says. We pull into Matt's driveway, tiny weeds poking through the gaps in the brickwork.

"Is anybody else coming in now?" Matt asks as we perform the disembarking maneuver, consisting of me getting out and pulling the passenger seat forward. The sharp stink of tobacco smoke greets me as Matt exits the car.

"I got to go home first," I say.

"Yeah, I have to grab that bottle of wine from my place," Jordan says. Colin slides his narrow frame across the back seat and out of the open door. Matt nods and heads for the house's side entrance with Colin following closely behind him. I re-adjust the seat and climb back into the car. "Is there anything that you have to do at home?" Jordan asks as we pull out of the driveway.

"Just shower and change, then try to snag some booze if possible," I say. Jordan nods.

"Okay, then I'll go by my place first, then we'll head to your place and I can chill while you shower and shit. Oh yeah, we have to pick up Sarah too," Jordan says. I nod and watch some scenery pass. I hope that Lisa doesn't come tonight. Talking with any other girls would be so much easier if she wasn't lurking in the shadows like some kind of sexual gorgon. Sarah's kind of hot, but I think she's into Matt. Jenny's super hot, but she's into anyone that's not me. This leaves the potential options for fraternization as Lisa, Megan and Heather, all hot in their own way. Lisa and I were going out about a year ago. I get the feeling that she wants to get involved with Jordan. It's just the fact that Jordan and I are good friends that keeps her at bay. The awkwardness would be too much for any of us to bear. Jordan and I shoot the shit as he drives to his place. Jordan lives about two minutes outside of town, brand new house, tons of vehicles. We pull up to the garage, the edge of the battered half-pipe jutting out from around its corner.

"I'll be right back." Jordan puts the car in park and turns off the engine. He then proceeds to twist the key backwards a small way to activate the radio. I flip through the stations briefly before settling on the classic rock station. Zepplin, Kashmir. I sit back and rock slowly to the rhythm. I'm anxious for some reason, it's not the party either. Most of Matt's shindigs involve the same twenty-five people, more or less. Maybe it's Lisa, our last interaction was slightly hostile on both of our parts. God I hope she isn't there tonight, of course she's probably thinking the exact same thing. Maybe this brooding anxiety is about the booze factor, the uncertainty of its acquisition is often a concern for those in my position. It's best to just try and ignore it for now. I spend five minutes waiting in the silky womb of Kashmir before Jordan returns to the wheel, new clothes on and wine-filled back pack in tow.

"Mike texted back, he's just staying at home tonight," Jordan says, as we begin driving to my house, he then adds, "and Sarah's getting a ride with Heather so we don't have to pick her up either."

I nod and say, "Cool, maybe I'll just change and try to get some booze when we get to my place. You can just chill in the car." I open the passenger-side window and let in a rush of warm spring air. The dulcet tones of "fat-bottomed girl" mix with the chorus of fast-moving air as we speed up the highway leading back into town.

We make it to my house in record time. Jordan likes to cut loose when he's driving, it can be frightening at times.

"Okay I'll be right back," I say as I leave the car. The mental preparations begin as I launch my domestic campaign of vestment alteration and alcohol liberation. My ingress will be through the side door, then a crafty descent to the basement, hopefully without eliciting too much attention. I brace the outer screen door against my knee, open the inner door and begin. The descent is rapid and quiet. I then stop briefly at the bottom. "Hey mom, just changing and dropping some stuff off. Then I'm going out with Jordan." I then immediately proceed to the basement storeroom fridge. A muddled response comes from upstairs. I'll shout something back in a second. First I deftly open the fridge and prepare for the alcohol extraction. Eighteen beer are inside, he won't miss two. I just have to return the empties. I expertly retrieve the bottles and instantly nestle them into the confines of my back pack. I can notice that the anxiety abates slightly. I head back to the stairs, as soon as my backpack's secure. "What?" I shout from the base of the stairs.

"I just said, 'Hi how was school?'" my mom responds, obviously standing in the kitchen near the side entrance landing.

"Fine, did you hear me before? I'm heading out with Jordan right away, okay?" I reiterate.

"Yeah sure, I was going to make pizza for supper tonight," she offers.

"It's fine, I'll get something while we're out," I say, while picking out a suitable shirt, pants, underwear combo.

"Alright, have fun," she says before returning to the living room, I nod at nothing in particular, but don't respond. A few moments later and I'm newly dressed, armed with two beers, and flush with around twenty-two bucks, all the vital ingredients for a mediocre night.

I lope back to the Sunfire and we get on our way. Jordan has his Mp3 player hooked to the radio. He's playing a selection of metal and hard rock, and by the time we're back at Matt's place "Ramble on" is just finishing up, another Zepplin classic. It looks like Ron Klassen is here, which means that Steve Anderson is here too, that big obnoxious bastard. We got in a fight two years ago and he's been a dick ever since. He split my lip and I gave him a black eye, I can still imagine the adrenalin surging through my veins. I shake my head. He can be ignored, if it's needed, and I can always hang out in the backyard near the fire pit.

"Alright, let's see what's happening. Maybe we can get in on a beer run," Jordan announces. He then exits the sloppily parked Sunfire. I step onto the lawn. Dead patches indicate where Matt's dog has relieved himself repeatedly, despite every effort to dissuade him. Nature will find a way, as Jeff Goldblum would say.

"We should walk to the pit after we get all fucked up," I suggest as we approach the house.

"Not much point if we got the house to ourselves though," Jordan shoots back.

I shrug and respond, "Yeah, I guess not, just something else to do later on." The pit is little more than a gathering of trees around a small pond. A picnic table was brought there years ago and now it serves as a sort of ad hoc meeting spot. Maybe I'm just feeling nostalgic. I've had some good times at the pit. Including the first time I smoked pot. I got so baked that I tried to climb one of the smaller trees. I soon ended up falling rather unceremoniously into the pond. Try explaining that to your parents. Stoned, soaking wet and stinking of beer at ten in the evening, not even a cloud in the sky. We reach the house and Jordan is about to barge in when the door swings inward.

"Gentlemen, ready to get fucked up?" Matt poses the rhetorical question then leaves the door open for us. We follow him up the stairs from the side entrance landing into the house's spacious living room. Ron and Steve are already parked on one of the couches, a fresh beer in each of their respective hands. Colin is entombed in the overstuffed armchair that sits in one of the room's corners. The large flat screen is showing a UFC fight. In place of the regular sounds of men pummeling each other are the desperately aggressive tones of some new punk band. Matt loves his punk bands. Jordan and I nod to Colin, Ron and Steve, who respond in kind. Steve seems engrossed in the match, no threat there, yet. "You guys bring booze or what?" Matt asks, while walking through the living room to the kitchen. We follow, crossing in front of the TV just as one of the fighters shoots to take down the other fighter. The defender barely manages to stay on his feet by splaying out his legs and sinking down his hips.

"I got a bottle of wine and Eric's got a couple of beer," Jordan offers, I just nod.

"You got cash? We're supposed to make a beer run when Jason and his brother get here," Matt says casually. Oblivious to the alcohol acquisition issues that I've been facing, I should have asked him earlier on, but I didn't think he was on speaking terms with Jason. I guess a lot can happen in a day.

"Yeah, that would be sweet, pick me up a twelve of Moosehead, bottles," I say, and hand Matt my cash. He grabs it and nods, then opens the fridge, revealing a random cross section of food. The fridge also contains about a dozen brown bottles, one of which he removes and greedily opens. I take a page from Matt's book (or bible in his case) and retrieve one of my pilfered beers. I then put my backpack down near the walk-in pantry. Meanwhile, Jordan's hunting through the kitchen's many drawers, looking for a corkscrew so that he can enjoy his prize, red wine. That doesn't bode well for Jordan; if he mixes he'll get sick for sure, it happens every time. "So it's just wine tonight then Jordan?" I ask, somewhat sardonically. He scowls and continues to search for the corkscrew.

"Where the fuck is your corkscrew man?" He then turns to me and says, "For your information it's not mixing that makes me sick, it's because I drink too much." I let out a guffaw and crack the top of my beer, an eruption of foam greeting my efforts.

"Shit," I say as I quickly clasp my mouth over the bottle top and move to the sink, trailing beer as I go.

Matt laughs then exclaims "First party foul of the night goes to Eric."

"Shit, you got any paper towels," I ask while rinsing off my hands in the sink.

"Yeah, just below the sink. The corkscrew's in that drawer." Matt points to the tool's elusive hiding spot.

"Are we going to have a fire tonight?" I ask while cleaning up the beer trail.

"Yeah man. I was going to start it later," Matt answers.

I look up from the floor and say, "I could get it going now if you want." I've always liked starting fires. Not in a creepy burn down a person's house then watch the terrorized occupants flee into the night sort of way, more like campfires and stuff.

"If you want, it's not even dark yet though," Matt says with a mild edge of annoyance in his voice. I don't really care though. Starting the fire will get me outside, and away from Ron and Steve, plus it gives me something to focus on.

"Okay, cool, you got matches?" I ask.

"Yeah, there should be a box in the drawer closest to the pantry there," Matt says before heading back into the living room.

"Fie-yah! Are you coming Jordan?" I ask before heading to the designated match drawer.

He takes a large swig from his wine bottle and says, "I'll be out there in a bit, yeah. I'm just going to bum a smoke and take a piss." I nod and head for the door that leads to the backyard porch.

The comforting smell of campfire smoke washes over me. Vibrant tongues of orange and yellow spring from the crackling blaze. Loud pops fill the air. The smoldering wood produces an array of sparks and hot embers, short lived sprites born from the heart of the conflagration. Jordan comes out after about fifteen minutes of being trapped in conversation. I'm finished my second beer by the time that Jordan has drained half of the wine bottle. I can tell he's beginning to get a bit messed up.

It's getting close to six when other people start showing up in force. Darrin, Tom and Suzzane, Patrick Sullivan and Cindy Despin, and a half dozen others. Music has infested the whole house and people are gathering in the usual spots: living room, porch, kitchen and fire pit. After another hour the party is in full swing. The beer run is soon successful and it doesn't take me long to drift into the state we like to refer to as "comfortably numb". Warm and fuzzy, I feel no pain and know no fear. Then, all of a sudden, I spot her moving out onto the porch. Lisa: Gorgon! Repellant Medusa of myth and legend! Foul, serpent riddled she-devil. I'm petrified instantly. I've turned to stone, and not in the sensual way. I thought I was in the clear. I was getting ready to speak with Jenny, who has been orbiting the fire for the past ten minutes.

"Hey man, can I bum a beer?" Jordan asks. His wine bottle is long since empty. I nod robotically and quickly look around. Derrin, Matt,

Ron, Heather, Steve and Colin, shit where did Jenny go? The porch! She's in the lair of the gorgon, lifelike statues parade around her. No! Damn it, alright just stay put, she'll head back this way yet. Just like the moth to the flame. Oh god, don't say anything like that if you talk with her.

"Hey man, I saw your latest painting in art class. Pretty fucked up. It's good though," Colin remarks as he shuffles closer to the fire.

I turn towards him and say, "Thanks man. Yeah I don't know, I just thought that Wolverine fighting Boba-fett in a primordial jungle would work somehow." I'm not a bad artist. I've definitely seen better, but I'm progressing. Colin laughs and takes a drag from his smoke before offering it to me. I don't normally smoke, but when I drink it seems like the thing to do. I accept the smoldering cigarette and take a drag. I can feel the smoke burn in my lungs. I take one more drag and hand the smoke back to Colin. Lisa creeps into the corner of my vision, the patio her perch. That's good. I can work with that.

"Hey man, I'm hungry. We should do a food run," Jordan says while wavering ever so slightly. He's a good enough driver when he's drunk, as long as we don't have to travel very far.

"I got four bucks left," I say.

"It's alright, I'll put it on the card. We'll hit the drive thru," Jordan says. He's lucky enough to have his own credit card. My parents just laughed when I asked for one.

"Rock on then," I say, before quickly downing my beer and accompanying him around the side of the house. I studiously avoid eye contact with Lisa or anyone in her vicinity as we progress to his car. I must not be turned to stone by her fearful gaze.

Our meal quest is rapid and successful, acquiring a sad pile of squashed hamburgers and an unhealthy profusion of over-salted fries for our efforts. When we return, it's totally dark out and the party has more or less moved outside. We're fortunate that the house to the left of Matt's is empty, while his right side neighbor consists of old Mr. Baxter who could give two shits about anything other than whiskey and satellite TV. If he had decidedly different types of neighbors, these little gatherings would be next to impossible.

We approach the bustling back yard. I can see the fire is choked with silhouettes. They're all drinking, talking and smoking. I take a seat far away from the fire and begin to dine on the contents of my food bag. I squelch down the passable meal as I scan the gathering around the fire. There, Jenny is sitting near Tom and Suzanne, who are sharing the beach chair. Alright, after this, just try some kind of conversation, somehow. Probably by using your brain, in order to form words, and then using your mouth to speak the words that your brain formed, yeah, that whole thing. That's the ticket! I look back to Jenny. My heart punches me in the ribs. Shit, this is going to be trickier than I thought.

"Hey Eric." A female voice, I freeze for a moment, no, not Lisa. I turn to see Sarah standing there.

I rattle off the standard greeting "Oh hey, how's it going?"

"Good, you?" she responds.

"Good," I say. The silence deepens. My lexicon fails.

"Have you seen Matt around?" she finally asks.

"Kitchen probably," I say somewhat tersely, the pending conversation attempt wearing on my nerves.

"Okay, I'll go look. See you later," she replies rapidly before departing. Matt doesn't normally stray too far from the kitchen and the source of the booze. Okay, food is gone, get a beer as a prop and then let's do this. I psych myself up as I head to the fridge. Five beers remain, gave two away, plus the other two, hmm seven. Let's see what seven and the beginning of number eight do for my performance. I grab the beer and take my circuitous route back to the fire, in order to avoid the patio where Lisa has been lingering all night. A shifting orange glow illuminates me as I position myself for the engagement run. I begin to move forward, mind searching for something to say. Standard greeting? No, too predictable. Smooth line? No, don't know any. I'm three feet and closing, it's now or never, begin interaction or break-off. Spontaneous joke? No, my voice doesn't want to cooperate. I fumble. My mind locks me into autopilot and I circle wide around Jenny. I come to a rest back at my selected chair. My head is swimming and I feel deflated. But the timing wasn't right. Too many beers also, seven is just too many. I'll definitely talk to her at the next party.

"Hey man can I grab another beer?" Jordan asks. I nod.

"Grab as many as you want man, I have to go for a foot-putt," I say as I stand up on shaky legs.

"What, the pit? Don't go, just stay here man. I think Brad's going to fire up a joint right away," Jordan offers. I just shake my head. "Alright man, see you later" Jordan says and waves before turning back to the party.

Well, that Jenny miller encounter went as disastrously as usual. Where's a wild animal when you really need one? I head up the dirt alley which carves a curving path behind the houses lining Matt's street. The pit's not that far, only two blocks, then across a field and through a small grove of trees. Maybe I *should* just stay. I could try talking with another girl, Heather was looking good tonight. But no, my head is swimming now, I need the air. I shouldn't have had the eighth beer. A shifting blur of images pass as my path unfolds before me. Unsteady legs propel me towards my new goal. The wind calms me somewhat. The cool caress has a sobering effect that helps me to refocus. I don't know what it is with Jenny: love, obsession, brain damage. It's probably brain damage. It feels like I'd imagine brain damage would be, all unable to think good and shit.

I'm almost there now. I've got to lie down, or something. I cross the expanse of ground to the trees. Moonlight filtered through the clouds casts a silvery pall over the field. The trees sway slightly as I approach, their bows heaving in unison. Leaves and branches rattle and shake. I step into the grove. Hard fingers in the form of twigs and saplings claw at me as I pass through the thicket. The smell of earth and fresh moss clouds the air. The woods begin to close around me. The buzz in my head filters my vision down to a tunnel. My body feels weightless. I'm walking on water now, no wait, air. I'm walking on air. No, not air, nothing, there's nothing at all beneath me. What's happening here? I'm pitching forward, no balance and no weight. I want to scream but I can't. I'm moving now. There's such a feeling of speed, it's impossible. What the fuck? I'm flying, no, not flying. Rocketing, faster than thought, my body is being torn apart, what's happening to me? Such velocity, I can't stop myself. I can't see anymore. No wait. What the fuck? There's an old man, skin stretched taught over his bones, and what is that, a top hat? I'm dreaming. I must have passed out somewhere. The old man is laughing. He's laughing at me. Fuck you! I want to scream, but I can't speak. This is a dream, it must be a dream, or acid. Somebody could have slipped some acid into my drink. The old man is gone now. Just speed, such a feeling of speed, and now color. What's happening to me? My body is apart, it's all apart. What the fuck? Wake up! Wake up! I can't speak. Wake the fuck up! My body, wait, I feel, pavement? What the fuck? I smell something very different here. There's garbage and exhaust, spices and some weird odor that saunters into my nose without identifying itself first. What the fuck? I'm slowing, no wait. I'm not moving anymore. I can see something. My vision swirls. Vomit erupts from my mouth without invitation or restraint. What the fuck? I'm on concrete. I slowly look forward, then to the left. I then look up and up and up... I vomit again, this time with real feeling, and a guttural wretch not before heard by man or beast. What the fuck?

"What the fuck?!" The words erupt from my expellant-spattered lips and reverberate off of the stone and glass of the surrounding buildings. They then proceed to echo up through a bewildering array of fantastical sights that could never exist anywhere on the earth that I know. Then, even before I can close my mouth, the supreme horror of a voiced response, soft, thickly accented and full of wonder. "What the fuck indeed!"

Grot Fastwhisker

What's it then? What's it that the city wants from us? What's it that's got all of the bugs upset, and the mices? What's it that's got all of the pigeons upset, and the goldfishes and stopwatches? What's it all coming from then? The city tells us? We can help with the mices and the rats. We can see the dreamers. They never come too far. Never to the city, is that what it means? Is it maybe something else? Move quickly or be devoured. Rat knows this well. Rat is wiser than some would think. Tell us then, why does the city cry out so? Tell us. Rat has hidden paths. The cat and the dog do not know. The crow cannot see what is beneath. Roaches think only of themselves, only of garbage and consume. Rat knows more. With feet and elbows moving rat will find truths. The city dreams too. Rat has seen, dark dreams. Dreams of metal, and dreams of lies, dreams of dreams, and dreams of flies, rat knows. Concrete whispers its own secrets, it is unreliable, trust it only for its purpose. This rat knows also. Come then, tell rat. Rat is here for the city. Rat is always here. Rat will always be here. Rat needs the city, and the city needs rat. Rat will make it all better. Trust rat now. What is that? The dream is real? This doesn't surprise rat. Rat knows the dream always, all, ways. Yes, yes, Rat will walk the path, if the city makes the trail. Rat will search for the dreamer, but so will others. Rat is strong but rat is not dog. Rat does not guard. What? What is that? A dreamer's purpose is to dream. What else could it be? The danger is real? Rat understands. Rat will then hurry to follow the path, if the city seeds the trail. But others will come too, others who are not rat.

A bundled body emerges. He steps into the graffiti-spattered tunnel then looks back and forth quickly. The small figure wears a shabby hooded coat, fringed with a dark fur collar. Countless oddities gild him, a large bird cage, several conspicuous forks, deranged folk art of every imagining and an over-stuffed, canvas backpack. His mid-section is encircled with a belt of leather pouches, the contents can only be guessed at.

The tunnel soon shrinks away behind him. He peers upwards. Bridges and overpasses mingle with the buildings and support girders that span overhead. He travels a brief way then nimbly scales the chain link fence pressing up against the right-hand wall. He swings over the top of the fence and drops down onto a catwalk, a raised sidewalk connecting to the Fourteenth Street overpass. Pedestrians look, but nobody says anything, nobody cares. He looks to the south. Uneven churls of smoke coil up there, marking "Reachers Hope" in his mind. The city is quiet for the moment, but his purpose still calls. He slows his thoughts for a moment. Breathing low and steady, he concentrates on the world in front of him. Gradually, the substance of reality peels back as he peers through the spectral veil. Shimmering unworldly sights illuminate the pulsing spiritscape. The focus of his vision strips away the buildings, streets and bridges, leaving a vast train of outlandish images in their wake. Animated trees surround laughing skyscrapers made of light, while effervescent hues dance across mouldering boulders of desperation. In the distance, stilt walking mansions romp with small surly ducks. The tenuous ground is alive with color. He gazes at the horizon. The spectral sky is wrong today.

Grot calls for his watcher spirit. Within moments a glowing green orb streaks through the spirit realm, stopping just shy of his face. The orb resolves into the form of an ethereal green rat.

"What do you wish of us master?" The spirits voice an echo in Grot's mind that instantly fades.

"Rat must be wary of dangers." He internalizes the standard mantra.

"And this one will always watch for them master." The tiny spirit replies in kind.

"Rat can see the spirit sky. Tell us, what do they say?" He asks the spirit while motioning towards the spray of discordant colors.

"This one has heard tell of sickness, this one has seen the crumbling sky." The reply comes back, as cryptic as ever.

"Where does it crumble from?" Grot asks, trying to follow the tenuous thread.

"A question, but the wrong one," the spirit responds.

"What is crumbling?" he asks.

"A question, but the wrong one," the spirit responds.

"Where does it crumble to?" he asks.

"There is only ever one place master, the city," the spirit responds. Grot sits for a moment, perplexed.

"And what has it heard of sickness?" he finally asks.

17

"Mug of 'Reachers Hope'," the spirit responds. This is not expected, little Mug Snerdz is known to Grot. One of his protected, the path is set then.

"Rat thanks you for your vigilance," he says.

"As always, this one serves," replies the spirit. Grot relaxes his focus. The world drifts back into its usual state. He can see the faint outline of the watcher spirit, a green mist that circles a wide perimeter around him. Grot eyes the distance to "Reachers Hope", a deep concern overcoming his features. He's known Mug since he was a baby, helped his mom Grenda out of a scrape more than a decade ago. They've been close ever since. Mug must have just become ill or she would have called Grot. He removes his backpack and rifles through the clutter of arcane reagents and shamanistic implements. Eventually he produces a battered cell phone and checks the holographic display. Panic grips him then, two days, no wonder he's so hungry. He was speaking with the city for two days! Three missed calls from Grenda. He seethes with agitation. An urgent desire wells up within him, a dread yearning to sprint through the vast urban maze with reckless abandon. *No, we can't be stupid now,* he thinks, *not now.* "Reachers Hope" is right near the warrens. Gangs and urban predators are everywhere, waiting for foolhardy prey of all description. He dare not step through the veil either. The spirit sky is crumbling and there's no telling what other dangers lurk in that realm today.

He calls Grenda back. No answer, he leaves a quick message then stashes his phone. An uncomfortable minute passes, and he's just resigned himself to taking the direct route when a thought strikes him. A spell that he put in place some days ago, its power might still remain. Becoming excited at the prospect, he scoops up the backpack and runs nimbly though the herd of citizens. He thinks back to the casting. The spell was affixed to a doorframe in a small shack. It was towards the Koshikawa mega-mart on Eighteenth Street, an old pumping station, long abandoned, with a sizable rat's nest in the basement. Dire rats no less, each the size of a small dog. That's why he picked the building in the first place. The city provides.

The "Elghar Market" lies directly in his path. The stalls of that great bazaar sell everything from clothes and postcards, to ammunition and hydroponically grown produce. As he ambles through the crowd the city presents an opportunity near the market's far end. A booth laden with large Acheri nuts is pressed right up against a guardrail. There's a catwalk ten feet below. Grot grins and slows his pace as he reaches into his coat pocket. He jogs slowly, dodging between different market patrons as he goes. Ten feet away now, the shopkeeper, a large human sporting a pistol on his hip, spots Grot, suspicion etched on his face. Before suspicion turns into justification, Grot produces a small marble, bound in a single copper wire. He then makes a series of arcane gestures. A flash of power erupts at the shopkeeper's feet, bringing with it a large mass of slick marbles. A brief look of confusion passes over the Human's face as he fumbles for his pistol. He then takes one unsteady step backwards, marbles shift, and he becomes airborne, one desperate foot momentarily framed in the stalls neon glow. He lingers in the air for a fraction of a second before he comes crashing down on his back. Meanwhile as this pratfall unfurls, Grot scoops up four Acheri nuts. He throws them in his backpack and bolts past the booth. Vaulting over the iron bars, he sails into the open air above the catwalk. The landing is practiced and perfect. He bends his knees, smacks his palms on the ground then he's up and running again, the distant sounds of consternation propelling him onward. An inner charge of glee overcomes him for a moment, just like old times. Rat has to eat after all. No signs of pursuit, still, he ducks into the mouth of an alley and scurries to the nearest manhole.

Soon he's safe in the cozy confines of the Tirileth city sewer system, part of the new system by the looks of it. The tube has a diameter of around fifteen feet. Smooth composite pipes line the walls, with dim LED lights at regular intervals. A raised metal grate acts as a service platform. Grot sits on the metal grate and places his backpack beside him. The birdcage clangs against the steel grate, sending a metallic echo up the tube. Grot lines up the four pilfered nuts. The genetically engineered legumes are each about the size of a man's fist. Good nutrient value, they're normally quite pricey. A brief acknowledgement is given to rat as he crumbles a necessary tribute onto the floor of the sewer pipe. He then begins to feast greedily on the stolen food.

The first nut is gone and he's in the middle of opening the second when a large black rat emerges from the gloom of the tunnel, red eyes shining in the dim light.

"Much and many greetings friend, you are welcome to join us if you wish." Grot hacks the nut open with his machete and presents a piece to the black rat. It stares for a moment, looks toward the crumbled tribute and then moves swiftly to the spot where it fell.

"Under sky, darkness grows." The incomprehensible tone of the big rat's intention sounds in his mind. Grot is surprised for a moment. Then he looks closely at the rat. Beneath his left hind leg rests a small square of glassy paper, a matchbook. A familiar sensation creeps through his scalp. The tunnel hums with dull reverberations, the soft voice of the city.

"If you please friend, could you bring us that square of paper," Grot asks. The rat nods then steps to the side and grasps the matchbook in its mouth. A brief scramble later and the rat's sitting next to Grot. "Platinum Under Sky Nightclub" is scrawled across the match book's holographic cover. A stylized silver building topped with a haze of digitally rendered clouds serves as the 3D backdrop. Grot does not know this place. He flips the matchbook over to reveal a weave address. The sight of it causes him to let out an inadvertent hiss. The matchbook does not have a physical address, some choice of style that he doesn't understand. The internet weave is another thing that Grot doesn't understand. He never learned how to use the electronic pathways of the digital worlds, the peculiar cultures and unnatural hacker spirits had always dissuaded him. He sits for a moment, absentmindedly petting the large rat's head and eating fake nut. "What is the darkness, friend? Could you tell us?" he asks after giving the rat a large piece of fake nut.

"Darkness of life, the story is not clear" is the only response that it offers. Puzzling, life to the rat means many things. It means garbage, shadows, tunnels, mating and luck. Rat doesn't know its own death until it happens. Darkness of life might be something unnatural. Something that rat does not have language for. Unusual that this rat would refer to a "story", that is another conception which is wholly foreign to most every rat.

Grot finishes his meal, leaving a sizeable portion of the stolen nut for the black rat. He then thanks it before departing with the newly acquired matchbook. *The city's first crumb bought for a crumb*, he thinks, *but what does it mean?* The trip to the pumping station proves to be uneventful and soon he arrives at the gleaming blue neon of the Koshikawa mega-mart. The massive building is surrounded by a large well-lit and well-guarded parking lot. The corporate shopping center sits as an ominous glowing beacon in the midst of dilapidation and decay. Shambling disabused apartment blocks sag between the massive support pillars, and old homes rot amongst the bones of the boarded-up store fronts. Grot knows that the city moves in cycles. This place may yet bounce back and re-grow, or it may just fester in this state, forcing the denizens to move to other, brighter parts of the city.

A giant transit tube connects to the top of the mega-mart building. The tube no doubt leads to an exclusive corporate enclave located on the level above this one. Grot doesn't like to venture up too high in "The Tier". Rat likes to stay in low places, where the shadows are welcome, and hiding is easy. He travels a bit farther before his objective becomes apparent. There, amid the architectural vexations, the pumping station; sitting blithely behind a useless chain link fence, time and circumstance making it entirely irrelevant. Grot approaches the empty door frame of the building, and stops. He slows his breathing and begins to focus. The substance of the material world falls away as the turmoil of the spirit realm coalesces around him. He begins to search for a hint of the spell's power. He looks past a shifting stack of deer skulls. Then squints, and tries his damnedest to ignore the nineteen thousand screaming toasters circling around him in a great, glittering torrent of chrome. A few moments pass as he adjusts. Then, a strand sticks out, as clear as day. It was definitely spun by him. He can tell immediately. His perception shifts back to the mundane world, and a triumphant smile crosses his face as he makes his way into the pumping station. A layer of filth blankets the building's interior. He looks to the basement stairs, dearly wishing that he could visit the dire rats dwelling there. But he's already lost enough time. A sense of urgency is now growing stronger by the minute. Instead, he hurls one of the Archeri nuts down the short flight of stairs as he utters a prayer to rat. He then turns from the entrance hall and walks to the main chamber. The room is all but stripped bare, with only a few odds and ends remaining. Grot then spots his true prize, a dented steel door frame leading to the station's storeroom. He crosses to the door frame and pauses to inspect the metal. The mark's intact. He lingers for another second before stepping through the door frame. An instant of no time and no space follow. The calm of oblivion gives way and he suddenly finds himself walking out into a bustling street full of goblins. He grins and looks back to see a number of confused faces framed by an old stone tunnel. Familiar smells assail him. He glances around: "Gintche's Sundry Unmentionables" sits just next to the "Stinking Weasel" tavern and, just up the street; "Ramshackles Food Hut" tries its best to give indigestion to the masses. He nods to himself, "Reachers Hope", now, to seek out Grenda, and define his latest purpose.

A short while later Grot is standing across from Grenda's multi-tiered apartment complex. The buildings in "Reachers Hope" are all connected in some way. Ladders, catwalks, old wooden planks and even stout ropes, which are used as zip lines or hand bridges. "Reachers Hope" has a Goblin population of around seventy percent. Most of the houses and apartments are squat and ugly by conventional standards. Street merchants are commonplace, serving as the reflection of an old Goblin custom. Grot stops and calls for his watcher spirit, the ethereal rat appears a few seconds later.

"What do you wish of us master?" The spirits eyes burn with green fire. Grot commands the spirit.

"Go to the apartment of Grenda Snerdz." He then sits cross-legged on the apartment's front steps. Closing his eyes he exerts the force of his will and touches the watcher spirit, engaging it. Instantly his vision resolves into a cloudy haze revealing the inside of Grenda's apartment. He focuses his will and begins to travel through the apartment in the watcher's body. He can see the familiar couch, the tables and furniture, no signs of life though, no telltale spark of a spirit. Grots concern deepens. He takes one last look around the apartment then releases his hold on the watcher and opens his eyes. The world takes shape around him. He quickly checks his phone again, no calls. He has to know. It's time to cast a spell. He needs space and time to prepare. Fortunately his den is close to here. *The diner,* he thinks, *we should check the diner first.* He calls the watcher spirit.

"What do you wish of us master?" the spirit says.

"Go to 'Iggy's Diner', search for Grenda Snerdz. If you see her there, come back and tell us," he commands the tiny spirit.

"It will be done master," the watcher spirit replies before it streaks off on its new mission. Grot stands and begins to head towards his den. Then a thought strikes him. Rifling through his backpack he grabs the cell phone, quietly resolving to keep it in a jacket pocket from now on. He activates the holo-screen and brings up his contact list. He pages through the display until he arrives at the number he was looking for, simply titled "Old green", he hits the connect button. A few seconds later and Grot's greeted with the dusty voice, and dustier face, of Karlmarg Greengerson or "Old green" to almost everyone.

"Grot? Is that you? Grenda's been looking for you." He lets out a cough and snort, following up with "Mug's been awful sick these past days, was bit by a sewer troll don't ya know?" Grot's stomach sinks, it's worse than he thought. He has to find them now or the disease may spread to the boy's nervous system, "Sewer Shakes", he's seen it before.

"Old green, it's very important that Rat finds them. Do you know where they went? Rat has been to the apartment, it's empty."Agitation is mounting now. Stupid, stupid Grot, how could he get so lost. *It wasn't even one of our episodes, or was it? We can't remember,* he thinks, *just the purpose, there is a new purpose now we can remember that clearly, the dreamer and the darkness of life.*

"I heard that she'd taken the day off so she could bring Mug to the Bio-doc's," Old green says in a languid tone.

"Which Bio-doc, Old green, there are thousands in the city?" Grots mind races to the nearest Bio-doc locations: Fifteenth Street near the Barbarossa gun shack, Sixteenth Street, just under the second level overpass, Eighteenth Street, one block past the Koshikawa Mega-mart. He can't focus, agitation beginning to take hold of his senses.

"I'd imagine it would be the Mazatech facility over on Thirteenth, she has a record with Koshikawa," Old green offers. Grot nods to himself; she was spotted trying to "liberate" some Koshikawa property. She's been on their official hit list ever since.

"Okay thanks Old green, if you hear anything else please call us alright?" Grot says rapidly.

The ancient Goblin responds, "Sure thing." Grot disconnects the call and consigns the cell phone to his jacket's inside pocket. He has to go through some ten blocks of the warrens in order to get to Thirteenth Street. That means that Grenda is travelling through ten blocks of the warrens too. Taxi drivers aren't stupid enough to traverse those labyrinthine streets. No auto-cab routes. No mono-rail either, of course. Most of those tracks ring the outer perimeter of the various levels of "The Tier", dipping downwards or veering upwards to connect several levels together.

Grot stands quivering for a moment before he remembers the spell. The spell will find her, it has to. He needs to know where she is, he needs to be certain. The watcher spirit returns to him as he starts to head to the den. No word means Grenda isn't at the diner, as suspected. He hurries on his way.

Grot snakes his way up the hilly streets of "Reachers Hope". His path takes him past "Reachers Square", a collection of shops all stacked inside a tottering mall-like construction. The uncertain arrangement of carpentry is always teeming with activity. It's also been the sight of countless gang brawls, including the infamous "Shotgun Axe showdown" of '72. Lucrative real estate is always murder-worthy in the minds of the various urban predators. There are times when more than half a dozen gun fights erupt each day. Enforcement is rare, as with other parts of the warrens.

Grot turns right and heads down a narrow alley. The tunnel way is created by a high concrete wall running next to a long row of square apartment blocks. Doors and stoops slip past. He walks by old boxes, disembodied doors, dumpsters overflowing with filth and a pair of shady-looking Goblins. He stops briefly to inspect an indeterminate mass of crawling things, scientifically poking it with a stick before moving on.

Finally he arrives at the cobblestone bridge that marks the old town sewer entrance. Unlike the new utilitarian designs, these passages have history and character. These passages remember the ages before neon and chrome. Grot looks around to see if he's being watched. Content that he's cloaked in the cities protection, he steps sideways through the illusory wall. A simple spell placed ages ago. The wall can even feel real to an outside observer, if they are unable to perceive the spell's design. The other side of the illusion reveals a tunnel which corkscrews down into the murky depths. Goblin eyes penetrate the darkness, allowing him to see the grainy grey tunnel unfurling before him.

He eventually enters into the large stonework sewers of antiquity. Vaulted ceilings curl overhead, and curved walls perch atop a flat stone floor. A central channel carries a slow river of run-off water and waste. Arced stone walkways bridge the channel at regular intervals. He stands still and feels the mood of the sewer for a moment. A jovial calm permeates the area, accented by the usual traces of fear and lethargy. He nods to himself and continues up the familiar sewer passage, turning left at the first junction and then right at the second junction. He approaches the end of the tunnel where three circular storm grates sit in the gloom, one directly ahead of him and one on either side of the tunnel. He briefly peers through the rusted metal of all three grates then steps through the illusory bars of the left hand grate. Proceeding up the slightly smaller tunnel, he soon comes to the notch in the wall that signifies his passage.

Approaching the wall, he peers upwards at the vertical tunnel travelling up into the ceiling. The tunnel features hand and foot holds carved into the stone. The trick is getting up the first ten feet. Fortunately Grot has done this many times before. He reaches into his backpack and produces a long, knotted coil of nylon rope. He then sits cross-legged on the stone floor and begins to chant, a low murmur at first, but slowly it builds to a deafening roar. He shifts his tone and focuses on his breath. Unearthly tones begin to pour from his mouth. The walls reverberate with pulsing waves of sound. A moment passes before a flurry of movement catches his eye. Then, from the murk of the tunnel, four dozen small rats come scuttling into view. They approach rapidly and snatch up the rope in a synchronized effort. They then begin to climb up the nearly vertical surface of the wall, small claws interlocking with the cracks in the stonework. Grot ends the chant as the rodent entourage reaches the den's floor. He then moves over to test the rope; it gives a small amount of slack, but then goes taught. Satisfied that it's relatively secure, he begins to climb. The pack of rats holds on long enough for him to shimmy his way up to the hand-holds. He then climbs up the rest of the way using the stone ladder.

Once he's inside the chamber's confines, Grot pulls up the rope. A portable light sits on the wooden table; it casts an orange glow as he switches it on. The chamber itself is only five feet high and about ten foot square. Rats cover every square inch. The room has rough hewn stone walls; it was created by a city spirit a long time ago. Grot then added a table, a small lockbox and a pile of soft blankets and pillows that can serve as a bed. The dens location keeps out most intruders, but the tunnel also features a number of arcane surprises. Grot created the ward and then tied in a number of spells, triggering them would be unpleasant, to say the least. He crosses to the lockbox and opens the lid, everything right where he left it. He grabs a large handful of Nutri-pet food pellets and sprinkles them on the ground for the group of rats. He then crosses back to the lockbox and retrieves a small glass jar of finely ground dust. The powder sparkles white and gold in the light. He removes his backpack and sifts through the contents, eventually retrieving an intricately carved wooden bowl. Images of rat swarms, streets and buildings festoon the bowl's exterior, while its interior seems to gleam with a faint green light. Grot puts his backpack on the table then places the bowl in the center of the room. He sits cross-legged in front of it, in the midst of the rats, jar of dust beside him. An undertone of miniscule mastication surrounds him as he slowly begins to weave the threads of the spell together. He draws strength from Rat and from the city. The arcane strands begin to radiate outwards as he pours a handful of dust into the bowl. The fine grains of the multi-hued dust congeal instantly into a tiny, detailed replica of the surrounding city. The dust forms into miniature streets, diminutive houses and microscopic people, all moving and shifting just as the city does. Grot isn't interested in what the sand is doing however, just the spell. Just the purpose that now compels him.

The threads spiral out. He can sense the power building. When he feels that it's time he begins to chant, a deep thrumming that surges from his spirit. He rhythmically calls back the threads and draws them into his core. Abruptly, his consciousness bursts free. He finds himself soaring through streets and alleys, blasting past buildings and stores. He can see the world clearly beneath him, throngs of people going to and fro. Focus now, think of her face. The soft dark eyes, gentle curls of auburn hair, full smiling lips. There, he has her. The spell lashes out with unerring tendrils. The power draws him inexorably to her. A building, now a room, his heart sinks. Not the Bio-doc's office. Not the Bio-doc's office at all.

Xanshudan and Kane

The plan seems to be working, so far. He glances down at the Barbarossa tech I.D. badge clipped to his liberated lab coat, then smiles and nods at a woman as she walks past. Dancer's forgeries, coupled with Kane's magic, got them past the first two security check points. Now he just has to remember the names from the dossier, the employees who know Mr. Gainsbrook personally. They could see that something is amiss before it's time to extract. That would be bad.

"Great Zool! Would you look at the honkers on that one!" Kane's juvenile rhetoric fills Xan's mind, causing him to momentarily focus on the research receptionist and her ample frame.

"Not the time," he internalizes, in an effort to add some gravitas to their situation. Kane continues unabated.

"Oh come on! Bring me over there, gimme just one squeeze. The tongue always surprises them."

"Maybe if this job works out I'll bring you over to 'The Cherrywood', get a private dance or two. But for now, the task at hand if you please?" Xan conveys the message internally to the perverse manifer spirit. He then turns up a short hall, opens the door to the Barbarossa "Advanced Nano-Tech Prototype Research Lab", and enters. The room sits past layers of electronic and physical defenses. The edges of the space are lined with a collection of small, glass-walled chambers all filled with testing equipment and experiment stations. The center of the main lab is occupied by a dozen powerful computers arranged around ten work stations. He can see that two of Mr. Gainsbrook's colleagues are already at their computers. The dossier comes to mind as he views their faces. The Human woman is Carla Brightmore, she's known Andy for five years now. The Elf man is Terry Sylvantus, a new researcher. He's been out for drinks with Andy twice. "Showtime," Xan internalizes as he moves into the lab.

"Good morning Carla, morning Terry." The voice of Kane comes through Xan's mouth as he relinquishes verbal control to the corporeal spirit. Kane's tiny face normally appears on Xan's left palm but just now the manifer spirit is resting inside his body.

Right now he only needs the parasitic spirit to speak for him. Kane can duplicate Andy's voice, and he's a better liar than Xan could ever be.

"Hey Andy," Terry responds, absorbed by a holographic readout.

"Andy, you're in early today. I thought you'd finished the new schematic?" Carla asks. She then turns from the work station to peer around the low half-wall.

"Yeah, pretty much, just tweaking some algorithms," Kane announces.

"That's Andy for you, always tweaking the algorithms," Carla mocks. *Good,* thinks Xan, *no suspicion.*

"You know me," Kane retorts. Andy's other close cohorts haven't arrived yet. Xan hopes that they can be clear before Greg Cranston arrives. According to the file, he and Andy were lovers; it's difficult to fake that type of intimacy, especially for Kane. Xan takes a moment and glances around the room. Four concealed ceiling turrets, clustered over the work stations, six obvious cameras and two low-yield particulate scanners. Silver Dancer should be in place by now. The others are set and ready to go. Now he just needs to wait for his signal.

Xan crosses to Andy's work station as naturally as possible. He sits down in front of the computer and boots it up, accessing the nano-schematic auto-sculpting program, just as Silver Dancer showed him. The archaic grids, commands and task bars of the advanced rendering program fill the confines of his holo-screen. Xan couldn't hope to comprehend the nuances of this software. He can fake it pretty convincingly though, as long as nobody looks too closely. The program chirps and clicks for a few minutes before the persona of a dancing silver sprite appears in the bottom left corner of the screen.

"I'm going to power up the nano-fabricator," Kane says, on cue.

"Sure thing," Carla answers, while working on some unseen problem. A series of lights begin to flash, followed by a rapid humming in one of the antechambers. Xan waits until the fabricator is fully powered before tapping on the small silver dancer icon on the bottom of his screen. As soon as he does, the cameras and scanners immediately deactivate. Suddenly the building's fire alarm begins to wail away as spinning amber lights jut from the ceiling.

"Oh shit," exclaims Carla as she looks around. Terry jumps out of his concentration and nearly falls out of his chair. Xan knows that fire drills are a scheduled affair, so this will appear as an actual fire, especially if the device triggers properly.

"Go, I'll be right behind you. I have to manually shut down the fabricator now," Kane says in an urgent manner.

"Right, shit. Okay. Hey, I think I can see smoke out in the hall!" Carla says as she looks towards the research lab's exit. *Perfect,* thinks Xan, *Cables handywork.* Carla and Terry quickly exit the research lab, propelled by the convincing facade.

Once they're gone, Xan immediately crosses to the small-circuit nano-testing room, opens the door and enters. He then crosses to the wall safe and removes the I.D. card obtained from the currently indisposed Mr. Gainsbrook. The card slides through the scanner and the wall safe emits a click. A yellow light appears. A keypad also unfolds from the safe's thick door. Xan punches in the illicitly acquired six digit code. He then waits while the final safeguard unfurls from the wall, an old retinal scanner. He aligns his eye to the scanner's optical reader, as a pulsing band of blue light passes over his face, scanning his arcane altered retinas. A tense moment passes as the reader digests the information. The light turns green, and he breathes a sigh of relief. The lock disengages and the door opens. Inside sits a series of small nano-coders, each about the size of a pack of playing cards. Xan quickly sorts through the coders and finds the one that they're after, simply labeled "Ring-cell prototype". The others are older designs, mainly back-ups. He pockets the nano-coder then closes the safe door and exits the testing room.

"Well that was easy, now all we have to do is walk out of the building with all of the other rubes," Kane proclaims. Xan crosses the room to the door leading to the main facility's hallway.

"Just don't say anything stupid and we should be fine," he retorts.

The door slides open to reveal a scene of structured panic. Employees are rushing to and fro, seeking unseen points of egress. Xan falls in and begins to play the part of a confused, frightened scientist.

"Aw, where'd those tits go?" Kane's lecherous voice once again fills Xans mind as he passes by the now empty reception desk.

"You're incorrigible," Xan internalizes as he glances about, searching for unknown threats. He has to move one hundred feet to get to the security check point. The wide hall is filled with bodies, all jostling for position and speaking in hushed voices. The check point is manned by two guards. The pair's standing near the card reader, assault rifles hanging indifferently. There's a bank of elevators recessed in the wall behind them. The hall continues on, to the right of the elevators, it eventually leads to the primary security check point. That check point divides the hall from the main lobby of the twenty-third level entrances, his current destination. Xan passes through the first security gate without incident, the pilfered I.D. card doing its job yet again. Turning to the right he proceeds to follow the flow of the crowd, trying to blend his movements and tone with the throng of humanoids. He can see a series of four security gates covering the width of the hall. The gates connect with two security check points which frame the hall's entrance. The other side opens into a large circular space surmounted by a second storey mezzanine. The upper level is accessed by two staircases lining opposing sides of the lobby doors. The second floor space also houses the main security barracks and arcane defense quarters. He's ten feet and closing. There are four armed guards manning the security check points, two per side. Kane's voice abruptly fills his mind.

"Something's wrong!" He stumbles for a second before regaining his footing.

"Don't fuck around Kane. I'm not in the mood," Xan responds internally while reaching for his I.D. card.

"No seriously! Some majicker is peeking at us!" Kane responds in a genuinely urgent manner.

"Shit!" Xan internalizes as he moves forward to scan the I.D. and pass through the gate. The card slides through the reader, and the whole world erupts. Claxon bells blare, dozens of voices cry out and the gates slam shut, held fast by strong magnetic locks. Before the guards have time to react, Xan focuses his will and opens his perception to the arcane weave. A whirling tide of color surrounds him, the walls and floor become grey blurs. A semi-translucent vagueness overshadows everything. There, on the mezzanine, just past the gates. The aura of a wage mage can be seen. "Plan B, now!" Xan yells as he raises his left arm, hand open and facing forward. Kane's face pokes out from his outstretched palm. The tiny face winks at the guards and instantly a bright flash of light overwhelms the area, blinding everyone with a fierce intensity. Hysteria grips the crowd and a mass of blind workers stumble back up the hall, away from the newly perceived threat. Meanwhile the guards have all taken cover. They're in the middle of calling for back up when a dark shape emerges, appearing seemingly from thin air. Her lithe form is outlined in ballistic weave and accented by composite plates. She blurs forward and expertly dismantles the blind guards, rendering each one unconscious with a single deft blow.

"Not quite as planned?" Eve quips, her lower face a metallic, screaming demon mouth.

"Show us your boobs!" is Kane's immediate inappropriate response.

"Shut-up Kane!" Respond Xan and Eve in unison.

"There's a mage ..." Xan begins.

"Rex is on it," Eve says as she unlocks the gates and begins to move to the main hall entrance. Xan passes through the gate and follows. He glances up at the mezzanine as he passes through the foyer. A conspicuous blood stain marks the place where the wage mage stood; as usual Rex is nowhere to be seen. He looks back towards the door. The sound of running feet signifies responding guards.

"Cable, do it." Eve conveys the order through her headset. The scream of a rocket engine precedes a shattering window. Glass hails through the foyer as the small missile streaks overhead and detonates on the second level wall. The mezzanine flares, guards dive for cover. A sudden blanket of fire quickly ignites the walls and floor. Waves of heat course through the lobby as Xan and Eve sprint out the door. They dart through the parking lot and quickly reach Cable's Z&X 950, which peels out as they pile in.

"Where's Rex?" Xan asks, even though he already knows the answer.

"He said he would meet us back at 'The Castle'," Eve replies while fastening her harness. Xan nods and snaps into his seat.

"There shouldn't be any response for at least five minutes. Silver Dancer said her smart-frames are up," Cable yells from the driver's seat.

"Good, at least something's going right today," Xan calls back.

The voice of Devlin chimes in from the passenger side. "Sorry boss man, I tried to get through their ward but it was too damn strong." His head pops around the seat corner, chiseled good looks framed by a wild mane of multi-hued hair.

"It's not your fault Devlin. I should have listened to Kane, for once," Xan says.

The triumphant voice of Kane fills the van's interior. "You all heard it!"

Devlin chuckles, looks back to Xan and says, "Please tell me that you still have the prototype." The van lurches forward and bounces erratically over some uneven ground.

"We do," Xan says and taps his coat pocket. Devlin nods and relaxes a degree.

"Hold on," Cable yells as the van banks hard to the left and then straightens out and decelerates. He then adds "route nine twenty-three, we'll blend right in."

The van moves smoothly up the wide roadway. A glimmering sports car edges past, the internal holographics making it appear as though the driver is a savage demon, wreathed in roaring flame.

"Good," Xan says as he sits back and closes his eyes. He focuses internally for a moment. "You can drop the disguise now Kane." The physical form of Andy Gainsbrook shifts and flows.

His human features melt away replaced by coal black skin, pure white hair and pointed Elven ears. Xan sighs and looks at the floor.

"I wouldn't worry too much Xanshudan, none of us were indentified. You were disguised as Andy the whole time. We can presume that they'll question the real Mr. Gainsbrook but he doesn't know anything. He would know even less of course if you would have let me deal with him," Eve says quietly.

"As I've said before Eve, I don't want to operate like that anymore, not if I can help it," Xan responds. He looks back to Eve, the dull shimmer of his white eyes gleaming in the low-light.

"Hmm, well it's not me that you have to worry about on that accord," Eve responds, while lowering her metal mask to reveal stern and attractive Elven features. Her short hair is drawn into a top-knot and a series of scars criss-cross her left cheek and jaw, the roadmaps of combat.

"Yeah, well, *you* try to control a sixteen-thousand year old demi-god! I'd rather try herding lions with a butterfly net," Xan says. Eve laughs.

"That's why they call it the terrible sixteen-thousands," interjects' Kane.

"Nobody ever says that," Eve responds dryly.

"Yeah I've never heard of that either, Kane," Xan remarks.

"That's just cuz ... well if you don't run in those kinds of circles ... every Asura knows ... never mind, just shut up," Kane exclaims before sinking back into Xan's palm. Eve laughs and looks to Xan again.

"Maybe you shouldn't try to control him, just try to guide his decisions, like an unruly child. I've heard that Asura are wild and free by nature. They often resent authority and disdain taking orders, even within their clan structure. If you want Rex's help, maybe just ask him for it, or try to attain it by other means," Eve offers, before sitting back to watch the streets move by. Xan lets that thought roll around his mind as the van continues along its course. They soon pass through the route nine-twenty-three junction, and arrive at the Tirileth city central level terminus. The terminus consists of a complex series of ramps, bridges, underpasses and overpasses. The winding roadways serve as a convenient route leading to virtually any of the more than thirty different levels that make up "The Tier." Traffic congestion can be bad at times. The only alternative however is to drive back and forth across more than a dozen levels in an attempt to find other ramps that lead either upwards or downwards. Alternatively, they could pay the exorbitant vehicle lift tolls. That route requires a valid credstick however, and the van is less than legal.

"Looks like it might take an hour or more to get down to level nine," Cable says as he inches the van forward onto one of the main down-ramp junctions. "The 'Steel Sharks' are playing the 'Slaughter Guard'. I'll put it on the holo-vid," he says. The holographic display springs to life in between the two front seats, bringing with it the harsh roar of fast moving motorbikes. Screaming engines harmonize with staccato cracks of automatic weapons' fire. Motoblitz players blast by one another on dangerous tracks, as they fire rubber bullets at every conceivable angle. Cable and Devlin are immediately engrossed.

"I'll call Cassandra," Xan comments as he produces a GII secure-com and begins the encrypted connection process.

"Nice, you did promise me some romantic action earlier," Kane announces, awkward as usual.

"Just stay quiet, please?" Xan responds as the cell phone connects to the custom com-hub. The palm-sized holo-screen engages, revealing Cassandra's dark features set against an ornate wooden backdrop. Xan smiles and nods at the small holographic projection. "Cassandra, as beautiful as ever I see." She laughs and smoothes her long platinum hair, hooking some of it behind a gently pointed ear.

"Well, well, Xan. I wasn't expecting to hear from you again so soon," she responds, a teasing smile creeping across her full lips.

"As it turns out, we could move sooner than I'd anticipated," Xan responds, then adds "We had a minor issue with the extraction, but we aren't compromised."

"That's good. I wouldn't want to lose someone with your skills," she retorts playfully. Xan smiles and waggles his eyebrows, a bad habit that he learned from Kane. Cassandra snorts and rolls her eyes then continues "Payment upon delivery as per usual. If I'm not around, speak with Marcus, he'll make sure that you're taken care of." She gives one last lingering smile then disconnects.

"Whoa, get a room you two," Kane exclaims as Xan pockets his cell phone. "Oh wait, you already did!" he adds, chortling at his own joke.

"Quiet you, or I'll start wiping my ass with my left hand," Xan responds, eliciting laughs all around, even from Kane.

"So what's up now boss man?" Cable asks while briefly taking his focus off of the Motoblitz match.

"Now it's time to get paid. After that, I guess we'll see," Xan says as he peers through the windshield, the sprawling city scene unfolding below.

A little over an hour later, and the van is passing through familiar turf. Medieval stone facades punctuate the landscape as they trundle down the curved streets of the ninth level warrens.

"All clear," announces Cable. The van turns into "The Castle's" alley. A neon glow coming from the nearby pawn shop's open sign acts as a signal, meaning that nothing is amiss. The alley itself runs between a row of stores and an abandoned warehouse, travelling seventy-five feet before culminating in a heavy steel gate. A reinforced wall connects to the gate and encases the medieval turrets and pitched roofs of "The Castle". Cable guides them up the alley and through the gate, which opens for the approaching van. He turns to the left, passes the guard house, then opens the steel overhead door and directs the van into the spacious garage.

"Honey, I'm home," Kane announces as Xan exits the vehicle with the others just behind him. Static erupts from the ceiling speaker for a moment, then Silver Dancer's voice fills the garage.

"And me without dinner ready."

Kane answers immediately, "I'll forgive you this once, if you show me your boobs."

"I think that I can live without your forgiveness. Rex got back a little while ago. He's in the garden if you're wondering," Silver Dancer responds, surveying the scene using the cameras and microphones mounted all around "The Castle."

"How does he always get here first?" Cable asks while retrieving a large bag of gear and weapons from the van. The barrel of his Stonefire auto shotgun pokes through the open zipper.

"Magic, brother," Devlin responds, and snaps his fingers. In a flash a small orb of scintillating colors manifests and floats beside his head. The mass of colors bobs in the approximation of a bow before a ghostly voice erupts from its center, repeating Devlin's words "Magic, brother."

"Quit it, you know I don't like that thing," Cable says, glowering at Devlin's arcane companion. The tiny spirit recoils from his wrath, first flying high up near the garage's ceiling, then passing through the stone wall.

"Now look what you did. You scared him," Devlin mocks. He then moves into "The Castle" through the garage's side door. Eve and Xan follow closely behind.

"I scare him? I've seen that thing literally melt the face right off of a guy before," Cable exclaims while following the others into "The Castles" main building. "Like right off of his skull, just like that!" He snaps his fingers to drive the point home.

"Yeah but he did it in a really cute way," Devlin continues his mocking. The group proceeds into the large open space that serves as "The Castles" main living room and kitchen. A pitched roof, shot through with steel girders, arcs overhead. Inside, a collection of couches, tables, chairs, desks and cupboards litter the floor and walls. Devlin slumps down in the largest of the couches. He then activates the oversized holo-vid occupying the better part of the north wall. Eve heads to the open kitchen area. Meanwhile Cable crosses to the northeast door leading to the long hallway of the "Murder Chamber". The halls other end contains the door to "The Castles" living quarters. Xan is about to head into the turret connected to the room's east wall when that very door opens to reveal Silver Dancer's silhouette.

"By Zool Would you look at that!" exclaims Kane upon seeing Silver Dancer and her signature minimalistic attire, a skimpy tube top and a pair of shorts that leave nothing to the imagination.

"Bite me Kane," she retorts.

Kane immediately responds, "You know that I will, anytime, anyplace. And I do mean *any place.* "

She snorts and heads to the kitchen then queries, "So, you're all in one piece and we have the prototype?"

"Yeah, thanks to you they didn't even manage to scramble a response," Xan says while removing the now purposeless lab coat.

Silver Dancer grins and says, "I wanted to try something new. I guess it worked out better than I expected." She winks and turns back to the kitchen. "Hey Eve."

"Hey," Eve murmurs as she peers through the fridge's contents.

"It made the ride home kind of boring though, you know?" Devlin says, eyes affixed to the holo-vid. The opening title of "Dr. Balthazaar & 'The V's' Big Game Hunt" is playing, a show about hapless mercenaries who are filmed while stalking some terrible creature which is stalking them in return.

"Gee, sorry Devlin, next time I'll let them sic the combat drones on you. You know, for entertainment's sake," Silver Dancer retorts, then sticks out her tongue at the now laughing Devlin. Xan grins and turns toward the northeast door.

"I'm going to talk to Rex, then shower and hit the sack for a couple of hours before I head to Cassandra's," he announces to the group, who nod and voice their assent in turn.

The heavy steel door slams closed and Xan enters the "Murder Chamber". He glances briefly at the concealed ceiling turrets, and the claymores that line the walls, before entering "The Castles" living quarters. The space consists of a series of five large bedrooms arranged around a central hall. The hall also branches south and leads to a stout door which opens to "The Castles" garden, Rex's living area. He turns down the short hall and opens the door. Outside, a tall turret rises up just to the left of the door. Dim UV bulbs irradiate the garden in grey light, carving erratic arboreal shadows in the soft grass. Xan stands in the garden for a while, looking everywhere for the Asura.

"Rex?" he finally asks. For a moment nothing happens. Then, the ground begins to heave upwards, creating a tufted plateau of grass which quickly melts back down again. The earth resettles to reveal the bestial, tiger-sized demi-god. Rex stretches and shakes the clumps of dirt from his rippling blue scales. He grasps the earth with his forepaws and hind leg talons as he turns towards Xan. An animated mane of shimmering red hair flows up from the Asura's head and neck, floating as though caught in an ever-present chaotic wind.

"Greetings Xanshudan, my travel has wearied me some, and so I find myself seeking respite within the cradle of the earth," Rex says, his armored, dog-like mouth not quite synching with the words that he speaks.

"Are you hurt?" Xan asks, even though he already knows the answer.

"It is difficult to kill that which is only partially here," Rex responds in his usual manner.

"Well, thanks for your help. But did you have to kill that mage?" Xan looks into the earth Asura's eyes, intense flashing colors radiating around points of infinite space.

"All paths are formed of chaos, identic to the branching frost forming on a pane of glass. The choice becomes inevitable in an instant, yet the notion of the other shall ever remain. And though exigencies may occur time and again, this path is never set, never certain, until that choice is made. The mage made his choice, and so the path was set in that instant," Rex responds, the deep growl of his voice drowning out the regular sounds of traffic.

"I see, anyway, I just wanted to make sure that everything was alright. I think I'm going to take a shower then lie down for a while," Xan says while looking past Rex to "The Castles" bath house just on the other side of the garden.

"When you awaken I shall be ready to accompany you to Cassandra's, should you feel that it is needed," Rex offers.

"Thanks that would be good, I was just planning on walking," Xan says.

"I shall shadow you, unseen," Rex adds.

"Good, you're ugly and nobody wants to see you," Kane comments from Xan's palm. Rex snorts, then smiles and vanishes from sight.

"See you later Rex," Xan says while crossing to the bath house.

"You shall, if your path allows for it," Rex responds.

After showering and dressing, Xan returns to "The Castles" living area. He then enters his private quarters. The large room has a bed, a dresser and a desk. A fair-sized weapons locker serves as one half of the walk-in closet. Xan crosses to the bed, undresses and climbs in. The wry voice of Kane fills the room.

"Not jerking-it today?"

"Shut up Kane." He then sighs and continues "You know, sometimes, I regret this little arrangement of ours." Kane laughs and speaks in a sugary voice.

"Oh come on, you know you love me." He then changes to a tone best suited for speaking with a one year-old: "Maybe you're forgetting about the 'Banewoods' incident; do you really think that you would have survived that without me?" Small kissing noises come from his tiny mouth.

"Yeah, yeah, thanks again, for the hundredth time, anyway, good night Kane," Xan replies before he rolls over and stuffs his left hand under the pillow.

"Good night," Kane responds internally.

Sleep overcomes him quickly and Xan soon finds himself in the midst of a vivid dream which grasps hold of his entire being. A thunderclap presents a flood of visions. Power clouds around a small sun, encased. Grotesque figures swirl, a metal skeleton, mutations, guns and helicopters. Explosions, fire and bullets, the buildings crumble to dust. Overwhelmed by the intensity of the imagery he soon awakens in a cold sweat. The stillness of the room invades. He stares at the ceiling, chest heaving rapidly. Then Kane's voice breaks the silence "What the fuck Xan, chill out!"

Xan doesn't respond, he just stares at the ceiling, breathes deeply, and tries desperately to remember what he just saw.

Grot Fastwhisker

Grot looks closely at the building. The imprint of an old ward remains. The reagents must have lost their energy, or maybe the ward was dismantled and never repaired. *Good,* he thinks, *that's one less thing to worry about.* He peers out from the rusted hole in the dumpster's dark blue metal. The pockmarked concrete of the Koshikawa enforcement center can be seen no more than a half block away. He calls for his watcher spirit. A moment later and the ghostly green rat is hovering in front of him.

"How may we serve you master?" The faint whisper of the spirit's voice drifts through Grot's mind.

"Rat must be wary of dangers." He internalizes the standard mantra.

"And this one will always watch for them master." The spirit replies in kind.

"Go to Grenda Snerdz. You will find her in that place." Grot motions to the Koshikawa enforcement center. The spirit departs immediately and flies towards its new goal. Grot waits for a moment, anxiety building. The dark folds of trash crowd around him as he sits still and listens to the city. He concentrates, eyes closed. Slowly, all around him, tiny voices begin to drift out of the quiet haze. He tilts his head in an effort to single one out. He needs a powerful voice now. A weak one will not do, he can't afford to be subtle. He slows his breathing. There, he can hear one. A soft voice, but a voice carved out of iron and steel, a warrior's voice.

Grot addresses the voice. "Rat greets you with all respect, mighty one. Rat stands in awe of your great power. Rat begs to ask a boon of one who is so mighty."

Nothing happens at first, then the screech of metal grinding against metal forms into a voice and speaks. "Rat may ask, this one shall respond."

"Rat gives you all of our thanks, rat is not worthy," Grot responds in a placating tone. He smiles inwardly and turns momentarily from the voice to focus on his watcher spirit. Grot closes his eyes and exerts the force of his will, touching the watcher spirit and engaging it. Immediately his vision transfers to inside of the building. Through the grey haze he can see Grenda and Mug.

Their auras are chaotic and hurt. He can see Mug's illness. A brief swell of rage overcomes him. "Bastards!" Grot snarls. "If Mug gets worse because of them, Rat will return and gnaw off their stupid feet." He seethes for a moment before he re-focuses on the watcher. A quick scout of the building reveals that it's a small, local enforcement center. He counts twenty-two employees. Sixteen of those twenty-two are armed with some type of firearm, mainly a collection of pistols and assault rifles. The center's containment cells are lined up against the north and east walls. He counts five prisoners in total, including Grenda and Mug. Those two are in a cell located on the east wall. *Perfect*, he thinks, *but we have to act quickly; they might take Mug to a juvenile facility soon.* Now he just has to warn Grenda, and cast the second part of the spell that he started while he was still in "Reachers Hope."

Grot releases his control on the watcher spirit. The confines of the dumpster materialize before him. He climbs out into the alley and stalks through the shadows, while clinging close to the stained wall. He searches around for a suitable location, and soon he finds what he's looking for, a door frame leading into the apartment block that dominates one side of the alley. Grot looks at the door. An old mechanical lock serves as the only deterrent to his ingress. He grins and slips off his backpack. A moment later and the door is standing open, thanks to a lock-picking gun that Grot acquired ages ago. He stops and listens for a moment in the open doorway. Content that he's alone, he removes a small glass jar from his backpack. He twists off the lid and lifts a dollop of dark paste from the inside of the jar. With a practiced hand he traces a series of sigils into the door frame. He finishes and murmurs three short words of power, sealing the sigils and linking them to the original markings back in "Reachers Hope". Grot then produces a rectangle of cardboard that he tore from a discarded box. He folds the cardboard and places it in the door frame at the level of the door knob, making sure that the cardboard prevents the door from shutting completely. Then, creeping low, he heads back up the alley to the safety of the dumpster.

Nestled once again in the steel cave, Grot produces a brown leather pouch. He tugs the top open and retrieves a tiny red pellet with his slender fingers. He then calls for his watcher spirit, and a moment later the tiny green rat is hanging in the air in front of him.

"With this offering Rat grants you speech." Grot intones the words of the spell as he crushes the red pellet between thumb and forefinger. "Grenda, it's Grot, stay clear of the rear wall and be ready to run." Grot conveys the message into the core of the watcher spirit. "Now go to Grenda and use your speech, use it quietly," Grot commands the watcher spirit.

"Yes master," responds the spirit. Grot wipes the red crumbs from his hand and tucks away the leather bag. He sits for a moment, trying to steady his nerves, before he begins to listen again. The voice comes quickly this time.

"Greetings again, oh mighty one! Rat grovels before your power! Rat would be ever grateful if you would help, Rat is so small and you are so big!" He then waits for a response. Suddenly, the stillness of the street is filled with the shrieking of twisting metal. The dumpster jumps as the deafening "boom" of heavy steel colliding with concrete overwhelms the alley. Grot shifts his gaze to the hole. He watches for a few seconds before a huge pile of dangerous metal lurches out through the alley. Formed into a roughly humanoid shape, the spirit's bladed limbs are made of jagged sheet metal. The rest of the fifteen foot tall monstrosity is comprised of a collection of pipes, nails, I-beams and girders.

A calm spectral voice fills Grot's mind: "This one shall serve." The words make Grot grin savagely. He looks to the enforcement center and commands the spirit.

"Strike a hole in that building at the spot where our watcher sits. Do not hurt the two living things in the room." As he speaks the words he extends his will and wraps an arcane tether around the creaking metallic behemoth. The city spirit complies and begins to lumber up the street. Heavy footfalls send tremors through the ground, causing windows to rattle and car alarms to wail. As the apparition nears the building the thunderous drumming of automatic weapons fire begins. Fast moving projectiles streak towards the steely spirit. Dozens of bullets flatten as they hit their mark, while others ricochet off and embed themselves in the surrounding street and buildings.

Grot sees the threat immediately. There are two Koshikawa guards wielding assault rifles, they're standing right near the building's entrance. They won't be able to stop it with those weapons, their bullets are actually adding to the spirit's mass, not taking away from it. They could hit Grenda or Mug though.

Grot growls and deftly reaches into his coat's inside pocket, producing an orb of compressed garbage. The orb measures about three inches across, yet it's surprisingly heavy. He holds the orb in an outstretched hand as he chants the song of the wisp. Within moments, a sickly orb of grey mist coalesces in the alley and begins to attract loose bits of garbage from everywhere. A swirling torrent of debris soon encases the orb. The whirling sphere is shot through with broken bottles, dirty diapers, busted microwaves and large bags of filth. Grot concentrates on the wisp and sends it hurtling out of the alley. The stinking sphere reaches the guards just as the metal spirit arrives at its destination. The whole world shakes as the spirit slams into the building and crushes a depression in the brick wall. Meanwhile the guards cry out as they are engulfed by the putrid ball of fast moving garbage. One of the armed men begins to retch, while the other is bludgeoned to his knees by an onslaught of solid trash. Grot keeps the wisp in place over the building's entrance. He then quickly climbs from the dumpster and moves up to the mouth of the alley.

Another massive "boom" rocks the ground as the metal spirit crashes into the building again. Vibrations from the impact shatter one of the building's windows and crack a second. The spirit recoils and pulls out a large chunk of the wall, it's immediately illuminated by the glow of the internal lights. The metal spirit steps back and Grot looks to the building's entrance again. The retching guard is dragging his unconscious comrade's body. He's attempting to get back into the building in a desperate bid to escape the whirling rubbish. Grot turns his attention back to the city spirit. He reaches for the arcane tether that binds them and sends a mental command. "Guard the two living things from that room and bring them back to us."

"This one shall do as Rat commands," the soft spectral voice responds. The metal spirit looks back to the building just as a small figure crawls through the rubble. The figure carries an even smaller body into the now empty street.

"Grenda!" Grot yells. She turns and looks to the alley, eyes wide with terror. Upon seeing Grot, she scoops Mug up in her arms and begins to run towards the alley. The metal spirit follows closely behind. Grot looks back to the building. The chaotic sphere of trash is clattering and banging against the main doors, the guards are inside somewhere. The sudden voice of his watcher spirit draws his attention.

"Master! A wizard is on the roof!" Grot looks up just in time to see a Human woman peek over the roof's edge. He acts swiftly and produces one of the egg shells that he keeps in his coat pocket. He growls out two clipped words and crushes the shell as he makes a series of arcane gestures that end with him pointing at the wizard. The wage mage begins to cast a spell. Then her hands stop moving and she looks around. She furrows her brow for a second then vomits a liquid stream off of the roof. She steadies herself and tries to cast again, but instead simply doubles over, out of view. Grot laughs. Soon Grenda and Mug reach him at the mouth of the alley.

He looks to Grenda and says "Go to the dumpster there, we'll be right behind you!" Then he turns back to the metal spirit "Stall them but do not kill anyone, do you understand?"

"Yes," responds the spirit.

Grot looks to the imposing figure and says, "When we are away from this place you may relinquish this form." He then adds, "You have served Rat well and Rat is grateful."

"Rat is strong. This one shall obey," the metal spirit responds, before turning back towards the building. Grot dismisses the rubbish wisp with a wave of the compacted orb. The pile of trash falls at the building's entrance. He then turns back up the alley and runs to the dumpster.

"Grot! I'm so glad to see you. Thank you!" Grenda begins.

Grot waves his hand then says, "Of course, but not here, let's go." He then leads them further into the ally and up to the chosen door.

"Where are we going? Do you know somebody here?" Grenda asks as they approach the door.

"Trust us," Grot says while reaching for the door. The smell of burnt gunpowder drifts into the alley, carried along by the sound of gunfire and loud voices. Grot opens the apartment door, the square of cardboard fluttering to the ground as he does. "Just walk through," he says, then smiles at her. Grenda clutches Mug, looks back briefly, shrugs, then steps through the doorway and instantly disappears. Grot grins and steps gingerly through the doorway. The familiar feeling of no time and no space soon end with him walking into the Snerdz apartment. Just in front of him stands a thoroughly puzzled Grenda. She shakes her head, puts Mug on the couch then turns and hugs Grot, tears welling up in her eyes.

"I don't know what that was but thanks Grot, Mug's so sick, he's not talking anymore. Those bastards wouldn't help." She chokes out the words.

Grot hugs her for a moment before saying "Don't worry Grenda, Rat will help him. Rat will use all of our power." Turning from Grenda he crosses to the couch and sits down in front of Mug. He breathes deeply and focuses his perception. Mug's aura is marbled with illness. *It looks bad, but there's still a chance,* he thinks. "We have to perform a ritual. We'll need you to get some things," Grot says as he continues to peer through the veil at Mug's spirit.

"Whatever you need Grot. Just please make him better?" Grenda responds. She then gets ready to leave.

Four hours later and the ritual is complete. Grot again peers through the veil into Mug's aura. He smiles triumphantly as he sees that the dark veins of the disease have disappeared. He looks over at the expectant Grenda.

"He'll be fine in a couple of days." Relief instantly floods over Grenda. She rushes to Grot and hugs him again.

"Thank you so much. I don't know what I would have done without you," she says as she steps back and moves to sit near Mug.

Grot stares at the boy and says, "It's Rat's fault Grenda. Rat should have been here for you. We shouldn't have gotten so lost speaking with the city." Grot looks down, then over to her.

Grenda smiles warmly and says, "You couldn't have known. Besides, if you didn't do crazy stuff like that you wouldn't be able to do all the other great things that you do, right?"

Grot laughs and touches his chin for a second before saying "We suppose, and, Rat wouldn't have billions of friends either." He gives her a sly grin and begins to pack up his ritual implements.

Grenda laughs. "Well, you'll have to let me buy you a bunch of lunches at the diner then."

"Rat would … I'd like that," Grot says as he finishes filling his large backpack. Grenda smiles at him then turns to Mug and kisses him on the forehead. "Rat will check on you tomorrow sometime. Call if you need anything, Rat keeps our phone in our front jacket pocket now," Grot says then winks.

"Thanks again Grot. Do something for me though? Take care of yourself," Grenda says.

Grot begins to head to the door then he adds, "We will if you do us a favour?" She tilts her head and smiles. "Stay away from Koshikawa buildings?" Grenda laughs and nods, while giving him a mocking look of innocence. He leaves and stands in the hall for a second. A tear wells up in the corner of his eye, brought on by a short pang of ancient grief. *Not now*, he thinks, *rat has another purpose, we cannot get lost again now.*

Grot attempts to re-center himself as he heads out of the apartment and into the busy streets of "Reachers Hope". He thinks about Mug and can't help but grin all the way back to his den. The trip is quick, and soon he's standing in the rat filled stone nest, scratched wooden table and sturdy lock box right where he left them. He mulls about, tending to his different hidden caches and preening the goods therein. After a while his cadre of rats leaves his company. Movement catches his eye then, and he looks to the pile of pillows and blankets. A large black rat emerges into the gloom. Grot blinks a few times then peers closely at the rat, the same one from the new-town sewer, he's sure of it.

"Warm greetings friend, aren't you the clever one to find us in this place," he says as he crosses to the lock box and opens the lid.

"The dreamer is the story." Grot stops dead in his tracks as the big rat's intention echoes in his mind. He turns, a handful of nutri-food pellets slipping between his fingers.

"What do you know of the dreamer?" Grot says while slowly placing the pellets in front of the rat and then sitting cross-legged on the floor.

"The dreamer is the old story, close to here. The darkness of life uses the path," the big rat responds. It then snatches up a pellet and begins to chew contentedly, as though its quest was complete.

Grot ponders for a long while as the rat eats its fill then returns to the nest of pillows and blankets. Eventually he removes his gear and most of his clothes, crosses to the warm confines of the nest and snuggles in. He lies on his back, scratching the black rat's head and thinking about what it said. After a long while he begins to feel drowsy. Then just as he begins drifting off he bolts upright, causing the rat to jump up and look at him.

"Apologies friend, we think that we know what you mean now," he says excitedly as he leaps out of the nest and begins to gather up his gear.

Not long afterwards he's back out on the streets of "Reachers Hope". Grot stops for a second and thinks about his destination. If he's right, it's only three blocks north then across an empty lot and up a short alley. There the west gate tower ruins can be found jammed in around a collection of buildings. The ruins have history, unlike the other ancient structures around here, there was an old story. Something about a demon, a prince and an unrequited love, it didn't end well. It's a famous legend; many hear it when they are children, as a fairytale. He begins to head towards the ruins. Cars and scooters speed by as he walks up the sidewalk. The smells from a nearby "street meat" van assail him briefly as he passes by. A group of Goblins and Orcs sits nearby. They're all feasting on their questionable meals while conversing in loud voices, glasses clink, bravado flows. Grot eyes the group over, then continues on. He passes a glowing strip mall, a bar called "The Cannibals Daughter" and several more low-rent apartment blocks. Five minutes later he arrives at the site.

The ruins are little more than a fifteen foot long section of stone wall, attached to the lower frame of a small stone tower. They are less than fifty feet away from a tall apartment building. The old stone wall connects directly to a chain link fence, which continues up the alley. There are thousands of pad-locks on the fence, some ritual display of love. A collection of roads and overpasses can be seen stretching some two hundred and fifty feet above the ruins. Grot looks around briefly before he sits cross legged in the middle of the frame of the tower. Countless pairs of names cover the ancient stone, hearts and addition signs linking them together. Breathing slowly and rhythmically, he peels back the veil and looks into the spirit realm. Roads and overpasses fade. The apartment block turns into a massive stone statue of a spear wielding warrior. The ground is painted an electric green. A haunting sensation slithers through his scalp. He can see swirling spectral forms hovering within the vast forests far in the distance. *We could find her still,* he thinks, *the woods are near.* Regret swells and he shoves the memory down. He then looks to the sky. There's a great vortex of sparkling clouds. They are alive with purple and red lightning bolts, pure mana energy. Grot sits transfixed, in all his long years he's never seen a mana cloud. Based on everything that he's heard, this one is immense. Yet there is something else as well, dark bands of mist that swirl about like the tentacles of a squid. There's something more subtle as well, something hidden. He looks closely for the source, any source. Vision blurs into pure intentionality, everything else fades away. Finally, a single thread stands out. There's a single black thread connecting the cloud to the ground. Grot can't tell where it leads exactly. It's too far away. He thinks for a moment. Not the dreamer, something else is using the cloud. *There is some force that bends dark magic to its will,* he thinks, *the "darkness of life".* The watcher spirit's voice breaks Grots concentration.

"Master beware, Orcs approach from your left. They have weapons." He immediately relaxes his focus and looks towards the mouth of the alley. A moment later three Orcs walk into view.

They are proudly displaying a variety of tattoos on their arms and throats. Two of them have the addition of a pistol casually stuffed in their waistbands. The third just looks like he enjoys punching things with the metal bands covering his meaty fists. The group stops a short ways away and the largest of the three addresses Grot.

"Sup Gobbo. Youz on 'Blood Knuckle' turf, what youz got for us?" He then bares his tusks in a display of aggression.

Grot looks up and says, "Blood knuckles? Rat's never heard of you." He sighs and continues "Rat has no time for this; it's already been a long day. You will go away now little blood knuckle. Do not make Rat cross with you!" He then stands and turns toward the group. The Orcs look to each other then they look to Grot and begin to laugh hysterically. After a short while the leader pipes up again.

"This Gobbo's nutz! Lets juss crack im down and filch im." The trio advances, cocky smiles etched across their faces. Grot grabs the fork and begins to focus his power. Then, out of nowhere, a park bench hits the lead Orc square in the chest and sends him skittering across the pavement. Grot tenses for a second, then wheels around to see the friendly face of Delrog, two curved horns sticking out of his mop of thick black hair and long tusks framing his wide mouth.

"Grot, I thought I saw yer," the huge Ogre bellows in a casual, booming voice. The remaining Orcs panic and begin to reach for their pistols. "I wouldn't do that if I wuz you fellas," Delrog says as he hefts a sturdy battleaxe designed to suit his twelve foot tall, eleven hundred pound frame. He then adds, "Sounded like Grots in no mood fer yer shenanigans, and I'd be much more worried bout im than 'Ol' Choppy' ere." The Orcs look to each other, then to Grot and Delrog, before they remove their hands from their weapons. They then move cautiously over to their fallen leader. "Don't come back neither. I'll be lookin fer youz, and next time I'll throw something more sharper den a bench!" he bellows as they remove their lifeless leader. Grot watches as the two conscious Orcs retreat up the alley. He sheathes the fork, then looks to the hulking Ogre.

"Many thanks friend Delrog."

"Youz ain't never needs to thank me Grot. I'll always owe youz," Delrog says as he reaches down to punch Grot lightly in the arm, to him, it feels like being kissed by a battering ram.

"How've you been?" Grot asks while rubbing his arm and moving back to his original position in the tower ruin.

"All better now thanks to youz. Thought I wuz gonna bite it," Delrog answers as he hooks his axe into a steel loop in his belt and covers it with his long brown coat.

"Rat is glad that we could be there," Grot says, then sits cross-legged on the ground.

Delrog stands for an awkward minute before asking, "Uh, watcha doing here Grot?" A confused look creeps across the big Ogre's face as he first looks to Grot then in the direction that Grot is facing.

Grot looks intently at the massive simpleton and says, "Rat has a purpose here. Please Delrog, Rat thanks you greatly but we must be alone now."

Delrog stands for another five seconds processing what was said before responding. "Oh, oh, oh. Sure, course, sorry Grot. I don't know too much bout magics."

"It's perfectly alright Delrog. Take care of yourself. Rat will always be there for you when you need us," Grot responds. Delrog smiles and nods, he then waves one last time before he lumbers back towards the street that he came from. Grot laughs quietly to himself as the humongous Ogre rounds the corner. *Sometimes the city provides in the strangest of ways*, he thinks.

With Delrog departed, he quickly scans the spectral sky yet again. Still, the black thread remains. The mana cloud looks bigger now. He shifts his perception back and looks around the courtyard. The minor ruckus didn't even attract any attention. He looks back up the alley. Steel doors, dumpsters and weave relay poles line the far side. He begins to fiddle with some small stones. Minutes tick by. The sounds of the city wrap him in a familiar cocoon as he waits. He sits in the midst of the ruins for a long time. One hour passes then two, and three. Before long he's beginning to doubt his revelation. Maybe he misinterpreted the rat's words. Another hour passes and Grot starts to get up when his watcher spirit's voice enters his thoughts.

"Master, the spirit sky!" Grot quickly shifts his perception and looks back in time to see a huge crack of searing light resolving into a globe of radiant power. A tornado of mana clouds races and roars around the orb. Huge waves of energy pulse off of it, irradiating the spirit scape in a collection of brilliant colors. Grot braces himself and looks closely at the orb. *No not an orb,* he thinks, *a tunnel.* As he watches, the tunnel buckles and belches forth a massive blast of light, causing Grot to recoil blind. He stumbles and shifts his perception back to the material realm. A few strained seconds pass, with color infected darkness as his only vista. Slowly, his vision begins to return through a field of sparkling lights. He hears the sound of someone vomiting and he turns toward the source. His vision clears and Grot sees that he's standing no more than ten feet away from a tall teenage Human.

The Human vomits again then he looks around wildly and screams in a northern Human dialect "What the fuck?!"

Grot stands motionless for a moment before he can't help but voice the very same sentiment "What the fuck indeed!"

Eric Gibson

I can't believe what I'm seeing, neon-glowing craziness. Buildings on top of buildings, around roads, on top of stairs, it's everywhere. It's all that I can see. Oh shit. Focus, this thing in front of me. What the fuck is it? It's like three feet tall and green. Large eyes with vertical slits, like a snake. What the fuck? It's covered in weird shit. What's that, a bird cage?

"What the fuck, you're small and green!" is all I manage to say. The thing looks taken aback for a second.

"No need to bring size and color into this. You're tall and sort of pinkish! There, isn't that hurtful?" he retorts in an impish sort of way. Despite myself I burst out with laughter, then instantly stop. Blackness overcomes me.

I fall into a dream. I'm at Matt's. The fire is roaring high. The party goers are dancing around it and chanting in unison. I look more closely to see that each of the dancers is small and green. They have snake-like eyes. They're all howling and throwing their hands around wildly. I can see them dancing in an intricate circular pattern. I can hear a voice ...

"Dreamer..." It's faint, far away. The dance intensifies. The figures are whirling and spinning, jumping and diving. The chant becomes a cacophony. Still the voice, it's urgent now ... "Dreamer, wake!" The dancers are gone. Just a hurricane of fire remains. Something rises from its center. An eye? "Eric Gibson, awake!"

I snap to. The dark smell of mildew greets me as I open my eyes. I'm in some kind of brick shack. A small card table sits at one end. A fridge-like construction is across from it. I'm on a couch. There are two stools near the table. I can't make out the light source, but the room has an odd glow. I twist and look around, nearly retching as my vision spins. I can see what looks like a steel door standing beside a boarded-up window. I lie back down. My mind races, it keeps resetting itself, over and over again. It keeps going through what I've just seen. A quick flash of color catches my eye. I sit up and look intently at the greenish glow. Is that a rat? I'm suddenly aware of the raw vulnerability inherent in my situation. The door opens and I'm on my feet and hefting one of the stools before I can think about what's happening. It's that thing again. It enters the hut. It seems oblivious to the stool that I'm holding.

"Watch it monster! I'll mess you up!" I say, trying to muster all the menace that I can. The threat still comes out as a quavering peep.

"No, no Eric. Stools are for sitting, not for hitting rats," it says, eyes gleaming with an odd inner light.

"How do you know my name?" The stool slackens in my grip. This thing doesn't seem concerned at all, or threatening for that matter.

"You dream very loudly in this place Eric. Rat can hear your name, it drifts to us in the spectral winds," it responds. What the fuck does that mean? Is this thing crazy? I put the stool down and sit.

"What are you?" I can't take my eyes off of it, long nose, pointed ears. Its arms almost reach the ground while it's standing. It smiles, revealing rows of shark teeth. It then sits across from me on the couch, shrugging off its large backpack in the process.

"Our name is Grot. We are a Goblin and a shaman. We follow the voice of Rat, the voice of the city." It grins and nods to itself as though that was the perfect answer. A Goblin? A shaman? What does that even mean? The voice of rat?

"Wait, the green rat?" I blurt out. The Goblin looks surprised.

"You can see the form of the watcher? Interesting." It seems to consider something.

"A watcher? What do you mean shaman? Like magic?" I ask. I'm light-headed and agitated, my leg's twitching hard.

"It's not surprising that you know some things. The dreamers touch the veil and so they see us as we see them. In fact your dream may have created ours, or vice versa of course," it says in a matter-of-fact sort of way.

"What?" I say. My head is still buzzing; I'm starting to feel sick again.

"Not important. This is important though," Grot says as he raises a necklace of sorts. It's made out of a thick twine with a small rodent skull dangling at its center. The skull is framed by a series of shiny black stones, four per side. "You must wear it or they will find you easily, and it will help you to understand." Grot offers me the necklace. My head swims.

'What? I want to go home!" The words cause me to heave for a moment. I can feel tears welling up. Don't cry you bastard. Not in front of this thing. Who knows what it would think?

"We do not know the way Eric. Rat is sorry," he says, sounding genuinely sympathetic. Wait, how does he understand me? I choke down the tears and look at Grot. Despite his savage features I can see a face worn with care lines. He seems so kind. Is it a ruse? What if he's just waiting for me to let my guard down? Then "Bam!", he like bites me and drinks my blood, or something. Shit! I don't know what I'm thinking. He could have killed me a dozen times by now. I can see a machete on him right now.

"How can I understand you?" I ask. Grot shifts on the couch, arms still outstretched brandishing the necklace.

"Rat knows several Human dialects, you speak a northern one. Rat also has a necklace," he says rapidly in a thick accent. A northern dialect? Wait! Humans!

"You mean there are other Humans here?" I ask. Grot bursts out laughing and nods.

"Oh yes. Humans and Elves and nasty Dwarves and silly-looking Halflings and great big Ogres and not so big Minotaurs and somewhat reticent Gnomes and..." It looks like he's going to just keep naming things. I hold up a hand and shake my head.

"What are you telling me? That all these things that don't exist, live here?" I say, incredulous.

"Yes, yes, and much worse than that," Grot says quickly. He then adds "Please Eric, the necklace," as he shakes the peculiar neck decoration. I look at it for a second, shrug and grab it. The skull rattles against the small stones as it swings gently in the dim light. I don't know if this is some kind of fashion statement here, but normally this type of necklace would just mark you as a future serial killer. I hook the string around my neck and let the skull dangle against my shirt. A strange tingling sensation briefly travels through my back and neck. An involuntary shudder grips me and the sensation passes. I grasp the skull and look closely at it. Small runes cover every millimeter of the bone.

"Is this magic?" I ask, immediately regretting the timber of my voice, somewhat reminiscent of an awed five-year-old. Grot laughs and slaps a knee. He then looks at me thoughtfully.

"You feel it, don't you?" he asks in a way that suggests he already knows the answer. I don't say anything. I just continue to stare at the small skull. The tiny runes seem to move about of their own accord.

"The necklace will also help you to speak, and to understand what is being said to you," he says. I sit for a moment thinking about what Grot has told me. Anxiety begins to wash over me. It starts to feel like panic. How can this be? How can I get back home? I can feel tears welling up again. I can't help it now, and before I can stop myself, I'm crying. My head in my hands, I'm heaving up and down. Then Grot speaks. His voice becomes a great soothing beacon that washes over me. "It will be alright Eric. Rat has you now, and the city does not want you to be harmed. Rat is not Dog but we will guard you for now. Do not cry Eric. You have power that you do not know, and the strength of the city will lift you now. Do not despair." Words slow and begin to blend into a beautiful rhythm that captures the whole of my mind. The song's splendor sears the fear from my thoughts. I cross to the now empty couch and lie down. Sleep overtakes me and, thankfully, I don't dream.

I awake with a start. My chest is heaving, unfamiliar surroundings. Where am I? I must have passed out at Matt's. I don't recognize this room though. It isn't Jordan's house either. Then it hits me all at once. The Goblin, the city, I remember. I bolt upright. I'm on a large couch, way too large, like it was made for a giant. There's a coffee table and an arm chair. A strange smell permeates the area. It looks like there are electronics of some type against the far wall. Everything's oversized, what's happening? Then a voice, it's close, just through the massive hall.

"Rat will be gone soon, the Human needs Rat's help." It sounds like that Goblin from before. I jump at the response, as a deep rumbling voice fills the room.

"Anytime, humie his age shouldn't be wanderin' round dem streetz. He weren't even armed." The voice sounds enormous, as if an elephant could speak. I look over the back of the couch. A huge bay window takes up the better part of the wall, thick curtains are drawn.

"It appears that our guest is awake," the Goblin announces, as it steps into the room across from me. What was his name? Grit, or something?

"Hey," I say while staring at the ground. Can't run, there's nowhere that I can run to. "Holy shit! What the fuck is that!" I exclaim as the small Goblin is eclipsed by a gigantic figure. It must be more than ten feet tall and its shoulders are like five feet wide. A monster with giant teeth and curved horns, it could twist me in half like a regular person twists the top off of a bottle of beer.

The Goblin lets out a laugh then holds up his hands and says, "Worry not Eric. Friend Delrog can be quite gentle. He is an Ogre." Gentle, that thing could break my rib cage with a sneeze. It's grinning shyly at me. It seems to have a childlike demeanour.

"Hullo," it bellows while lifting a ponderous, ham-sized hand and giving a single wave. I can't think of what to do so I just wave back stupidly.

The Goblin laughs again then says, "You must be hungry. You've been asleep for some time." Oh shit, how long have I been here? My folks will be freaking out, not to mention Jordan, Matt and everybody at the party.

"Oh shit, I have to get back," I say, and begin to climb from the couch. My head swirls and I sit right back down.

"Slowly Eric, stay there, Rat will get you something to eat. Friend Delrog, keep Eric company please," the Goblin says before it heads into the hall past the behemoth. Maybe I can call home, yeah, my phone. I quickly take my cell phone out of my pocket and activate it. I try to connect to each and every number without response, or any real function at all.

"Ain't never seen dat type phone afore." The bass of the Ogre's voice jolts me out of my despair. I try to say something, but all that comes out is a faint sound of acknowledgement. I follow it up with a nervous smile. Oh bloody hell, it's coming over here! Two long strides later and Delrog is sitting beside me on the couch. The impact of the Ogre's weight settling on the furniture shakes me violently. I'm breathing heavily now, my heart is beating quickly. I look over briefly and am greeted by a head nearly as large as my torso. Those tusks must be four inches long. His breath could make a brave man weep. I try to smile, and show him the phone, flipping through a couple of screens as I do. "Looks kinda old, kinda real old," the Ogre says. Old? This phone is brand new, state of the art. He grins broadly and follows up with "youz wanna watch 'Drone wars'?" I just nod. I'm too petrified to do anything else. "Holo-vid on," the Ogre says in a loud voice. A second later, the wall with the electronics virtually disappears, leaving behind a crystal clear three-dimensional video. There's like tanks and helicopters and crazy looking robot things. They're all shooting at each other and driving around at insane speeds. What kind of show is this? There's some kind of scoring system, it's in a different language that I can't read. I can understand the announcers though. They're commentating like at a UFC match.

"Oh! Did you see that shot? 'Firewing's' in trouble, it seems like 'Iron lady' is looking to end it," the one announcer says, as a large explosion overtakes one of the flying drones. Immediately afterwards a series of tracer rounds strike the disc-like construction. The drone twists and banks down into the ground before shattering into a giant fireball.

"Ouch! Now you know Alex will feel that one," the one commentator says.

The other responds with "He sure will Mike. I bet he'll be sick for hours." They both laugh at the "joke". I find myself momentarily absorbed. The show is mesmerizing.

The Goblin returns with a plate covered in what looks like pieces of fruit or vegetable. There also appears to be some kind of cured meat and he's holding a bottle full of orange liquid in his left hand. I snap out of the trance and begin to recall my surroundings again.

"I have to go. My folks will be looking for me," I say in a meek voice. I'm trying my damndest not to get choked with emotion.

The Ogre responds first . "Oh, where's it choo live den? We'z can help yer get back in no time," he says in a languid tone. I look to him briefly, then look back to the Goblin.

"We are sorry Eric. Rat does not know your purpose. A dreamer has never come this far before. Rat does not know the way back," the Goblin says. He then places the plate and bottle on the oversized coffee table. What dreamer? What does that mean? I can't get back home? I start to panic again. I look back to the Ogre. He's focused on the flickering 3D images.

"What am I supposed to do?" I say as I look back to the Goblin.

"For now, eat and drink. There are those who we may speak with. They are far from here and you do not understand the nature of the city. We must be cautious now. Others may have seen your arrival," the Goblin says, as it sits on the carpet in front of me. Others?

"What does that mean? And what does it matter, I don't have anything of value," I say while inspecting the plate of food. The orange-tinged bottle sweats on the table next to the plate.

"You may be wrong there Eric. Rat sees something in your aura. We have not seen its like before," the Goblin says cryptically.

"What does that mean?" I say while prodding one of the pieces of what I've decided are vegetables.

The Ogre laughs heartily then pipes in "Ye see Grot, I ain't tha only one what can't understand ye."

Grot laughs and responds, "Rat has been told that we have that problem." He follows up by saying "all will be clear after we speak with Elindriss."

"Who's that?" I say. I then pop a piece of "vegetable" in my mouth and chew briskly. It's kind of sweet, not bad.

"She is someone who is skilled in reading auras," Grot says. What does that mean? I guess I'll find out. What choice do I have really? I eat more of the "vegetable" and some of the meat. It's pretty good and the drink tastes kind of like orange soda, only different in some intangible way.

"Will they be able to get me home?" I say between bites and sips.

"Rat does not know. She is skilled in many magics, Rat hopes so," Grot says, then smiles. I wonder if he's actually crazy. He keeps calling himself "Rat". He must know magic though, the necklace, the green rat.

"Why are you helping me?" I blurt out the words without thinking.

Grot seems to consider for a moment before responding, "Rat is part of the city. When the city suffers, so does Rat. The city told Rat about the dreamer, you. The city told Rat that you must be put under protection. If you are not, the city will suffer greatly, it may even cease to be," Grot says. The words raise hairs on the back of my neck. Okay this Goblin must be crazy, the city? How do you speak with a city? It's crazy-person talk. Yet he seems so sure. Maybe you can speak with a city in this place, whatever that means.

"Whatcha talkin bout Grot?" the Ogre says as he glances over.

"Not important, friend Delrog. We must leave soon, but first Rat must ask two more favors of you," Grot says. He then stands and begins to clear the empty plate and bottle from the table.

"Course, anything for youz Grot," responds Delrog. I find it strange that this giant should be so eager to please the little Goblin. Maybe he put a spell on the Ogre or something. Delrog does seem kind of spacey.

"Many thanks, friend Delrog. Firstly, Rat is not fond of guns, but Eric must be safe. Rat does not have a 'Merc card', does friend Delrog know anybody who sells them?" Grot says as he quickly takes the plate and empty bottle to the hall and out of sight. Wait, what did he say? A gun?

"Oh sure! 'Beetlefoot's' got a good selection. He has em in a cube van. Should I call im?" the Ogre responds in a lethally casual tone. I've only ever shot a rifle a couple of times. Mostly .22s when we'd visit my cousin's farm. I've played a bunch of first person shooters, maybe that will help. Shit, what am I thinking, who am I supposed to be shooting?

"Yes please," Grot calls from what must be the kitchen.

"A gun?" I say nervously as Grot re-enters the living room.

"Hopefully you will not need it. But you have come to a dangerous place Eric. You cannot imagine the terrors that lurk in the dark stretches of these streets," Grot says, as he removes his backpack.

"Beetlefoot? Yeah, was hoping that youz could swing by. Whatzat? Yeah, same place. Oh good, good, see youz inna bit." The Ogre's loud conversation takes over the room. He then turns to Grot and says "Said he's not too far, be bout forty minutes er an hour." Grot nods then produces a thick fold of what looks like money, except fancier and more colorful.

"Thank you greatly friend Delrog. The last favor Rat asks is that you do not mention Eric to anyone. It is very important, do you understand?" Grot says while looking sharply at the Ogre. There is something about this small Goblin. I can't quite put my finger on it. It's like he has a presence or something, he's hard to ignore.

"Course Grot. I'll take it to my grave," Delrog says in a loud, solemn voice. He then adds "I could go wit youz if youz need protectin? I gotz gunz, an 'Ol Choppy', an his brothers and sisters."

"You are too gracious, friend Delrog. Rat and Eric will be less noticeable without you, and Rat does not want to place you in the path of danger," Grot responds.

"Whatever youz want Grot, youz know I ain't scared o nuthin," Delrog says. In contrast to when other people make that statement, I actually believe the Ogre. Whether he's fearless or just plain stupid is another question all together.

"Thank you again friend Delrog. Rat wonders, does friend Delrog have any of the 'Stunty Stan's Study Stuff, Stupid!' series of holo-vids?" Grot asks.

"Naw, but I could getz it off da weave," Delrog replies. Stunty wha? The weave?

"Could you please? The urban creatures series should work," Grot says, then touches his chin thoughtfully.

"What's the weave?" I ask as the large Ogre moves to the holo-vid and bellows "Computer on."

Grot looks over at me. He then seems to drift off for a moment before he waves his arms around and says, "Digital cities all around, but also in small computers. Get much information from all around the world." He points to the holo-vid. I get the feeling that he doesn't really know what he's talking about, but it almost sounds like the internet back home. I look at the holo-vid. The holograph now displays a series of menus, prompts and folders, all floating in mid air. Delrog taps on a few files, then collapses the sphere before bringing up a display that looks like a media player.

"Whatcha lookin for Grot?" Delrog says, his wild features highlighted by the holo-vid's glow.

"If you could just play a slide show of images, standard street critter stuff," Grot says.

"What's this?" I say as I look towards the holo-vid.

"Rat wanted to show you that your dream might be very different than ours," Grot says. He then points to the holo-vid just as a sickly monster appears framed against a brick wall. The thing's skin is peeled back from a mouth full of sharp fangs; it looks like it was Human once. Long black claws jut from the monster's hands, and milky eyes skulk in its recessed sockets, grey leather skin encases it. Some text appears below but I can't understand it.

"What's it say?" I ask while pointing at the words.

"Delrog, change the language to Human, northern dialect would you?" Grot says then sits cross-legged on the floor across from the holo-vid. The Ogre fiddles with the display for a second before the word "Ghoul" appears at the bottom of the screen. There also appears to be some series of classifications or genus. I look to Grot, who returns my gaze briefly before pointing to the holographic images again. The image changes, now there's some small ugly thing. This creature is covered in patchy body hair and warts. It looks tiny. The thing is holding a butcher knife that's the same size at its body. The words "Sewer Troll" appear underneath the image. The holo-vid continues. Next a sort of dog with chameleon skin called a "Bargheist". Then a cat-like creature with creepy glowing eyes. The word "Bastet" appears beneath it along with warning text saying "Extremely dangerous". The holo-vid continues. The large display shows one monster after another, all real, all in this place.

The slideshow plays for a while longer before Grot speaks. "So you see Eric, if you do not know these things from where you came from, then you have entered into a very different dream indeed." He then turns to Delrog. "Thank you friend Delrog, you can watch holo-vid again if you wish." The Ogre nods absentmindedly then activates the holo-vid, the roar of "Drone wars" filling the room once again. I swallow hard and think about what I just saw. What the fuck was that one thing? It was like a giant mutant octopus crossed with an eagle, it was bigger than a car.

"Yeah, maybe a gun would be good," I say while staring off into space.

Grot laughs then says, "Rat will get you two." I can't help but laugh. After a minute or two of watching drone wars I calm down a bit. Damn it, nature calls. Well I'm going to have to go sometime.

"Is there a bathroom?" I ask, somewhat sheepishly.

Grot chuckles then says, "Yes, but it is very big. Don't fall in." I laugh again. He then adds, "Last door on the right", and he points to the hall. I walk in the indicated direction. As I suspected, a large kitchen is on the right-hand side of the hall. Across from the kitchen, a poorly painted door stands closed. I travel further. Two more doors line either side of the end of the hall. The one to the left looks like an external door. I enter the right-hand door and I'm greeted with a plethora of peculiar sights and smells. I almost feel like I'm a little kid again. Everything is massive. I actually do hope that I don't fall in. That toilet is huge, and I don't even want to think about the ways that Delrog befouls it on a regular basis. Just climb up and hold onto the edge. Keep my legs wide. This will be fine.

One awkward balancing act later and I'm feeling a bit better. I walk back to the living room, dawdling briefly to look at the kitchen as I pass. A grimy smear of empty food containers covers nearly every surface. The giant appliances look as though they've never been cleaned. It'll be a wonder if I live through the meal that Grot fed me. I enter the main room and cross to the couch.

"Is this a house?" I ask Grot. He's once again sitting cross-legged on the carpet in front of the couch.

"Yes, Ogre house. House made for one Ogre," Grot replies while gnawing at what looks like a handful of seeds.

"Are there lots of Ogres?" I ask, while gazing at Delrog. His large yellow eyes are staring intently at the explosive action unfolding on the 3D display.

"Not so many. There are very few Ogres in this part of the city, more on the edge, outside of the hive," Grot answers.

"The hive?" I ask.

"Yes, yes. Tirileth city, the middle is sometimes called 'The Hive' or 'The Tier'. There are cities on top of cities, more than thirty levels that go up into the sky. There are even many levels that go down beneath the ground." Grot motions downward with both hands. I think of the streets and bridges that I saw. Thirty levels?

"Wait, how big are these levels?" I ask, in an attempt to understand exactly what Grot is telling me.

"Levels are bigger at the bottom, smaller up at the top. Rat thinks maybe thirty miles across at the bottom and maybe one mile at the top?" Grot says, then pops some seeds in his mouth and chews noisily. Thirty miles across! That's just one level? This place is enormous.

"What level are we on?" I ask, not that it matters much.

"We are near 'Reachers hope' on the city's second level. There are those who call this level 'The Gauntlet', but Rat has no use for such silliness."

"Where are we going?" I ask, as I remember what Grot said earlier.

"We must reach Cassandra's mansion. She lives high up on level nine, we have not seen her in a long time; we hope that she is not upset with us," Grot responds. I just nod dumbly.

"Okay, right. But first we wait for the guns?" I say.

"Yes, first we wait for the guns," Grot retorts. I sit back on the colossal couch. Maybe five minutes later Delrog's phone rings. I can see the holo-screen from here. The infamous "Beetlefoot" has arrived.

"Beetlefoot" turns out to be a small shifty Goblin. He looks like he has cameras for eyes. His right arm is like some kind of advanced prosthetic, it looks kind of brutal, like it's made for hurting people. He's wearing a long coat and I can see a gun dangling under his arm. I suppose that's to be expected, still, it freaks me out. We're right on the street in front of Delrog's Ogre house. Nobody seems to care. I see all sorts of Goblins and Orcs walking around, it's surreal. They're everywhere. Tall ones, short ones. Shit, look at that Orc, he must be eight feet tall. Oh why couldn't Delrog come with us? I look back towards the van. Grot is haggling loudly with the augmented Goblin. Delrog stands just to the side. Above us a cluster of roads and pillars connects to create a vast urban hall. After a minute or two "Beetlefoot" packs up and drives his van back down the narrow street. Grot approaches. He's carrying a duffle bag in one of his long arms. He grins and says, "Good deal, come back inside and we will show you."

Delrog and I follow him back up the front steps and then into the relatively small Ogre house. We gather again in the living room. This is kind of exciting. Is he really going to just give me a gun? Grot places the bag on the ground. He then unzips the top and hefts out a nasty piece of metal. It looks kind of like an Uzi or something, holy shit. He grins and says, "You must be careful with this, Eric Gibson. What do you know about guns? You have them in your dream?" I look at the firearm, as Grot slides a magazine into the handle.

"I shot some rifles back home. Nothing serious though," I say, still staring at the weapon.

"Here," Grot says as he steps near. He then continues, "This is the charging handle, put in magazine, pull like this and gun is loaded. This is safety. Push like this for safe, push here for one bullet only and push here for many bullets. This is the magazine

release, push when empty of bullets. This is a good gun, reliable."
He smiles and holds the gun in his outstretched hands. I grab the
weapon—it's heavier than it looks.

"Are there more bullets or clips?" I ask.

"Yes. Rat's got three more magazines there, eleven millimeter
rounds, same as the pistol," Grot says as he points at the duffle
bag.

"There's a pistol too?" I ask while I look at the bag.

"Yes, yes help yourself. Just remember, same as submachine
gun. Chamber one round, use safety, magazine release makes
clicking noise, you know, bang, bang," Grot says as he waves at the
bag. I walk over and peer inside the bag. Sure enough, a compact,
sturdy-looking pistol sits at the bottom. The firearm is surrounded
by a number of magazines. I can see three longer magazines for the
submachine gun and three smaller ones for the pistol.

"Thanks Grot," I say as I lift the pistol out of the bag.

"Maybe just take the pistol and leave submachine gun in the
bag, then carry bag?" Grot suggests.

"Oh, yeah right. I guess this is illegal or something?" I say
while placing the submachine gun in the bag.

"Well, most Marshalls won't care about the pistol.
Submachine gun might be different, although, not where we're
going. Hmm, on second thought, carry both," Grot says then
laughs to himself. Something about his laugh makes me nervous. I
take the submachine gun back out of the bag and sling it over one
shoulder using the attached strap. I find a spot for the pistol at the
small of my back, jammed in my waistband and held tight with my
belt. "That reminds Rat. We got this from a street vendor earlier,"
Grot says. He then quickly exits the room before re-entering with a
large black coat. "It should fit," he says as he hands it to me. The
coat's quite heavy. The material feels kind of like leather.

"Thanks again Grot," I say as I put the coat on. It fits well
enough. The coat's bottom travels down past my knees, it covers
the submachine gun nicely. It has deep front pockets that can be
used to hold the extra magazines as well.

"Rat could not afford a better coat, but this one has some ballistic weave, to protect the dreamer," he says, motioning towards the coat as he speaks.

"Cool! I mean, well thanks," I say as I smooth out the pockets and get ready to fill them with the magazines. Grot nods and looks at Delrog, who has been watching with infantile fascination. He then addresses the Ogre.

"Friend Delrog, Rat cannot thank you enough. Rat will bring you a present when we next head this way." Delrog smiles like a massive child and nods his head. Grot then turns to me and says "Are you ready? We must not linger here." I look to Grot, then to Delrog, then back to Grot. I swallow hard then nod as I feel for the new weight of the two guns. "Good. Worry not Eric, for you are with Rat now and Rat has great strength within these streets and alleys," Grot says. He then checks his bizarre collection of accoutrements. Satisfied that everything is as is should be, he heads towards the hall. I follow as Delrog stands to see us out. We exit through the large door and walk down the concrete steps. We start up the street and I look back to see the Ogre framed in his doorway. I can see a simple grin carved across his enormous face as he waves goodbye. I wave back and can't help but wonder what it would be like to be him. Massive, simple, and happy, doesn't sound so bad really.

We haven't gone far when Grot stops then peers up and to his left. He seems to be staring off into space. No wait, the green rat, it's there. He's saying something to it, but I can't hear any words. "Hurry Eric, we must go, this way now!" Grot says. I follow him up the street. We turn right at the first cross street. He's fast for his size. I can barely keep up. He turns to the left and darts into a path between two buildings. I follow and find a staircase heading up to a catwalk. We make it to the catwalk before he slows and says "Come, we are not safe here. Someone was watching you. We must get to Cassandra's."

I pant and try to catch my breath before responding. "Who's watching me?" I follow Grot as he moves swiftly over the catwalk and back out onto the bustling street.

"It is not clear. But they have strong magic; they have performed a ritual, a powerful ritual," he says as we continue up the curved street. I just follow along and hope, yet again, that this small Goblin isn't completely insane.

Grot and I continue on for some time. The city is astounding. I imagine that I'm experiencing some type of culture shock. I can't tell—I've never really traveled anywhere before. A crazy patchwork of streets, roads, bridges and buildings surrounds us. Strange flying machines bask in the glow of outlandish holographs. Alien signs and sigils festoon the landscape, and the crowds... The crowds are everywhere, an insanely captivating blend of life. I can see Humans in their number as well. But they're all wearing weird clothes, and lots of them have metal implants in their heads and bodies.

"So, what's the deal with the metal eyes and arms and stuff?" I ask Grot, as we turn into a wide pedestrian walkway.

"Cybernetics, there are many who give up parts of their body and spirit so that they can see better and be stronger," he says as we round a bend. He then adds "To Rat it is unnatural, but there are many who do not feel that way."

"So, what? You can just buy better eyes or stronger arms or a new brain?" I ask.

Grot laughs then responds. "Yes, yes, many things for one to buy. One can buy bones and arms and feet. Buy blades in fingers and lasers in eyes. There are some who have no body left. Their spirits are warped and often mad." I think about that for a minute, it's almost like this place is a snapshot of some future version of the earth. Only with the addition of crazy shit walking around everywhere.

"Stop! No! Rat should have seen. Be still Eric. Do not make a sudden move!" Grot says as he holds out a hand towards me. I look up and around. We're at the elbow of a wide alley, it branches to the left. Square apartment blocks line the alley. Some of the buildings are stacked on the others at odd angles. Then I see them. What the fuck? How did I not see them before? Four heavily armed men are fanned out at the alley's corner. Two are covering the left hand passage while the other two are directly in front of us.

They're wearing advanced looking armor and carrying assault rifles. I hear movement behind us. There's another man. No wait, he has pointed ears, an Elf. His clothes are different, they're covered in odd symbols.

The Elf speaks. "Run along little shaman, this doesn't concern you. Give us the boy and we'll let you live." The words send a shiver down my spine. We're fucked. My heart begins to race. Why me?

Grot looks to the Elf, a savage gleam in his eyes as he speaks. "Live, die, it's all the same really. But first you really should meet Rat's friends. They would be ever so glad to meet you." He finishes speaking and abruptly he transforms into a large ghostly rat. He's floating in the air and a shining green mist surrounds him. He begins to make a bizarre sound. He's chanting but the sound is coming from everywhere. I can see waves of power radiating off of him, like the ripples on a pond's surface.

"Kill the shaman! Don't harm the boy!" The Elf barks out the order. He then begins to make a series of elaborate gestures with his hands. The armed men raise their weapons and begin to move into position. Shit! I have to help Grot. I step quickly between the ghostly rat and the Elf while I fumble for my gun. The armed men hesitate. I'm in the way, I now realize. The Elf looks at me and smiles cruelly. His hands begin to move in a different way than before. Streaks of light are coalescing in his hands. Shit! I'm panicking. I can't reach the gun. Then, the whole area begins to buzz with an indescribable sound. The Elf stops moving his hands and looks around. Suddenly the sound reaches a terrifying crescendo and rats come from everywhere. The Elf spins back towards us but Grot is nowhere to be seen, just rats. There are so many rats. Rats of all description. I see brown rats, grey rats and white rats. There are red-eyed snarling rats and large black rats. Rats the size of dogs bound out of the alleys and, what are those, flying ghost rats? Gah! Flying ghost skeleton rats! What the fuck! The men are screaming and firing on the rats. I can see scores of them being shot down, maybe hundreds. It doesn't matter though, a sea of rats, never ending. An explosion goes off and I'm thrown to the ground. My ears are ringing. The smell of burning fur fills my nostrils. I look over. I see a muted screaming Elf, he's covered in rats. Rats and blood. I shut my eyes, I'm dizzy. My head throbs. My hearing is a high-pitched wail. I open my eyes and look up the alley. Everything is rats. No buildings anymore, no streets. No armored men, no screams, just rats. I fade to black.

The Ballad of Grimmfang

A querulous "Den" of life made terse. I am the god of this universe. This scabrous king that beckons me in is neat and rich and guarded. He feels it's his place to sit cross from this face, to speak with the skull of the god head. The night's cool and crisp for my rooftop tryst with the entire world down beneath me. So eyes alight with a scanner's sight the story unfolds discretely. Twenty-seven inside as no-one can hide before the tech of the devil. These lists of light, the tale of their might, show a pitiful plight in the rubble. And so in due course they'll all be made worse, if they should choose to cause trouble. Snap back to my mind I find that slight grind that turns my hearing electric. I pat the black cat of neural synapse and hearing made thought scampers back. Transmission to mind I find with that grind a coiling bright mass of signals. I pluck from the bunch a sumptuous lunch, corp. security and Marshalls, their vigils. So as long as I grind, from time to time, they won't catch the white skull of the devil. Lest cold steel bone arm and "Fates" trusty form could bring "Retribution" to revel. So if I must I'll crush them to dust as long as the grind chimes a warning. But all in due time, I must first show them mine to test of their plans and their daring.

I descend.

I stop all mirth with my plummet to earth, shrouding the spot completely. From fifty feet high I fall from the sky, cracking hard ground beneath me. My mechanized thighs cause great surprise, people drawing guns, nearly. As terror struck fools yammer and drool I cross the ground immediately. Now panicked eyes cause me to surmise that all of my life's deeds precede me. I keep them in place with a slow grinning face, followed closely by words they heed dearly.

"Hold tight your minds you spurious swine, your 'clever' din that spirals so thin. I'll stop the clout that you all flout should I see your guns come out! So flee with your bones to your fetid homes if it's a bounty you're seeking. Cause I'll shred all your spines leaving only behind no more than a puddle of reeking." I deliver my rhyme to gauge all in kind. I'm met only with false smiles and greetings. If I had the time, it comes to mind, I'd deliver on them savage

71

beatings. Pale forms of fright run through the night as up to the door I creep as a blight. Yet others exclaim, "Look there! He's insane!" The corpser, the cancer, the mech-necromancer, but they'd never say, as from bone I'd flay, their skin and muscle and lives. So I stride as all must abide into the place where drinking thrives. I first check the grind and find no sign of my lunch having any hunch, so it's inside I decide to confide, eyes scanning side to side. A room filled wide with the rude and the snide. I see, sitting with three, he who has sent for me, corporate, suited and wee. He spots my face in the haze of this place a stark white apparition; I just smile and all the while continue my peregrination. Upon reaching his booth I see, forsooth! No room has been made for the devil! I eye up the others, and forgetting my druthers, I speak with a tone low and level.

"If I wanted you dead, I'd claim your head and be free and clear. Now let them roam, these cronies of chrome, before my ire appears here." He mumbles, he moans, he drops his cell phone, to a shower of "sorrys" am I treated. They're sent to drink foam, his cronies of chrome, so down in the booth am I seated. Now across from his face I cut to the chase, as my temper is getting quite heated. "You brought me here, to this dank cave of beer, when money transferred will do. Now tell me why, before I decide to cut 'Fates' thread just for you." He quakes, he squirms, he writhes like a worm. He says he's a fan from the Koshikawa clan, he offers five zeros to end just one man. I ask of the sport as it's of more import than money received, to one of my sort. He vents and compliments he laments some "poor gent", he comments that "failures don't pay the rent". In house cleaning is what he's been scheming. It turns out this "gent", all "twisted and bent", tragically lost spousal fealty. He took out a knife and cut up his wife, making him "a liability". I've already grasped it will be my task to track him down and inflict his last gasp when with a rasp that's what he asks, I consider a moment, my hands they unclasp. "Ill advised ways shade your forays. I know well your brand. You're my fan, and a small stupid man. Wanting to scan my white skull was your plan, a prospect so rude that it darkens my mood causing my next move to become somewhat crude." I shock the room with a sonic boom shattering glass, booth and table. Time slows to my will, "Fate" trills to the kill, no-one but I stand able. I cross the room in front of the "boom" faster than sight "Fates" keen thread bites. Cold steel bone arm sweeping to harm, "Retribution" foresworn, leaving necks shorn through a sudden blood storm. Found falling down a resounding dread sound, as three heads smash to the ground. As reactions set in fear and noise spread within, the bar crowd thins as exodus begins. I casually bend down to take from each crown that which is mine due and proper. I gouge my toll from each eyehole, an electronic optical stopper. My grim task done, with a modicum of fun, I turn to the man from the Koshikawa clan. He's bruised, confused and missing a hand. "I'll take your job you pathetic slob, but you'd do well to remember. To get your fill of excitement and thrill stay away from those who dismember. If you want this job done you'll transfer my funds into that spot you know well. But never again dare this type of ensnare or you'll beg for the sweet fare of hell." He vomits and groans, he falls and lays prone. I find the grind comes to mind yet still there's no sign and so by design my escape is benign.

I ascend.

Sounds of life drown, a bright spectrum surrounds. My rooftop flight cuts a course quick and tight. I fly through the sky un-seen by the eye, a hound on the town while making no sound, un-scanned, un-known, all stealth abounds. So first must be found this gent "gone to ground", the cad, the killer, the dead-eyed suit filler. The mark in my mind that burns, sparks and shines, his info refined is sent down the line. The path of the line, through channels designed, arrives in due time at a dear "friend" of mine, his keen mind aligned to purpose defined. Find in all haste the man now debased, through internet spheres craft many smart ears to tirelessly search through and hear gossip for you, traverse each avenue whether false or true. My "friend" Fhaligun "the wonderful one" a Gnome that sheds bizarre with the power of a sun, he croaks and tokes and tells the worst "jokes". He stinks and he sweats and he pees when he bets, and once on a whim he ate his neighbor's pets. Small "quirks" aside this "thing" takes great pride in maintaining his motto of "NOTHING CAN HIDE!" So with info consigned and fee sent down the line it's just a matter of time before the "mad gent" is mine.

Rebecca Arliss

"Don't blow smoke up my ass Matthews. A five man squad gets eaten by rats in the heart of the warrens and you're trying to tell me it was part of a corporate training exercise?" Rebecca says. She puts her hands defiantly on her hips, flustered by the spokesman's inability to lie. A slight zoom with the eye cameras catches some sweat forming on his forehead.

The Human looks at her and says, "Yes ma'am, as I've stated, this was simply a Koshikawa corporate training drill that ran afoul of a large and dangerous brood of rats." He can't even convince himself of this bullshit. Rebecca just shakes her head and remains on point.

"There are only three reasons that a five man squad would have for entering the warrens. Reason the first is if they were openly punishing transgressors. Reason the second is if they were trying to retrieve stolen property, and reason the third is if they were secretly eliminating some *problem*." Before Matthews can answer she presses on "and since we all know how much corporations like to announce the punishment of any who would openly defy their will, I was wondering—who is it that you are planning on murdering?" A tight zoom on the man's face, his shifty eyes betray his nature. He gives Rebecca a venomous stare.

"I've already detailed what has transpired. You should choose your questions more carefully Miss; you might give the wrong impression." Rebecca snorts her derision. He then sits back in his chair and continues "I would however like to offer my deepest sympathies to the families of the deceased soldiers." Standard placating statements follow. He must have been coached by a P.R. rep. She sighs. *No point in continuing, he's not going to betray his corporate head masters,* she thinks, *I can't blame him really.* If he made a truthful statement he'd be murdered on principle alone. In fact, he probably doesn't even know why they were there in the first place. She casts a quick glance down through Koshikawa's public interface office. A glowing waterfall flows past the curved front window, creating an elegant curtain of glittering light. The lobby is filled with plush furniture and exotic plants. A large holo-vid displays the usual Koshikawa propaganda while a hefty security station divides the lobby from the various offices. Rebecca gives her most sarcastic of thanks and turns to leave the mezzanine office. She heads down the staircase and out past the security checkpoint, stopping briefly to retrieve her pistol.

Passing through the main doors, she emerges into the U.V. glow of Koshikawa's twenty-first level shopping districts. Rebecca stops for a moment and accesses her cybereyes' visual modes. She activates the weave optics. The eyes obtain and convert localized graphical data, creating a whole world of digital constructs which flicker to life all around her. Advertisements in the form of glowing whales and annoying pigeons fly through the virtual sky. Tiny pirate ships sail in the distance. Digital store fronts advertise the daily specials and availability of goods for their material world counterparts. She can see a weave hub serving as a connection point between distant digital locales. All types of fantastical avatars are flying about in the virtual space. She walks up the street as she peers through the digital landscape. Eventually she finds what she's looking for, a local slave node used to access the "Tirileth City" central camera system. She knew that there was one near here. Her mind sweeps that intrinsic feeling and the weave optic's software is deactivates. A couple of blocks later she arrives at a small public park.

The park has a large field, several carefully tended trees, and a few hedges, all arranged around a number of twisting paths. There are benches at regular intervals and the space is illuminated by tall U.V. lights which cast a yellowish glow. She finds a spot without any obvious camera coverage and sits on a wide stone bench, producing a small circular porta-comp and a tiny button camera in the process. She adheres the button camera to a light standard and angles the lens towards herself. The lotus position comes naturally as she draws up the porta-comp into her lap. Opening the porta-comps side panel, she produces a thin fiber optic cable, which unspools from the computer's innards. She takes the cable's lead and searches for the metal port located at her temple, then plugs it in. Two key strokes later and her meat shell is left behind. She's now a being of pure thought, rendered digitally as the persona of a white garbed ninja, her chosen avatar. The ninja scans the area with glowing purple eyes. She then springs forward through the electronic air, flying through and around the countless weave constructs that clutter the digital space. A quick masking check conceals the ninja from the prying eyes of other avatars. She continues on.

Countless other weave travellers pass by, oblivious to her presence. A quick scan brings up a local map. There's a weave bar, "Shifty Sam's", it looks popular. If it has a large corporate presence it might be a good spot to ask some questions. She checks the feed from the button cam; a picture of her slumped over body coming through clear as a bell. She drags the camera feed image to the top left corner of her sight so that it doesn't obstruct her vision too badly. She then begins to move back towards the camera node. Hopefully, with some luck, she'll find some answers and some kind of story.

The simple metallic node appears as a spherical building with the words "Tirileth city property" etched on its structure. The ninja gazes around briefly. Dozens, maybe hundreds of different avatars flit about. Silver knights fly by on onyx horses, while giant dogs trot along beside animated cleavers. She looks back to the node for the camera system. The weave construction is protected by six soldiers, smart-frames. The inside will be worse. She moves smoothly towards the node. The smart-frames don't react to her approach, her custom programming working to conceal her avatar's presence. She reaches the node and places her digital hands on it. Instantly the weave constructions coding becomes visible to her, as does its encryption. A "Code Cleaner" program comes to hand and she begins to disassemble the nodes encryption. Slowly she pries apart the lines of code; it's tricky but not ultra-grade, over the counter stuff really. Less than a minute later and she's by-passed the encryption. She peers into the node again. This time the roaring static of a firewall greets her, a simple enough defense to by-pass. A smart-frame based on the template of a standard civic requisition order will work. She then attaches a digital line to the bait and drops it into the constructs coding. A moment later and the automated acquisition system inside the node has ratified her request. The system pulls the smart-frame through the wall of the weave construction. The digital line snaps taught and she's drawn through the hole in the firewall along with the phoney order.

Instantly she's transferred into the main camera hub which serves as the central storage site for all of the city's public camera feeds. She stops for a moment and looks around. The nodes internal space is crafted as a giant hall, complete with huge pillars and ornate marble tiles. The walls are lined with steel drawers. They stretch up for hundreds of feet. The hall itself extends off into an infinite blackness.

Now she has to beware. The central system is teeming with counter measures, as well as government hackers who are paid to keep intruders out. Then an idea strikes her. She quickly accesses her computer's smart-frame schematics and extracts a "Brigand" template. She can make it look like a standard camera feed attack. A fake assault might draw off some of the digital defenses and take some of the heat off of her. The ninja rapidly constructs the smart-frame. The piece of programming ends up looking like a small red demon, complete with horns, a wild mane of hair and cloven feet. An inadvertent laugh bubbles from her avatar. She thinks about her destination for a second. The camera feeds from near Fourteenth Street and Clove Street on the fifth level, that's where it happened. She won't be able to access the central storage controls so she'll have to find the files' actual digital locations within the hall. She peers at the wall for a moment; they all seem to be arranged chronologically and by level. *Good,* she thinks, *that makes things easier.* She calms herself for a second before launching the demonic smart-frame. The stylized piece of programming begins to streak to its new goal, and she leaps into the air. The ninja quickly reaches the fifth level and then begins to fly laterally. Soaring through the digital space, she soon reaches the drawers containing the stored video feeds from the Fourteenth Street cameras. She begins to download a number of the camera feeds when an internal alarm starts to wail. The ninja looks around quickly and prepares a "Decoy" program. A tense few seconds pass. Nothing happens and she returns to her search. *The alarm was for the smart-frame,* she thinks, *just weird timing.*

Next she finds and downloads the camera feeds from Clove Street. A triumphant grin creeps across her face and a shot of adrenalin overcomes her. She looks down through the hall. A number of the soldier smart-frames are still moving towards the little demon. She sees her moment, and quickly descends to move back to the nodes access point. The ninja steps through the gate. A moment later and she's once again flying through the expanses of the internet weave. She's gone a small "distance" when she stops and produces a small ribbon, which she then hangs in mid-air behind her. The ribbon vanishes, indicating that the "Line lock" program is in place. She thinks for a moment about what to do next. The weave bar springs to mind. It might be worth a shot. Its address appears in her navigator and suddenly she's flying unerringly at great speed towards "Shifty Sam's".

The bar appears as an overwrought version of an old west style saloon, almost cartoonish in its extravagancies. The garish swinging doors sway slightly as she moves into the digital hangout. She quickly checks on her meat body as the ninja sits next to a buxom tavern wench and a robot dog. She sits still and listens for a short while. Several of the patrons are using sound blocking privacy filters. Most of the others are discussing various inane topics, mainly surrounding celebrity culture, sports and politics. There's also some talk about the standard corporate and gangland crimes, the usual stuff. The bartender approaches, his avatar is the caricature of a stereotypical old west saloon keeper, long whiskers, bowler hat and even a six shooter on his hip.

"Howdy li'l lady. What can I get you? We have a whole range of S-drinks." She considers for a moment then shakes her head and says: "Not interested in that. I would buy a round for the bar if anybody knows anything about the fifth level Koshikawa incident that happened last night. Rumors, theories, anything?" The brazen approach causes a few of the avatars to move away from her. The bartender looks back and forth.

"I'm not even sure what you're talking about, some corpie crime?" She quickly peers around the bar. No obvious Koshikawa employees, maybe she was wrong about this place. Its proximity in the weave doesn't mean much, when you can go to bars half way around the world in the blink of an eye.

"Just a Gargle Blaster then." She mutters, while accessing her digital funds. The ninja stays and asks questions for a few more minutes. Soon it becomes clear that nobody knows anything, or cares. She leaves the bar and heads back into the weave. Vast buildings pillar around her, selling their services far into the digital sky. She drifts listlessly for a few seconds, when the internal tone of her cyberear's phone fills her hearing. She mentally connects to the phone as she checks the button cameras digital display again, finding the same park scene as before.

She shifts her focus back as the voice of her boss, James Jackson, filters into her audio receptors. "Arliss! Did you get that interview that I sent you for over an hour ago?"

She musters her most sardonic voice before responding. "You mean did I get that pack of poorly crafted, bald-faced lies squeezed through the clenched teeth of a brainless corporate peon? Why yes, yes I did."

"Cut the crap Arliss, what did you expect from a corporate spokesman, the truth? If you have some kind of proof that he's lying, then show me and we can run a story about it, otherwise you're going to be late for the breakdown meeting. So get your ninja butt back to 'The Tower', upload that video, then get to the meeting room!" He disconnects without another word. She flips off the afterimage and floats above the maze of digital constructions for a little while longer. A dark castle sprouting up from a floating island drifts past. The words "Devon's Naughty Dungeon" flash in neon on the outside of the black stone. She smirks to herself and types in "The Towers" weave address. A second later and the silvery monolith of "The Tirileth City Chronicler" is shining in front of her.

The ninja passes through the front door, her digital I.D. tag granting her instant access. The inside of "The Tower" has a layout similar to that of a regular office building, only the floors line the outside of the walls while the entire center of the building is totally open. The construction allows for easy access to any of the numerous floors. The building's "windows" are actually rendering programs which display the internet weave surrounding the building itself. The overall effect makes it seem as though they are real windows made of glass. She quickly flies up through the center, briefly toying with the notion of sneaking into the meeting so she can surprise "Oldtop" Jackson. He really doesn't like that though, maybe if she finds a better story. This rat attack could be something, five man squads are normally only sent when the corporation is ninety-nine percent sure that they will succeed. The fact that it failed is interesting in and of itself. The ninja moves quickly to her office. She can see Daryl's platinum warrior avatar sitting at his desk. The other offices are mainly empty, no doubt at the meeting already. The interview is quickly uploaded from her head computer. She then messages the editing department to let them know that it's there. A moment later and she ascends to the abnormally large meeting room, an expanded internal digital space. More than two dozen avatars sit around the long, glass table. She can see Sally's cartoon sloth avatar, and Jeff's four-armed mutant sitting next to her. The head of the table is taken up by James' avatar, made to look like a more handsome version of himself. James is speaking as she moves into the room.

"… meaning that Roy and Malthias will cover the McMillan rally. Next point of interest: the "Warp Marsh" exposé is going ahead as planned whenever we receive the drone footage. I'll need Derrick and Thalia to do some research, background, histories, you know, the usual stuff. There's been a lot of attention given to this latest airplane disaster, so let's try to link that to the "Warp Marsh" piece. somehow. Alright, next on the agenda, nobody groan but there's been another Grimmfang sighting …" The name of that infamous murderer causes a number of the journalists to sigh and shift in their seats, including the ninja, "… I said stow it! The incident happened in a bar called "The Den", in the sprawl, of all places. Primary sources state that there are three dead and one wounded, the dead and wounded are said to be Koshikawa employees, but the corporation hasn't mentioned anything about the incident as of yet. Jeff, you're on this one, see if the story is credible, talk to the bar owner, track down patrons, you know the routine. Stories about this freak sell; he's got some kind of demented fan base, so try to find something out." A number of journalists relax when they realize that they won't have to follow that lead, it'll end badly no matter what happens. James continues "Finally, a shipment of artifacts from 'Orcanthus' was stolen late last night. The shipment is thought to be worth nearly one million credits, it is unclear how they were stolen at this time. Celene you have this one, find out something will you?" James looks to her avatar, the half-snake half-belly dancing woman nods. James then concludes the meeting with his usual rallying call "and the rest of you find something to report on! This is 'The Tier', there's always something going on out there!" The various avatars begin to leave the table. "Arliss! Did you upload that interview?" James yells as the ninja turns to leave.

She swings around quickly and says, "Yes boss, the editors should have it now." James nods then points at her.

"Good, now go find something to do!" She gives him a false salute then drifts out of the room and floats back to her floor, which is now buzzing with activity. Her office door closes just as her cyberear's phone begins to ring. She concentrates for a moment and creates a small display window which hangs in the digital space in front of her. The phone connects and her mother's face fills the screen.

"Hey 'Becks', how are you doing?" she says in her usual manner.

"Good mom. Just at work, as you can probably tell. How are you?" the ninja responds.

"I'm good. Yeah, I see that you're in your ninja clothes. So is anything interesting happening? Any major stories?"

"Not sure yet, I'm looking into something right now, but I don't know if it will turn into a story or not," she says while glancing at the button cameras screen.

"Well, be careful. Anyway I was just calling because Robert was going to be in the city this weekend and I was wondering if you could make it down for supper one night?" She considers for a minute. She doesn't get to see her brother too often since he moved from the city.

"Sure mom, just let me know which day works better for you guys. I'm sorry, I really should go. I have to move my body," she says while peering at the screen. There are people walking past. It's a good neighborhood, but still, she should head home anyway.

"Alright, good. Yeah I'll let you know when I hear from him again. Love you honey. Be safe." The ninja peers back at the screen.

"Love you too mom, I'll talk to you later, bye." She then disconnects and hovers for a moment before she retraces her digital path, and deactivates the weave interface. The physical world springs into existence all around her. Sounds and smells assail from every angle. Rebecca takes a moment and re-orientates herself. Tracing her digital line back to her physical location saved her from the dreaded "dump shock", but she's still always been a bit groggy after entering the weave. A quick look around reveals that a couple of corpies entered the park at some point, there are some kids hanging out at the far side. They're all looking at one electronic device or another. She stands and stretches her athletic frame while shaking out her cargo pants. She quickly checks her image in the button camera. Her hair's a collection of short purple spikes, sticking out a random angles, piercings in both ears and her nose. Her cyebereyes are tiny impenetrable purple orbs. She grabs the button camera, deactivates it, then tucks it away in an inside pocket. Her weave optics activate as she puts her porta-comp in her backpack. She calls up a map of the level and performs a quick search for the closest public transit tubes, soon finding a group which could take her down to level ten. The tubes are twenty long blocks to the northwest. Her cyberears come to mind and she activates her phone.

"Connect to 'Hive Taxi'" she sub-vocalizes, and a few seconds later the automated taxi service is responding in the standard way.

"Select the send command to have a taxi sent to your current position or, if you'd prefer, enter a desired weave destination." She mentally activates the send command and sits down to wait.

The taxi shows up a short while later. The car's a new style automated cab, limited travel routes, but it will work for her purposes. She approaches the rear door and inserts her credstick into the slot just above the handle. An interior light winks green and she enters the cab. A pleasant digital voice soon fills the confines of the taxi.

"Greetings, Rebecca Arliss, and welcome, where is it that you would like to go today?" She cringes slightly at the thought of her name being fed to the machine.

"The Rathiss street transit tube station please," she responds, the pleasantry occurring as a force of habit. The cab whirs to life and immediately proceeds to travel up the well tended streets, as the digital voice confirms the destination.

"Rathiss Street transit tube station. Very good, enjoy the ride." She lets out a snort and looks out the window.

The beautifully structured buildings, roads and bridges edge by as the cab moves smoothly up the street. The imagery washes over her for a moment before she turns her attention to the pilfered data. When she gets to her apartment she'll write a smart-frame to search for Koshikawa symbols and a second to track rat activity. Hopefully with both smart-frames in place she'll be able to scan through the video feeds much more thoroughly. The cab slows to a halt and the fare appears on the door near the internal credstick slot. She slots her stick and the light blinks green, unlocking the door in the process. She exits onto the busy sidewalk. The massive transit hub stands in front of her. The structure spans between the two levels, making it appear as a giant square column. There are clear lift platforms travelling up into the twenty-first level and beyond. She's heading the other way though. Her credstick slots in the transit gate and she passes through the now open gateway. A short while later she's moving from the station's platform into the large elevator space. A diverse cross-section of citizens already occupies the interior of the massive lift. Soon, the steel doors close and the transit elevator begins to descend. Rebecca watches as the elevator passes into the twentieth level, the cluttered city scene unfurling like a glass banner.

The lift stops briefly at each level, letting passengers on or off respectively. Rebecca continues to watch the slow descent through the increasingly grimy tubes. They reach the tenth level and she disembarks with a small group of passengers. She exits the station and once again calls for an auto-cab. A short while later and she's stepping out in front of "The Titan Arms" apartment complex. The familiar glow of the "Wellglades" coffee shop can be seen just up the street. She enters the twenty story block and walks to the elevator. A swipe of her mag-key calls the elevator, which she enters. The doors close behind her and the elevator begins to move, soon arriving at the twelfth floor. She exits into the hall, one more swipe of the mag-key opens her apartment door to reveal the familiar mess inside. The lock engages behind her as she activates her custom made security system. The camera concealed outside her front door winks on as she yells "computer" and enters into the apartment's main room. The space is a square, about fifteen feet on each side. Her bedroom door sits opposite the door to the bathroom, while an archway just to the right of the entrance leads to her compact kitchen. She tosses her backpack on the couch and unclips her holster and spare magazines from her belt. The pistol is deposited on the coffee table before she walks to the fridge, its contents revealing an uninspiring arrangement of leftovers. She rummages around briefly and retrieves a carton of noodles and a can of "Ol'Grog" then heads back into the cluttered living room and sits on the couch, across from her second holo-vid.

"Vid on" she says while diving into the cold noodles, following with a chaser of beer. The wall transforms into an image of the plastic-faced Trisha Stellar sitting beside her moronic co-host, Tanner Stevens. The clock in her retinal display reads 6:10 lunar, the news just started. She watches half-heartedly and eats the noodles while she plans the programming for the smart-frames. The news broadcast blurs into background noise as she begins to figure out one of the smart-frame's designs. Scanning for Koshikawa logos is only part of the design. A true special ops team won't be sporting any logos. They do tend to use the same equipment, usually type-A light combat suits and bull-pup assault rifles, for close quarters manoeuvrability. Koshikawa favors black and grey, a bit of urban camouflage. She just has to add these variables to the smart-frame's scan. The second smart-frame will be far simpler to create. The corporate pest control scanning software can be used as a template; it should only take a few minutes. The news rolls on for a while longer as she finishes the noodles and the can of "Ol'Grog". She then grabs her porta-comp and heads to the computer in the living room's corner.

A short charge of adrenalin passes through her as she uploads the pilfered data into her apartment's computer. She then sits in her armchair and reclines slightly before she unspools the computers cable and connects it to the port in the side of her head. The apartment melts away as she calls up the computers interactive media software. The purple-eyed ninja surges to life. The software's room is designed as a large simple cube, there are drawers lining the flawless walls. The many drawers are each labeled and as she looks at the walls the titles of the files light up and spring forward. She looks them over briefly. "Rihley trip", hunky Elven surfers and a never ending supply of deadly island liquors. "Robert's wedding", dad was so drunk that Matthew and Uncle Jared had to carry him out. The ninja lingers, thinking about Matthew. She deleted those sweaty files already though. Finally she spots the new camera feed files. They're labeled by the camera's location and the recording time-frame. She concentrates for a second and accesses her head computer. Her vision transfers to the control panel and she quickly selects the file labeled "rat attack witness". The file begins to play and her senses are overtaken by the recording. She can see the stout, grungy woman; the street noises hum in the background, voices and vehicles mainly, filtered through her cyberear's microphone. Then her voice cuts in.

"Yes. I'm sorry about that. Anyway you told a member of our staff that you saw hundreds of rats attacking and then eating a bunch of armed corporate troops, is that correct?"

The woman looks back and forth then stares at Rebecca and says, "That's right, hundreds or thousands, maybe even millions of em. Came from everywhere, then all of a sudden they was gone, just like that. Only bloody bodies left, and then one got up and left." The camera tightens on the woman's face for a moment.

"Are you saying that one of them survived the attack?" Rebecca asks.

The woman looks hard at her. "I never said it was one of them, anyway I didn't get a good look. I was trying to get out of there; I didn't want to get ate up by the rats!"

She hears her voice chime in again. "I was in that alley and there weren't any bodies."

The woman looks at Rebecca likes she's touched in the head. "Of course there ain't no bodies. The corpies meat wagon fetched 'em not ten minutes after the rats ate em, five bodies, almost skeletons."

Rebecca's voice breaks through the buzz of the street noise again. "What corporation?"

The woman looks back and forth then answers. "Koshikawa, they'd taken off their K symbol but I knew it was them, black vans, same as they always look."

Rebecca follows up by asking "What time did this all happen?" The woman seems to consider for a moment.

"It was around three lunar, I remember because I was watching 'Win or Die'". The ninja nods to herself and cancels the head computer feed. She'd only found three witnesses, and the other two were even less reliable. *Still,* she thinks, *the only reason that Koshikawa admitted that this incident even occurred was because they knew that they'd been identified.* The corporate meat wagon would have been a dead giveaway, even if they had removed their logos.

She considers her approach for a moment before she re-activates the media software. She quickly sorts through all of the camera feeds and discovers that only two cameras are close enough to the alley in question to be of any use. One camera covers the mouth of one side of the alley, while the other camera covers a section of the street near the alley's opposite side. The alley itself travels up a short ways and then doglegs to the left in order to create a shortcut through the buildings that are piled all around. She accesses the camera feed of the alley mouth and prepares to integrate into the recording.

A moment later and the ninja is immersed in the silent street scene. Groups and crowds walk past as she waits and watches for her timeframe. A river of ghostly digital images passes through her. One of her smart-frames flashes several times as Koshikawa employees walk past. The corporate logo that they sport attracts the program's attention momentarily before it continues on. The second smart-frame flashes a number of times as well as it outlines a rat here or there. The feed continues. Suddenly, she is encased in an impenetrable wall of static as the world disintegrates around her. She steps back out of the immersion software and sees that the camera feed has been scrambled. She advances the recording. The feed is scrambled for more than half an hour, a difficult task to say the least, especially since the scrambled feed wasn't discovered. If they had been discovered, the feed would have been pulled and a full investigation would have been launched. She transfers the second camera feed into the software and dives in. A completely different scene greets her. She can't see up the alley from this angle but she could tell if somebody walked into the alley entrance. The feed rolls forward and she scans the scene. Both of the smart-frames flash a number of times as they detect a logo or rodent, but no armored men, no hordes of dangerous rats. She continues to study the feed, when her rat sensing smart-frame flashes and flickers as though it's glitching out. The coding and the template are still sound, she can see the construction clearly. She then rolls back the recording a few seconds and looks more closely at her surroundings. The smart-frame is flickering on two humanoids in the crowd. They walk up the street. One of the humanoids is a male Goblin and the other is a young Human male. The ninja studies them closely. They're both wearing the same necklace, that's what's setting off the smart-frame. The necklaces each feature a rat's skull. She feels somewhat deflated. Then, she spots the pair turn into the alley. A second later and the world is crashing into static around her. The ninja leaps from the immersion software and lands in front of a scrambled camera feed. She rolls back the feed a few seconds and freezes on the two figures. *There's no way that it's a coincidence,* she thinks. *Those two are travelling somewhere, and there weren't seven bodies, there were five.* Not really any other leads at the moment. She'll have to track their movement, somehow. There is one way to do it, but it would mean that she'd have to head back into the central camera node, providing that they haven't jacked up their security too much since her last little dalliance.

Cassandra

Cassandra narrows her ice blue eyes at the large Orc. He's sweating. He smells kind of like cat piss. She puts her elbow on the chair's plush armrest and leans her head against her hand.

"Tell me something Marmuk? What am I supposed to do with this?" She points to the silvery porta-comp sitting on her large desk. He looks to the circular computer then to Cassandra.

"Well, I thought youz wuz lookin for info on a Marshall? This is a Marshall comp," the big Orc says triumphantly. Cassandra glares daggers at him. He instantly stops smiling.

She continues. "Marmuk, you are what we like to call 'a blunt instrument'. Like a hammer or a crowbar. You are very good at the tasks required of such a tool. These tasks rarely, if ever, have anything to do with computers however. I would also like to mention, just as a side note, that if you ever bring a Marshall's stolen porta-comp into my mansion under false pretenses again, I shall have Marcus emasculate you and feed the leavings to the rats." The Orc crosses his hands in front of his crotch and glances over at the Dark Elf. Marcus just grins, the geometric lines etched across his face rippling silver in the soft light. The Orc swallows and looks back to Cassandra.

"I'm real sorry. Juss thought ..." he begins.

Cassandra cuts him off by holding up a hand. She then says, "Don't think anymore Marmuk, it is not an action that is required of you. You're just lucky that the computer hasn't been damaged or tampered with, we'll simply have to arrange to have it returned." The Orc looks surprised but doesn't say anything. Cassandra then adds, "You seem surprised? You've never dealt with a true Marshall before Marmuk, local enforcers don't count. For something like this they'll send out one of the true order, and that's some trouble that I don't need. Now get the fuck out of my sight." She points to the door to put an accent on the final statement. Marmuk leaves without another word. The richly carved doors close behind him as he exits.

"So what's the plan?" Marcus asks. Cassandra peers up at the huge spherical aquarium occupying the ceiling. A school of

90

luminous spirit fish swim through the spectral waves, runes etched in the glass constraining them.

"Simple, the Marshalls are already aware of us. That being the case, we say that some misguided individual brought the computer here seeking recompense. I told them that I do not deal in such illicit materials and that they should return the computer immediately. We then pay somebody to return the computer to the nearest enforcement center," Cassandra says and turns her chair back towards Marcus, two knife handles stick out from the folds of his pin stripe suit.

"Why do we have to tell them at all? Couldn't we just pay some bum to return it?" Marcus says as he crosses to the red leather couch pressed up against the west wall.

Cassandra smirks and says, "Don't know much about Marshall porta-comps do you? I wouldn't even be surprised if they show up at our door sometime soon."

Marcus nods then looks to the porta-comp. "What, like a GPS or something?" he says while producing a Celsior ultra-lite. The slim cigar flares to life with a flick of his thumb and forefinger.

"Yes, or something. Our usual counter measures will have worked; still, the trace will be quite close. They can easily infer." She ponders for a few seconds then adds, "Put a stop on the Marshall info hunt for the time being, we'll see if 'Devilfish' comes up with something. If he doesn't then we can start farming it out again." Marcus takes a drag and nods, two columns of smoke stream from his nostrils. She then looks at the computer and taps on her desk. The desktop instantly resolves into a large holographic display. "Phone on," the computer flashes and transfers to the secure-com hub. She then continues, "Connect to captain Gromgir Broadis." She smoothes her hair and flaunts an inch more cleavage. The phone flashes a number of times before the call is answered by a young, attractive Human woman.

The Human glowers at Cassandra and says, "Marshall Enforcement center 9-A, Captain Gromgir Broadis' office. How may I help you?" Cassandra smiles cooly.

"I'd like to speak with Captain Broadis. Tell him it's Cassandra Seelie. I have something for him." The receptionist frowns then the screen goes black for a moment. Soon the carefully manicured beard and bald head of Captain Broadis fills the holo-display. "Captain Broadis, a pleasure as always," she says while smiling at the stout Dwarf. He grins broadly and flushes ever so slightly before responding.

"Why Cassandra, this is a surprise. I swear you become more beautiful each time that I see you." He smiles coyly and blinks a few times. Cassandra laughs to herself. Dwarves are always so smitten by Elves, Dark Elves especially, the most forbidden of desires. She leans forward slightly and continues.

"I see you're as formidable as ever. How have you been? I imagine that the job keeps you pretty busy." His smile broadens.

"I've been good. Yeah, you know, there's always something happening." He then seems to compose himself slightly before continuing. "So apparently you have something for me?" Cassandra smiles, *he's remembered who I am, it sometimes takes them a little while,* she thinks.

"Yes. It seems some misguided fool thought that I was the type of Elf who would buy a Marshall's stolen porta-comp. I of course corrected them and then immediately contacted you so that I could arrange to have the porta-comp sent over." She presents the half-truth with a convincing air.

Captain Broadis looks hard at her and says, "Possession of stolen Marshall equipment is a mandatory ten years in the stacks. I can't let that slide." He glares at Cassandra as she responds.

"I never said that it was in my possession. I could however convince the individual who stole it to return it to you, out of gratitude, for your years of selfless service." She grins and touches a finger to her throat. Captain Broadis gives her a wary smile.

"I suppose you didn't say it was in your possession, now did you? Well, mighty kind of you to want to help. What's in it for you?" He raises his eyebrows and waits for an answer.

She smiles sensually and says, "Just as I said captain, I'm a fan of your work, your courage is inspirational. These streets are dangerous. I grew up with that danger, I know it well." Captain Broadis nods and seems to consider something. She grins to herself.

"Still you might want to make sure that nobody important returns the porta-comp; there may be some … uncomfortable *questions*." He then points, furrows his brow and adds "This doesn't remove you from my radar by the way." He looks sternly at Cassandra.

She grins and replies, "I wouldn't have it any other way captain," then winks and disconnects the call. Marcus laughs, an explosion of blue-grey smoke bursting into the air. Cassandra looks over and begins laughing as well.

Marcus takes another pull from his cigar then says, "So, should I pick a patsy or did you have someone particular in mind?" He raises his brow at the last statement, exposing more of the red lenses that serve as his eyes.

"Hmm, whoever, it doesn't matter. Just make sure that they know who you are. Also, wrap the computer to make sure that they don't know what it is," Cassandra responds.

"You got it." Marcus stands, grabs the computer and leaves through the double doors.

Cassandra looks back to the ceiling. A giant luminous blue fish slowly drifts past, then a glowing green fish, followed by a school of ethereal yellow minnows. The spectral colors gradually drift around the ornate room as she once again activates the holo-display in her desk. She peers through her itinerary for a minute. There are six active jobs, two that are in need of operators and three which have been completed but payment is still pending. Whisper should be here soon. She'll have a sample of the "Orcanthus" artifacts with her. Then there's Xan, who knows when he'll decide to show up, it'll be good to see him again in person. She lingers on that thought for a moment. That obnoxious spirit will be with him, but she can ignore it easily enough. The prototype that they stole will net a tidy sum. Finally there's Sam Lockwood, that'll only take a few minutes. He'll be picking up his team's share for the Dr. Michaels extraction. A unique payment request, which was fine, it meant that she could negotiate his price down some. She then brings up the open jobs menu. Two smaller folders appear inside. She opens the top one which instantly explodes into a sphere of information. This job came in yesterday, still no takers. It's in the warp marshes, pretty much just looking for a corpse. Still, they're willing to pay well. Maybe Sam will be interested. She collapses the folder back down then unfurls the second folder. This job is much more straightforward. Sabotage one corporation's facility so that another can profit. She's seen it dozens of times. She thinks for a moment, Xan might be interested, if not maybe "Hellion" and his crew or "The Broken Brigade". There's a never ending supply of mercenaries in "The Tier", if you know where to look.

She collapses the sphere back down into a folder. She then calls up the internal camera feeds. Instantly, a patchwork cross-section of screens fills the holo-display. She looks at each one in turn. There's the front driveway, the guard house and the gardens. The back patio with its large pool, hot tub and bar, a pair of guards can be seen there, they're part of the regular detail of twelve. She looks to the cameras at the mansion's sides. The building sticks out from the edge of this level's precipice, appearing to hover above the sprawling city below. She continues to look at the various screens, finally settling on the camera displaying the front guard house. The computer's phone begins to chime. The screen displays a number, an old number. She hits connect and the cross-section of screens disappears. The new image reveals the rugged features of Gerald Wright or "Mountain Man" to most everyone who knows anything. Cassandra smiles broadly and says "This day is just full of surprises! The illustrious 'Mountain Man', everyone thought that you had moved on or retired, or something." The Human smiles, a shaggy grey beard lining his face.

"Lying low for a time, that's all. Anyway just calling to let you know that 'Grey owl', 'Steel rider' and I are back in the game, we got bills to pay and all that." She nods and looks at him thoughtfully. He was known as a top notch tracker and field expert. She only ever employed him on three missions, and the last one went belly up in a bad way.

She smiles again and says, "Well it's good to see you back in action. I do have a job even now if you're interested. It would be perfect for someone with your skills; it is outside of the city however."

He grins. "I would be interested, yeah. You know the wild lands always suited me better anyway. So what's the job? Can I record?"

"Certainly, I was recently approached by a corporate by the name of Anderson. He's been vetted, no ulterior motives. Anyway, this Mr. Anderson has a son who went missing when flight 27 went down last week. You may have heard?"

He shakes his head. She shrugs and continues, "It's not important, as it turns out Mrs. Anderson consulted some powerful psychic who said that the boy was still alive, in the 'Warp marshes'." The mention of that place causes "Mountain man's" eyebrows to rise. Cassandra continues "Now whether it's true or not I don't know. I'm told that certain psionic practitioners can actually tell that a person is alive at those distances. Regardless, the Andersons will pay handsomely to have their son, or his remains, returned to them." She finishes and raises a questioning eyebrow.

"Mountain man" considers for a moment before responding: "You don't mess around do you? Warp marshes eh? What's the job pay?"

Cassandra considers for a moment. Somewhat telling that he's so interested in the money. Most would ask about leads or known threats. She gauges the man for a moment more before answering. "Two-hundred K, they're expecting a two week time frame. If you can't find anything by then you get one quarter instead."

He grimaces a bit and seems to do some internal math before he responds with "What leads do you have? Is there anything in particular that I need to know?"

She grins inwardly. "I have a fairly extensive dossier. It includes a GPS co-ordinate of the downed plane, DNA sample of the boy and more," she says while leaning back in her chair. She then adds "I was about to contact one of my other operators to see if they were interested, but if you want the job it's yours."

He considers for a while longer before responding. "I have to speak with the others. Can I get back to you?"

She pretends to be somewhat annoyed and says, "Sure, but make it quick. You called me, remember?" She gives him an evil smirk and disconnects. He's desperate enough to press the issue with his crew. She laughs, two-hundred K, she would have had to give anyone else three-hundred and fifty K at least. That leaves her with two-hundred K for herself. A satisfied smile creeps across her face.

Crossing past the gilded mirror hanging behind her desk, she grabs a glass and one of her crystal decanters from the south wall. The bright red of the "Tselith Ambrosia" soon fills the confines of the receptacle. The spicy aroma fills her nose as she downs the liquor in one swallow. A pleasant fire spreads through her chest and she places the glass back on the bar top. Soon the desk computer is chiming that it has an incoming call. She slowly crosses back to the desk and then waits for another moment before she connects. "Mountain man's" gruff features once again appear in the holo-display.

"Make it two-hundred and fifty K and we have a deal. We also want twenty K up front," he says, then tilts his head, waiting for a response.

She considers for a moment. "Two-hundred and thirty K and you can have fifteen K up front." She sits back and looks off to the left in an attempt to appear disinterested in the conversation. His jaw tightens and he looks off for a moment.

"Alright, deal. We'll take the job," he says.

She smiles and opens her arms then says, "Terrific, I'll send the dossier. If you have a credstick attached I can also send the funds right away, unless you prefer cash?"

He grins and answers, "I'm old but I'm not that old, yeah a stick's in place now." She nods and quickly accesses her electronic funds.

She then transfers the dossier and the fifteen K before saying, "I wish you happy hunting. Try to come back in one piece."

He laughs and says, "No guarantees" before disconnecting. She leans back for a moment. The spectral lights dance and play against the walls and floor. She closes her eyes for a moment and relaxes. *Always something,* she thinks, *now to call Mr. Anderson.* She quickly connects to the corporate V.P.'s personal holo-vid number. The tired, drawn features of Mr. Anderson soon fill the confines of the display.

He looks hopefully to Cassandra before saying, "Have you found someone who's willing to go?" He licks his lips and looks just to the right. She can hear the sound of soft crying, indicating where Mrs. Anderson is no doubt sitting.

Cassandra smiles brightly. "Good news! I've contacted a skilled tracker. He's agreed to search for your son for the two weeks that we had previously discussed."

He puts on a desperate smile and looks back and forth slightly before saying, "Good, good. Like I said, four hundred thousand, but only if they find him, otherwise one hundred, for their time." He nods to himself as if confirming the purchase of a new car.

"Payment upon delivery, I'll keep you apprised of the team`s progress, it shouldn't take too long. Take care," she says. He nods briefly then immediately disconnects. It seems like the father believes that his son is dead already. Her door chimes.

She activates the camera display again. Just outside the wooden double doors, she can see one of her guards. She thinks for moment. His name is Brad Davis. He's been on the team for maybe five years now? She purses her lips and speaks into the computers intercom.

"Enter." She opens the door remotely and waits. The young human walks in timidly. Cassandra motions to one of the chairs sitting opposite her desk. The guard quickly obliges, making sure that his weapon doesn't scratch anything as he sits. After a moment Cassandra speaks, "Brad, what can I help you with?" He shifts in his chair and looks around the room. His gaze lingers on the spectral aquarium for a while.

"Umm, it's like the other one, from the living room. Beautiful," he says while pointing at the ceiling and smiling sadly. Cassandra peers upwards.

"Yes, they are. They're very expensive as well. What can I help you with Brad?" She adds a slight edge to the question. The young Human swallows hard and speaks while staring at Cassandra's desk.

"I was just wondering if I could take next week off. There's some personal stuff happening and I have to deal with it." She considers for a moment, it would be easy enough to find out what he's talking about. She studies him for a short while, gauging his mannerisms. It's probably some kind of tragedy, maybe a death in the family.

"Of course Brad, speak with Marcus when you have a chance and he'll arrange for someone to cover for you." She then stands and motions towards the door.

He quickly stands and says, "Thank you Cassandra, I'll make sure that I speak with him." Cassandra nods and watches the guard leave. She shuts the door and brings up her desk's holographic display again.

Soon, she's delving into the data stores of the internet weave. A quick local search finds a short obituary dedicated to a Stephanie Davis, beloved wife and mother of two. She was twenty-two, doesn't say a cause of death. Cassandra collapses the weave display and stares up at the aquarium. He's still in shock. She remembers that feeling all too well, even if it was more than a hundred years ago. That night filled with fire and rage. The sight of her parents burning. She shudders then looks back to the holo-display.

"Phone, connect to Marcus, " she says.

A moment later and the sub-vocalized voice of the augmented Dark Elf fills the room. "Cass, what's up?"

"A guard named Brad Davis is going to approach you about taking next week off. I want you to give him the time off as well as a bonus, a year's salary," she says in a business-like tone.

Marcus responds, "Should I ask why?"

Cassandra smirks, blinks innocently then says, "You're a clever boy. I'm sure you could figure it out if you wanted too." She then disconnects and looks back to the aquarium. The wispy spirits are all coursing along, following some unseen pattern. Her eyes close for a minute and she relaxes. The familiar chime of her holo-vid rouses her from the short respite. She peers back to the ornate mirror. Coal black skin framed by a flowing crown of shining platinum. She fixes her hair briefly and re-applies her subtle lipstick, then looks to the holo-vid which is still chiming at her. She breathes deeply for a moment and hits connect. Darius' handsome face fills the holo-display.

He grins seductively and says, "Cassandra my love, your beauty constantly overwhelms me!" Cassandra smiles while silently groaning. She went out for drinks with the Elven SIM star a few times. She's starting to regret the decision. A brief smile creeps across her lips.

"Darius, how have you been?" He grimaces and grabs his chest before responding.

"I've been in constant agony without you!" She can't help but laugh quietly.

She then rolls her eyes and says, "I'm sure that you'll live." He smiles and raises his eyebrows.

"I don't suppose you'd want to put me out of my misery by coming out with me tonight?" She looks at the ceiling. *I could put him out of his misery,* she thinks, *although, not in the way that he intends.*

She laughs at her own joke then says, "No, I don't suppose that I would. I'm sorry Darius, I'm terribly busy at the moment, I can't really talk now." He seems deflated.

"I wouldn't dream of intruding. I would love to talk again soon, take care of yourself," he says before he blows her a kiss. Cassandra disconnects and shakes her head. He seemed much more interesting in his SIM's. She crosses over to the bar and pours another shot of "Ambrosia". The expensive liquor radiates heat through her chest as she swallows. She then crosses back to the desk and activates the holo-display. The job folder springs into view and she quickly updates the Anderson file before moving it into the pending job pile. She collapses the folder and activates the camera feed again. This time she focuses on the front gate camera. There are two armed guards manning the external post, the other is in the shack no doubt. She then leans back and watches the road. It shouldn't be long now.

Sure enough, no more than five minutes later and Whisper's sleek motorcycle is approaching the mansion's main gate. The holo-vids intercom flashes and Cassandra answers immediately. "Let her in," she says and disconnects. The motorcycle passes through the gate and drives up to the parking lot at the front of the mansion. A minute later and Cassandra lets the short Human into her office.

"Heya Cassandra. How's tricks?" Whisper says, in her usual low-toned voice. Cassandra motions to one of the seats opposite the desk. "Good. How's everything with you?"

Whisper crosses to the chair and sits in one smooth motion, her implanted cybernetics causing her to move with an unnatural fluidity. "Good, good. We managed to pull it off. No alarms or anything. Nice score, real hot stuff," she says as she nods happily to herself.

Cassandra grins and motions to her desk. "You said that you brought a sample?" The Human smiles and nods, she then removes a canvas bag from her shoulder. Whisper opens the bag and produces a small statue carved into the shape of a whale. The rock that it's carved out of is glowing with a bright green light. Cassandra gazes at the statue. It's beautiful. The carving has small intricate swirls and designs which catch the inner light. The whale looks like it's swimming in a tiny luminous ocean. Dancing colors slowly begin to manifest on her desk. She looks up at the tank of spectral fish. They're all sitting eerily transfixed by the small green statue. None of the spectral fish are moving at all. They're all just pointed at the green whale.

Whisper looks up, twitches a bit then says, "Well that's weird." Cassandra nods. She looks back to the statue and a thought strikes her. She covers the statue with the canvas bag and looks back to the ceiling. The spectral fish immediately go about their business. She smiles, it makes sense now.

She then looks to Whisper and says, "I believe that I have appraised the statue. You said that you had more of these?" Whisper nods and holds up both hands, palms out.

"We got ten more, eleven in total," she says then nods to herself. Cassandra grins; she can sell off ten of the statues and keep one for herself. Cassandra's all business.

"Let's talk price. If they're all in good condition and around the same size I can offer you two hundred and twenty K for lot." She says. Whisper thinks for a moment, she shifts in her chair.

"They`re all around the same size yeah, different animals mainly. These are hard to come by though, super rare, call it two hundred fifty K and we got a deal." Cassandra considers for a moment. She could turn around and sell them at one auction or another for fifty to a hundred K each, maybe more if there's a bidding war.

She looks back to Whisper and smiles then says, "Two hundred fifty K it is."

Whisper grins broadly. "Great, great, I'll bring the other statues by tomorrow, you can hold onto that one for now."

Cassandra nods and says, "Good, payment upon delivery. If I'm not around, speak with Marcus, he'll take care of you." Whisper nods and stands. She then heads briskly to the door, as she reaches the exit she looks back.

"I'll see you tomorrow then." Cassandra nods and watches her leave. She then looks to the covered statue, then bundles it up and carries it to the wall safe. The safe itself is concealed behind a hinged painting located on the offices east wall. The statue is slipped back into the canvas bag. She then places the bag in the safe, locks it and swings the painting back into place. She crosses back to her desk and sits for a minute, thinking about what to do next.

The flash of the holo-vids intercom breaks her concentration. She brings up the front gate camera and activates the intercom. She's about to ask who it is, when the camera springs to life and the words get caught in her throat. *It can't be!* She thinks. Her hands begin to tremble. A static charge of emotion wells up through her core. The fire flashes through her mind. The smell of smoke and the sound of screaming overwhelm her.

"Ma'am there's some grimy looking Goblin and some Human kid. The Goblin said that his name is ..." Cassandra interrupts him, bursting out with a brief flurry of tears in the process.

"Grot ..." She quickly composes herself, "I mean Grot. Yes of course, let him in."

"Yes ma'am, the boy is armed." Cassandra furrows her brow. She looks hard at the boy, he doesn't seem familiar. He doesn't look like the type who would know how to use a gun. *But Grot,* she thinks, *Grot would never harm me*. It's been so long, but things couldn't have changed that much, even in all this time.

"Let them through," she says.

"Yes ma'am," the guard responds. Cassandra watches as the small Goblin and the tall boy pass through the gate. Her eyes sparkle with tears. She couldn't even imagine what would have happened to her if not for Grot. She would have been dead within a week, or worse. A tense minute passes before she sees Grot and the boy round the corner and walk into the hall. She can't help herself and she runs to Grot. The Goblin looks somewhat haggard, but still overjoyed to see her. She bends down on a knee and hugs him, grasping him around an awkward assortment of bizarre items. The recognizable smell of the Goblin washes over her and she heaves for a moment as he comforts her.

"Grot! I can't believe it, how is this possible?" she says after their embrace is complete.

He looks at her timidly and says, "Rat is sorry Cassandra, Rat became very lost. We usually don't travel this far up in the hive, but we always kept track of you. Rat was so glad that you are doing so well, rat never abandoned you, not entirely." *What's happened to him? He's calling himself "Rat" and "We"*, she thinks, *there's something off about him*. Cassandra stands and looks down at Grot.

"You should have called or something. All this time, I thought you'd died. I thought that you were dead. How is it that you're still alive?" She looks him up and down. He looks almost the same as the day that they parted ways some seventy-five years ago. Cassandra knew that the Goblin was a powerful shaman, one of the most powerful that she's ever seen, but he hasn't aged at all. She remembers the last week that she saw him. That last job. It went really badly and everyone that he knew and loved died. Cassandra and Elindriss were the only ones left. She thought that he had died as well, he never came back. Grot looks at the floor and kicks a foot.

"Rat is so sorry, we thought that you'd be better off without us. Rat went looking for them, you know? We looked in the spectral fields for a long time. We saw them once, near a forest, but they did not want to be found, they did not want to come back to us." His eyes brim with tears for a moment. He then adds "These things must wait, Rat has purpose. We beg for your help." Cassandra looks fondly at the old Goblin.

She wipes her eyes and says, "Anything for you Grot, I owe you everything." She then looks over at the Human boy. He seems entranced. There's something else as well, he has a glazed look, like a shell-shock victim. She extends a hand. "Where are my manners? My name is Cassandra Seelie, welcome to my home."

He shakes her hand and manages to say "Hi" in a small voice. Grot then motions to the boy.

"This is Eric Gibson. He is why Rat has come to you now." Cassandra considers for a moment then motions towards her office. They follow her into the luxurious room. The boy is immediately engrossed by the spectral aquarium. He stands motionless, mouth agape. Grot follows her and sits cross-legged on the floor just to the side of the desk. She smiles at the familiar sight of the old Goblin, sitting on the floor in a room full of furniture. The intercom interrupts with a bright flash.

"Apologies, just one moment please." She then switches to the front gate camera as she activates the intercom. Xan is standing there. He's with that creature that he travels with sometimes. She shudders. Asura have always given her the creeps. "Let them in," she says. Before the guard can respond she disconnects and collapses the display. "I'm so sorry Grot. This will only take a minute," she says while looking at the Goblin.

His eyes gleam with a soft inner fire as he responds. "No, no, this is perfect. Rat approves."

Eric Gibson

Everything is so pretty, and Cassandra's so hot. Grot never said anything about how hot she was. She's like ridiculously hot. How the hell does that stinky, weird little Goblin know an Elf as hot as she is? She's like if you managed to mix a dozen hot chicks together and somehow the result became the sum total of their overall hotness added up. Like that level of hot. Her skin is coal black, not African black but like actual coal or obsidian. Her eyes are shimmering blue pools of inner radiance, even her hair is like liquid platinum. I can't help but stare, enchanted. My vision spins. I'm still dizzy. I think I'm concussed. Grot said that I'll be fine. Apparently he's a doctor as well, or something, I don't know. I look up at the aquarium. Colorful ghost fish drift through the smoky waves. My mind flips back to the rats. I convulse and a tremor surges through my hand. Just calm down, breathe deeply. I look around the room. All the walls are richly carved, the furniture too. That desk looks like it costs more than my house back home. Shit, my parents are probably going crazy right now. I feel tears well up for a moment. Choke them down you bastard. I shake my head, my vision swims and I catch myself before I stumble over.

"Eric, are you alright? Here, sit on the couch," Grot says as he stands and motions to the piece of furniture. I cross to the red leather couch and sit. Grot looks over to Cassandra, "He might have a mild concussion. We were attacked, there was an explosion."

Cassandra glares at him and says, "Grot! Why didn't you say something?" She then touches her desk. A holographic display springs to life and she taps on a small icon, she then continues "Who attacked you?"

"It is uncertain, they were corporate though," Grot replies. Cassandra touches her chin thoughtfully. The office doors buzz open and I look over to see a Human woman walking briskly up the hall.

She reaches the office and curtsies then says, "How may I help you Ma'am?"

"Hi Katie, could you bring us four 'Ensilade' waters, a flank of Elk steak and the jar of Xelic paste?"

The woman laughs and says, "Well it's not the strangest selection of items that you've ever had me get, but its close." Cassandra thinks for a second, smiles, then nods her assent. The woman turns to leave just as a man enters the far end of the hall. No wait, not a man. He's an Elf, with the same skin color as Cassandra but his eyes are pure white, like pits of oblivion. He's dressed in a hooded long-coat. The hood is down revealing short, stark white hair. He's wearing tall armored boots that clack against the stone, but there's also something else moving out there. It sounds like the clicking of claws. The Elf moves smoothly, he seems dangerous. I don't know why, but he seems really dangerous, like he could destroy somebody with his bare hands. I can see something like heat waves surrounding him, or is that my imagination? Cassandra stands and moves to the door. I'm instantly entranced. She moves like a goddess, grace personified. She addresses the Elf in the hall.

"Xan, it's good to see you, is Rex here or did he stay at the gate?"

The Elf known as Xan replies, "Cassandra, I see that you have guests. I didn't mean to interfere." He then looks at the empty hallway to his left and says, "Rex, show yourself please, you're being rude."

A voice erupts from somewhere: "Yeah, and that's my job. So, Cassandra? Show us your boobs?" I stifle a giggle, where did that voice come from?

Cassandra replies in a flat tone. "Kane, it's good to see that you're a mild annoyance as always." Then suddenly a monster appears, and I damn near shit my pants. I'm at the other end of the room before I know what's happening. Grot quickly turns from the group.

"Eric, it's alright, calm down, we should have warned you." I can't respond. I'm spellbound. I'm staring at a living nightmare, bigger than a tiger. What am I seeing here? It's like a blue-scaled dog-lion. It has massive bird's talons for hind legs and … its mane! What's happening? Its mane is like glowing red fur pouring upwards off of its head and neck. Those eyes are intense, they're like tiny universes.

The monster speaks. "I did not mean to startle you young one. I often travel unseen. I am unaccustomed to such social nuances." I feel like I'm in a dream, its mouth isn't matching the words. The timing is slightly off. I swallow and try to speak but nothing comes out.

Cassandra looks at me and smiles. "Apologies Eric, I wasn't thinking. Please sit, everything is fine. These are friends of mine, we have business to discuss." I stand frozen for a moment longer. I then feel myself nod and watch myself walk to the couch and sit. It takes a moment for my mind to repossess my senses. I keep staring at the creature. It's difficult to look at somehow, almost like I can't tell how far away it is. I feel like I'm falling towards it one second and the next second it's rushing away from me.

Grot sits next to me and says, "Come Eric, we will let them discuss business, Rat can see that Katie is returning with the salve, it will help your head." I look up the hall to see the woman carrying a large tray in each of her hands. A bloody steak adorns one of the platters, while the other has four blue glass bottles and a small jar. I nod meekly and follow as Grot stands. "Cassandra, is it alright if we sit on the balcony for a while? Rat thinks that Eric needs to relax for a bit."

"Yes of course Grot, I'll speak with Xan and mention what we had discussed," Cassandra replies. Grot nods and smiles, revealing rows of serrated teeth.

"Many thanks, come Eric, grab two of those bottles and the jar if you please?" I nod and follow. The woman stops and offers me the contents of the left hand tray. She's pretty, maybe early twenties? She has a metal implant in the side of her head. I fumble slightly as I edge the bottles and jar off of the tray. I smell blood from the steak. The woman walks past and enters the office. Cassandra motions for Xan and the monster to enter. She then looks to Grot.

"The first door on your right will take you to the living room. You'll see the balcony from there." She turns back to the office. I follow Grot as he opens the right hand door. The room that greets us on the other side probably cost more than my whole home town. The space is elegantly arranged and filled with works of art. One of the walls is taken up by a living mural. Not a holograph, but moving stone carvings covered in shifting colors. The whole wall is writhing about. The designs are travelling through a complex pattern, with creatures and animals, plants, trees and mountains all flowing together. There's another 'spectral aquarium', that's what Cassandra called it before. This one covers the whole floor. I can see past it, is that a city? It looks like a tiny city, hundreds of feet below, weird. Grot crosses the room to the windows that cover the far wall. I can see a balcony beyond them and what is that? Sky? A beautiful sky, I haven't seen the sky here yet. Grot slides one of the panes, which turns out to be a door, he then looks at me and motions for me to come over. I nod and slowly cross the expanse. The balcony is massive, there's a pool and hot tub at the far end. It also looks like there's a bar or something. There are two guards out here. One's a Human and other looks like an Elf. Grot waves then approaches the balcony's edge. I grin awkwardly and follow. I peer over the handrail's edge and nearly drop the jar and bottles. There *is* a city down there, a huge sprawling city. There's more too, I can see the edges of the different levels, sticking out here and there. I look up and the world swirls around me. The city stretches upward for hundreds of feet, a wave of vertigo hits me. I try to recenter myself by closing my eyes. I smell car exhaust and flowers. I open my eyes and look down. Grot is looking up at me.

"You see Eric. Now you understand?" I nod dumbly.

"But why? Why is it built like this?" I ask while staring out across the city. Grot ponders for a moment then responds.

"It began many thousands of years ago. The stronghold of Tir'Ileth was all that stood here. It guarded the farms and villages around its base. For a while everything was good, but the people soon found that the land was dangerous. The forests and mountains were even more deadly still, so the old masters of Tir'Ileth began to expand their stronghold so that it could protect more of the surrounding land. But soon the land fought back and as they pushed outwards more horrors were awoken and innocent people were slaughtered. The old lords then thought of other ways to expand, as more and more people flocked to the safety of the city. They began to build upwards and downwards. The foundations were tempered and made strong with earth magics and the stronghold grew and grew until it stretched hundreds of feet into the sky. These days the lands are just as fierce, even more so, the edges of the sprawl are as dangerous as any place in the world. Most fear to expand outwards and very few live in the forests that surround the city, and so they keep building upwards."

I sit for a minute in silence. I look at Grot and ask, "Are there other cities?" He laughs and reaches for the glassware in my hands. I relinquish a bottle and the small jar.

"Yes, yes, many other cities all around the world. There are small towns and villages too." I nod and sit on a cushioned chair. I feel the mass of the pistol at the small of my back.

"Are they like this too?" I ask.

He shakes his head and says, "No, Tirileth city is unique, though the Rihley Archology is similar."

"The monster in there, what is it?" I ask, as Grot places the blue bottle on a small stone table. He then uncaps the jar and I'm overwhelmed by the sharp tang of some unknown substance. I blink a few times as he approaches.

"He might not appreciate being called a monster. He is an Asura. He is not of this place. He is a native of a place called 'The Realm of the Eternal Flux,'" Grot says as he smears some of the paste on my forehead. The substance burns my eyes for a moment before it subsides. Within seconds my head feels better. The dull throb is gone and I'm not dizzy anymore. I think about what Grot just said for a second before responding.

"What do you mean? The realm of what?" Grot smiles and recaps the jar. He points to the blue bottle in my hand and speaks.

"Drink, you'll feel better." He then continues as he uncaps his own blue bottle, "'The Realm of the Eternal Flux' is a separate place, what some would call another dimensional reality. It does not have the same physics as this place. There are paths that one might take to travel there. The natives are known as Asura. They are powerful creatures. They are very different from Humans and Elves and Goblins. They are born of elemental power, elemental power and chaos." What the fuck does that mean? Maybe it doesn't matter. Hopefully I won't see that thing again. I look at the blue bottle, uncap it and drink. It's like water to the power of ten, though maybe I'm just imagining it. I was thirstier than I thought. I look over to the guards. They're speaking amongst themselves, assault rifles slung over their shoulders. My mind returns to a river of rats running through an alley of desiccated corpses. I shudder and retch softly. My hand shakes with a slight tremor.

"Relax Eric, it's alright now. Rat has found your guardians. We have almost completed our purpose here," Grot says as he sits cross-legged on the balcony near my chair.

"What do you mean?" I ask.

Grot looks up at me and responds, "Rat cannot stay with you. We have seen a foul darkness and we must find its source, it is important, we can feel that it will be our new purpose, soon."

"But wait, no you can't just leave me! What am I going to do?" I exclaim, my voice cracks with emotion. Grot smiles in a comforting way.

"We will find out. Rat trusts Cassandra, she will ensure that you are safe. She will help us to find answers."

"But couldn't you stay here anyway? You said it's important, for the city," I say, anxiety building.

"No. Rat is sorry, but, we must follow the path, it is all that is left to us." I nod solemnly, my mind races. What now? He's weird and kind of smelly but Grot's the only one I sort of know here. Grot and Delrog. Oh how I wish Delrog had come with us. Grot could've commanded him to be my bodyguard or something. Now what's going to happen?

"Worry not Eric, when Cassandra is ready we will speak with Elindriss. She will be able to see more." I nod and put the empty blue bottle on the stone table. Then I remember something that was said.

"Wait! You said that you found my guardians? Who?" Grot smiles and is about to respond when the glass door slides open. I'm utterly distracted by the sight of the goddess, framed in light. An enchantress outlined in a wondrous backdrop.

109

"Elindriss is ready to see you now Eric, if you're ready to see her?" Grot looks to me and nods. I nod back and swallow hard. I stand and walk to the goddess. She smiles and says "I'll be right back Grot. Eric, follow me please." I follow her. I'd follow her anywhere.

We head back into the lobby, but this time we walk to the double doors directly across from the hall to Cassandra's office. I don't see the dangerous Elf man or the monster. Maybe they left. I'm somewhat relieved at the prospect. We approach the door. It's lined with shining silver metal. I can see runes carved into the metal, they seem to glow and pulse with an inner life. Cassandra stops in front of the doors. She smells exquisite. Careful now, don't get aroused. That would be embarrassing. Think of the rats. I shudder and instantly regret thinking of the rats. She turns around and gazes at me, pools of incandescent blue. I smile stupidly. She motions to the door and speaks.

"Elindriss waits for you inside, do as she says, everything will be fine." I nod. I try to say something, but it's like Jenny times a million. I just smile and pad aimlessly as she walks back through the lobby. She disappears through the door and I regain my senses. I lift my arm to open the door, but it swings inward just in front of my hand. I recoil for a second and peer into the room. It looks almost like an old library. I can smell leather mixed with some kind of incense. There are peculiar statues and masks covering the table tops. Odd sculptures are hanging from the walls. I can see a large complex statue in the center of the room. It almost looks like a planet but there are lines attached to it which lead to small, highly patterned circles. The center planet is surrounded by a strange mist-like substance. A voice shocks me back to awareness.

"Well come in or leave, it's impolite to just stand there and ogle." I nod quickly to the unseen voice and step through the threshold. The room is stacked with bookshelves. Nearly every square inch of the shelves is filled with old looking tomes. I slowly become aware of a presence to my right. An Elven woman is sitting in a fancy wooden chair. She has the same skin and hair color as

Cassandra but her eyes are violet. She's every bit as beautiful as Cassandra, they could be sisters.

"Take a seat. Let's have a look at you." I comply and sit across from her. I cross my arms in front of my stomach and look around the room. I look back to Elindriss. She's staring at me. She has a strange look in her eyes. Wait, I think her eyes are changing color. They're casting off light now. They're so wonderful. I can't look away. I don't want to look away. I must stare at her, it's all that I've ever wanted, it's all that I'll ever want. I realize that now. Everything else melts away. I can only see her eyes, my only world. Nothing else matters. Nothing else will matter. They are everything to me. I don't even want to blink. I can't miss one second. She exhales and suddenly her eyes fade away. What's happening to me? I recoil and begin to stand. "Sit!" she says sternly. I comply. I look up and muster my nerve.

"What was that?" I ask. She smiles and shrugs.

"I just needed to see something before we continued. Take off the necklace." The necklace? Oh, right, Grot's necklace. I reach up to my neck and feel the rat skull.

"But I won't be able to understand you without this," I say. She grins and points to the necklace.

"Don't worry about that, just take it off." I nod and quickly remove the necklace then put it on the small table beside my chair. She produces a silver chain that unfurls to reveal a small, eye-shaped crystal. She dangles it in the air between us and she begins to mutter something. I can't quite hear what she's saying. She closes her eyes and holds the crystal at arm's length. When she opens her eyes they each resemble the crystal. In fact they are crystals. She stares at me and I feel a great well of energy surge through my core. I can see something in my mind. A radiant ball of energy, it's burning like a small sun. What the fuck is that? She screams and drops the crystal. She covers her eyes and yells. "Damn it! Go get Cassandra, now!" My heart skips a beat and I'm up and running before I know what's happening. I burst out into the lobby and run for the beautiful room. I pass through the door and run across the spectral aquarium. There, Grot and Cassandra are talking. I run to the sliding door and open it. Grot is on his feet before I say anything.

"What is the matter Eric?" he asks. I stammer and point to the library.

"I ... I don't know! Sh ... she said to get Cassandra!" Grot looks to Cassandra and they both begin to move to the sliding door. I step out of the way and then follow as they run to the library.

Cassandra steps towards the seated Elf and asks, "Elindriss, what's wrong?" Elindriss turns towards Cassandra.

"Well I'm blind, so there's that. Oh yeah, and I'm pretty sure that the boy is carrying a fragment of the true power." What does that mean? Cassandra looks at me with surprise etched on her face. What's happening?

Grot moves into the room and says, "Rat can help. Sit still Elindriss."

She nods and smiles at a point near Grot, she then says, "Grot you bastard! Cassandra told me that you were alive, what the fuck?" she says.

Grot laughs and replies, "It is good to see you again Elindriss."

She laughs and responds, "Sure rub it in." She then sticks out her tongue. Grot laughs.

"We shall cure this pesky eye thing and speak afterwards, yes?"

Elindriss grins and nods then says, "Yes. Thanks. It would be sort of awkward trying to cure myself. I just wasn't sure if there were going to be any secondary effects, you know?"

"Are you sure it's the true power Elindriss?" Cassandra asks.

"I've never encountered this before but I've heard legends. The essence of the true power blinds, it can build worlds or tear them apart. It was the instrument that created the other realms. It has never been seen, not in its raw state anyway. The legends always allude to the after effects or the side effects," Elindriss responds. Grot begins to apply a green paste to her eyes.

"When Rat first saw the dreamer we too were blinded by a bright flash in the spectral sky."

112

I step back into the lobby. What are they saying? I hear Cassandra's voice but, for some reason, I can't understand her. She's speaking a weird foreign language. What's happening? Elindriss' voice responds. I can understand her.

"The power seems to be contained, whatever it is. We must not assume, it could simply be a side effect of the form of trans-dimensional travel that Eric experienced. Regardless, we need to find a way to safely extract it." I begin to breathe rapidly. I hear clicking on stone and footfalls. I turn back towards the hall as the monster comes bounding up. It takes every ounce of willpower that I possess to not give in to the fight or flight response. I'm so glad that I don't have to pee right now. The Elf is beside the monster, he speaks but I can't understand him, he seems to be asking a question. He's glaring at me. I manage to point a shaking finger at the room. Cassandra meets the Elf at the door and says something to him, I can't understand her. She then looks over at the Asura. The monster bows and smiles, revealing rows of razor sharp teeth framed by four massive canines. It speaks but the language is bizarre, like deep toned chaotic gibberish. The necklace, it's because I don't have the necklace.

I try desperately to think but my mind keeps resetting. I try to focus on the conversation. Grot says something about Elindriss and her sight returning, I feel relieved. Cassandra thanks him, I think. I'm feeling light headed. Cassandra asks a question, beauty framed in light. The monster speaks but I can't quite hear anymore. I feel tired, so very tired. Grot says something, he's panicked. Everything's so hazy. He rushes over to me and pulls me down. What's happening? He slips the necklace on. A fog instantly lifts from my mind.

I look around, startled, then stare at Grot and exclaim, "What's going on? My head ... My head was feeling really weird." He pats my shoulder and helps me to my feet.

"The ward was breached; somebody was trying to enchant you. Please keep the necklace on, it is important."

I nod and respond, "But she told me to take it off!" I point at the room and look over. I'm abruptly aware that Cassandra and the monster are looking at me. I draw back and look at the ground.

Grot nods and says, "It is needed to see your aura clearly. We should have warned you to wear the necklace while you are outside of the library, Rat is sorry, we did not think." Cassandra looks to Grot and speaks.

"We have a powerful ward in place Grot, are you sure they dismantled it?" Grot shakes his head.

"Not dismantled, they followed Eric through, our watcher saw the thread, somebody has performed a ritual. They are still performing a ritual. They have great arcane resources to do so." Cassandra nods. The voice of Elindriss drifts into the lobby.

"If they have a ritual in place, they've seen him. He needs to leave while we do more research. If we find out exactly what's happening we can figure out how to extract the power safely." Leave? Where am I supposed to go? Cassandra steps to the library's threshold and responds.

"Do you think that you can figure out how to do that?" The voice of Elindriss drifts back into the lobby.

"Someone will have to. You don't realize how dangerous this power is supposed to be. According to some legends, if it is released in the wrong way it can 'change all of reality'." I let that thought sink in for a second. I remember the feeling when Elindriss looked at me. The feeling of that small sun was indescribable. My mouth twitches and a tremor rolls through both of my hands. Grot nods to himself, he then looks to me and smiles.

"Then it is settled. Eric will go with the guardians until answers can be found." He claps his hands and looks at Cassandra. She looks over at Xan and the monster.

"Well? What do you think, sounds like something that you'd be interested in?" I swallow and look over at the pair. Them? The guardians? What is Grot thinking? They'll just sell me to those corporate guys the first chance that they get. Wait. Maybe that would be better anyway. Maybe the corporate guys would be able to get me home. Though, that Elf that got covered in rats seemed kind of like an asshole. I shudder again, thinking about the sound of thousands of chewing rats. Xan puts a hand under his chin, his swirling white eyes moving back and forth.

He then looks to Cassandra and says, "What about you? If somebody is tracking Eric they're going to be coming here, are you going to be safe?" He seems to be genuinely concerned.

Cassandra responds, "Don't worry Xan, we'll increase security, don't you have faith in Marcus?" Xan laughs and nods his head.

"Fair enough, as long as you have it under control, I think I would be very interested, I'm sure that the team will be on board as well, standard rates?" Cassandra nods, he continues "Who's picking up the tab?"

She smiles and looks affectionately at Grot before saying, "I am." Xan raises his eyebrows then shrugs and nods. The monster looks at me. Its eyes are whirling spheres of chaotic colors. I lose my balance for a second as its voice fills the lobby.

"We shall see the task through. It feels imperative that we do not falter. It feels as though failure in this shall bring the bedlam winds. They shall be the corrupt reeve of our doomed village. They shall surge and topple our fragile house of cards, emptying the detritus of catastrophe upon us all." What the fuck does that mean? It then looks to Xan. The Elf returns its gaze and nods. He then turns back to me and extends his hand.

"We haven't been properly introduced. I'm Xanshudan and this is Rex." Rex bows. I wave feebly at the monster. I still can't look at it for too long. I turn to shake Xan's hand when a tiny face appears on his palm. I recoil and gawk at the miniature face.

It winks at me and says, "And I'm Kane. It's alright, I don't bite. Do I Cassandra? Well, maybe just that once." I can only stare as a response. What am I seeing here?

"Get bent, asshole" is Cassandra's response, causing the small face to burst out with laughter. I laugh and wave at his hand awkwardly.

Xan grins and says, "Don't worry, he's harmless, mostly." I nod and watch as the face disappears back into Xan's palm.

Grot chortles and pipes in, "Rat has not seen a manifer spirit in many years, randy little buggers." Xan snorts and laughs. Grot then looks at me and motions towards the lobby. Cassandra turns back into the library with Xan following closely behind her. Rex sits on his haunches and seems to stare off into space.

"Are you sure that they can be trusted?" I whisper to Grot. He looks past me to Rex before he answers.

"Yes, Cassandra trusts them, they have history together. We trust Cassandra; there is history between us too." I nod and furrow my brow.

"What is your history with her, if you don't mind me asking?" Grot looks away for a moment as if considering something. He then looks at me and smiles.

"She is Rat's daughter." I can't help but recoil in shock.

"What? Seriously! Forgive me but I don't see the family resemblance!" Grot laughs and shakes his head.

He then says, "Rat adopted her when her parents were killed. Rat kept her safe and raised her. Rat helped her to make a life for herself." I nod and calm down a degree. He continues "Then Rat got lost one day, we had difficulty returning. We thought that she would be better off without us, it's not important, things change. Rat will visit her now, she is adamant." I nod and look back towards Rex. Maybe this will be alright. I sure wouldn't mess with that thing. I'm about to turn around when Grot's voice comes from behind me, an ethereal whisper "We must go now Eric. Remember what we told you and worry not, Rat will always be there for you when you need us, Rat has billions of friends. We are never too far." I look back towards Grot and much to my surprise he's not there. I quickly twist around and scan the area, nothing, just Rex. No wait, something's on the floor. I bend down and pick it up. Three rat tails braided together, they're twitching and slowly writhing like worms. An involuntary shudder grips me. I feel a static charge creep through my hand then up my arm. An image of the small sun passes through my mind. I look at the tails again, three tendrils of light, dancing to a beautiful song.

"Thanks Grot." I whisper to nobody in particular.

Moag

We see you, disgusting insignificant malefactors. Putrid filth, peel back your flesh and dance in your guts. Show us your blood, little stupid things. Show us only your suffering. We need nothing else. Worms. Vile, stinking worms all. Whore yourselves and be strangled by perverse lunatics. Enjoy your precious parties. You shall soon dance on blades while shit rains down on you. We see you, from the shadows we see you. Ungulate against apathy you blind ugly garbage. Your days are numbered. We see that number. We hold that number in our dark red hands. So dance now. Dance little meatlings, for we shall soon set tableaus of gore. We shall soon bask in your misery for you do not see us. We sit in the dark stone of your ignorance. The long night time of your incomprehension shall be your downfall. From here we shall begin our plan. From here we shall begin the rituals. Blood shall do for the first ritual. Easy blood, the blood of rats or the blood of infants, we shall eat their eyes. We shall rejoice in their agony. So dance now beneath your "Platinum Sky". Soon your sky shall be a different color, stained by the horror of our dark desires.

We flit back into the underground and become a shade. Rats, everywhere, rats. They shall serve. Their blood shall serve. We cling to the stone and head deeper into the sewers. We kill one and two, we kill more. Twenty shall do. We need twenty, or an infant, a mewling babe that we could peel the flesh from. It would take too long to find an unguarded baby though. We have been exposed for too long already. Rats are easy. Rats are everywhere. Crush their spines and break their heads. Just as with the dancers, filth running through the sewers with fur in place of impotent clothes. Fifteen rats dead and broken, it does not take us long. Five more shall do. Five more and we shall begin. We shall vomit forth the bile of disillusionment. Soon we shall watch them wither and break. Two more rats, careful, save the blood. The first ritual shall guard us. The first ritual isolates us from prying eyes. It shall also serve as our dark heart, the font of annihilation. It shall grant us the time that we need, and eventually we shall be able to twist the intention of the frail. We shall be able to cause them to slaughter and then despair. We shall cause them to dance to their own ruin.

Three more rats, it never takes long. Rats, everywhere. We clutch them with our long tail as we run along the wall. We clutch them as a bouquet. We must now find a bastion. We must find a hidden place to bleed our victims, a place that can become a slick coppery womb. We shall paint it in blood. We shall decorate it in bones. The sewers deepen. We must be careful to remain near to the club. It shall serve as our festering wound. It shall spread our diseases. It shall corrupt the multitudes as they seek to corrupt themselves. Gyrate now against our poisoned spines. Gyrate now on broken glass.

There is an open place. We can see a passage. It's an old passage that is not used by the city. We enter cautiously, clinging to the ceiling and shrouded in shadows. The passage opens into a tunnel, an old tunnel, a subway. Something lives here, some creature that hunts in the darkness. We can see it now, a spider, as large as a horse. We lick our lips. Brazed spider is our favorite. We call the fires of Ing'tha and the vermin ignites. The vermin writhes and dances. We delight in its suffering. The vermin shudders and coils into a ball. We are elated as it expires. We shall now explore this den. We shall reclaim this black pit, this hunter's cave. We crawl through the nooks and crannies. We defile this place. It shall serve us well. Vicious runes shall be carved in the passage. We shall trap our dark heart and it shall become a killer as well. Blackness encases the stone. There is one passage, only one. The rest is collapsed, clogged ventricles. The dark heart doesn't care; its blood comes from elsewhere. We stow our bouquet, then move to craft the rune. We must be cautious now. If we were sent back we would be flayed. They would skin us then gift us with our flesh. They would laugh and say "stitch it back on little Moag. You cannot walk about without any skin on little Moag, it isn't proper." Then we would. We would grin and we would stitch it back on, and we would wait, as we have all these millennia. We know that our chance shall come, but it shall come sooner if we are not sent back. We move to the passage. Our sharp claws glow red and we begin to carve. The rune is fire etched into stone. Ing'tha burns in this place now but we are drained. We must feast. We return to the charred spider and we dine. Legs and legs then squeeze out the eggs.

Crunch and munch when it's spiders for lunch. What, no eggs? Bad spider! We torch it, we rend it asunder. Its carapace is strong but we pry it apart anyway. We reduce it to ash so that it does not spoil our dark heart. Then we sit and we watch. We feel the infernal ground. Soon the place is clear, the ritual place, as with the other. We shall craft this one differently though. We shall craft this one for ourselves.

We gather the altar stones, destined to be red, destined to reek of death. We pile them and make a flat top. We carve the circle beneath, born of slaughtered innocents and bound by the dwoemer of fire. We desecrate the circle. We bleed ten of the victims and wait in the blackness. The circle glows scarlet. The circle glows with rage and we laugh, bathed in red. We tear apart the other ten. We spread their gore across the altar and stain it. We feel the thread come down. The black line anchors to the stone and we laugh. We feel Ing'tha and we are renewed. Our dark heart beats and we laugh. We think to the second ritual, "The Magzzoroth Announcement". Not rats now but infants. We need infants, innocent blood. Twenty shall do. Where do we get them? We are not large and powerful, yet. We must slink through the shadows and poison the innocent from the darkness. Still, we shall find them. We have the time now. The first thread has appeased the masters. They have their own bloody designs. They use the old dwoemer as well but their victims are the throng of life, bloated, vapid cattle. When "The Announcement" is complete we shall gain our station. We shall be closer to them then. It shall allow us to mutilate the throng with our own loathing. We shall sculpt them into a shambling theatre of brutality. We shall gift the great old masters with countless thralls, herding them with fear and malfeasance. First we must prepare. We must retrieve our treasures and bring them to our dark heart.

We head back into the passage. We run through the sewers, killing some rats for fun. The treasures are not far. They are hidden in our old lair. We glimpse the nightclub as we approach. Dance with your horrors now, for they shall soon be made manifest. You contaminated parasites, brainless chattel. We wish for the acid rains of Ing'tha. Melt off your faces and grant you no identity. We find our treasures, stowed in a bag made of Human flesh. We snatch them up and slink back to our dark heart. We return and the heart is warm now. The dwoemer of fire is strong. We laugh and we store our treasures. We hide them up high, and are surprised by a sudden crimson flash. The master's gem is glowing, demanding horrorshow, near to a god. We cringe and wince. What does he want? We did our part, there is nothing else. We rage and fight. The call must be answered. We are compelled, it cannot be resisted. We grasp the gem and he fills our mind.

"Insignificant insect, cower and grovel else be thrashed by stinging barbs and flensed for your insolence!" Towering daemon, fire, horns and fangs, absolute dread radiates from him. We cower and grovel. We plead and beg. He abates. "What have you been up to my repugnant emissary? Lie to me and be rent to pieces by crawling insects!" We lie. We lie well. We speak of corrupting mortals and eating babies. He laughs and mocks "little Moag with his far reaching goals, the power of a gnat and the balls of a chicken!" We grovel. We agree. Inside we seethe through a pall of fear. We shall finish "The Announcement". We shall show him. One day we shall be the one to peel his flesh. The great one continues, "I have a job for you little Moag, a job that even you can perform. We have undertaken a blood sacrifice at the great altar. Velgrin has seen that a Human has come through the rift. You shall find him little Moag, Velgrin has need of the Human's blood. He has need of the Human's spirit. If you find the Human you shall use 'The Black Hand of Setterack', we shall do the rest. Is that understood you feculent little maggot?" We agree. We praise his wisdom and power. Inside we kill him with a chainsaw. He continues, "Velgrin shall send you a telepathic imprint of the Human's last known location. The Human disappeared shortly after his arrival and Velgrin said that there is powerful warding dwoemer in play. You had better not get sent back before you use the hand, you mongrel, or I swear that I shall devise a torment for you that shall make a flaying seem like a gentle breeze! Do you understand me you feeble, stunted deject?" We bow and scrape. We agree to everything and we promise to do our very best. Abruptly he is gone. The fear lifts. We swear at him. We promise our eternal vengeance with a flurry of curses. Velgrin's impression overcomes us. We fall to the ground and grasp our head. There is a path, it is very clear. The path leads to a small ruin then to a nearby shack. The vision subsides. We stand and bristle. We curse their names. "The Announcement" shall have to wait. We shall find and butcher infants later. For now, we must find this Human. We shall find him quickly so that we can return to our plans. We shall find him quickly, so that the masters don't suspect us.

We scurry from our dark heart and pass by the nightclub. Enjoy your reprieve, filth. Enjoy the petty circumstances of your existence. Drink and fuck and shit and die. We shall return. We shall see you all buried beneath an avalanche of putrescence. We shall shove excrement in your nostrils and scar your very being with our cruelty.

We leave the shadow's embrace and transform ourselves, on the outside we now look like them. Our flesh is that of a Human. We walk amongst them. Bile wells within us and our heart is full of venom. We wish to cut their throats. We wish to hear their life draining away and to breathe in their final breath. We restrain ourselves as we walk.

Miles pass. We do not tire, but we wish to perform this task quickly. We shall steal a car. We shall murder someone and steal their car. We become giddy at the prospect. We walk for awhile longer, until we see a mark. Our hand moves quickly, and we steal a man's credstick. We see the man and we remember. We move out of sight and become the man. We put on his flesh and we walk back into the street.

Soon we find a pawn shop. Desperation encased in brick and glass. There is a blade in the display case. It is a sharp blade that snaps out quickly at the push of a button. We are pleased, it shall do. We buy the blade with the credstick. The shopkeeper does not see our true nature. He is blind to our loathing.

We move back to the street now. We need a victim, a driver, distracted. The streets become our hunting ground. It is not long before we see our prey. He sits unaware. His car is running near an apartment block. We move rapidly to the car door, knife in hand.

The prey does not notice us until it is too late. We quickly open the door, and then we open his throat. The wound yawns wide. He sits in shock for a moment. We bubble with ecstasy. He sputters and spouts blood. We hear someone scream but we do not care. He convulses and pours red as we put him on the street, filth into the gutter. We drive away. The smell of blood surrounds us, and we are ecstatic. We are sticky with lovely blood and we are in ecstasy.

We drive through the streets sitting in our abattoir. We grin and laugh sitting in a puddle of red. The car moves onward. Some look and become frightened, others don't care. It does not matter. We abandon the car and the flesh when we get close to our goal. We hide and then become a new Human, one not covered in blood. It saddens us to do so. We grip the knife and we laugh. Maybe we shall find another, just for fun.

Goblins, many Goblins are here, a different type of filth, smaller and dirtier. Bags of stinking sludge. We wish carnivorous bugs in their brains. We pray that they choke on their own entrails. The ruins appear before us. They are small, no more than a frame and a pathetic wall. We know the story well."The Fall of Errigose", a petty corruption. The legend persists due to romance, disgusting *love* between two Humans. We sneer and look up the alley. The shack is there. We find it quickly and we enter. It is a sad little room with a couch, table and fridge. We sniff the air. We begin to search. We scour the walls and table. We peek through the fridge and look underneath. We tear apart the couch, and find something. It is a tiny metal disc. It has raised patterns, one side has a face and the other side has an animal. It is similar to the burning coins of Ing'tha, but it is foreign. It is from a different place. We take the coin. We might use it to cast a spell. Not us exactly. We must contact a devotee of "Ignis Infernus". They shall aid us, we shall use them. A laugh bubbles from us. This might be easier than we first thought. We remember where a church of "Ignis Infernus" resides, hidden from prying eyes.

We begin to move to the church. It is quicker to walk these streets. We don't steal another car, but we still watch for a chance to murder. The filth here is wary. They can see predators. We could kill them in our natural form. We could poison them and burn them. We could make their eyes bleed. But, no, first the task at hand, we must not enrage the masters. They have others that they can send, even a "Faceless". We could not fight the others, not yet. The "Faceless" would slay us without effort, and then laugh at our mangled corpse.

We continue to move through the city. Putrefaction surrounds, break their legs and set loose the hounds. We head down. Level by level we head beneath the ground. We see pain and desolation. We laugh at the unfortunate, mocking their hunger and kicking them when they draw near. Run from us, filth. Cower and give us our due. We pass other predators as well. Muggers and gangers, they don't bother us. They see something in us. We let the fire come through our eyes and they recognize us. They see our murderousness.

Time passes, miles pass. We are untiring. The faster we finish the quicker we can begin. As we walk, we watch for infants. We could steal them away. Put them in a box, save their bodies for the ritual. We look up and down, left and right. Red light screams at us, greens and blues anger us, the city is colorful. We wish it to be black and grey. We wish it to be bathed in ichors of decay. Salesmen approach us. Step away small mongrel. We want none of your wares. We'd kill you if we could. You twisted vendors of the street, merchants of exploitation. We applaud your selfish efforts but we want nothing from you, nothing, but your unending torture. We remember the path now. We are not far. Soon little Human, soon you shall wish that you hadn't come to this place. Soon you shall know suffering. We shall find you. Moag shall find you, and then pain shall be your constant companion. We see the church. It's an old warehouse. Mephistopheles' skull marks the wall. We grin. We shall present ourselves in our natural form. Our Human flesh is shed. We leap to the tall roof, become shadow and enter. The church teems with dark figures, sycophants and willing victims. We watch unseen. Down beneath us we see puss. Malignant wretches all, useless crawling whelps. Wait, maybe not all. There is one. We see one with the old power. He practices blood dwoemer.

We rape his mind, and announce ourselves. He stutters, his thoughts are in turmoil.

"What the fuck? Who are you? How are you speaking to me? What do you want?" We draw him out. We lure him outside. "What power? What do you mean? Show yourself, I'm warning you!" This one has courage. This one thinks that his dwoemer shall save him. We reveal ourselves. We bow and we smile. We do not tell him our true name. We call ourselves "Reaver". He cowers and snivels, he looks to us and he speaks "Apologies oh mighty Reaver! I am not worthy to be in the presence of one of the true lords, native of Ing'tha and power that we all serve. I am your willing servant in all matters." We acknowledge his groveling. We bait him with words. We cajole and lie. We speak of fire and power. We make him obscene promises. His eyes betray his desires. He is hooked. We ask him of scrying. He speaks. "Yes of course. Do you have a blood sample?" We shake our head, we show him the coin. He speaks. "Yes this will work. Do you have a name?" We shake our head. We propose a naming ritual. We can fetch the heart if he can craft the ceremony. He nods and speaks. "We can use the basement, there's a room." We acquiesce. We command him to prepare the ritual. We command him not to tell any others. We give him the coin and warn him of reprisals, should he fail. He nods and bows. He returns to the church. We laugh and sink back into shadow.

We stalk off in our natural form. We stalk off in search of a sacrifice. A fresh bleeding heart, we delight at the thought. We wish for a bed of fresh bleeding hearts. We wish for a tidal wave of them. We travel through the darkness. We leap from roof to ledge from ledge to pole and onwards. We are vapour and suggestion. The darkness becomes us. We run along the walls and cling underneath bridges. We soon find a mark, a young Human female, alone, unaware. She's staring at a phone. She's standing in the shadows. We pounce from on high. We latch onto her throat and bite. We inject our poison and we wrench her to the ground. She fights and screams. We rend out her eyes. She squeals in horror and pain. We tear off her jaw. She makes delightful noises with her tongue. We squeeze the life from her as our poison takes hold. We are ecstatic as she expires. Our sharp claws dig into her and soon we have our heart. Our hands are dark and red, and we are in ecstasy. Voices can be heard. We leap to the roof and melt back into shadow. We clutch our fresh bleeding heart firmly. We clutch it with our long tail as we return. A broken red trail marks our passage but we do not care. The city does not care. We bring the fresh bleeding heart to the church, then into the dark basement. We approach the room. The smell of death greets us, and we are pleased.

The heart cracks and pops. The heart sizzles and steams. We smell burning flesh and we are comforted. The Human performs the ritual. His bloodstained hands form patterns. We shall not murder him. He may be of use in the future. He may be of use when we perform "The Announcement." We sit and remain patient, keeping an eye out for interlopers. The door is locked and the room is soundproof. There are drains in the floor and chains on the wall. Blood grime edges the room's corners. We like this place, it reminds us of home. Soon we shall have your name little Human. When we have that, we shall find you. Then we shall watch your limbs as they are shorn away. We shall caper and sing as you choke on centipedes. We shall laugh, as we serve you up to be slaughtered in the worst of ways. But now we wait. We must think to "The Announcement." We must plan the other factors. We shall need the steel for the altar. We shall need a hound from the black pits. We must find and steal the metal. We must coax a hound to our service. There shall be time after we find the Human. We shall have time to find the infants. Perhaps a hospital, we could become a nurse. Steal one and two before we continue on to the next hospital.

We look back to the Human as the ritual nears completion. The heart is nearly ash. Its core shall never burn. We watch and remain patient. We look to our small belt. "The Black Hand of Setterack", we have had it with us for one thousand years now. It was given to us by the masters in case they wished to come to this place. They do not even need a portal, only the hand. We must guard it closely now. The Human has seen it but he does not know what it is. He does not gaze at it with desire. He would covet if only he knew. We shall distract him. His service shall be compensated with meaningless trinkets. We shall gift him with the knife and the man's credstick. If he's convicted of murder because of them we shall laugh. The ritual reaches its end and the ash flares crimson. A soft and tortured scream fills the room.

"Eric Gibson!" We laugh and clap our hands. We congratulate the Human and gift him with the trinkets. He is pleased, bowing and thanking us. He then speaks.

"I will start a scrying ritual right away." We warn him of the powerful warding dwoemer. He smiles in a way that we like. He speaks. "Well then, we're going to need some more hearts. Six would be ideal." We return his smile. We are filled with glee and perform a small dance. We then promise to return soon. We promise to return bearing a bouquet of fresh bleeding hearts.

Rebecca Arliss

A shift in the breeze brings the smell of earth and trees. Rebecca steps from the sidewalk and enters the park. Nearly three square miles of cobbled paths, trees and gardens, the space also contains dozens of stone bridges and old tunnels. Rebecca's been here many times before. She used to live about a mile away. She frequented the park then, went jogging and hacking. The park is large enough to get lost in, a good spot to launch her avatar from. This way, even if she is traced, she can just wipe her porta-comp and ditch it, then walk away. Although that would suck and be expensive, the alternative is decidedly worse. She thinks about the variables again. No way to get access through regular channels. It would raise tons of red flags with Koshikawa. If they do have something to hide, they might just cut their losses and give up the chase. Unless they have a lot invested in the prize, in which case they might just send a five man squad for her. She winds her way down the familiar paths of the park, while thinking about the story. The stolen footage can't be used directly, that's obvious. She could still track the Goblin and the Human. There seems to be something about them. Then it hits her. She could craft a smart-frame based on a simple facial recognition template. Like the Marshall tracking systems. Corporations use them as well. Koshikawa is probably tracking the pair already. She might be too late. But her instinct is screaming at her about this story, and the more she pries, the stronger the feeling gets. Her "independent" dug up some good info on the deceased Koshikawa troops. It turns out that the Captain was some kind of hotshot wizard known by the name "Fire Sight". Apparently he was a real pro in tracking and acquisitions. The other four were all Black Ops, not Special Ops, a slight difference but a telling one. They no doubt have airtight manufactured identities, so it's useless to dig too deep into their backgrounds. Still, that type of a group is only sent after something of great value, since it failed, Koshikawa won't be nearly as subtle the next time. She continues on through the park until she reaches her favorite hacking site. She sits up against the massive trunk of the old oak tree. Two stout roots frame her sides, forming her nature chair. A stone bridge spans the creek that snakes through the shallow valley just in front of her. Clumps of trees accentuate the different grassy fields and U.V. standards dot the landscape at pre-determined intervals. There's a small group playing Torus in the field far to the right. She closes her eyes for a moment and inhales. She smells fresh cut grass and pollen. The hum of insects surrounds her and she hears birds singing in the distance. The city's traffic sounds like some far-off ocean. She opens her eyes and produces her button camera. It's time to get to work.

The ninja springs into existence and checks the button camera feed, serene park, no problems. She then activates the motion sensor smart-frame and adds it to the camera software. The ninja looks back to the weave just in time to see a great host of avatars, all around her. She leaps into the air and readies her defenses, as a shot of adrenalin surges through her. Wait, it's a carnival. The ninja laughs. She should have checked her weave optics before engaging. She's been here too often, assumed that it would be the same as it always is. Not today, it would seem. The digital landscape of the park is transformed. It has become a massive medieval carnival. She laughs again and looks around. Her ninja garb isn't too out of place. Many of the avatars are dressed as old time warriors or heroes. There are games of archery and jousting, she can see a large arena for dueling, and tents selling all sorts of paraphernalia. She lingers for a few minutes before she plots her route. She could head straight to a slave node as she did before. However, they might be on high alert now. It would be better to bounce her weave line through at least a dozen hubs then add a line lock. She sighs, it will take a while, but still, it pays to be safe. She calls up an international hub grid and begins selecting different hubs at random. It doesn't take her long to find twelve, plus her final destination makes thirteen in total. The ninja carves in the first hub address and blasts off at the speed of thought.

A new relay is created at each hub that she stops at. Just to be extra careful, she decides to put a line lock on each relay. The encryption should block up any trace when it reaches each new hub. She'll then be able to gauge how skilled her pursuers are by how quickly they bypass any given hub. That should give her plenty of time to jack-out and beat feet if she needs too.

It takes her the better part of an hour to set up all of the relays. Her motion sensor chimes twice, first for a jogger then for a group of joggers. Finally, with all the relays and locks in place the ninja once again finds herself standing across from the dull grey of a Tirileth City slave node. Not the same one as earlier, this one's on the sixth level. Not that it really matters, the whole system is linked. If they upgraded one part of its defenses they upgraded every part. It's the inside that she's really concerned about. One can never tell what's there until it's too late. There is a Federal decree in place that restricts the city from employing countermeasures that use lethal bio-feedback, except for the military of course. Still they could get her port I.D. and completely fry her comp in the process. She'd be extremely screwed then, more than likely a couple of years in the stacks at a minimum. The ninja gazes at the slave node, twice as many soldiers outside, that's not a good sign. She quickly engages her "Sleaze" program and writes a custom masking program for her avatar. It will have to be a different approach this time. She has to assume that internal security found her last phoney requisition order. They might be wise to that ploy. She could try to "piggyback" an employee, it's risky though. Last time she tried that she nearly fell into a trap. She has far superior software now, but she'd still have to put a snare on the node. That could be tricky as well. Most nodes are set to scan for them. Government hackers also perform routine searches. She could probably fool the node's detection algorithms, but a hacker is another matter entirely. The ninja sits and ponders for a minute. Then an idea strikes her. She could infect the node with a series of minor smart-frames based on a spam template. Then, when an employee attempts to enter, she could quickly place the snare while they're dealing with the spam. That way the snare's only in place for a few seconds.

She activates her smart-frame sculpting sub-program. The spam-frames are easy enough to make. Four should do. She rips four local weave advertisements and stitches them into the smart-frames. She then compresses the collection of spam-frames and gets ready to connect them to the node. They'll be instantly destroyed as soon as the first avatar enters the address, but that's fine. They only have to work once.

The ninja then breathes deeply and moves forward towards the node. No reaction from the soldiers, it seems that they don't have detection upgrades. She positions herself within arm's reach of the node, then touches it and accesses its structure. The encryption's been upgraded, that much is obvious. *This might take a little while,* she thinks. She launches her "Code Cleaner" program and begins working.

The ninja slowly slashes through the code. She keeps expecting an alarm, but the soldiers are still unresponsive. She returns to dissecting the encryption. More than thirty minutes pass as she works on the node. Her motion sensor triggers only once as an Elf on a scooter drives past. Finally, she cracks the last part of the code. The ninja reaches into her satchel and produces a neat stack of letters. She then attaches the letters to the nodes construction, and watches as the spam-frames disappear into the weave constructs coding. The "piggyback" snare is readied and a tense few minutes pass as she sits in the digital shadows, waiting for her chance. Then, just as she's beginning to get fidgety, the letters spring to life and the spam-frames activate. The ninja moves quickly and flings a grappling hook into the weave construction. A few seconds later and she's flying through the wall of the node, directly on the heels of a plain looking governmental avatar. *Hopefully they aren't a digital security expert,* she thinks, *that would be unfortunate.*

The ninja holds her breath as they pass into the digital hall of the central public camera system. She cuts the line and sits perfectly still. The employee continues on their way and they are soon lost to the ninja's sight. She peers around. There are definitely more smart-frames, something else as well. There are banners on the columns and the walls, they weren't there before. She activates her detection software. The ninja's eyes flare, and the hall transforms before her sight. A latticed grid of three dimensional lights greets her. She focuses on one of the banners. The grid opens to reveal a familiar coding pattern. A "Cyber Net" program, the banners are traps, they're everywhere. They don't seem to cover the entire area though. There are routes in between them. She looks to the wall of cabinets. Banners line the walls. She knows that the program occupies a limited virtual space, but it looks like they overlap in a way that covers each drawer. If she had a digital I.D. tag she could just waltz past them without any trouble. Wishful thinking isn't going to help now however. The smart-frame distraction won't work either. She'll still have to get through the nets anyway. She concentrates on her breathing for a minute. This will have to be a slow walk. Remain patient, access each databank independently and make sure that she doesn't activate a single net. The ninja pulls a short black spike from her satchel, a smart-frame she wrote with the facial recognition software. The program should track the Goblin and the Human anytime that a camera clearly captures either of their faces. With any luck the total combination of the images will build a clear picture of where they've been within the past three days. If it works, it should give her a number of different canvas locations. The ninja looks at the wall and slowly advances. She steps sideways through the construction of the first "Cyber Net". Good, no alarms, no activation. Now only who knows how many more nets to go. She sighs and accesses the central tracking system, a sort of digital schematic of the camera layout in the city. Her jaw drops as she sees the design.

The ninja slowly slinks between the nets, creeping past soldiers and plain-faced avatars in the process. This system is immense. The central tracking system displays 78,642 active public cameras. She narrows her search to ten levels. One to ten, the best bet as the incident happened on the fifth level. They could've come from above or below. Still 28,275 cameras, she narrows the search further. The same levels but three square miles per level instead, near to the incident. They were on foot. Hopefully that was their primary mode of travel. Down to 2,125 cameras, that's a manageable number. She's about to begin when her motion sensor lets out a warning and she looks to the button camera image. A little girl is running by, she's with a dog. The dog runs up and sniffs Rebecca's body eagerly. *Don't you dare hump my leg,* she thinks. The girl calls out and the dog bounds out of sight. She lingers on the camera for a moment more. The ninja shakes her head and looks to her new route. This is going to take some time. She slinks back to the drawers and expertly glides past the net. It's becoming easier each time. They must have all been set by the same bored techie. No variation, at least not yet. She begins to stab each of the required drawers. An hour passes and she's struck just over four hundred drawers with the black spike. The park is full of activity but nobody seems to be paying close attention to her body.

The ninja drifts through the hall. She walks up the wall, stabbing drawers as she goes. Another hour passes and she's pierced five hundred more targets. She's starting to feel a rhythm, and the nets are getting even easier to bypass as she goes. There are fewer avatars around here. Still, she performs regular scans.

Hours pass as she works her way through the grid of drawers. With a digital I.D. tag she could've done this in seconds by accessing the controls of the central system. Her nerves are beginning to fray. The intermittent adrenalin surges are starting to wear her out, and her body must be as sore as hell right now. She considers buying an auto masseuse once again, if only she had twenty grand to blow. The ninja looks back to the grid, fifty to go. She won't actually know whether she has anything of value until she compiles the data. That won't take long though, and it can be done at her apartment. The ninja dances on the drawers, stabbing each one as she goes. Five minutes later and her task is complete. The node's entrance beckons, a white speck far in the distance. She quickly pulls up her scanning interface and creates a map based on the placement of the "Cyber Nets". She studies the map for a moment before tracing a path between the nets. An ethereal blue trail appears in the ninja's vision. She then launches into the air and follows the trail precisely and at great speed. Dozens of avatars streak past, they don't seem to notice her, and soon she reaches the node's entrance. The ninja toys briefly with the notion of putting a "Mole" program in place. Problem is that they can be used as a trap as well. It would be nice to have a back door into this system however. She struggles with the decision for a moment more before a trio of nearby avatars begin to make her nervous, and the ninja quickly departs. She moves a short distance from the node, there's still no alarms, no pursuit. She smiles contentedly and enters the hub address where she started. One or two jousts, then, to work.

The ninja strikes down three jousters before succumbing to an Orcish knight's lance. She laughs. She'll have to return next year. Hopefully she'll be less busy by then. Her optical clock reads 9:30 lunar. The ninja retraces her digital line and disengages the weave interface. She stretches. Sore points announce themselves in her shoulders and back, her legs and ass are numb. She shakes the blood back into them and looks around. There's a dog walker crossing the bridge. Beyond them she can see a pair of Zealots slowly plod up the path. The symbol of Zool is prominently displayed on their lapels. She nods to them and they return the greeting. The pair is here often, it's best to remain on good terms with the "Zoolots". Their order serves as the parks primary custodians, though it is still technically public land. The Zealots offer a level of protection that the Marshall's couldn't hope to match. Most gangers avoid this place like the plague. She stands and stores her porta-comp in her backpack, checking her pistol and pockets in the process. Her headphone buzzes, causing her to jump. The call display winks in the lower right hand field of her vision. She laughs and connects the call.

"What's happening you mug, are you drunk?" Rebecca sub-vocalizes. Anastasia's voice erupts in her cyberears.

"Becka! What's up? No, not really. I wouldn't call it drunk. Anyway you should come out tonight!" Rebecca considers for a moment. She can't really afford to lose any time on this story, and she's already really tired.

"Oh yeah, what's on the agenda tonight?"

"We're going to hit up 'Dante's Inferno'. A bunch of us are going there." She considers for a moment. It would be fun to unwind, though it would take like two hours just to get into the club.

She begins to head out of the park as she replies, "You know, I'm super beat, I've been working on this story all day. I think that I'm just going to go to eat something and go to bed."

Anastasia makes a pitiful whimpering sound and says, "Aww, it won't be any fun without you! This better be one hell of a story! Is it going to make you rich and famous?" Rebecca laughs.

"Not bloody likely, at this point it just better turn into something or else my boss is going to tan my hide for wasting his time, anyway have fun tonight, I'm just going to head home, I'll talk to you later."

"Alright, fine. Enjoy your food and sleeping. I'll talk to you later, party pooper," Anastasia says before she disconnects.

The park's on the ninth level, not too far from her place. Still, it takes more than forty-five minutes to get back to her apartment. A pair of drunken Elves stumbles out of "The Titan Arms", the smell of alcohol wafts through the air as she catches the door and heads inside. She enters her apartment just as she realizes how hungry she's become. The security system activates and she throws her backpack on the couch. She stows her pistol and activates her cyberear's phone.

"Call 'Fat Catz'." She takes off her pants and shirt as the phone chimes in her head.

"'Fat Catz' delivery, one moment please." A short span of dead air greets her before the voice resumes, "I've got you at 'The Titan Arms', tenth level, west forty-second street, apartment 12-C, is that right?"

"That's right, yeah," replies Rebecca as she takes off her bra and panties.

"Can I take your order?" the voice responds, male, probably early twenties.

"Yeah I'll get one order of Tilhine and one order of barbeque chicken." Half Elven and half Human cuisine, just like the restaurant. The Human half of the menu tends to be way better. That could just be because she's actually had authentic Elven cuisine. There's no comparison. The voice announces the usual total and time to arrival.

"That'll be 24.78, it should be there in forty-five minutes to an hour."

"Thanks. Have a good night," she responds. The voice returns a pleasantry as she disconnects and crosses to the small bathroom.

The water pours over her as she tries to work out the sore spots in her muscles. Soon she'll put the pilfered data through a map grid. She begins to get nervous as she thinks about the infiltration. There was no alarm though. The real problem may be the complete lack of usable information. She closes her eyes and washes her hair and body, working through the purple spikes which then reform thanks to a nano-particle treatment. She towels off and puts on some lounging clothes, pajama pants and a "Screaming Robots" T-shirt. She then heads to the couch and retrieves her porta-comp. A moment later and the info is loaded into her apartment's computer. "Vid on," she says as she crosses to the couch and puts the porta-comp in the backpack. The holographic display winks to life just as a Marshall leaps across a bullet-riddled table, guns blazing. Some old vid, it will serve as adequate background noise. She crosses back to the computer and calls up the Tirileth City map, then activates the grid software. The software is a variation on the cities GPS and weave pole grid locations. It displays the entirety of the hive, as well as the surrounding sprawl. She stares at the enormity of the digital map for a few minutes. The great tear-shaped construction hovers before her, in all its complexity. Fortunately, she won't need to immerse herself this time. The program will create two trails based on the captured images and their relation to one another, one trail for the Goblin, and one for the Human. The program will also create a time table and display the precise moment of the captured image. She accesses the computer's holo-display and retrieves the camera data. She then transfers it into the grid and lets the smart-frame do the rest. The program starts, and her heart skips a beat as nothing happens at all.

Then, after a few seconds of terror, a green dot appears. Green was for the Goblin. She lets out a breath. The dot moves and soon turns into a line which begins to stretch through the heart of the hive. The line hops erratically; it even disappears altogether a

135

number of times or jumps between levels within a seemingly impossible time frame. The Goblin must have been avoiding cameras, or something. The line continues on for more than a day before the second dot appears. Red, red was for the Human. It first appears near "Reacher's Hope", on the city's second level, curious. That makes no sense, unless the Human is very skilled at avoiding cameras. But then why the sudden lapse in vigilance? The lines then travel together for some time. They're heading upwards until they're lost again on the ninth level. She's familiar with that area. It's a rougher neighborhood than where she lived. There's definitely a higher criminal element. The dots don't reappear after that. She thinks about the path for a moment, glancing at the holo-vid as she does: the Marshall spouts some cheesy line before he mows down a dozen bad guys with a wall of lead. She looks back to the grid. Two points of interest then. "Reacher's Hope", she highlights the area and enlarges the image. There's a huge Goblin population, it's a stone's throw away from a particularly bad stretch of the warrens. She feels a slight pang of anxiety. The other spot isn't much better at all. She quickly performs an image search using the Goblin and the Human, setting their pictures against news stories and posted bounties near "Reacher's Hope" over the past ten years. Nothing, she tries the same thing regarding stories and bounties near the ninth level location over the same timeline. Nothing there either. She searches through the other news stories from both of the areas. Minutes pass, then half an hour. Finally something stands out. There's a story about a suspected fixer operating right in that area. Like suspiciously close to the last area that the lines appear. It's dated from seven years ago, it say's her name is Cassandra Seelie, there's a picture of a huge mansion and a beautiful Dark Elf woman. The mansion is perched right on the level's edge. That kind of real estate is exorbitantly expensive, hundreds of millions of credits. She performs a search on Cassandra Seelie. A number of sites appear. They all pertain to a local business woman and philanthropist. According to some of the articles, she's an importer of rare goods and arcane reagents. She contributes to several charities, including more than one local orphanage. No doubt it's all a cover. She thinks about it for a moment. The Goblin and the Human could be working for this Cassandra. Maybe this was all about a botched theft. Still, Koshikawa wouldn't want to keep it a secret. They'd be posting the pairs images as known thieves, in an attempt to elicit the help of bounty hunters. She could try to get an interview with Cassandra, but first she should follow the more solid lead. She sighs. "Reacher's Hope" it is then. If she can't find anything there she'll try the Cassandra angle. If that doesn't work out then she'll have to ditch the story and start from scratch somewhere else. That would be annoying, and it would make all that good hacking irrelevant. She sighs again then retrieves her porta-comp and uploads the map grid with the newly plotted routes. She then places the small computer on its charging pad before slumping down on the couch, eyes unfocused, holo-vid Marshall dispensing justice. She's about to head back to the computer when her cyberear's phone rings.

She answers "Yeah?"

"'Fat Catz', your food's here," responds a young male voice.

"Right, one sec." She adjusts the computer's display, the hall just outside her door flares to life. She then strikes the lock icon on the bottom of the display. "Door's open, head on up."

The delivery boy is paid and she heads back inside with her meal. She wolfs down the food in record time. As usual the chicken outshines the noodles, but she doesn't care too strongly, just glad to be fed. She stares at the holo-vid with glazed eyes. The Marshall gets shot, but he keeps on fighting as submachine gun wielding Orcs assail from every angle. She starts to think about the next day, a nervous energy washes through her. She looks at her pistol, there's some special ammo that she bought a few years back. She'll load that up tomorrow. Right now though, it's time for a small amount of mindlessness and then bed.

Cassandra

The sky ripples with drops of water. A strong smell of rain permeates the air. Cassandra lounges on the deck chair, staring out at a world of falling water. It's been a long day, maybe the auto masseuse? She gets hints of citrus and melon as she drinks. It's been a long, strange day. She smiles again at the thought of Grot. She remembers running through the alleys with him, breaking into shops and snatching food from vendors. She recalls his tricks. He always had something up his sleeve, always some way to get out of any situation. He'd better come back as he promised. He'd rushed out so quickly they didn't even exchange phone numbers, if he even has a phone. She has some of his hair now though. She'll be able to find him, even with his skill in warding magic. Still, she'd rather that he returns willingly. He's so different now, the grief changed him. Though, he's still the same where it counts, his heart is still the same. That didn't change at least. She looks at her drink then back to the wall of water. Xan and Rex took the boy to "The Castle". Elindriss is recovering, she's rarely wrong when it comes to her visions. That boy could be a ticking time bomb. Bump into him in the wrong way and all of reality changes, whatever that means. She takes a drink and laughs.

One of the guards at the far end of the balcony looks over and yells "Did you say something Ma'am?" Cassandra shakes her head, platinum curls glistening in the soft light. Her phone blinks and lets out a soft tone. She looks to the stone table, a holographic gate icon floats above the phone. She snatches it up and engages the front gate camera. The image of a guard standing beside a bulky Human appears. The Human is somewhat portly, obvious cybereyes, Sam Lockwood. She thinks about the scene for a second, then sits up. That's right. She completely forgot that he was coming. She hits the connect button as she stands.

"Ma'am, a Sam Lockwood is here, he says that he has business. He's armed," the guard announces. She enters the living room and crosses to the hallway's door.

"Yes of course, let him in, it's fine," she answers as she passes through the door and walks up the hall. A moment later and she's sitting behind her desk. She swivels in the chair and looks in the mirror, smoothing her hair and adjusting her curves before resettling at the desk. The spectral aquatic dance continues as she waits. Her computer buzzes and Cassandra opens the office doors. Sam swaggers through the doors, all bravura and nonchalance. She looks him over. He's somewhat dirty. He's wearing a coat of heavy armor with a large pistol under the left arm. She flashes him a business smile and points to an empty chair. He bows slightly and sits with a groan.

He adjusts himself then says, "Cassandra, what's happening?" She considers him for a moment. He's a talented enough mercenary, a bit sloppy, but he's tenacious and more dangerous than he appears.

She responds, "Oh the usual, you know, always something going on."

He nods and says, "I hear you. So you got the payment?" She shifts in her chair slightly.

"A bit of an odd request, your payment method I mean." She studies him as he responds.

"You think? Well, I suppose so. We're planning on doing some work out that way is all. There's tons of opportunities, good money, good action, the craziest parties." He laughs at the last statement. She puts a finger to the side of her mouth and leans against her armrest. She motions towards him as she speaks.

"You've been there before then?" He nods.

"I was there a few years back. We had a contract with one of the clans, a protection detail."

She considers for a moment. "Had a contract, what happened?"

Sam shifts uncomfortably in his chair. "Most of the company was wiped out in an ambush, some bad shit. After that I came back, needed to find another crew after all, still, tons of money to be made there."

She nods and adds, "That's true. There's money to be made here as well, but first, old business, so you're sure that you want demi-gold? Asura trade in credits as well you know?"

He nods and says, "Yeah, I know, but they prefer gold, and I don't like to give em any fucked up reason to be angry with me.

They're random enough as it is, you know?" She smiles and nods. That's something that she knows very well.

"Alright then, thirty thousand coins, they are stamped with the Hishiken clan symbol, I trust that isn't a problem?"

"That's fine; fire gold's as shiny as any other," he says.

She nods and continues. "The coins will be divided into three duffle bags. Do you have a vehicle?"

He hooks a thumb back over his shoulder. "Chopperface is parked over on Elgin. I'll hoof the bags over there, vehicles hot, didn't want to bother you with it." She lets out a short laugh.

"That's considerate of you." She then accesses her desk's computer for a moment and sends a ping to her vault guard. She looks back to Sam and continues "Your payment will be in the lobby shortly". She then leans forward and adds "I do have another piece of work available, if you're interested?" He tilts his head from side to side, as though physically shaking the notion around in his mind.

"Alright let's hear it, we'll see," he says as he leans forward, forearms on his knees.

She nods and says, "I can't discuss the actual particulars but I can tell you that it is a standard infiltration and sabotage job, an urban based facility. Beyond that I can't disclose further details without a contract." He considers for a moment before leaning back in the chair.

"Fair enough, espionage eh? I'll have to get back to you. I'll need to run it past the guys, but I'll give you a call tomorrow sometime with the answer." She nods. That's fine. She wasn't planning on doing anything else tonight anyway. She smiles and stands while motioning towards the door.

"Very good, your payment should be ready by now, and I'll speak with you tomorrow then." Sam nods and grunts as he stands.

"Yup, alright. Thanks for the demi-gold by the way. It would have been a pain in the ass to find a money changer that doesn't gouge you senseless."

"Well you're just lucky that I happen to have a few Asura clients, a few operatives as well for that matter." She winks and follows him as he leaves, closing the reinforced doors manually as he exits into the hall. Just past him, three large black bags sit near the entrance. *He must have strength augmentations,* she thinks, *maybe bioniflex muscle clusters.*

She rolls her head back and forth as she returns to the desk. The jobs folder materializes at a wave of her hand and she strikes Sam off the pending list. She then thinks for a moment. No file for Eric. There shouldn't be any possible trail. She has significant countermeasures built in, not to mention a powerful degauss device should the need arise. It's still too risky though. The guards are already on high alert. Whoever is tracking Eric knows that he came here. They might try to get info on him by breaking into the computer. Failing that they might try an actual physical break-in. If it's a corporation they might even try to plant evidence in order to have a "legitimate" reason for laying siege to the mansion. She taps on the desk and brings up the phone. "Call Marcus," she says as she leans back in the chair. The phone winks twice before Marcus answers.

"Cass, what's up?"

She clears her throat and says, "A bunch of crazy crap, I'll tell you about it when you get here. Where are you?"

"Was taking care of that other business, then I found a guy to deliver the thing, just heading back now, be a half hour maybe?"

She nods to herself and says, "Good, good. I'll see you in a little while then."

"Is everything alright?" Marcus asks, his digital voice edged with concern.

"Yeah, I mean there was a minor thing earlier but Elindriss is fine. She'll be able to see again by tomorrow," she responds. Marcus laughs.

"Minor thing? Oh yeah, I've heard that about blindness."

She laughs and replies, "Well it's fine now. Just get back here soon."

"Yeah, yeah, I'm on my way," he says before disconnecting. She smirks, he's getting cocky. He's been around for ten years, and has been in her bed a few times. That entitles him a small amount of leeway. Elindriss is the only one left over from the original crew however. From back when they were breaking into labs, blackmailing diplomats and stealing gem collections. Cassandra remembers the thrill of hiding from unknown pursuers on dark roof tops. The adrenalin afterglow when she completed a successful maneuver, and the mortal terror of combat. There were botched runs and big scores. There was her time with Xan and his old crew, before things got complicated. She looks at the desk and locks the computer with a few deft motions then walks to the hallway. She looks at the kitchen, just to the left as she exits the office. She turns right instead and enters the living room. She sits in the auto masseuse and activates the nano-fibers of the chair. The Arnoch carving rolls and changes in front of her, outside the rain is slowing. She thinks back to the carving. The Arnoch was one of the strangest creatures that she'd ever met. They are a different type of Asura than Rex, very different. She remembers when it created the work of art, payment for her involvement in a job. The massive demi-god had the body of a huge ant topped with a monstrous humanoid torso. Its head had the features of a hawk and an elk, with radiant green gems for eyes. The Asura was huge. It barely fit in the room, and it had to walk through the wall to get there, some feat of magic. Its name was completely unpronounceable.

She still shudders to think of its prophecy: "Tragedy shall come in three, first shall be the family, then shall be the heart and finally the home shall be taken, destroyed utterly." She'd already known the first two tragedies, she hoped. The third still dangled above her head. Arnoch seers were never wrong. They may be able to see something in Eric. She ponders that for a moment as the auto masseuse works its magic, and her neck and shoulders begin to relax. The problem is, Arnochs don't usually leave "The Flux". And travelling there could be fraught with all sorts of unknown dangers. It would no doubt cost millions upon millions of credits to convince one to come to the material realm. At this point it might be worth it. They're not really known for their greed however, unlike certain other Asura. Arnoch are notorious for having enigmatic motivations. They might not help simply because they don't want to. Then it wouldn't matter the amount of Asura gold that was offered. She sits for a moment longer before she heads to the kitchen. She grabs an Ensilade water and piles some

Nelmas bread on a plate. She then places the plate and bottle on a tray before leaving the kitchen. To the north of the lobby, the winding staircase leads to the mansion's second floor. She heads up the stairs then into the second floor hall, turning to the right after a short distance. The original "Delray" greets her as she rounds the corner and moves up to Elindriss' door. A voice calls from within.

"Come in, it's open." Cassandra pushes the door open. She smells vanilla and incense as she enters. The room is infested with arcane implements and reagents. Elindriss is sitting on her bed, some soft music is playing. Elindriss looks towards Cassandra, bandages covering her eyes. "Don't know if I'm hungry, I'll take the water though," she says. Cassandra peers around. Elindriss must be using her familiar to see the world. The little cat is hiding though. Cassandra nods and puts the tray on an empty section of the desk. She then hands the bottle to Elindriss. "Thanks," she says as she uncaps it and drinks.

Cassandra sits on the edge of the bed and says, "I know we spoke about all this earlier but are you sure of what you saw in that boy?"

Elindriss takes another sip and says, "I can't say for sure. All I can say is that I've never seen anything like it before. When my sight returns I'll start going through the old tomes. Do you have somebody performing digital research?"

"No, Xan said that he'll take care of that. I presume that he'll put Silver Dancer on the job," Cassandra says. Elindriss nods.

"Alright, yeah, that works. I'm sure between the two of us we'll be able to find out something."

Cassandra nods then says, "What if you can't?" Elindriss laughs.

"Well, we're going to have to do some real work then, aren't we? Track down some real experts." She then adopts a more serious tone and continues, "It's not even really for that boy's sake. Corpies might be able to extract the power eventually but then what? What would they turn it into? Medicine, healing, something beneficial? Weapons of war? What happens if it's not a corporation? What happens if it's a madman or a power-hungry monster of some type?"

Cassandra nods and replies, "I know El, just kind of wish that I didn't, you know?"

Elindriss laughs and says, "You wish you didn't know? I'm the blind one here, remember." She then sticks out her tongue, Cassandra laughs.

"Right. I guess you do know." Elindriss takes another sip.

"How are you doing? I mean with Grot and everything?" Cassandra swallows and thinks for a moment before responding.

"It's shocking, that's for sure. I don't know, we barely got a chance to talk, he was babbling about some purpose. He seems different. I'm glad that he's not dead, but still kind of pissed, you know? He didn't visit in all this time, he didn't even call." Elindriss nods.

"I'm sure he had his reasons Cass. You weren't there, during that job. I was, remember. Nobody should have to see that." Cassandra nods slowly.

"Yeah, I know, I know. I don't know, I mean I guess I am glad that he's back. He'll be visiting from time to time." Elindriss nods. She shifts on the bed causing it to creak and shake.

"Good, although I could do without the smell." Cassandra laughs, he was a bit ripe.

She stands and says, "Well a simple spell can cure that. Anyway you should rest. I'm going to wait for Marcus then go to bed."

"With him?" Elindriss asks, a droll tone seeping into her voice. Cassandra laughs and reaches for the door.

She looks back and says, "No, not tonight. Sleep tight." Elindriss grins.

"Good night." Cassandra closes the door behind her as she steps back into the carpeted hall. She returns to the living room, a cloud of colorful spirit fish swim beneath her feet as she walks. Outside, the rain has slowed to a patter. Wet silver nails streaking down towards the city. She sits on the couch and says, "Music on". The rhythmic sound soon surrounds her. It's a selection of classical compositions, mainly Elven and Human, though there are a number of rousing Celestial numbers and one intense Asuric piece. The music pervades her thoughts. It has a cleansing effect. She listens to the crashing percussion and the thunderous brass, the subtle woodwinds and the energetic strings. Some compositions use voices of haunting clarity. While other songs feature the enigmatic tones of the other realms. She sits and listens for a while until the door opens to reveal Marcus, with his silver face tattoos and short, stark white Mohawk. He saunters over and sits in an armchair opposite the couch.

"Hey Cass, so, what was this crazy crap all about?" She smiles, takes a deep breath then looks to him and begins to relate the tale.

Soft music fills the lull. Marcus sits still for a moment, seemingly lost in thought.

"Shit, that's fucked up," he finally says. A short silence follows.

"That's all you have to say?" she says. He shrugs.

"Well shit I don't know. I mean obviously we'll jack-up security but other than that? I'm not a majicker, I don't know about that shit. And I don't know what to say about the Gobbo. I mean you've mentioned this Grot a handful of times, he was like your dad or something?"

She nods and says, "Yeah, or something. I thought he was dead for the longest time." She feels a tear form in the corner of her eye. She wipes it away with the back of her hand. Marcus leans forward.

"Cass? Are you alright? I mean it's a good thing that he's back right? It's not like he's an asshole who's come to borrow money or something?" She laughs.

"Yes, it's good he's back, he's not an asshole, and he doesn't want money or anything. He's just a bit odd." Marcus grins.

"Well, aren't we all?"

She laughs and says, "You are, that's for sure. Anyway, I'm stupid tired. I'm going to shower and sleep." Marcus raises his eyebrows.

"You want company with either?"

She laughs and says, "Not tonight, lover boy." She then stands and exits the room. Marcus sighs as the door swings closed.

She laughs to herself as she ascends the winding staircase, enters the hall and turns immediately to her right. She enters her spacious bedroom and closes the reinforced door, punching in the security code as she undresses. A short while later and she's showered and dried. She heads to her bed and slips between the covers. "Lights off," she calls out as she rolls over and closes her eyes. Her mind races for some time as she reflects on the day. *Tomorrow will be less stressful,* she thinks, *just another day at the office.* Soon, she drifts off to sleep.

The morning comes. Cassandra stretches and performs her regular routine, then chooses a skirt and blouse combination from her closet. She adorns various pieces of jewelry before appraising herself in the mirror. Satisfied, she exits the bedroom and peers up the hall towards Elindriss' door. She'll let her sleep, if she isn't up already. The poultices can take some time to fully set. They can also be somewhat draining. She descends the staircase, spotting Katie on her way down.

"Hey Katie, I didn't know that you were working today?" she says.

Katie curtsies. "Yes ma'am, I'm covering for Amanda. She said that she was sick." Cassandra rolls her eyes.

"You're too nice Katie. Well then, now that you're here, can you make me the usual breakfast, I think tea today as well if you please?" Katie nods then curtsies and heads to the kitchen. Cassandra waves to the lobby guards, part of Marcus' increased security.

"Brad, Jesse," she says as she heads to her office. They respond nearly in unison.

"Morning ma'am." She opens the office doors and enters, leaving them open in expectation of Marcus and his usual morning debriefing. She taps on the desk and activates the computer, then performs a quick search for local news stories. Nothing really, some gang nonsense over on Fourteenth Street, that's about it. She calls up her itinerary. Appointments are limited to Sam and "Whisper" so far today. She could begin searching for buyers for the statues. The sound of footsteps makes her look to the hall as Marcus comes striding up into the office.

"Are you expecting somebody?" he says coyly.

She smiles and retorts, "Yeah, the same sarcastic prick that shows up every day, so, anything to report?" He laughs then shakes his head.

"No. We're going to change to the lobby protocol for now though. I think that would be wise, until things settle out a bit." She nods and looks into the hallway.

"You'll be out there with those two then?" she asks.

"Yeah, plus at least one more whenever Lana decides to show up."

"Alright, I suppose I'll keep the doors locked between meetings then," she says. He nods and raises his eyebrows.

"You damn well better!" She laughs, and points to the door.

"Out! My breakfast will be ready soon. I don't want your ugly mug spoiling my appetite before it gets here." He laughs and gives a short bow before leaving, closing the doors behind him. Cassandra peers at the computer. She calls up the hall camera and puts it at the bottom left of the screen then sits back in her chair and stares up at the spectral aquarium. The red skeletal fish floats past and a shiver travels up her spine. She closes her eyes and thinks about the statues. She'll have to go through her contacts and make a list. Try those avenues first. They'll pay a higher premium than a typical auction. If they don't pan out then she'll start hitting up the auctions.

A smile settles on her face, when, she's jolted from her planning by the high-pitched wail of the house's alarm system. It's a red alert. She quickly looks to the camera. Static, she flips on the camera grid. They're all static. There's muffled assault rifle fire. Marcus' emergency ping lights up the desk and her heart begins to race. There's a sonic boom and the room shakes. She snaps open the right side of the desk and hefts her custom T-90-SD. Loaded with specially made ammo, one burst will tear a gorilla in half. She breathes hard and looks to the door. "Phone on," she says, no response. There's more gunfire, then nothing, just the whine of the alarm. Agitation begins mounting. "Phone on," she whispers urgently, still no response. She crouches and aims at the door. She waits. She waits for what seems like an eternity. Then, a deafening explosion rips the doors from their hinges. She squeezes the trigger, strafing the dust and debris. Casings pour from the gun as she empties the magazine. Suddenly a powerful shockwave overcomes the room, her mirror shatters and she has the wind knocked out of her. Her ears are ringing and she's gasping for air. She looks down. Her gun is split neatly in half. It falls to the floor, useless. She looks at her hands, no blood; all of her fingers are still there. She steps back and blinks. Her heart is racing. Her breath is coming in gasps. She glances up. There's a crack forming in the spectral aquarium. She swallows and peers into the dust. Then a voice splits through the destruction.

"Cassandra, you're mean! Have I lost your esteem? You primp and you preen, dark queen of the scheme, you carouse and career while staying unseen. But I'm trying to deem, how long has it been?" Cassandra tries to respond but she's frozen, petrified. He continues, "Twenty years of gore, at least by my score, but all that's a bore I've come for much more. A titular score, a name you'll soon whore! Don't make me implore or I'd soon become sore." That voice, those rhymes. Utter horror envelopes her. Grimmfang! Mortal terror pours over her like a thunderstorm. *No! Not him,* she thinks, *what has he done?* A hooded figure emerges from the dust. A pair of blades is sheathed on his back, "Fate" and "Retribution." That's what he calls them. That's what they're known as. She quakes and gasps for breath. Metallic skeleton hands, dripping blood, armored greaves and metal tipped leather strips hanging from a monstrous steel face serving as his belt. She swallows hard, choking down her grief. She looks him in the eyes, one is pure white, the other has a silver cornea. A black x sits at its center. His white skull tattoo flexes as he smiles and laughs. Her breath catches in her chest then, and she is lost in pure dread.

Xanshudan and Kane

A rich coffee fragrance pervades. Xan crosses to the kitchen and refills, for the third time.

Kane's face breaks the surface and says, "Careful now, I hear that stuff's addictive."

Xan laughs and says, "You want a cup?"

Kane snorts. "Are you trying to overdose or something?" Xan crosses the kitchen and opens the fridge door. "Just go outside. I'll eat some dirt if you're hungry," Kane says in an annoyed tone.

Xan laughs and says, "I'd like to actually taste something for a change. Don't get me wrong, your unique appetite has saved me a small fortune over the years, and my life once or twice, but I saw that Eve picked up some Eldar berries. I'll grab some Nelmas and some jerky and I'm set."

"Suit yourself. It all tastes like ash to me," Kane responds.

"Did you say ass?" Xan mocks as he retrieves the stated items and consigns them to a plate.

Kane laughs derisively and says, "You know exactly what I said, we share a telepathic bond, jackass." Xan grins and crosses back to the table. "The boy's still sleeping then?" Kane asks. Xan nods and begins to eat.

"Yeah, I think he's in love with Silver Dancer, they spent some time talking yesterday. Apparently that's a big deal for him."

Kane laughs and retorts, "Anybody with eyes is in love with Silver Dancer, stray dogs are in love with Silver Dancer, I've seen a rat propose to her. Hell I'd be surprised if he wasn't in love with Silver Dancer." Xan snorts and continues eating. Kane sinks into his palm and internalizes "You know, I bet that boy would be worth a lot of money to the right kind of people. Like buy an island off the coast of Kalai type of money. Like hot and cold running nubile island girls type of money. You see what I'm saying?" Xan stops eating and focuses internally.

"Well first off, his name is Eric. Secondly, are you trying to say that you want us to sell him off? Like to the highest bidder?"

Kane whines. "What? Do you really think that he's better off with us? Shit, you heard Elindriss, he could burst apart at any minute. Kill us all, what then wise guy? Who wins then?"

Xan shakes his head. He knows all too well how most corporations operate. Especially corporations who send a five man hit team to retrieve one boy. "Well if that does happen it doesn't really matter where Eric is, everything will change, if you believe what she said."

Kane groans. "Yes but if we do it my way we get very, very rich first. How can you not see that?" Xan laughs humourlessly as the "Murder Chambers" door opens.

"Oh baby! What are you doing to me?" Kane announces as Silver Dancer enters the room, the nipples of her ample breasts poking through her small shirt.

Xan shakes his head but his gaze lingers for a moment before he says, "Good morning."

Silver Dancer smiles and yawns then says, "Good morning Xan. Fuck you Kane!" Xan laughs and continues to eat.

Kane pipes up again. "You know, if you ever wanted to sit on Xan's hand I would be totally cool with that."

She laughs and shakes her head. "I do know Zealots who'll perform a banishing ritual for free you know," she retorts.

Xan laughs and says, "Don't think that I haven't thought of that, apparently it doesn't work."

Kane chuckles and responds. "Yeah, we're way harder to get rid of than that, kind of like crabs. You think that you got them all and then BAM! Like a thousand little eggs, and you're all itchy down there, and you need this special shampoo and a tiny comb, and you have to make all these awkward phone calls ..."

Silver Dancer scoffs, holds up her hand and says, "Hey I'm about to eat here, can you gag him?"

Kane immediately retorts, "I do have a ball gag, if you're into that type of thing?" Silver Dancer snorts and shakes her head. She then walks to the kitchen, perfect hindquarters stuffed into shorts one size too small. Xan looks back to his plate.

"I need your help with something," He says.

Silver Dancer opens the fridge and replies, "Sure. You know I was thinking more about that facial recognition tracking software and I think that I could totally fuck with it, if you wanted me too, that is?"

Xan laughs. "Oh yeah? How?"

She begins to empty part of the fridges contents. She then glances over and replies, "It's so simple, I should have thought about it before. All I'd have to do is hack into the central camera system and infect their construct with a facial mapping algorithm. Once it's in place the program would put Eric's face on any number of random people that we chose, or just one if that's what you wanted. Then any search using standard facial recognition protocols will begin to track our chosen targets and not Eric."

Xan laughs quietly, doesn't sound easy. He trusts her though. Silver Dancer is a certified genius. He nods and says, "Do it if you think that it'll be a cake walk."

She smiles and ambles back to the table with a cup of coffee and a bowl of something. "The public camera system? I was hacking that for fun when I was six years old, created a vid of a boy that I had a crush on when I was eight." She says. Xan laughs, it's no doubt true. She's one of the few hackers that have ever made it into a military grade system and lived to tell the tale. There's only one system more insidious then those deadly militaristic domains. That system resides in another dimension however, and normally there's no need for a hacker to travel there.

Xan continues eating. He finishes and reaches for his coffee while saying, "Before you waltz into the camera system, I was wondering if you could find us a fortress?" The term "fortress" is used amongst the group, a synonym for "safe house".

She looks up from her breakfast. "Sure, yeah, is there a particular area that you had in mind? What's my timeframe?"

Xan considers for a few seconds then responds, "Anywhere except the ninth level, and the quicker the better. Cassandra deleted all of her video with us on it, and we avoided the cameras on the way back here, but I still don't think that we should stay; we're only six miles from her place after all. It's better if we're completely hidden: look for abandoned areas, preferably a fortified structure." She nods and returns to her breakfast.

Kane clears his small throat and says, "Also look for structures with kinky basement additions, ample drainage, and at least a dozen voyeur cams, mainly in the bathrooms, I think that would be best."

She smirks and says, "Sounds like a church to me." She then waggles her tongue and smiles wickedly. Xan laughs.

Kane makes a shocked sound and says, "Don't mess with me woman, you're trifling with powers that are beyond your ken! I would rock your world! I would perform acts of such wanton carnality that they would be considered illegal on mere principal alone! I would find a shaved weasel ..."

Xan puts his left hand under his right armpit, he then says, "Just like a parrot, go to sleep now."

Kane yells a muffled response. "Ooo ashtard ul git u fer iss!" Silver Dancer and Xan laugh.

"You should invest in a single, soundproof glove," she says in a matter of fact sort of way. Xan laughs and rubs his chin with his free hand.

"That's a good idea," he says. The clank of the "Murder Chambers" door closing fills the room. Xan looks over to see Devlin stumbling through. He grins from beneath an unwieldy tangle of untamed locks and begins to head to the kitchen.

"Morning." Xan and Silver Dancer respond in kind while a muddled sound comes from Xan's armpit.

Devlin laughs and says, "Oh is Kane being bad again? I love his little time outs."

Xan pulls his hand out from his armpit. "Next time I *will* invest in that soundproof glove, or maybe just some sturdy tape."

Kane unleashes a tiny raspberry then sinks back into Xan's palm. Silver Dancer finishes eating. She grabs her coffee and says, "I'll get to work right away, shouldn't take too long to find an adequate fortress." Xan nods as she crosses to the door to the turret. "The Castles" electronic brain and hacking center resides at the turret's pinnacle, a small reinforced room teeming with augmented computer equipment. Xan watches her walk to the door, her curves bouncing slightly as she moves. He sits for a moment more, lost in the throes of biology. He then shakes his head and looks at Devlin.

"Did you happen to see if our guest is up yet?"

Devlin nods and says, "Yeah, I was going to tell you, Cable was showing him the bathhouse." Xan nods and considers his approach for a moment. He should meet Eric in the garden. That's a good spot to begin.

"Eve's out on her run?"Xan asks, even though he knows the answer.

Devlin nods and answers, "Rex went with her this time, said something about hunting."

Xan laughs. "I can only hope he does it invisibly."

Devlin shrugs and laughs. He then retrieves some "Tri-crisp" cereal and says, "With him, who knows?"

Xan nods. "True enough. Alright I'm going to meet Eric in the garden, maybe give him a small tour."

Devlin pours some juice and closes the fridge door then says, "Kid seemed pretty freaked out, might want to try to calm him down some." Xan nods, he saw that too, on their walk back here. He also learned some things about Eric and that place that he's from. No wonder he's freaked out, it sounds very different, very different indeed.

Kane chimes in. "We could get him laid. You promised me a trip to "The Cherrywood" yesterday, remember?"

Xan laughs. "Yeah, I guess that was technically yesterday wasn't it? You really believe that he's thinking about that right now?"

Kane replies in a flat tone. "He's seventeen, he would be thinking about that if he was being eaten by a pack of ravenous ghouls." Xan and Devlin laugh. Xan thinks for a moment. Eric needs to learn some things about this world. Grot wasn't very clear about what he does and doesn't understand. Cassandra said that he kept calling Eric "The dreamer". Like that was supposed to mean something. Xan looks back to Devlin as he crosses to the "Murder Chambers" door.

"Maybe we'll do a bit of target practice instead. I can show him a thing or two."

Devlin nods and says, "Yeah, shooting guns seems to calm down a lot of people." He then laughs and sits at the table.

Kane adds, "Well, the kid will get to shoot one type of pistol anyway." Xan smirks and Devlin chuckles, Xan then exits the room. He crosses into the living quarters and then exits into the garden. The door to the bathhouse stands shut just across the small expanse. He leans back against the tall oak tree and waits.

A minute passes before Kane's voice breaks the silence. "So Xan, do you often wait around outside bathrooms looking for teenage boys?"

Xan laughs and says, "Shut up Kane, you know exactly what I do."

Kane continues. "I'm just saying it's a little creepy." Xan rolls his eyes and looks at the tower attached to the living quarters. The tall, conical building is filled with spare weapons and gear, some stuff from past jobs, no ammo or explosives though. All the volatile stuff is stored beneath the garage, far away from the inhabited areas. Kane melts back into Xan's palm and internalizes "So have you given any more thought to what I was saying earlier?"

Xan focuses internally. "Yeah I have Kane. It's not going to happen. First off, without any other considerations, it's dangerous, we have no idea who or what we'd be selling him to, not to mention their intention with such a power. Secondly, and more importantly, it's really scummy; I'm talking like bottom of the barrel scummy. Also, I gave my word to Cassandra and that Grot guy. That type of thing actually means something to me you know."

Kane groans then continues, "A dead man's word is worth about as much as anything else that he brings to the table. You don't think that they're going to keep coming? What? We're just going to take all comers?"

Xan laughs and says, "Phrasing?"

Kane snorts. "Shut up!"

Xan then continues. "Just let it go Kane, we have a job now. Treat it as any other; we do not break a contract, that's what keeps you alive and active in this business." Kane whines and sputters for a minute before the bathhouse door opens. Cable steps out wearing his combat boots and cargo pants, the chiseled lines of his well-muscled torso gleam in the grey light.

Cable nods upwards. "He's in there, had a shower, now he's just sitting in the stall. Maybe shitting, I didn't stay to smell."

Xan laughs. "Good recon, maybe I'll give him a minute or two." Cable crosses the carpet of grass. His corded arms flex as he reaches for the gate to the courtyard. Xan looks over and says "Would you mind setting up some targets? I'm going to show the kid some shooting basics."

Cable looks back and nods then says, "I was going to prep the sentries too, bring them to the fortress to serve as perimeter defenses, if needed."

"Good thinking, check with Silver Dancer, she said something about creating a new piece of scanning software for them," Xan responds. Cable nods and heads into the courtyard. The large Human then crosses to the garage and disappears through the side door.

Xan stills his mind and breathes deeply for a moment. He concentrates on his senses and feels the familiar charge of energy. The world around him swirls and morphs. Colors and shapes coalesce into a smear of life and inanimate material. Living things glow brightly with green, orange, yellow, red and blue. Brick buildings are greyed-out, blurred as though being seen from a great distance. He looks around. The bright candles of his teams' auras light up the cold stone of "The Castle". He peers through the grey of the garden wall, and past the iridescent ward. A colorful tide of life flows there, moving to and fro based on their own inclinations.

He looks back at the bathhouse. He concentrates, then frowns. It must be Eric's necklace. He can't see him at all, no hint of an aura. *This Grot is a skilled magician*, he thinks, *it's difficult to conceal an aura so completely*. He peers overhead. The shimmering dome of "The Castles" ward pulses with subtle shifting hues. He relaxes his focus and his vision returns to its usual state. Minutes tick by as Xan leans against the tree. After a short while he begins practicing "The Art". He latches onto his arcane core, and wraps it around his will. The ground shudders as he starts his routine. The air cracks and booms as he strikes with fist and foot, he blurs as he moves from one point to another. He can feel the channels of power travelling through each limb, points of energy flashing out and back in like the pistons of an engine. A door closes and he's aware of a presence. He re-centers and looks to the bathhouse. Eric's eyes are wide. He may have seen some of the routine. Xan watches him closely. The boy is tall, he's unsure of himself, no significant muscle mass. He's not an athlete or a warrior.

Eric shuffles his feet. Xan walks closer and says, "Are you hungry? We can get you something from the kitchen."

Eric nods. He holds his stomach and looks back towards the door. He then looks to Xan. "My stomach's kind of messed up."

"That's understandable. We can get you something for that as well," Xan says as he points to the living quarters' door. Eric nods and walks slowly across the yard. "When you're feeling a bit better I thought that I'd show you how to use that T-90 that you've been hauling around everywhere, even to the bathroom I see," Xan quips as Eric approaches. Eric manages a weak smile in response. The pair enters the living quarters and passes through the "Murder Chamber". The blare of the holo-vid signals their arrival in the main room.

Devlin looks over from the couch. "Well then, look who's decided to grace us with his presence. Good morning." Eric nods and mumbles something inaudible. Devlin laughs and says, "Yeah I know what you mean." Eric lets out a short laugh. Xan crosses to the kitchen and retrieves a stout bottle from one of the cupboards. Eric slowly drifts to the kitchen, an uncertain puppy lost in the wilderness. Xan hands him one of the small white tablets and a cup.

He points to the sink and says, "Water or if you want there's juice and other stuff in the fridge. Look around and grab whatever looks appetizing ..."

Kane interjects with, "Just stay away from the Gulduni, might as well call it fart paste." Eric laughs and pops the tablet in his mouth. He downs it with water from the sink.

Xan nods and says, "It is not good. Eve likes it though, Tempus knows why." He finishes speaking as Cable enters the room from the garage door and looks towards the kitchen.

"Targets are set, is there still coffee?"

Xan looks at the pot and nods, he then says, "Thanks Cable." Eric stands to the side and clutches his cup as Cable walks up. The boy is nothing like Xan at that age. When he was Eric's age he was already working for the "Venom Lords", he'd killed his first man when he was ten. He remembers when he was seventeen, barely. It was one hundred and ten years ago. The city was a much different place then, cybernetics was in its infancy, the first weave constructs were being created, and there was a pall of intolerance. Perpetrated by racist bands who sought to kill and destroy any Dark Elves that they found, amongst others. His jaw clenches and he looks back to the kitchen. Cable's fixed himself a coffee and some type of breakfast. Eric enters the space timidly. Cable sits at the table and looks to Xan.

"Is Dancer in her tower?" Xan nods.

Kane exclaims, "I swear she was hitting on me earlier, she even made lewd gestures and everything. Xan back me up here!" Cable laughs, Eric smiles. The voices of Trisha Stellar and Tanner Stevens drone on in the background. A repeat broadcast, old news. Eric calls over from the kitchen.

"Is this like breakfast cereal?" Xan looks over. He's grasping a box of "Tri-crisp". Xan nods. Grot had told Cassandra that "The Dreamer" would know certain things. He told her that Eric's dream touched ours, whatever that means. Xan hasn't had a lot of dealings with Shamans or Witch Doctors. The spirit realm should be left to spirits, that's what he was always taught. Eric slowly assembles a breakfast as Cable eats.

Xan looks over at the holo-vid. A close up of Tanner, his rent-a-tan Elven features framing the display. He prattles on, "In other news, a recent increase in ghoul activity on the city's second level has prompted a change in bounty prices from fifty credits per head to seventy-five credits per head. Hunters should be wary of course, as several large populations have been reported in and around "The Warrens"". Xan grins to himself. He remembers those jobs, smelly and terrifying with shitty pay. Still, anyone with a gun and some guts can make a living at it. There are definitely enough monsters in the city to go around. Cable finishes eating and crosses to the "Brain door." Xan stands and joins Devlin on the couch as the news rolls on.

Eric slogs through his breakfast as Xan sits and speaks with Devlin. By the time he's finished with the food he seems to have perked up a bit.

Xan looks back over the couch and says, "So? It's all edible?"

Eric grins and puts down the bowl. "Yeah, tastes like 'Captain Crunch'." Xan laughs.

Kane pipes up and says, "I assume that's a breakfast cereal from where you come from? Not like some weird sexual thing?" Eric and Devlin laugh.

Eric then says, "I think it might be both?" The group laughs, Eric seems to shed some anxiety. Xan stands and stretches. "Are you ready to do a little target practice?"

Eric nods, then looks back and forth before saying, "Is Silver Dancer around? I just wanted to say good morning."

Kane laughs and says, "I don't think anyone in this room, 'just wants to say good morning'", to Silver Dancer, if you know what I mean?" Eric blushes and looks away.

Xan brings his left hand to his face and says, "That's enough out of you; don't make me get the tape!" Kane laughs and sticks out his tongue, he then disappears into Xan's palm. Eric blinks a few times and looks away. "Dancer's busy right now, don't worry, we'll see her later." Eric nods bashfully. Xan crosses to the garage door while motioning for Eric to follow. The buzz-hum of neon illuminates the darkened space. The Z&X 950 and Dancer's "Night shadow" crouch on the floor. A pair of steel mounts. One armed and armored, the other fast and agile. Eric lingers for a moment inspecting the space and the vehicles.

"Nice car," he finally says. Xan looks over from the garage's side door.

"Yeah, it's Silver Dancer's, some light armor but it's fast as hell." Eric laughs and a goofy smile creeps across his face. Xan pushes open the side door and says "this way." They head into the courtyard; more or less a square framed by the buildings and walls that make up "The Castle." The targets are placed up against the solid, reinforced stone of the "Murder Chamber." They'd need to be firing armor piercing shells from a thirty millimeter cannon to even put a dent in that wall. Xan grins and says, "One second, I'm going to grab my pistol and some suppressors." He then fires two lines of arcane power down through his legs and surges upward thirty feet. He arcs through the air and performs a perfect backflip before landing on the other side of the garden's wall. A muffled sound of awe seeps through the stone as he crosses to the living chambers' door. He quickly retrieves his custom TTM4 and a number of empty clips. He then crosses to the turret and finds three suppressors, one for each of Eric's weapons and one for his pistol. He returns to the courtyard where Eric is standing. Xan grins and says "I'll grab some boxes of ammo from the garage." Eric nods dumbly, he turns towards Xan.

"How'd you do that?!" Xan stops and looks back at him.

"I use a type of magic known simply as "The Art", it is an internalized form of magic."

Eric nods and says, "Can anybody learn it?"

Xan shakes his head. "Only those with an arcane connection can train in "The Art", as with most other magical practices." Eric seems to consider that for a second before responding.

"How do you know if somebody has an arcane connection?"

Xan grins and says, "Well you need to read their aura."

Eric laughs bitterly and says, "I guess that's not going to happen for me then."

Xan shrugs. "There's still time yet, if it's something that you're interested in I'm sure that we could test you when this is all over."

Eric then seems to sober to his situation. "You mean if I live and I'm not sent back home."

Xan bobs his head from side to side. "There are certain factors which are out of our hands, there's no point in worrying about that right now, but we can do our best to protect you Eric, and to that end we should probably see if you can shoot straight." Xan grins and turns towards "The Castle".

He quickly enters the garage and retrieves a number of boxes of ammunition, regular rounds for the eleven millimeter weapons and sub-sonic ammo for his thirteen millimeter pistol. He heads back towards Eric and hands him the two suppressors. "Here, like this." Xan says as he retrieves his pistol and his own suppressor.

"So what else can you do with "The Art"?" Eric asks as he screws one of the cylinders into place.

"The results become an expression of your efforts. I've seen an Elf slip through the folds in reality, and a Gnome who could catch bullets. I've seen great masters who could pop your head like a grape from three hundred feet away and others who could stand in a blazing fire, unscathed." Eric laughs then looks at the ground.

Xan continues. "Practitioners can see auras, the natural form of the core of life. They can control their breath and bodies, their focus." He finishes the statement, slaps the clip home and fires off twelve perfect bull's eyes across four targets in an instant.

Eric stares, mouth wide. "No way! That was crazy!"

Xan grins and says, "I've been doing this for a while."

Kane interjects. "Stop showing off! I'm the real power here!" Xan laughs and reloads instantaneously.

"Hah, some power, you don't even have arms, now, be quiet! There's a new shooter on the range." Eric laughs and hefts the submachine gun. He hesitates for a second then pushes the safety to semi-auto. *Good,* thinks Xan, *he's not a total loss.*

Gun powder wafts through the courtyard and brass litters the ground. The muffled cracks of the suppressed weapons sound like stones being thrown against a concrete wall. Xan watches and teaches as Eric fires round after round down-range. He has Eric switch to full auto-fire mode, and he has him use the pistol as well. Eric proves to have better aim than most beginners. The boy mumbles something about "first person shooters" as an explanation. Eric eventually begins to find a shooting style that fits his constitution. Xan nods to himself and holds up a hand.

"Good, that's probably good for now. I can see you're beginning to feel more comfortable. Just remember, don't hesitate, if there are armed men or something's coming at you, just let them have it. Silver Dancer will attach a monitor to your T-90 so we'll know immediately when you use the weapon and where you are when you use it. We'll also fix you up with a laser sight and a tactical light, maybe a modified barrel and some special magazines as well."

Eric smiles and says, "Cool, yeah, I think I was starting to get the hang of it there."

Kane interjects, "Shit kid, you have better aim than Devlin, remember that day?"

Xan laughs and nods. "It's true. You see that building over there? He accidently shot it, had to pay a tidy sum to calm the owner down." Eric laughs and looks at the wedge-shaped building. A moment later, Xan hears the telltale sound of two forms land in the garden, one on two legs and one on four legs. He glances at the gate and says "Eve and Rex are back. Why don't you head inside, find Cable and give him your T-90, tell him to outfit it with 'The Works'". Eric smiles and nods, he then walks briskly to the garage's side door. Xan can tell that Rex makes the boy uncomfortable, it makes sense—Rex even makes Xan uncomfortable sometimes. The garden's gate swings open and Eve walks through. Hard, athletic body encased in skin-tight ballistic weave. She isn't wearing her full combat regalia however. Xan senses that Kane is about to make a lewd comment so he quickly shoves his left hand under his right armpit. A torrent of muffled gibberish follows.

Xan and Eve laugh, she then says, "Thanks for that. You doing some target practice with the kid?"

Xan nods. "Yeah, not a bad shot either. So we're going ahead with the fortress search, might want to get some things together."

Eve nods and walks towards the garage's side door. "How long until we leave?"

Xan turns toward the garage and says, "Maybe an hour? I want to be gone as soon as possible, Dancer's on the hunt now." He removes Kane from his armpit.

"Alright, I'll have time to shower then," she says.

Kane immediately responds, "I can give you a tongue bath, it'll take a while ..." Xan shoves him back in his armpit, ending the rant mid-perversion. He stands for a moment with his hand in his armpit before Kane's telepathic voice fills his mind.

"I'm not there anymore, stupid." Xan laughs and lowers his left arm. He hears movement and turns to see Rex, no more than six inches away. Xan jumps and then grins in embarrassment.

"Xanshudan, for shame, I could have eaten you twice without you even noticing," Rex says in a playful tone.

Xan laughs and says, "I was speaking with Kane telepathically, that's why." Rex nods mockingly while sticking out his lower lip.

"Excuses are the doctrine of the fool, the poor man's ally. You should not bandy them about so callously."

Xan snorts and says, "Yes but a *reason* is simply cause and effect, the cause here being Kane's intolerable personality and the effect being that I could have been messily devoured."

Rex laughs, an eerie sound that sends a shiver down Xan's spine. "Cause and effect painted by our own inadequacies readily transform into excuses, and so when shall we differentiate?"

Xan smiles and says, "I suppose that would depend on the nature of how we perceive ourselves, and what we would consider to be inadequate within it."

Rex raises his eyebrows and retorts, "Ah, but perception is only a rendering of the truth of the matter, it ignores cause and effect as much as it acknowledges it, and so we find ourselves trapped within an arbitrary construct of understanding. How then shall we quantify our qualities?"

Xan laughs and says, "*That* is a question best posed to a more intelligent Elf than I. How was your run?" Rex sits on his haunches.

"I do not tire, I merely observe. And I have seen that a stain swirls through the spectral sky. I cannot place its genesis but it is an ill omen."

"Is it near to us?" Xan asks. Rex shrugs.

"It is difficult to tell. The spectral sky is in turmoil. I do not rightly understand the subtle aspects of that place. I merely view it, because of my sight." Xan nods. Rex once spoke of his vision, as though everything is in immaculate detail, even at great distances. He can even see through illusions and view invisible creatures. Apparently he can make out the details of a person's face at a range of two miles.

Xan then motions to the main area. "We're just getting ready to leave for a fortress, Dancer will find something soon."

Rex tilts his armored head and says, "No one can hide, it may buy us time but we should be seeking answers, there are seers within the gardens of entropy."

Xan cringes and says, "I think we should hold off on any type of extra-dimensional travel, I mean we don't know how Eric will react. Plus many of your kin are ruthless, mercenary and ridiculously deadly, what if they have designs on the power contained in Eric's body?" Rex sways his head from side to side.

"Perchance you are correct, but if we cannot find answers in this place we may be left with little alternative."

Xan considers that for a moment before saying, "I'll keep it in mind, for now though is there anything that you want to bring to the fortress?" Rex nods his head.

"Yes, the redwood chest that is stored in the vault, therein lay items of various import."

"Sure, we'll grab it and put it in the van." Xan says.

Rex begins to walk to the garden gate, he looks back and says, "I shall be in the garden, feasting upon my repast." Xan inhales sharply and walks towards the garage's side door. He's seen what constitutes a "repast" for Rex. He just hopes it isn't someone's dog this time. Xan enters "The Castles" main room. Everyone except Rex is present. Cable is using the table to modify the T-90. Eric is watching with marked interest, leering intermittently at Silver Dancer who is sitting at her porta-comp across the table. Eve and Devlin are on the couch. Eve has some kind of power drink. He lets the door close behind him and Silver Dancer looks over as he crosses to the table.

"Hey boss man. You know how I was talking about a church earlier? Well I think I found the perfect fortress, our very own converted cathedral. It was turned into an enforcement center years back, fourth level, near the southern edge. The whole area is abandoned now, corp lockout looks like, might be some critters but that's no worry really, as long as it's nothing too nasty." Xan nods and lets out a short laugh.

"Which deity was the church dedicated to?"

Silver Dancer thinks for a second then says, "Zool, so you know that the building's going to be sturdy. I think that it will work, what do you think?" Xan smiles and looks at the schematic.

"Yeah, I think that you're right. This looks like it will work just fine."

Eric Gibson

I can't believe she's talking to me, and what's more, I'm talking back. Well, I mean, not like right this second, but still. She's appallingly gorgeous. She's actually managed to change my entire ideal of beauty, the girls that I've been fantasizing about look like Grot by comparison. Shit, I miss Grot. These people are all weird, except for her. That silvery cybernetic arm just makes her hotter somehow; it matches her tall silver Mohawk so well. Her cybernetic eyes seem so exotic. They're hypnotic, like dozens of tiny silver concentric circles. Her body is the exemplar of sexy. I can't even look at her without getting aroused. Just use the armored long coat. Great, now I feel like a pervert, hiding an erection in my filthy long coat. Just think about the rats, no wait, not the rats, just look at the gun. Shit, that's not really helping. Just relax; Xan just said something about leaving in thirty minutes. They found some church somewhere. It's supposed to be safer then this place, or less obvious, I guess. Cable has taken the gun completely apart now. He was talking about adding a new barrel as well as adding something else so that it could withstand some kind of forces, maybe a spring? I guess I wasn't paying attention. Eve stands and walks to the "Murder Chamber's" door. I try my best not to stare at her ass, and I fail. She's crazy hot too. What is with this place? All these hot women everywhere, maybe it's just because they're Elves. They aren't coal-skinned like Xan. Silver Dancer is pale while Eve is more tanned or something.

"Looks like the 'Broken Spokes' beat the 'Devil's Brigade' last night, thirty-one to twenty-two," Devlin announces.

Cable nods and says, "Trounced them, I thought so, what with Murray being out, on account of being dead and all." I laugh. Motoblitz seems like an awesome sport. It's got motorcycles, drones, guns, jumps and ramps and some kind of javelin-based scoring system. We only watched for a little while yesterday, but I'm already hooked. I look back towards the door with the picture of the brain on it, that's where Silver Dancer is, she's hacking or getting some gear or something.

I begin to day dream when Xan says, "Eric, would you mind helping me with something?" He's standing near the door to the garage. I nod and stand.

Devlin deactivates the holo-vid and says, "Better get ready I suppose." He then crosses to the "Murder Chamber's" door.

Cable says, "I'll be finished here right away then I'll load up the trailer." Xan opens the garage door as I approach. He then looks over to Cable.

"Bring six extra claymores. Do we have any more of those Spyder mines?" Cable shakes his head.

"Used them all during that 'Bane Woods' cluster fuck, haven't picked up anymore yet. They're kind of hard to find right now."

Xan nods. "Right yeah, alright that's fine."

Cable grins in a feral manner and says, "I am bringing "Gerty" though, the gyroscopic harness is already packed."

Xan grins and replies, "Good, that's good, alright Eric, this way." I nod and follow. We walk past the van and Silver Dancer's sweet ride. He steps in front of a long workbench, the back wall is covered in tools and a large cabinet stands against the far wall. Xan looks at me. His eyes are pools of eternal white.

"What I'm about to show you must remain a secret. Only the other members of the team know that this is here, do you understand?" I nod solemnly. I wouldn't tell anyone. Shit, I don't even know anyone *to* tell.

Kane interjects, "And if you tell anyone we'll feed you to ME! And, also, Rex might have some too, so, watch it buddy!" I laugh. The little face is weird. Xan called it a manifer spirit. He said they "bonded" like thirty years ago. I guess Elves age way slower or something. He said that Cassandra was like a hundred and thirty years old! She's one hundred and thirty and still crazy hot. I thought she was like twenty, or something. Xan grins and looks back to the cabinet.

"Polygonal opportunist," he says. I nearly burst out laughing but instead watch as a small keypad unfolds from the front of the cabinet, cleverly concealed beneath a drawer's handle. Xan punches in a series of numbers. I can't read the sigils on the keypad. They're gibberish, like most everything else that I try to read. A soft beep comes from the cabinet as it rolls smoothly back into a recessed portion of the wall. I peer over to see a staircase curving down into the darkness. Xan begins to descend, motioning for me to follow. The staircase is wide, there's the faint smell of mildew. We progress down the stairs. It's lit by a series of halogen wall lights. We must be like thirty feet below the ground by now. We finally enter into a long room filled with crates and steel boxes. There's a huge steel door at the far end of the room. I glance around. The labels on the crates are all gibberish too. There seem to be numbers on them, maybe quantities of something. Xan crosses to the large metal door.

"What is this place?" I ask.

He looks back from the door and says, "This is 'The Castle's' storage and vault; it used to be a dungeon." I look a bit more closely. I can see metal rings in the walls, and what look like round holes in the floor and ceiling at regular intervals.

"What are in these crates?" I ask. Xan is doing something at the wall, after a second he turns around, the deep whoosh of the steel doors hydraulics accompany his response.

"Different munitions mainly, forty millimeter grenades for the 950's turret, some crates of twenty millimeter missiles for its vertical launcher and a large number of high explosive fourteen millimeter rounds for 'Gerty'. There are also other volatile items, hand grenades and a variety of explosive rounds in different calibers."

"Oh, okay," I say. It's strange. They use the same measurement systems. I wonder if it was they who copied us or if it was we who copied them? Maybe it was neither, but what then? Random cogent mathematical expressionism, or something? I look around. I begin to see a difference between the crates after a while. The ammo crates have handles right on the top. They're tall and narrow and made of steel. The other crates are more substantial, they're also metal, but it looks different from the ammo crates somehow, more shiny, and striated. I look back over to Xan. The vault door is huge. It's like three feet thick. Xan waves me over. The room beyond the door is slightly smaller than the storage area. Its square shaped, with smooth steel walls. The room itself is filled with a number of strongboxes. It's illuminated by overhead lights. There is an epic looking sword mounted on one wall. The scabbard is covered in intricate patterns wrought in some strange looking metal.

Xan notices me staring and says, "The sword is called 'The Edge of Night', it has been in my family for generations now."

I nod and say, "It looks pretty fancy." Xan laughs and takes the sword down from the wall. He unsheathes it and strikes a half dozen times in one second, the sword blurs and leaves a smoky trail through the air, it almost looks like a liquid. He stops and holds the blade sideways. The sword is curved, like a saber but the metal looks like oil on water poured across the darkest black that I've ever seen. "That's crazy! What is it made of?" I ask. Xan turns the blade.

"It is a special type of spectral steel, bound by a number of ancient runes." A magic sword? I guess that makes sense, shit loads of other magic here, why not swords? Hell they probably have magic machine guns. I laugh to myself, then stop abruptly, wait that's not funny. They might be used against me. Xan re-sheathes the sword and returns it to the wall.

He then points to an intensely intricate red chest and says, "Grab one end, it's not too heavy, just awkward with one person." I nod and approach the chest. The wood is covered with metal patterns, it looks like fire and trees and clouds and rivers all tangled together. There are also faces and figures. They're all bestial and freaky-looking. The chests lock is actually a metallic face. The keyhole is in its gaping, fang-filled mouth, it almost seems like it's about to bite down at any second.

"What's in this?" I ask as we heft the chest. The handles dig into my hand and my arms strain. It is very heavy, but I try not to let on.

"I'm not sure, it's Rex's." I blink with surprise and look back at the chest. Weird that the monster owns something like this, I wonder why? We manage to shuffle the chest up through the winding staircase. My hands and arms are killing me by the time we load it into the trailer. I can see a bunch of other gear already inside. I jump a bit and my heart begins to race as Rex emerges from the garden.

Xan looks at him and says, "We're nearly ready to go, are you riding with us or are you going to meet us there?" Rex considers for a moment.

"Perhaps it is best that I travel there using my talents, I have trod on the ground near to the church in the past, it is a simple matter to return to that place. I shall perform a perimeter search upon my arrival, and make certain that our fortress is not ensconced in crafty predators." Xan nods.

"Good, yeah that would be helpful, thanks."

Rex bows and says, "We have purpose now Xanshudan, whether you see it or not. But as we craft our fragile machinations, contrary wheels are turning. And with them flow the subtle waters of entropy, seeping into our midst as an uninvited river. We must stay the course, whatever that course may be. Else we capsize, and drown within the murky seas of impending avarice." I blink a few times. Rex speaks in such an odd way. I don't even know what he talking about most of the time, not to mention that watching him speak is mesmerising. Like he's in slow motion but his words aren't.

"I know Rex, there's more at stake here than any of us want to think about. It might be time to call in any favors that are owed, my pool is dry." Rex laughs. The sound makes my skin crawl, it echoes and distorts. It sounds like a mutant hyena put through an auto-tuner.

The Asura then says, "Well I believe that you owe me a favor." Xan laughs and I can't help but smile.

Rex then says, "Beyond that my ties were severed when I renounced my oath. I still have a few friends, but they shall not leave the flux, they are stubborn in that way."

Xan nods and says, "When we reach the fortress I'll call Cassandra and see if she can drum up some extra support, even in the form of someone to run interference." Rex grins and walks closer.

"Very well then, I shall see you at the fortress." Then without any fanfare whatsoever he's just gone. No puff of smoke or bright flash of light, just gone. I blink and look around.

"Is he still here?" I ask.

Xan laughs and says, "No, he's gone. He'll be at the fortress when we get there." I blink and furrow my brow.

"Some type of magic?" I ask.

Xan smiles and says, "Some type, yeah. Asura are unique, in case you hadn't noticed. They are born from a combination of pure chaotic energy and one of the four elements of earth, fire, air or water."

I nod and ask, "Yeah, it's pretty hard not to notice. But what does that mean exactly?"

"Well as far as I know it means that when Asura have offspring, instead of a spirit occupying a physical form as with other creatures, say like, a goat. A young Asura is formed out of a combination of pure energy. One half is the chaotic power that serves as the canvas of life. The other half is the pure essence of one of the four elements. The resulting Asura takes the form of their parents and grows normally. Only they are, by all rights, immortal. And, so long as they are not slain within their native realm or through the use of powerful magic, they'll live forever."

I sit in silence for a minute before Kane says, "It also means that they're random, magic spewing douche bags."

I laugh and say, "Takes one to know one I suppose." Xan and Kane both laugh. I consider what Xan said for a while longer.

"So how old is Rex?" I finally ask. Xan thinks for a second.

"Sixteen thousand eight hundred and twenty one, if I'm not mistaken." I stare for a second, stunned. What the fuck? That's crazy. No wonder he's so weird. I'd be really weird too if I was that old, all crotchety and shit. I look over to see Eve emerge from the garden's gateway, a large duffle bag in tow. She's wearing a skin tight black body suit; it has metal plates along the shins, elbows and one of the shoulders. She also has a metallic face mask, though it isn't in place. The mask looks like the mouth of a screaming demon. She has a series of throwing knives strapped to each thigh and there's a short blade sheathed sideways across her lower back.

"Ready to go Eve?" Xan asks. Eve nods and puts the duffle bag in the trailer. Xan told me that she practices "The Art" as well, but differently. He said that she can become invisible and move faster than a person can see. She once created a sonic boom just by moving, apparently. He said she could break me in half with a kick. I don't know if I find that hot or not. I find myself staring at her.

She looks over at Xan and says, "Yeah I showered and put some things together."

Kane pipes up and says, "Does that mean that the tongue bath is off of the table?"

She smirks. "It was never on the table in the first place, letch." Xan and I laugh.

Eve walks to the garage's side door as Xan says, "Oh right, I nearly forgot, here." He's holding something that looks like a grenade in one hand, only it's tall and skinny, more like a cylinder. His other hand has a pile of three plastic pouches. They have some symbols on them, as well as a red sunburst design.

"What are these?" I ask.

He holds up the grenade and says, "It's called a "Flash Bang", pull this, pop the hammer and throw. It's good for disabling a bunch of people, or if you need to run." I nod and take it, putting it in my inside jacket pocket. He then holds up the packages and says, "These are called 'Surgeons patches', they contain a large expendable colony of regenerative nano-bots. They can be used to heal severe wounds in a matter of moments. They won't bring somebody back to life, but they can save a life if they are used quickly enough. Here take three, to use them just pull the strip and take out the patch, then peel the side that says 'peel here'. Apply the newly open side to a spot near or on the wound, the patch will do the rest." I grab the three packages, they're way heavier then they look. I place them in my right front pocket and close the flap. Xan grins and says, "I also found a vest and ammo harness, if you want. You can use it instead of that coat. I mean that coat has some armor but the vest is high grade, it'll stop a large caliber round, the coat won't." He points to the coat, bulky with magazines.

I nod then say, "Still, I'd like to keep the coat if that's cool?" Xan nods and points to the trailer.

"Just empty it and stick it in the trailer, we'll get you a duffle bag too, so you can carry some more stuff with you." I nod. I wonder if I'll be able to keep all this stuff if I'm sent back home. That would be cool, although totally illegal and I'd have to hide it from everyone. And nobody would believe where it came from. I think about home again and feel a spasm of anxiety. I don't know anymore. This place is terrifying but it's also crazy, way more exciting than back home. Yeah right, what am I thinking? It'll be exciting right up until the point that I'm eaten by some freakish thing, like Rex or Kane, or that giant, eagle-octopus. I shudder, my mind flashes to an image of a cocoon made out of thousands of rats. I involuntarily shake my head, damn it Grot, I'm going to be traumatized for years because of you, if I survive. Xan walks to the garage's side door and I follow. He retrieves the vest and harness, it's a combination deal, rows of magazine pouches on the chest and either hip, there's also a large pouch on the left side and a holster for the pistol on the right side. The vest is heavy, it fits decently though.

"Thanks again Xan." He nods and looks at me.

"Sure kid." I know that they're being paid to protect me but Xan seems like a nice guy or Elf or whatever. I mean even if he could kick my pelvis right out of my body without even knocking me over. The others seem nice too, except Cable. He seems kind of cold. And Rex, he seems kind of mindbogglingly terrifying beyond anything that I could have possibly imagined or dared to fathom in my wildest nightmares. But I'm relatively certain that he won't eat me, so that's a good thing, I suppose.

I finish adjusting the vest. Xan gave me a bunch of special magazines for both of my guns, they fill the pouches now. I guess the magazines have extra bullets or something. Only Cable is absent from the main living room. Devlin approaches the garage door, large backpack in tow. Then I notice it, a small multi-colored orb is floating just beside his head. I swallow and take a step back. Devlin looks at the orb then over to me.

"Oh I forgot, you haven't been introduced, Eric this is Immoth, Immoth this is Eric." The orb floats closer. I can now see fine veins of purple and red within its core. My heart races, my mind flashes to an image of the small sun at my center. Tendrils lash out from the blazing orb. I wince, then blink and stumble backwards. "Hey, chill out," Devlin says. What am I seeing? There are colors everywhere. Everyone is made of color and light! The walls are grey and foggy. Immoth glows with a peculiar luminescence. I shake my head and close my eyes. When I open them Xan, Devlin and Silver Dancer are standing in front of me, no longer made of colors and light. They're normal again. An unnatural pressure leaves my head.

"Is everything alright?" Xan asks. Silver Dancer smiles and I forget about being afraid.

"Yeah, just, I don't know."

Xan continues, "What?" I look between the three of them.

"If something's happening we need to know Eric, it's alright, it might be important," Silver Dancer says.

I'm enveloped in a warm feeling and I say, "Okay, yeah, right. I saw the small sun and you guys all looked like colors, colors and light. The walls were grey, it was freaky. And I know that sounds crazy." Xan furrows his brow and looks at Devlin.

"A spontaneous astral perception, it might be a side effect of the power," Devlin says.

Xan nods; he looks at me and says, "Remember what I told you about 'The Art' and a practitioner's ability to see the core of life? That is what you experienced just now, though in an uncontrolled state." I nod, stunned. My mind locks into a loop and I find myself unable to form cogent thoughts. I sit for a minute, looping. Eventually I seem to readjust, as thinking resumes.

"Does that mean I can learn it? 'The Art' I mean?" I finally ask. Ever since I saw Xan creating small explosions with his fists I can't stop thinking about it, and other magic, like the type that Devlin uses. Apparently he can do some pretty amazing things too.

Xan looks to Devlin who shrugs and says, "I'm not sure Eric, it might just be temporary." I nod, somewhat deflated.

"Still it could be the beginning of your arcane connection, you never know," adds Silver Dancer. I smile wide. I'm entranced, she's so nice. Her words instantly make me feel better. She smells like cookies.

She then turns to Xan and says, "The facial mapping software's in place and "The Castles" sentry programs are active." Xan nods. Silver Dancer's so gorgeous, she's crazy smart too. I couldn't even follow what she was saying half the time, just glad to be part of the conversation. I did try to understand though, I really did.

Xan looks at me and says, "Let me know if that happens again, are you sure that you're alright now?" I just nod. It was disorienting, but beautiful at the same time. Xan then looks around. "Alright, so is everyone ready to go?"

"Yeah," says Eve as she walks up. Devlin and Silver Dancer nod.

"Yeah," I say.

"Okay, so Cable, Eve and I will take the van and the trailer. Dancer, you and Eric will take the 'Night Shadow'. If there are signs of pursuit proceed as we discussed, if we lose them continue on as planned, if it doesn't seem possible then switch to the fallback plan, alright?" Silver Dancer nods curtly. I suddenly can't think straight, my heart is racing. I'm driving with her? Damn! Thank you Xan, I want to scream. Just chill out a bit, I'm starting to twitch here. Just try to remain composed.

Dancer smiles at me and says, "Don't worry boss man, I'll see that he's taken care of." She then winks at me. I glance at her breasts and feel a flush overcome my face. Kane's voice breaks the awkwardness, by making things far more awkward.

"You stay away from my woman Eric! I will fight you! I've seen the way that you've been staring at her boobs. It's disgusting!" He then completely changes his tone and says, "So? Silver Dancer, show us your boobs?" I must be fire engine red right now, a six foot kid with an apple for a head. Silver Dancer just flips off Kane and heads to the garage.

She looks back and says, "You coming Eric?" Xan suddenly shoves his left hand under his right armpit and a muffled sound emerges. Devlin laughs and claps his hands. I grin and head towards the silver-armed siren, totally enthralled and utterly embarrassed.

We depart after the van and then stay close. Silver Dancer plugged into the car, she called it jacking-in. I could be jacking-off right now. The car's small and she's poured into that racing harness. Her large, perfect breasts are dancing everywhere. It takes all of my willpower to not stare every second. Just a few good stares, for later, if there is a later. Her electronic voice comes through the speaker, "It should only take around thirty minutes to get to the fortress. So what you were saying earlier about the computers where you come from, it sounds like they're maybe fifty to a hundred years behind ours, depending on how they progress of course, there are other variables at play."

I smile and nod then say, "Your computers sound so cool! I'd love to try it, the freedom must be amazing."

Her digital voice laughs and says, "Yeah there's nothing quite like it, a digital body, moving at the speed of thought. You're right, it is freeing." I grin and look out the window, they're heavily tinted. Dancer said that they are "bullet resistant" as well; at least she's honest about it. "Hold on Eric I'm getting a call." I nod to where I think the camera might be. She said that there is one inside camera and four outside cameras, omni-vision, she called it.

The car abruptly shifts to the right and accelerates. G-forces pin me to the seat. I can't see the van anymore. "Hold on Eric, take out your gun, we've got company!" I immediately begin to breathe heavily. My heart is beating so quickly it feels like it's about to burst from my chest. I sloppily un-hook the newly refurbished T-90, the laser springs to life and puts a red dot on the dashboard. Meanwhile, the car drifts expertly around a corner, we're travelling at a frightening speed. I hold on and nearly retch. My heart is a jackhammer being worked by a gorilla. "Cable's drawing off the main force but there's a TAC 'Quickrider' coming up on us fast, it's a drone, it sort of looks like a motorcycle. I'm going to try to bring it by your side!" I swallow and nod. I feel like throwing up. Just choke it down, you bastard. My window opens halfway, sidewalks and store fronts streak by. We're going fast, really fast, dodging through traffic and taking corners at suicidal speeds. Jordan would love this chick. She could drive him under the table. I try to aim out the window. "We need to deal with it quickly; here it comes,

175

get ready." I'm panting, my finger trembles and I look back out the window. I can see it. It's somehow highlighted in the car's rear window. The window must have a holographic display or something. The drone looks like a motorcycle except its very sleek and low. The top of the drone flips open and to my horror a gun turret appears. The gun begins to chatter, bullets spark off the back of the car and panic ensues. I see a white truck slam into a parked car. Men and women and other things dive for cover, some with an obvious amount of expertise. The drone continues to roar towards us, gun belching an erratic stream of lead. All of a sudden the car decelerates and Silver Dancer says "now!" The car swerves expertly into position some twenty feet from the drone. My heart skips a beat when I pull the trigger and nothing happens. The drone's turret tracks towards me. The safety! I quickly flip the switch to full auto and pull the trigger. A cascade of deafening explosions follows as a series of rounds strike the drone. I realize now that each bullet is detonating. The stream of bullets blasts a smoking line through the front of the drone and then disintegrates the front tire. It performs a clumsy high speed cartwheel then rapidly grinds to a flaming halt. "Yes! Awesome shooting Eric, alright reconfiguring the route, one second, I have to call Xan." I grin broadly as the window rolls up and the car turns off into a narrow alley. My body is buzzing with adrenalin, a tremor travels through my hand. I put the gun down in my lap and put the safety on. I don't know if there are even any bullets left in the magazine. Silver Dancer laughs and says, "Seriously, great work Eric, Xan agrees, he said they're just dealing with the other drones then they're going to take a modified route to the fortress." I nod and swallow, my heart is still racing. She then adds, "We'll head straight to the fortress, as quickly as possible."

"Who was that? The same people as before?" I ask.

"If I had to guess I'd say yeah, but then again word travels fast in 'The Tier', there might be more players joining the fray now. You never can tell," she says. Great, just what we need more complications. I clumsily reload the T-90, the magazine was empty, well three rounds left.

"Did we lose them?" I ask.

"Yeah, I've been checking the cameras, no aerial recon either," she responds. I smile, even if I do get back, nobody is ever going to believe any of this. Car chases, shooting guns at drones, beautiful Elven women. Maybe I can get some pictures before I go, if I go. "It won't be long now, I found an alternate route," she says. I nod and stow the gun. I sit back and try my damndest not to stare at Dancer's breasts. This time I succeed, for a while.

The fortress looms, wrapped in grimy dark stone reinforced with steel braces. The surroundings are desolate, mainly old buildings and warehouses. The fortress was apparently from another time, then modified somehow. We park a short distance away and she unplugs the fiber optic cable from the port in her temple. I make a point of looking the other way as she un-straps from the seat. It might be too much to bear. And I don't mean to be rude. It's just so difficult not to stare. I exit the car as she does. It smells musty here. A layer of dust covers almost everything. There is a small amount of air movement. Xan said that the different levels have certain systems to help regulate their air flow, temperature and water content. Dancer retrieves a duffle bag from the trunk and closes it with a thud. She has a pistol belt strapped to her sexy hip.

She turns to me and says, "Got a couple new pock marks in the back there, I'll need to get the armor repaired when we get out of here. By the way don't touch the car. I activated the security system, the shock can be lethal."

I laugh then remark, "Shit, back home they just make an annoying sound that causes dogs to bark." She laughs and begins to walk towards the church. I follow closely. The main doors look sturdy. There's some type of electronic locks, and what looks to be a deadbolt. She peers intently at the building then at the lock.

"Just as I thought, no power. It's okay, the trailer has a high end generator. Anyway I've got just the thing for this old mechanical lock," she says as she holds up her cybernetic arm and raises her pointer finger. The top of the finger opens and a series of small articulated wires poke out.

I laugh and say, "Cool." She smiles and puts the finger up to the deadbolt, within seconds the doors are standing open. We move inside and close the doors behind us. She locks the deadbolt with a sharp click. It's dark inside, not really any windows.

She looks back and says, "This whole area is embroiled in a corporate deadlock. A number of different corps are vying for the rights to the space. No plans for development for at least three years, not sure what first drove the people away though, no records on that, which is kind of odd. The church was converted into an enforcement center back when people used to work and live here." I look around. The front of the church is divided into a spacious lobby framed by a wall which appears to be comprised of a long desk guarded by a "bullet resistant" window. There's also a steel door that's embedded in the desk-wall, it has the same electronic and mechanical lock combination. This time the mechanical lock is in the door handle. Silver Dancer quickly has it open. Beyond the door the main area of the church has been converted into a large central work room, a few scattered desks remain as well as a dusty office chair. There's also a small room in the corner, it has a large interior facing window in one wall. Beside it is a pair of doorways leading to the station's bathrooms. There are a set of stairs against the back wall which lead up to the second level, a second set of stairs lead down to the basement.

Silver Dancer cups her hands over her mouth and yells, "Rex?" We both wait for a response. After ten seconds of silence she says, "He must be somewhere outside, checking out the perimeter." I nod.

"Wait, how would he get in if the door is locked?" I ask.

"He has his ways, don't you worry about that," she responds. I nod. Some kind of magic no doubt.

"This place is intense," I say.

She moves to the stairs and says, "Yeah, standard local enforcement layout, the containment cells are in the basement in this design, upstairs there's a kitchen, living room, storage room and a sort of employee lounge. That's where we'll be sleeping." I nearly faint, but then rapidly recover. She must have meant the collective *we,* not her and I. We head upstairs. It's pretty much just as she described, there's also a steel door against the far wall.

"Where does that lead?" I ask.

She thinks for a second then says, "The bell tower, there's also a porch up there I think." I nod. There's a pair of couches and a table in the living room. She looks over and says, "That's sort of the main living room and kitchen, over there is the door to the storage room, and that's the employee lounge." I swallow. It must be all of us sleeping in there. It's the only space that would work. The lounge proves to be a large room stripped bare. She looks around and says, "It's alright, we brought folding beds." I nod dumbly and try to say something witty, but nothing comes out. She turns towards me. She smells like sunshine. She kisses me quickly on the cheek. I flush and nearly fall over. She laughs and says, "That was for earlier, thanks for saving my butt."

I smile from ear to ear and say in my coolest voice, "Anytime." She laughs again, sweet music. I want to tell her how great she is, I want to scream it from the bell tower. I want to write it in the sky, or on the roof I guess, in this cities case. I'm about to say something potentially regrettable when a voice fills the room.

"Greetings Silver Dancer, Eric, I have encircled the perimeter and found naught amiss, where are the others?" I twitch hard and twist around to see the monstrous Asura. Silver Dancer looks at me and smiles. She then turns to Rex and begins to explain what happened. I sigh, just my luck.

Josh Berg

Grot Fastwhisker

The cockroaches are wearing cummerbunds. It was good of them to come. They fill out the groom's side nicely. Mice hop on the dance floor, their two-step is immaculate. A choir of pigeons roosts nearby. They practiced for hours to get the songs just right. Everything's set. Everything's perfect. We just need to get the dress. The rodent crowd is outfitted in petticoats and tophats. Oliver is wearing his finest spats. The cake took hours to make. With its tiny sugar bride and groom, their tails entwined. Banners and garlands string between the dumpsters. Bouquets of wilted flowers line the runway. Rodney is gnawing on them. He might have been into the wine dregs already. He is giving away his little girl after all. Grot smiles and wipes away a tear. A table of toads speak in hushed tones. The bride adorns the dress, perfect, it fits perfectly. Grot claps his hands. The music begins in tandem with the choir. The alley is full of revelers. A crow bobs to the beat. The procession begins. Daphne is lovely. The long train matches her tail nicely. On the other side, Jeffery is anxious, cold feet. Grot spoke with him earlier. He's just afraid of commitment, that's all. The pair soon assembles at the altar: an old coffee tin made into something beautiful. Grot raises his hands and the music stops.

He then says, "Dearly beloved, we are gathered here today before the sight of Rat to join Daphne and Jeff in the bonds of holy matrimony." Grot paces as he continues, "In these dark alleys, and during these dark times, it is good that we can find solace in the comfort of each other. Rat knows when the end will come and so we must live for these happy moments, these good times, between loved ones. Now we believe that the bride and groom have prepared their own vows, so we will let them continue." He steps to the side and clasps his hands behind his back. He's forgetting something, but what? Daphne begins her vows, they're heart felt. A gadfly sniffles. Grot tries not to cry. The words are gentle and kind. She delivers them with humor and grace. But the feeling still persists, like he's forgetting something. He can't quite remember. Daphne finishes and the revelers cheer, he smiles. Now it's Jeff's turn. The groom is nervous, Grot encourages him. Jeff begins his vows. They start slowly but then the words begin to have real meaning. Grot nods his approval. A hedgehog in the back row begins to weep. Still, something nags at him. Some part of his mind is in a muddled haze. He looks at the crowd. The rodents are dancing with the arthropods. The ring bearers are here now, tail rings carried on plush pillows. Jeff finishes his vows as they arrive. Daphne has tears in her eyes. Grot claps his hands together and says, "Wonderful, now if we can have the rings?" The pillows are set before the betrothed. He seems to hear a voice now, no wait, it's nothing, or is it? The fleeting tail of a memory passes through his mind, like recalling a dream. *What is it?* He thinks. *What are we forgetting?* Grot shakes his head and he continues, "Jeff, put the ring on Daphne's tail and repeat after us: with this ring I thee wed." Jeff follows the instructions. Daphne mirrors the ritual when it's her turn. A couple of shrews in the front row embrace. Grot grins broadly and says, "If anybody wishes to object to this marriage, do so now or forever hold your peace." He waits for a half beat. Then the voice seeps in again, it's far away. It must be someone in the city. It probably has nothing to do with him. A green blur passes before his eyes and he blinks a few times. He looks back to the altar and proceeds, "Then by the power infested in us, we now pronounce you Rat and Rat. You may kiss the Rat." It's a long kiss, full of love, Grot tears up. He promised himself that he wasn't going to cry. Wait, it's that voice again. It's closer now. He looks around. Beetles are throwing confetti. A weasel is performing a lop-sided dance, as the pigeon choir continues to sing. Grot shakes his head. He hears it again.

"Master ..." That voice, he knows that voice. It's quiet, but he knows it. He looks to the revelers. The crowd is eating the cake. They're not being civil anymore, not one bit. A crow devours a cockroach, cummerbund and all. Mice flee from the dance floor; one is torn apart by a shrew. Grot blinks and stares into the distance. A dark forest is there, he can see somebody right at the edge. He knows them. He puts out a hand. *Come back,* he thinks, *please, just come back to us.*

"Master!" He looks up sharply. There's a rat, a green rat. He remembers then, and is overcome with a flood of images. Eric, Cassandra, the spirit of the city and the darkness of life. Where is this? He looks around, a decorated alley, a crowd of different animals, birds and insects. They're all moving frantically. The alley's in turmoil, the spell is broken. Grot blinks and shakes his head. What happened? He stands for a moment. *It was another episode,* he thinks, *we get lost sometimes, somehow.* He quickly looks at his phone, just hours, many hours, but not days this time. He can remember leaving Cassandra's. He then stole a stack of holo-vids from a shifty street vendor, gifted Delrog with the stolen goods, and went to check on Mug and Grenda. The boy was healing nicely, Grenda said something about the diner but he couldn't go, then nothing. He shakes his head again and looks at the watcher.

"Rat must be wary of dangers." He internalizes the standard mantra.

"And this one will always watch for them master." The spirit replies in kind. The watcher then continues "You were not responding master. This one feared that you were ensorcelled." Grot smiles, *if only it were that simple,* he thinks.

Grot replies, "Rat is fine, thank you. We must return to our purpose." He then sits cross-legged on the ground. A few rats still mull about, tiny suits and fitted hats. The cake is in ruins. Grot focuses his will. He reaches out and grasps hold of the watcher. His vision shifts and he sees his own body sitting on the ground before him. He then soars up and over the buildings. He looks down at the streets and roads until he finds a familiar landmark. He's not too far from "Reachers Hope", but for some reason he's on the city's third level. He releases his control of the watcher and commands it to return to him. Grot hesitates for a minute. The banners and garlands sway slightly, pushed by an artificial breeze. He remembers Cassandra and he smiles. He should have gone to see her years ago, but time seems to slip away in fits and starts. Now his original purpose looms, the "Darkness of life". He must find this "Platinum Under Sky" nightclub, he must find out everything about it. He thinks for a second. It is unfortunate that he had to use all of his money to help the dreamer, Eric. He needs more money before he can do anything else. Then an idea strikes him, an old idea. Rat's purpose is important after all. A minor break-in is a petty thing by comparison. He grins, time to do some scouting. Just like in his "youth", Cassandra's influence returning. Grot laughs and stands. He looks back once as he leaves the alley. *Too bad,* he thinks, *we'd picked out the perfect honeymoon spot too.*

He creeps through the city. Most shops are open right now. That makes things a bit trickier. He keeps his eyes peeled as he moves through the Gromgir District. Restaurants, bars and store fronts clutter the narrow streets. Most are of no use though. He needs to find a store that still uses cash, or a store that deals in small, valuable goods. Like a jeweler's or an arcane merchant. He continues on through the District.

Soon he passes a store window displaying rings, earrings and necklaces. A glowing sign saying "Callwell's" is mounted above the door. Grot cases the store as he walks slowly past. One of the displays near the rear wall has some expensive merchandise. He's seen those types of stones before. "Callwell's" is a corporate chain; they'll have good electronic security, but their arcane security should be mediocre at best. He moves a short distance up the street and leans against a lamp post. He then focuses on his breathing and slowly peels back the veil. The spirit realm here is like a massive cavern, interlaced with tunnels. He looks to the building and refocuses slightly. The form of the store drifts through the spectral haze. He can see a ward; it's not a powerful ward though. It was created by a novice, he can tell right away. He could easily create a breach without alerting anyone. That would let him cast spells into the building and, more importantly, while he was inside the building.

He looks around the street. A restaurant is across the way. There are a series of brownstone apartment blocks surrounding it. The "Callwell's" sits in an old factory building that's been converted to house a number of small stores. Grot looks back up the sidewalk. There, an alley and a dumpster. If anyone sees him they'll just think that he's homeless, that or he's "dumpster hunting". He quickly moves to the steel container, grabs the lip and leaps inside in a single motion. The dumpster's nearly empty; it must have been dumped recently. The top falls shut as he huddles in the comforting metal. He then calls for his watcher spirit, and a second later the translucent rat is hovering in front of him. He occupies the body of the spirit, flies through the metal wall of the dumpster and travels into the alley. He looks around. Only the store seems warded. He flies forward. The ward covers the whole building. Across the street, he spots a potential base of operations. One of the apartment buildings has very few sparks in it, not many living things. The building might only be partially habited. He travels in and through the apartment building in the watcher's body. Some of the apartments are definitely unoccupied, but he soon finds what he's looking for, an empty one with windows facing the street. He can see the old factory's ward from inside the greyed out apartment. His focus shifts and the watcher spirit's perception shrinks away, leaving the smell of decay and old coffee grounds. He ponders for a moment, then laughs and snaps his fingers.

Scurrying from the dumpster, he crosses the street and moves between the buildings. There's an alley that runs behind the chosen apartment. He cloaks himself in the city's shadows and he creeps to the building's back door. It has a combination mechanical/electronic lock. He grumbles and tucks away the lock picking gun, then thinks for a second while gazing at the locks. They're both attached to the door knob; in fact they are a part of it. They are made of metal. There is some plastic in the electronic lock, but not much. The door is metal too. He grins and fishes around in his belt of pouches, soon producing a single rusty nail. He palms the nail and starts to move his hands as he hums quietly. An arcane strand begins to coil around the nail as he spins it in his hand. The strand slowly forms into a ball. He ties off the pulsing strand with his other hand and he leans close to the door. The nail touches the door handle and the ball flares with power. Instantly, the door knob and most of the door are reduced to a pile of brownish rust. A wooden core teeters for a moment then falls, Grot catches it before it hits the ground. He laughs to himself, too much power. *Now we'll have to hurry*, he thinks, *this is kind of conspicuous.* The wooden plank falls with a thud and he enters the building. He moves nimbly through the halls. The suite's door is soon in front of him; it's guarded by a similar set of locks. He grins. The spell is crafted again, and soon just the door knob and locks stain the carpet with brown dust. He moves into the apartment and closes the remains of the door behind him. The entrance is simple, no electronic security, unless there's a non-function alarm. They can be set to register a non-functional mag-lock, this building now has two. He hesitates for another second. Even if there is a non-function alarm he'll be long gone before anyone shows up, as long as everything goes to plan.

He moves to the window and opens the curtains, glancing briefly at the pane to make sure that the glass is intact. Satisfied that there aren't any cracks, he breathes low and peers into the veil. The mist of the spirit realm super-imposes itself over his sight. He can see the ward through the window. He concentrates on it then, and reaches out into the river of arcane power. Slowly, he hooks the threads of the ward around his finger tips. Lines of colorful light stream towards him as he begins to work. He carefully tugs and loosens the threads, skillfully unraveling the pattern. Gently, he creates a breach in the ward. A hole for him to cast spells through. He's positive that he didn't alert the wards creator, he was subtle enough. Grot lets his focus drift back. He looks at the store again. One window has a display in it. The other window shows part of the checkout counter. There is a security guard but Grot doesn't think that he'll be a problem, not after he casts the first spell. He watches the storefront for a second longer. There are a few customers inside. That's fine, they might get sick, but there will be no lasting damage. He fishes around in his pouch belt and soon produces an eye dropper. A small amount of the fluid stains his finger and he wipes it under his nose. His lip tingles and a second later he can't smell anything. He stows the eye dropper and pulls an eggshell from his pocket. He looks towards the shop and steadies his nerves. He then growls out two clipped words and crushes the shell as he makes a series of arcane gestures that end with him pointing at the shop. A few seconds tick by. Then, the doors of the shop burst open and a stream of people rush outside. They're all staggering, retching and vomiting. Grot covers his face with his bandana and puts up his hood, waiting patiently for his chance. There, the clerk and the guard, they're locking the door as they exit. He smiles and moves closer to the apartment's window. Focus now on the store. The window near the checkout counter will do. He chooses a spot and chants the words of power as he touches the pane of glass in front of him. A swell of energy flows through him and he streaks towards the chosen spot in the shops window, appearing on the inside of the shop a second later, just on the other side of the chosen point. He runs to the previously identified display case and shatters the glass with a single swing of his window hammer. Muffled calls of alarm can be heard as he empties the contents of the display case into his backpack. The internal alarm begins to sound. He quickly glances around. There's nothing else that can be grabbed quickly, probably a small amount of cash, if any. The guard is trying to open the door. He's fumbling with his mag-key and holding his breath. Grot runs back towards the window. The employee is staring, the guard is cursing. He focuses and looks through the window. He can see the apartment building across the street. The spell's power bridges the two panes of glass and Grot steps through the channel, and back into the darkened living room of the suite. He pants and shakes out the adrenalin before running out into the hall. Fleeing quietly from the apartment building, he sinks back into the alley and before long he's deep in the undergrowth of the city, another crawling thing lost amongst the clutter of life. He grins contentedly to himself, giddy with endorphins. Phase one complete.

"So where'd you steal this from exactly?" asks Sid "Stacks", his green optical lens shining in the light of the bustling back room. Dagga smoke creates a pleasant haze. There's a "Tablet" game going on in the corner. Gangers and low-lifes sit in a large circle there, Goblins and Orcs mainly. Alcohol flows, someone laughs.

"It does not matter, they will not be traced. You know very well that the stones can be reset and the metal can be melted down, it's all pure," Grot responds, he's done this many times before, long ago. The rotund Goblin looks Grot up and down.

He then nods and says, "Alright, I can offer you five thousand credits for the lot." Grot tilts his head and shifts in his chair.

"Do not presume that we are stupid Sid, that makes Rat upset. You're offering us half of what we think is fair, why is that?"

Sid laughs and says, "Because for all I know some Marshall will show up not two minutes after you leave saying 'We observed a smelly little Shaman steal a bunch of high end jewelry. Said Shaman then ran directly to this establishment, which seems slightly dubious owing to past encounters in this very back room!' Then I have to not only give the shit back, but also bribe a Marshall as well, and that's just not good for business, you know?"

Grot laughs darkly then responds, "Now friend Sid 'Stacks', we like you greatly, but you are beginning to insult us. Rat is not some two-bit hood, we are not traced. We are not followed. If we give you our word then that is the truth that we know."

"Yeah right, I've known other Rat shamans you know, liars, thieves and backstabbers the lot of them," Sid responds.

Grot nods and says, "Yes, but Rat is not them, Rat is Rat. Now on the other hand, if you choose to remain obstinate, Rat will go to Martha and get the ten thousand credits that we deserve. It's just that she is an inconvenient distance from here and we were in a bit of a hurry." The pudgy Goblin snorts and leans back in his seat. A small table sits before him, sparkling with the purloined jewellery.

Sid remains quiet for some time before saying, "Alright, fine, you win. Ten thousand it is." He then laughs and continues, "You know I haven't seen you in a while, I kind of thought that you were out of the game."

Grot grins and says, "Not that out of it; now pay us!" Sid scowls, but soon retrieves the money.

"Physical cash, we only keep it because of the tables," he says as he hands over ten folds of ten bills each. Grot flips through the cash then stores it in his backpack. He grins and stands.

"Nice doing business with you, see you again sometime." Sid nods and begins to round up the jewelry. Grot exits through "The Stinking Weasel's" back door.

He crosses to the concrete park that on the opposite side of the street from that famous tavern. The park is "Tunnel Ratz" turf, which is fine. He's on good terms with that gang, for some reason. It could be the mutual love of rats, or it could be the magic. They're primarily a Goblin gang, and Goblins tend to be highly superstitious when it comes to magic users, either revering them or persecuting them. One common belief is that it is very bad luck to attack a spell-caster of any stripe. He laughs to himself; of course that belief could've arisen from the fact that an angry spell-caster will explode you with fire or cover you in a blanket of scorpions. Whatever the reason, the gang doesn't bother him. He sits at a concrete picnic table. Bright graffiti covers every square inch. The city's chorus surrounds him. He lets himself drift for a moment. Small voices begin to speak up, all around. Some of the voices are forceful and angry, others are scared and alone. Some are healers and teachers, while others are warriors or thieves. He opens his eyes and looks around, a voice is not needed right now though. Right now he needs to make a phone call to another old friend, providing that he's still alive. He produces his cell phone and finds the contact then hits the connect icon.

It not only turns out that he's still alive, he's still living in the same dirty old hovel that he was congealed in. Grot moves briskly through the city. The second level is well known to him, even locations outside of "Reachers Hope". Melvin or "Metal Head" lives far from the core. The ancient Goblin sounded tired. He may have just woken up. Grot considers the advantages of getting a forged credstick yet again. He could've paid through the phone then, and not have to travel anywhere. He sighs and continues down the sidewalk.

After some time he arrives at the corner of Twenty First Street and Fortune Ave. The massive glittering temple of Fidgerith gleams like a great beacon of decadence. Known as "The Luck peddler", he's the patron deity of Gnomes, confidence men, gamblers and tricksters. The temple is also a lush casino. Grot grins. It's a far cry from "Reacher's Hope". He turns up the street and continues to Melvin's shack. The house is leaning at a dangerous angle, with a small yard encased in progress. Tall apartments and newer strip malls mainly.

Grot opens the gate and begins to approach the front door when a speaker activates and a voice announces, "You take one more step and they'll be finding pieces of you all over this block, buried claymores, facing upwards. They're everywhere." Grot stops and looks around.

He then says, "It's us Metal Head, Grot, remember we called?"

A short pause follows before the voice says, "Oh, yeah, sorry about that, come on in but stay on the path." The steel door buzzes and pops open. Grot navigates the stone path then ascends the stoop. He opens the door and enters. The house's interior is far nicer then the exterior would suggest. It's obviously been up-graded substantially over the years. Grot stands and stares for a bit. The house is ultra modern, really clean. "So Grot, it's been quite a few years, hasn't it?" Melvin comments. Grot looks over to see the shrunken old Goblin, a metal port gleams in his temple.

Grot nods and says, "Too long Melvin. You are looking good." Melvin laughs.

"Bullshit. You, on the other hand, haven't aged a day."

Grot shuffles uncomfortably and says, "We have some business to discuss." Melvin perks up his eyebrows.

"Oh do we? What did you have in mind? I'll quote you a price once I know what I'm dealing with." Grot nods. Melvin then continues, "Well come on, don't stand there like a beggar at the door." Grot grins and follows him into the living room, expensive furniture, works of art. The far wall is a holo-vid display showing a serene island scene. Melvin sits on the chair and motions to the overstuffed couch across from it. Grot sits and looks around. Melvin seems slightly put off.

He looks at the couch lamentably, clears his throat and asks, "So, what business are we talking about here?"

"We wish to know as much as we can about a place called the 'Platinum Under Sky' nightclub." Melvin blinks a few times and considers something.

"I'll charge you the usual fare, two hours upfront."

Grot thinks for a moment and says, "It was two hundred per hour yes?" Melvin nods casually. Grot produces four crisp notes, one hundred credits each. He hands the money to Melvin.

The old Goblin pockets the cash and says, "You can wait here if you want, it might take a little while to compile the data." Grot gets the sense that Melvin doesn't actually want him here, he's just being polite. Grot stands.

"No, thank you Melvin, we have some other errands to perform. If you could please call us as soon as you are finished we would appreciate it."

"Yeah, sure, no problem, I'll start right after I eat." Grot nods. Melvin walks him to the door and reiterates "I'll call as soon as I get everything."

"Thank you Melvin, we will speak soon," Grot responds. The door closes behind him and he looks north. That's where he has to go next.

"Madame Mystra's" isn't very far, only an hour by foot, through a part of the second level that's far nicer than the neighborhoods that he normally frequents. He's nearing the shop, when a Marshall's armored cruiser matches his speed and eyes him hard. He holds his breath and readies an egg shell, then walks as casually as possible. A few tense seconds pass, when suddenly the patrol car accelerates up the street and disappears from sight. Grot lets out a breath and hurries on his way.

He soon enters the arcane shop. A rich collection of odors fills his nose as the jingling door slams shut behind him. The shop is brimming with potions, unguents, scrolls and wands. A long wooden counter lines the shop's far side. Behind the counter are hundreds of small shelves filled with different reagents. The curator looks to Grot. She's an Elf by the name of Giselle. She is known to Grot. He smiles and nods as she addresses him.

"Greetings Rat Shaman, Grot 'The Timeless', grandmaster of the tenth circle and walker of the endless fields."

Grot bows and says, "Greetings Giselle Starshade, initiate of the old way, daughter of the Golden Light and singer of the truth."

She returns the bow. He approaches the counter. A pickled demon tongue wiggles in its jar.

"So, what brings such a distinguished Shaman to my humble shop?" she asks.

"Rat needs a few things, we made a list," he says triumphantly as he produces a crumpled piece of paper. She laughs, the sound is pure music. She takes the list. Her eyes dart back and forth as she reads Grot's nearly indecipherable script.

"No problem. I'll fetch a bag and start getting these things together." Grot nods and glances around the shop. A display case sits just to his left. It's filled with portal gems, seven thousand each. The case beside it is large and low. He grins and walks over, vermin grenades. He looks closely at the preserved rat carcasses. A row of stitching bisects each of their stomachs. He puts his hand to his chin. Giselle begins to assemble the items in the listed amounts.

"What type of vermin grenades are these?" Grot asks.

She looks up from the bag and says, "It's based on the stitching. Black is for spectral rats, red is for centipedes and blue is for spiders." He nods, three thousand apiece.

"What do you say to selling one with black stitches for twenty five hundred, because of our other business?" She stops bagging items for a minute as she thinks.

She then responds, "For you Grot, sure, we'll call it four thousand even?" He grins and nods. The transactions are completed and Grot leaves with his bag of goodies. He then wanders for a little while before finding a restaurant with the words "Nora's Diner" scrawled across the brick. There's a badly painted mural of a Goblin woman at a stove, presumably Nora. Grot moves into to the diner. Inside it's dirty and smoky, the walls and tables don't match. The food consists of the standard greasy spoon menu with a few traditional Goblin dishes thrown into the mix. There's nothing too great, not even a "Nora" in sight, rather some uninspired Orc woman name "Chenga" sweats behind the grill. Grot languishes for a while. He eats his meal and drinks his red tea. An hour passes. He pays his bill, leaves and begins the return journey to Melvin's, about half an hour from here.

The memories of Cassandra return as he walks. He smiles to himself again and thinks about when he'll see her next. In a week maybe, that would be good. Hopefully this stuff with Eric will have been dealt with by then, of course if it goes wrong there might not be a next week to get to.

He reaches Melvin's street without receiving a call from the old hacker. A quick survey of the area reveals that there's a raised monorail platform just up the way from his house. The station has benches and he won't seem as suspicious. He moves to the station and looks up the stairs. There's a camera dome at the top. He hisses and looks around the base of the platform. There, a collection of concrete blocks and boxes. He walks under the platform and sits down. It looks like this area is used by somebody, a street shelter of some type. Grot glances around briefly then retrieves the arcane reagents and distributes them about his person. A handful of marbles, bound in copper wires, a small, expensive jar of spectral dust. Ten red pellets made of an unknown infusion, a pouch of oiled snake teeth and a gold plated cockroach. He then waits patiently. Several hours crawl past before his phone rings. He eagerly looks at the screen and is pleased to see Melvin's number being displayed.

"Melvin?" he says as he answers.

"Yeah, it's me Grot. You can come by anytime, I'm done," Melvin responds. Grot stands and begins to walk.

"We'll be there right away Melvin," Grot says. He then disconnects and makes the short trip to Melvin's house. The steel door buzzes open and Grot once again enters into the rich interior of the house. Melvin ushers him into the living room. A clear plastic covering has mysteriously appeared on the couch. Grot grins to himself and sits on the slick surface.

"So it ended up being more or less five hours of work in total, that's another six hundred."

Grot nods and says, "First what did you find?"

Melvin looks him over. "You do have the six hundred?" Grot rolls his eyes and makes a scoffing noise. He then produces six of the crisp new bills. Melvin nods and points to the holo-vid. The display explodes into a sphere of information, pictures and videos.

Grot approaches the glowing globe and looks through the files. The club was established ten years ago by Telmar Sylvaris and his partner Tony Grossi, pictures and bios follow. Nothing of interest, one's an Elf playboy with a rich daddy, the usual. The other is some business major, a Human with more of a modest upbringing. No mention of magical talent in either file. The rest of the files outline the history, finances, returns and several incidents of note, including a high level assassination that occurred in the club's lobby. It looks like the target was a corporate scientist, thirteen bystanders were also killed. The perpetrator was never found. Grot pours through the files. The most interesting thing that he ends up discovering is the nightclub's actual physical address. It's on the city's sixth level. He pays Melvin.

"Thank you muchly Melvin, we must go now." Melvin pockets the money.

The small Goblin stands and accompanies Grot to the door while saying, "Sure, anytime Grot, call me if you need more work done. Take care now." Grot opens the door, hops down from the stoop and walks to the sidewalk through the claymore garden. He thinks for a minute, it's not quite clear what he's looking for. There's something there though. Like the thread, the black thread. He's going to have to find out. He'll only know for sure when he gets there. Whatever it is, he'll know when he feels the city there. *We just hope that we don't get lost along the way,* he thinks.

Rebecca Arliss

The whole area looks like a strange geometric spiderweb. Buildings of all description are connected by a chaotic grid of materials. Laundry lines, foot bridges, banners and neon signs swarm above. A quick appraisal of the area indicates that she sticks out like a sore a thumb. There have only been a handful of other Humans since arriving here. And she's been shopping the image around for hours now. The Goblins here are tight-lipped. She was afraid of that. It's a closed community, distrustful of outsiders.

"Heya pretty lady, I got a nice selection here, make you a good deal." The gruff voice of a street peddler draws her attention. She'd prepared for this by going to the bank earlier and getting some actual cash. These peddlers often know a great deal about the surrounding neighborhoods. She stops in front of the Goblin. His wares are displayed on a small folding table that turns into a briefcase. The merchant is sitting on the stoop of an abandoned apartment block. Great throngs of Orcs and Goblins surge through the area. The smell of smoke wafts from a nearby barbeque. "Here, fine spectral steel, isn't that lovely, it is said to bring good luck," the Goblin says as he holds up a thin chain with a medallion dangling at its center. The design is of the "Ouroboros", a snaky, dragon-like Asura of tremendous power, some think that it's actually a deity of sorts.

"May I?" She reaches for the necklace.

"Certainly," the Goblin says as he hands over the chain. She holds the medallion close to her right cybereye and sends a single pulse from her metallurgic sonar software. The sound waves bounce off the medallion and return with a precise measure of the metal's density. She glances at the readout in the bottom left side of her field of vision; it's 95% pure, spectral platinum. She looks at the table of goods. It's a random assortment of items. She can see a number of engravings as well, they're different from each other. There's a good chance that they're all stolen. The Goblin might not even know what half of the stuff is worth, or what it even is.

She peers at the pendant a while longer before saying, "I'll give you one fifty for it." The Goblin puts his hand under his jaw. He then motions towards her.

"Two hundred," he responds. She grins and produces a palm display.

"One sixty, you wouldn't happen to know this Goblin?" She holds up the display, an image of the mysterious Goblin flickers to life above her hand. The foot tall holograph shows the stooped figure in profile, fur collar, hood, large backpack covered in oddities.

The Goblin peers at it for a second then says, "If I do know him, does that mean that the necklace is worth two hundred?" She smiles.

"Well, that's kind of steep but I'm sure we could figure something out. I would like to find him."

The Goblin grins at her and says, "I know him alright, could even tell you where he might be found." She furrows her brow and sways her head, a ruse of an internal debate.

"Alright, two hundred for the medallion and what you know." She says as she deactivates the palm display and stores it away.

The Goblin considers for moment then says, "Alright, where's the cash?"

She tilts her head. "Info first."

He laughs and says, "Hey, no pay no play sweetheart." He then snorts and spits on the ground, a sawed-off shotgun dangles just under his short coat. She considers for a minute then produces a wad of twenties and counts out five.

"Put the medallion there, just so we have an understanding," she says, and puts the five bills on the table; the goblin weighs them down with the necklace.

He then leans closer and says, "Alright, fellow that you're looking for goes by the name of Grot Fastwhisker, he's crazy, a rat Shaman or some such. Or maybe he just thinks that he is, anyway I sometimes see him near 'Iggy's Diner' over on Stillbog Street, and that's all I know about that." He then sits back and grins in expectation of the rest of his payment.

She considers for a few seconds before saying, "Just how do I know that you're telling the truth?" He sits up and spits off to the side.

"You don't, you can check it out for yourself though, if you don't believe me, but first, the other hundred?"

She frowns and stands resolutely for a few seconds. Not much of a choice, no other leads, and at least she'll get the medallion out of the deal. Another five bills are slapped onto the table and she retrieves the necklace.

The Goblin grabs the money and asks, "What did you want to talk to him about anyway?"

"I just wanted to ask him some questions, that's all," she says as she pockets the medallion and her remaining money.

The Goblin snorts and says, "Sure, well good luck, like I said he's crazy." She laughs quietly and turns from the table. *A rat Shaman would fit,* she thinks. Now she has a potential name to go with the picture. It's time for another weave search, one with a wider parameter and a longer timeline. Grot, if that is his name, obviously had something to do with this rat incident, some kind of magic. She twitches and feels a shock of adrenalin as she remembers the blood magic story that she covered. They'd discovered a cult of Ignis Infernus operating right in the city's core, hundreds maybe thousands of victims. She remembers the smoldering ruin of their "Church", a massive force of Marshalls and Zealots laid siege to the complex. She'd never seen magic like that before, horrid torrents of energy stripping matter apart. There was fire, poison, lightning and bladed chains manifesting at random and without warning. There were explosions, illusions, even fantastical creatures called in from dark and disturbing realms. She recalls the Zealot that saved her life after she was hit. A swell of magic closing the gaping wound in her side. She winces at the thought and shakes her head.

Then there's the kid. She's shown his picture to dozens of Orcs and Goblins, with no result. He might be some corporate runaway. Maybe he's an executive's son who's now being pursued by his father's corporation. *That would make a good story,* she thinks, *especially if there was some kind of romantic angle.* She walks on.

The roads here are cramped with a mix of small and large buildings. Signs of dilapidation are evident, and some of the taller buildings lean at unhealthy angles. She walks a short distance, finds a bench and adjusts her pistol so that it's easier to reach. The porta-comp slides from its protective case. No port this time, no avatar, just a smart-frame search will do. She engages the programming software. A basic search-frame will work. She'll just add the images and now the name, Grot Fastwhisker. All institutions, all levels, she'll start the search with a fifty year timeline. The Goblin might be that old.

The coding soon comes together as she listens to her surroundings. Guttural Goblin words drifts in from all around. Many of the denizens here speak Street and Corp Common as well, the name of the standardized language adopted by all corporations more than a hundred years ago, based on Human, Elven and Dwarven primarily. Rebecca doesn't know any of the "Beast tongues" as they're called, Orcish, Goblin or Giant. She'd thought about getting a universal language translator implant, and the accompanying sub-dermal microphone, they're really expensive though. Those implants would really help when it comes to performing interviews however.

She finishes programming the search-frame and activates the construct. Within seconds the program returns a file filled with all of the digital data related to Grot over the past fifty years. The file is very slim, but the name is real. The timeline begins thirty-two years ago with a break and enter charge on the city's first level, it made news only because Grot managed to escape custody somehow. He even retrieved his DNA profile so that he couldn't be scryed. She looks at the mug shot. It's definitely him. She flips through all of the pictures, there are four including her camera capture. She studies them closely. He looks exactly the same in each picture. He hasn't aged a day, or at least it looks that way. Wait, there's something else. She suddenly feels like she's been punched in the guts. One of the searches discovered a Q & A article quoting one Cassandra Seelie as saying "If it wasn't for an old friend I wouldn't be in a position to donate in this way." The interviewer asks who it was and she simply replies "Grot". Rebecca exhales a snort of disbelief, it can't be a coincidence. The interviewer's next question is "Where is this Grot now?" Cassandra answers "He passed away." Rebecca frowns and finishes the article;

it's mainly superficial details about Cassandra's daily routine and social life. Passed away? That's not true though, maybe it was an intentional lie, a way to help the Goblin to disappear.

She swims through the other material. There's one mention of a Grot helping at an enormous fire in "Reachers Hope". The article stated that "he helped get everyone out safely, saving more than three hundred lives. The Goblin, who some called 'Grot', then disappeared before he could be questioned." That was twelve years ago, no picture. She considers for a moment, before re-calling her search-frame and loading it back into the sculpting program. She quickly expands the timeline to stretch back one hundred years and the search-frame is re-launched. A few seconds pass and the file grows by a small amount. She peers back into the folder. The search found one more item, based on the image. It looks like a copy of an ancient photograph, like an actual physical photograph. The picture is of Grot and a Goblin woman, their arms are around each other's shoulders and they're each wearing a genuine smile. She looks at the text; Grot and Daphne, it's dated over ninety years ago. She enhances the image and zooms in, he looks exactly the same, how is that possible? The picture was from an art exhibit entitled "Lost Loves", it doesn't list the image's origin. *One more search,* she thinks, *just to make sure.* She modifies the search-frame again, another hundred years back. The program returns quickly bearing one additional file. She shakes her head in disbelief and blinks a few times, then looks at the file. It's an old article from a hundred and twenty three years ago. The clipping is part of a racist newsletter, "Friends of Humanity", there's a blurry picture of Grot and some writing about his interference in their dispensing of justice.

It was without morals or conscience that this degenerate, bestial villain stalked into our company and despoiled our virtuous justice. This wretched fiend has allied himself with the forces of evil in our midst; the Dark Elves of the cursed mountain depths. They are no better than the savage Orc, the murderous Ogre or the arrogant Dwarf, all of this filth should be treated as such. A call has been sent out for the faithful to act. The Goblin's name is unknown; it is thought to be hiding a Dark Elf girl of seven years. They were last seen in

"The Warrens" of the city's second level. *Should they be found they are both to be subject to the justice of the righteous. Humans for humanity!*

She shakes her head, despicable hate speak. She looks at the picture closely. Still, exactly the same, he hasn't aged a day in more than a hundred years. She collapses the sphere and sits in thought. *That's how they know each other,* she thinks, *that little Elf girl was Cassandra.* She smiles, now she has a firm second lead. But first, it's time to go to "Iggy's Diner". After all, she could use a cup of coffee.

The diner is in a long, low building. Windows wrap around the front of the structure. A flashing pink sign brags "Iggy's" over and over again. She follows a meandering, hilly street to the front door. A pair of teenage Orcs barge into the diner just ahead of her, they're each close to seven feet tall. She enters the restaurant behind them and walks to a larger booth. The fake red leather squeaks as she slides into the seat. She glances around the diner. Looks like more than a half dozen patrons. Apart from the Orc teens, they're all Goblins. Most of the seats and tables are designed for smaller frames, low and stout. She smells grease, roasting meat and frying potatoes. The waitress approaches. Her name tag says "Grenda", she's pretty, for a Goblin.

"Hi hon, what can I get ya?" she says. Rebecca glances at the menu briefly, a large holo-display behind the counter.

"Just a coffee for now thanks."

"You got it," the Goblin responds before she turns back towards the kitchen. Rebecca considers her approach. She looks at the staff. Two waitresses and two cooks, there's probably another two to four waitresses and one or two cooks who aren't working right now. That makes seven to nine potential employees total. She thinks for another moment. The one article made Grot out to be a hero of sorts, at least around here. Maybe she could use that fact, say that she's doing a piece on Goblins of note in "Reachers Hope". That approach might backfire however, many of the Goblins that she spoke with said they didn't even know who he was. His likeness is unmistakeable. She did get the feeling that one or two of the Goblins she talked to were lying or hiding something.

If Grot is involved with Cassandra, which now seems quite likely, he might be a criminal. Wanted by corps and Marshalls alike, the break and enter record supports that theory. That would likely mean that he doesn't want to be found by anyone. He might have coerced the Goblins around here to remain silent. On the other hand they might be guarding Grot out of some sense of loyalty. She's heard that many Shamans are skilled healers. They could be protecting him if he acts as a sort of local medicine man. She stares at the table, eyes unfocused. The clack of the mug breaks her concentration, waves of steam jut from its lip.

She grabs the handle and says, "Thanks. Say, would you mind if I ask you a question?" The Goblin woman immediately looks suspicious.

"What kind of question?" Rebecca produces her "Tirileth City Chronicler" I.D.

The Goblin stares at it for a while then says, "Nothing on camera, I do not give you permission to use my image." The woman seems slightly agitated.

Rebecca puts the I.D. away then holds up her hands and says, "Hey, no problem, no audio either. I just wanted to ask if you know a Goblin by the name of Grot Fastwhisker?" The Goblin woman reacts visibly, she then quickly looks away. Rebecca produces the palm display featuring the various images of the Shaman. The waitress glances at it, purses her lips and shakes her head.

"No, never seen him before." Rebecca narrows her eyes, the Goblin's lying, she's almost positive. She nods and pockets the palm display.

"Well thanks anyway," Rebecca says. The waitress nods and flashes a quick smile before walking back to the counter. Rebecca looks at the mug. A few sips reveal that the coffee's average in all respects. She drinks casually and observes. A number of pick-up orders come and go. After a while she approaches another waitress, "Wella", by her name tag. She decides to take the official approach this time.

"Hi, Rebecca Arliss from the 'Tirileth City Chronicler', I was wondering if you know a Goblin by the name of Grot Fastwhisker?

He looks like this." She produces the image array. Wella glances at it briefly then shakes her head.

"He's never been in here," she says. Evasive, no eye contact, Rebecca stows the palm display.

"Thanks anyway," she replies. Rebecca looks at the other staff members. After a few minutes of questioning, it seems like nobody knows Grot, or at least they say that they don't know him. She orders a refill and sits in a different booth, near the window. There's a crumbling apartment block across the street, and a staircase leading down. There aren't many vehicles on the road, mainly scooters and motorbikes. She jumps slightly as a series of pops are answered by a barrage of weapons fire. The sounds cease as abruptly as they began, and most of the patrons didn't even look up from their meals. The employees were laughing. She glances out the window and begins to reconsider her new choice of seating, when a waitress approaches. The first one, her name was "Grenda".

She tops up Rebecca's coffee and says, "You know I gave it some thought and I think that I have seen that Goblin, what'd you say his name was?" Rebecca pulls the mug towards her.

"Grot Fastwhisker."

The waitress nods and says, "Right yeah, if it's the same Goblin, I used to see him at the abandoned living complex over on Salter." Rebecca tilts her head and considers for a moment. She had a strong feeling that this Grenda knew Grot on sight. Why would she suddenly offer up this location?

She smiles and says, "Thanks, I'll check that out."

The waitress lingers for a second then asks, "So what did this Grot do?" Rebecca takes a sip of the coffee.

"No, it's nothing like that. I was just trying to write an article about notable locals, apparently this Grot is some kind of Shaman."

Grenda slowly nods her head then says, "I mean I don't know if that was him or not, lots of homeless Goblins there you know?"

"Sure, well I might walk by there anyway, thanks," Rebecca says. Grenda nods and slowly returns to the counter. Rebecca calls up the map grid loaded in her head computer. A latticed sphere of the city superimposes itself over her sight. She imagines the search construct and the words "Reachers Hope", second level, Salter Street. The program responds and unfolds into a detailed street scene, the neighborhood looks desolate. It's in the heart of "The Warrens". Rebecca snorts, she scans up and down the street. It takes a moment but she finally locates the complex. The entire area is a series of townhouses and apartments, all built around courtyards and catwalks. The structures are disintegrating. She can see a series of shanty towns in the courtyards. She looks at the map's image capture; it's dated five years ago. The waitress might be lying. She might be trying to ward her away, thinking that she won't actually go into the heart of "The Warrens". She may even be trying to lure Rebecca into a trap. Still, a large homeless population could be a good, inexpensive information pool. She expands the map. There's a direct route leading there as well. The weight of her pistol comes to mind. She has Stonefire Hydro-blast HEI rounds loaded in all of her magazines. She also brought her old ballistic knife, a gag gift from one of her past birthdays. The knife is still quite functional, nano-sharpened blade and everything. She downs the coffee and hits up the washroom before heading to the front counter. Grenda meets her after a few seconds. Rebecca pays and leaves a twenty dollar tip.

She smiles and says, "For your help." Grenda nods, staring at the money.

The Goblin then says, "I was just thinking maybe you shouldn't do this story, some Goblins around these parts don't want any recognition, you know?"

"Well, I can let him decide that when I find him. I'm not going to force a story on him."

Grenda makes fleeting eye contact then looks down again and says, "Yeah, sure, just be careful if you go over to Salter Street. That neighbor hood is dangerous."

Rebecca nods and says, "Well it is in 'The Warrens' after all, but thanks I'll keep my eyes peeled." Grenda nods and looks away as Rebecca exits the diner.

The sidewalks are bustling. A group of Goblin kids are playing some kind of stone throwing game. The streets crawl by. She walks past prostitutes of each sex, and nearly every race. She passes by hulking Orc gangers and tiny Goblin hucksters. She even sees a massive Ogre, large even by the standards of that race. The streets and alleys eventually lead to the cramped urban caverns of "The Warrens". She stops and confers with the map then looks around. There's an S.O.T tag, that's bad. She starts walking again, glancing back briefly as she does. The crowds are thinner here, meaner looking. Sections of the street are blacked out as well. The lights are broken or missing, never to be replaced. The low-light augmentation in her cybereyes will compensate well enough, as long as it isn't pitch black. The living complex isn't far now. She quickly passes by a large group of rough looking Goblins. A diverse selection of visible firearms can be seen amongst them. She glances back again. *There's another huge Ogre,* she thinks, *it can't be a coincidence.* She looks closer. He has black hair and a long brown coat. It's definitely the same one from before. She speeds up then walks carefully through a long, lightless tunnel, emerging on the other side with a slight edge of adrenalin. The four stout towers that frame the living complex slowly slither into view. She glances back and starts into a slow jog. *Maybe I can lose the Ogre,* she thinks, *he might be a mugger.* She looks back to the towers. They're connected to the third level above, and they're all linked by a series of enclosed catwalks. She glances around, no signs of a population, no crowds. That's strange. She looks back again, no Ogre. There might be a crowd near the living complex; he probably wouldn't attack her there. There are no Marshalls around this area, that's for sure. They might show up after she's murdered, if at all.

She jogs on. Her breath quickens with her pace, and soon she's close to the complex. She begins to run, turns a close corner and instantly regrets the decision. She freezes. There are dozens of them. Grey skin, oversized jaws, long black claws. Ghouls! It's a den of ghouls! Her heart begins to pound. She unholsters her pistol and glances back, no sign of the Ogre. Then, a loathsome screech causes her to jerk around towards the courtyard. They're running at her, fast. They're scaling down from the buildings and leaping out of the townhouses. They're carrying weapons; knives, metal pipes, machetes and axes. Fear wells up inside her. She rapidly surveys the area. There, further up the street, a raised catwalk, it's encased in metal fencing. Only one or two could fit in the stairwell at the same time. They might get stuck in their haste. She sprints towards the catwalk, peripheries full of monsters. She bounds to the top of the stairs and spins around just in time to see a wretched Orcish ghoul, slavering at the base of the staircase. *Breathe low*, she thinks, *just like dad showed you, "The double tap"*. The pistol roars twice. The first round blasts a fist sized hole in the pavement. The second round opens up the ghoul, leaving it with a grotesque crater for a chest. The reek of decay and gore flood up the stairs. She takes a moment to look up the street. A rush of ghastly Goblins and Orcs are running at her, mortal dread wraps around her. Fear turns to action as a Goblin ghoul sporting a butcher knife stomps through the Orcs remains. The pistol roars twice and its head disintegrates. The remains skid to a stop. Her heart is hammering in her chest now, she begins to pant. She looks up again. *Too many*, she thinks, *there are just too many*. The tide rushes forward. Her pistol roars in groups of two. An Orcish ghoul loses a leg. She fires again. Two pipe-wielding Goblins are reduced to quivering meat. The pistol barks and a lanky ghoul woman is transformed into limbs and a head. She reloads, only one more magazine. She can see a multitude pouring into the staircase. She fires rapidly into the group, small detonations reducing the first row to shredded flesh and bone. One slips past and crawls over its dead compatriots. It quickly reaches the stairs and hisses at her. She readjusts and fires, the ghouls flank explodes revealing its ribcage. More are getting to the stairs now, she has to fall back.

She glances up the catwalk; it travels more than two hundred feet before opening up again. She'd be trapped, who knows what's at the other end, maybe a locked gate. She reloads, last magazine. She swallows hard and looks down the stairs, just as she's shocked by a great bellowing roar. Then, thunder envelopes the street as the wreckage of a family sedan crashes through a giant swath of the ghouls. She watches in horror, and joy, as the twisted metal barrels through the crowd, leaving a trail of carnage in its wake. The hoard stops, seemingly in unison, nearly all them peer hungrily towards the street. Then the bulk of the horde begins to move away from her. She's puzzling over this new development when an axe-wielding Orcish ghoul charges her, and she looks back to the stairs. The pistol barks twice and the ghoul loses the left side of its body. She grimaces and tightens her jaw. An anemic teenage ghoul darts through the gore next. It erupts grotesquely as it enters her firing line. She tries to steady her nerves. A bisected corpse tumbles violently into her awareness. She looks back towards the street. The Ogre, there he is. He threw the car! *By Zool,* she thinks, *he's far more horrifying than the ghouls.* He's wielding an axe that probably weighs more than she does. The impact of his blows shudder her ribcage. He's completely devastating them, every bit as much as her HEI rounds, even more so. He swings once, and four ghouls are horribly mutilated. He kicks another and sends it skidding sixty feet. A ghoul jumps and latches onto his back, he just tosses it, one handed. It cartwheels through the air and splatters against a brick wall.

She swallows hard and looks around. Another group is heading her way. She takes aim as the lead ghoul enters the slaughter room floor. The pistol roars and the ghoul's anatomy is instantly displayed. Two Goblins follow in suit but the last ghoul turns and runs. She glances towards the Ogre. He's surrounded. They're beginning to hack at him. He bellows and lashes out, a dozen crumple to the ground, wrecked beyond recognition. She eyes her pistol. The display reads two rounds remaining. An Orcish ghoul smacks the Ogre with a bat. The large figure recoils, then instantly ripostes and obliterates the ghouls head. She blinks a few times in shock. The Ogre is extremely skilled with that axe, it's somewhat disquieting. She ignores that thought for the moment, and tries to hold her breath as she descends the stairs. The spongy path still brings the stench of rotten death, and she tries not to gag as she moves to the street.

More than a dozen ghouls remain. They're being more cautious now, trying to wear down the Ogre. They're moving in and out like a pack of wolves surrounding a bear. She breathes low, takes careful aim and fires off one round. A small, rotted Goblin is immediately reduced to hamburger. The pack looks sharply in her direction. The Ogre uses the distraction and pounces. He instantly closes on one half of the group and destroys them with a single swing of his giant axe. An arm sails past her. One of the ghouls springs forward. It's running at her, twisted knife at the ready. She tracks and fires, but the round goes wide. Panic hits her. It's ten feet away. The Ogre is busy fighting with the remaining six ghouls. She throws the gun and draws her knife. The Orcish ghoul smashes into her, stabbing with a jagged blade and clawing with its free hand. She fends off the attack and slashes with her own knife. The keen edge carves a line through the ghoul's chest. Then iron claws grab her knife hand. The ghoul begins to wrestle her to the ground; it's very large, more than seven feet tall. It's strong too. She tries to twist to the side, but the ghoul hauls her over. Its claws dig in hard. She cringes and looks over to see the small bones of her hand peering out from the torn flesh. The jagged steel of the ghoul's knife pushes forward. It's reaching for her throat. The ghoul slams her into the pavement and drives its knife downwards. Her vision swims but she forces the knife up with all her strength. Still, it's slowly coming down towards her. The ghoul shoves hard on the blade and it touches her throat.

A rush of adrenalin hits her then, and she surges upwards, aiming her knife in the process. She thumbs the release. The blade springs from the handle, soars into the ghoul's eye socket and disappears with a wet slap. The Orc seizes for a few seconds before it stops moving. She sighs with relief and begins to pant heavily, while heaving up at the corpse. It must be more than three hundred pounds of dead weight, right on top of her. She can't move, not at all. She can hear grunts and growls, weapons are being swung. Black blood seeps past her head, the stink is unbearable. She heaves up at the corpse again, her hand stings like fury; it's not working properly anymore. A slow hysteria begins to creep in. Then she hears the sickening smack of something hard hitting something that's not. The sound is followed by a series of bellows, it's some other language. It sounds like Giant. Her heart is pounding. She shoves up at the Orc as hard as she can, nothing, she can't even wiggle out. Claustrophobia's now mounting. No choice, she'll suffocate or be eaten if she doesn't say something. She shoves up again and yells as loud as she can.

"Help! Please help!" A few seconds tick by. Then the sound of boots on pavement, large, armored boots. She puts on her friendliest smile. Her field of vision is completely overcome by a massive visage. Long sharp tusks, a set of curved horns and shaggy black hair, his eyes are bright yellow. He's scowling. "Hi, could you please help me? I'm stuck, I can't get out!" she says in a strained voice. The Ogre looks at the Orcish ghoul then back to her. He leans close, fresh cuts cover his face and hands. He then speaks in a tone so casual that he could've just awoken from a nap.

"Yup, we could help yer alright. But first youz gunna tell us why youz been askin questions bout Grot." She blinks a few times and composes herself. His breath smells worse than the dead ghoul.

Moag

We hear you, fragile squalling sack of need. Small dirty contamination, smother you to death and defile your corpse. Your mother shall not always be near. We shall remember this place. We shall return when we have found the Human, Eric Gibson. The six hearts have tracked him. We know where he has been. The beginning point is not far, and we shall find him soon.

We wear the flesh of a Human now. The pawn of Ignis Infernus gifted us with a pistol, in exchange for the blade that he believes to be enchanted. We laughed at the fool then accepted it, he shall still be used for "The Announcement", but then we shall tear out his throat when it is complete. He is stupid and useless beyond that. We walk on, past buildings and roads clogged with living excrement. Flush it all away, or better still, purge it with fire. Create a world of flesh searing agony and watch them cavort in despondency. They gaze at us as we walk. What are you looking at? You insects. You odious youth full of energy and ideals. We wish a pestilence upon them and all that they know. Be blanketed in sickness and terrible events, peons. We want their hopes to be crushed by constant disappointment. We wish them to become bitter and hateful. We wish for them to die, alone, angry and afraid.

The earlier killings come to mind and we laugh. The last two were fucking. They did not see us through the blinders of lust. The woman died first, we were subtle. The man did not notice at first, not until the blood pooled. Then we broke his neck using our long tail. We leapt from the open window and pulled hard. We simmer with pleasure at the memories. The ninth level of the city soon encroaches, another layer of rottenness. The place we seek is inside the rancid core. It is in "The Warrens", a maze of urban perdition. We like those streets, murder is easy there. We grin and move through an alley, checking our pistol as we do. We have not shot someone in a long time, it seems like fun. A "machine pistol" is what the Human called the weapon. He gave us three magazines for it, "bullets that burn". We shall use the pistol at the very first chance we get. Perhaps some gangers shall accost us. That would be pleasant.

We continue through the streets. It is many miles from here, but we do not feel like stealing a car. It may give us away, and we may need to stay in the area for some time. We must be careful to follow the trail, and it begins on this level. There are things that we may yet learn for the masters. We have the Human's name but not his face. We know his path, but not who he travels it with. We must be careful not to slight the masters with insufficient information. They would not be pleased. They would cast us down into the Stalker's Pit and bet on how long we would survive. Perhaps they would lash us to the flanks of their siege beasts as they march off to war, meat shield for their precious behemoths. We are getting close now. The buildings are decrepit here, hundreds and even thousands of years old. We see gang markings as well, 41T. We do not know them, but we very much hope that they come to us. We move the pistol to the front of our belt, real clothes, not figments fashioned out of dwoemer. We must seem real. They may be watching for our kin, or others. And there are clever technologies that can be used to see through some dwoemers. The street continues on. We walk past a robbery, Human teens in a store. One stares at us. We put up our thumbs and smile. He laughs and looks back at the cashier. We encourage your larceny. Murder as well, leave no witnesses. Perhaps the guilt of the deed shall crush you, or, perhaps instead a new monster shall be born, a thing of habitual selfishness. We know many such a creature. They are our "friends". They shoot us with crossbows and jam spiders in our ears. At times they hurl us from fast moving cars and hit us very hard with bricks. We, of course, return the favour, and on it goes, the grand "friendship" between us, which, after "The Announcement", shall change to subservience. Then we shall play a new game. We shall call it "Don't get raped by the Hellcat!", and they shall always lose.

A familiar landmark sticks out in our mind. A support pillar ringed with a shanty town. Platforms and hovels spiral up for hundreds of feet, disdain overcomes us and we swear under our breath. We fervently hope that the pillar was designed by morons.

Crumble down and squash these vermin. Bury them all beneath the rubble of idiocy. According to the map the place is only a mile away from here. We begin to move more cautiously, peering into alleys and up at rooftops. We soon pass by a street festival, wild music, dancing and barbequed food. We could easily murder here, but no, we mustn't dally. The masters expect quick results and we already forgot the gem. He shall be very cross even after we find the Eric Gibson. We may even be imprisoned for a century or two. Unless we find the quarry quickly, he may have already sent others. Many of our kin skulk in the shadows, for one reason or another.

The sound of celebration fades. Malodorous scum, may your beds be made of electric eels. We shall unleash a pack of hell hounds so large that it shall blot out your streets. Celebrate then, waste, on flames and snapping jaws. The roads roll and pitch, there are many hills and old stores. We are not travelling long before we see another landmark in the form of a large apartment block. The building is not tall. It is three stories, squat and long. It is half a block from the spot where our quarry spent one night. That is where we must start. We move up through the alley and turn onto a desolate street. An abandoned warehouse obscures the base of our target but the top can be seen, medieval turrets and pitched roofs. As we move towards it, we get a feeling, like eyes on our back, it's never wrong. We continue but we glance behind us. The blood heat of three can be seen. One is perched on high, while the other two sit in a room beneath. The building is a small, blocky apartment, far up the street and long abandoned. We continue, peering up the alley as we pass. At its end we see a heavy steel gate and a wall. Then it strikes us. The building shall be secure. The three are not looking for us. They wait for our quarry. We turn to the left and head up the sidewalk, past more desperation encased in brick and glass, not open. We see the wall of the place, past a few more sad little stores, it is tall. There are sensors and other electronics that we do not recognize. But then we smell the air, and we are struck by a scent that we do recognize. An Asura, demi-god, it smells of earth. We cringe and move quickly up the street. They are not there now, the group in this "castle". We seethe and swear under our breath. Asura can be very dangerous, even more dangerous than our kin. They are chaotic and unstable. We have met their kind before, though this one's scent is not entirely familiar. We must report this new development to the masters, oh how we wish that we hadn't forgotten the gem. We were in such a hurry. But we can't return to our dark heart now, we cannot lose the time. Then we are struck by a thought. If the three are waiting for the Eric Gibson they will probably know what he looks like, him, and the others who live here, it is not just the Asura. There were other scents present. We laugh and quicken our pace, moving to the end of the block then turning back up towards the three. We must be crafty. They shall have weapons as well. We shall murder the one on the roof and then take his flesh. Then we shall use it to murder the other two. Once they are all dead we shall steal their intelligence and use it. We shall also find a place that we can use to observe the "castle", if we need to. One of these surrounding buildings shall serve; many of them are empty and devoid of life.

We reach the cross-street leading to the three. A small group of Humans sit on an apartment stoop across the street. They are busy with some gambling game using cards that are placed on the stairs. Yes, cultivate greed and discordance imbeciles. Strike out at one another with foul rapacity. We laugh and move to the building occupied by the three. As we approach we see it immediately, a camera is perched above the door. We quickly walk past and turn into the alley. We stop and look around, squat apartments on one side, fire-gutted house beside it. We are not being watched. We undress and take our natural form. The pistol and magazines are retrieved and put in our small leather pouch. The shadows cover us and we jump to the wall then scurry up it, making sure to avoid the pools of light. A Human male is on the roof. He is using a viewing device. He is not obviously armed. We are sure that he has a weapon though. We look around the roof. A tiny shack contains a grey, steel door. There is probably a staircase just beyond. We grin savagely and pick up a cracked brick. The shadows erase us as we slink across the tar then climb up onto the staircase shack. The Human is down in front of us. We twist around and toss the brick down, behind the staircase shack. The Human reacts quickly, drawing a submachine gun and turning in one fluid motion. We wait patiently, aiming the pistol while shielded by the shadows. The Human says something, we cannot hear. He looks up, but he does not see us for we are a part of the shadows. He moves to the door and peers around the corner of the shack. We grin and put the pistol away. Our long tail is lowered as a noose. We garrote him and leap from the building. He coughs and falls, we swing taught against the front of the building and we pull hard. A satisfying crunch lowers us another three inches as his spine breaks. We quiver with delight and leap back to the roof, gamblers none the wiser. We gaze at the Human, implanted cybernetics, he may have warned the others. We grin maliciously. Soon it will not matter. We transform our flesh, on the outside we look like the Human. We laugh then steal his clothes and weapons, a large knife and the submachine gun. It is more dangerous than our gun. We make sure that it is loaded and we head inside through the door. The smell of dust and decay is strong. We smile and descend the stairs. The two in the room are the only other blood heat in this building. We find them easily. They may see us now, but it does not matter. They shall not know, until it is too late. We move to the door, it opens as we reach for it.

"Damn it Jenkins, you're not supposed to leave ..." His face turns to surprise as we shoot him. Bullet after bullet strikes him, his armor stops some of them but we adjust, and his brains strike the ceiling. We squeal in joy and aim at the other, an Elf female. She rolls and fires her weapon at us, bullets hit the door and wall near us. We shoot her. A handful of bullets split her head like a melon. We laugh wildly, then stop, glance around and listen. We need not be worried, not here. The Marshalls shall not be called. We shove the Human male further into the room and close the door. It is a small apartment devoid of most furnishings. There are two computers and a display however. We reload the submachine gun and retrieve the corpse's magazines, piling them in the pockets with the others. We smile at the new weight. We wish for a billion bullets. We wish for an ocean of them. The holographic display is on. We move to it, change dialogues and begin to look through the images. The first appears. *"Xanshudan", Dark Elf, Male, said to be the host for a Manifer Spirit, extremely dangerous practitioner of "The Art", leader of the mercenary team know to some as "The Decided".* We cycle the image. *"Eve", Elf, Female, a dangerous practitioner of "The Art", thought to have acted as a high level assassin, unconfirmed.* We cycle the image. *"Devlin", Human, Male, a talented magician of the sorcerer style, accompanied file lists arcane background and current family status.* We cycle the image. *"Cable", Human, Male, former special forces, veteran of more than a dozen campaigns, accompanied file lists known cybernetics, may be incomplete.* We cycle the image. *"Silver Dancer", Elf, Female, file pending,* we scratch our head then cycle the image. *"Rex", Asura (Shi Guardian), Male, a more powerful than average example of this species of Asura, use extreme caution. Do not engage without magical support.* There you are Asura. We have not seen your type before. But now we know what you look like. We cycle the image. A tall Human teen, the words *Eric Gibson* then *the target, live capture only.* We grin. We perform a little dance on the corpse of the Elf woman. Now we have your name and your face Eric Gibson. Now we shall curse you to a brutal destiny. Now we shall find you, no matter where you go. We steal the display. It is small and easily carried. A search of the room reveals nothing else of interest. We must not linger here. The Marshalls shall not come, but soon others from this Koshikawa place shall know that these ones are dead. We laugh and walk to the hall, closing the door behind us. Now, to find a suitable perch to watch this "castle" from, just in case our trail leads nowhere. This is their home. They shall inevitably return. After we find the perch we shall go to the place where the trail ends, the spot where the scrying stopped, an abandoned church of Zool on the fourth level of the city. We shall go to this church once we have found a tricky place to watch their home from, we must consider every potential if we are to succeed. We must ensure that this Eric Gibson knows perpetual torment soon. We must serve him up to be sacrificed, so that we can return to our great plan.

Silver Dancer

The lights flicker to life revealing green-grey walls. White iron bars encase the cells. The paint is flecking badly. She looks at the generator, some minor patchwork, that's all. Containment cells occupy most of the free space around it. She checks the leads again before locking the cell door, offering the generator some minor protection anyway. Her metallic fingers clack against the handle of the tool box, and Eric's voice drifts down the stairwell as she ascends.

"Hey, sweet, it looks like the power's on."

"Good, yeah that generator will give us twenty-four hours of juice on a single tank, give or take, just don't use tons of electricity," she responds as she turns off the basement lights and looks over at Eric. He's standing shyly. She can tell that he has a thing for her. It might be superficial like so many others, maybe not. He's sweet though and kind of cute. "Follow me. You can help me set up the sensor turret." He nods eagerly and follows. *He's probably staring at my ass,* she thinks, *it's normally all part of the strategy.* She once used the half-second of a cleavage stare to draw her TTM4 and blast three gangers to bloody chunks. Another time it allowed her to use her finger razors to slash a large Orc's throat; he was leering right till the end. She shakes her head. Sex becomes a tactic as well. "The Warrens" are unforgiving in that way, no room for mistakes. You need to use every edge that you have. They reach the second level. Devlin's in the living room working on a ward. Xan and Eve are getting the employee lounge ready, folding beds and strongboxes.

"Good job with the generator," Xan says from the lounge's open door.

"Sure, no problem, where are Cable and Rex?" Xan points to the balcony door.

"Rex is outside taking another look around, he seems uneasy about something." She nods. Rex is fascinating, but she doesn't trust him. He is an Asura after all. Xan continues, "Cable is fortifying the factory to the north east, he's setting up some claymores and one of the sentries there. We figured that the other sentry could be placed in the central office of the first level. We'll position it to face the front door and then conceal it in some way." She nods, makes sense, it will then serve as an alarm system that'll cover the basement as well. She points to the sensor turret.

"Eric and I were just about to set up the overwatch turret."

Xan looks at Eric then says, "Take Eve instead, Eric shouldn't step outside, especially right now." She considers for a second then nods her assent. That makes sense too. Eric seems defeated. She smiles at him and he perks up a few degrees. "Hey Eve, you mind helping Dancer for a sec?" Xan asks. Eric wanders over to the living room and sits on a couch. Eve soon strides into the main room.

"The turret?" she says as she points at the collection of parts.

Silver Dancer nods and says, "Yeah, can you grab the tower? I'll get the sensor head, the cord and the base." Eve nods and hefts the stout post. Silver Dancer grabs the base and cord with her left arm. She grabs the flat, black sensor head with her right hand. Eve begins to move to the porch door while asking.

"Out there right?" Dancer nods. Eric crosses to the door in a chivalrous effort. He can't seem to figure out the mag-lock though. She laughs to herself.

"There's a button on the frame, just beside the door knob," she offers. He fumbles for it and then opens the door, T-90 jangling under his arm. Eve steps into the stairwell and begins heading up. Dancer smiles as she passes and says "Thanks".

He blushes and responds with a quiet "You're welcome." The winding staircase culminates in a second steel door. She opens the door and walks out onto the large balcony. The bell tower is empty and boarded up. The stairs leading to its pinnacle are clogged with stones and pieces of old wood.

"Rex?" she says. A moment passes before the porch is suddenly occupied by the bestial demi-god.

"You called, my lovely?" he says. She smiles, his scales are beautiful in this light, each one a tiny sapphire cave.

"I was just wondering if you were out here, can we get past?" she says as she points to the peak of the pitched roof.

"Surely, but be careful now, don't fall," he taunts as he bounds nimbly to the roof and then abruptly leaps to the neighboring building, some thirty feet away.

She laughs. "Show off."

Eve grins and says "I don't know, his landing was kind of sloppy." She then leaps to the center of the roof and lands perfectly on the peak, holding the pole laterally like a tight-rope walker. Silver Dancer laughs.

"You're a show off too though." She then sticks out her tongue.

Eve tilts her head and says, "Yeah, yeah, so is that base even going to work on this type of roof?" Silver Dancer walks cautiously out onto the roof, one foot on either side of the peak.

"Yeah, it's fine, you can fold out some braces to accommodate a pitched roof," she says as she slowly approaches Eve. The turret is anchored and set after a few minutes. She then unspools the power cable and leads it back across the roof to the porch. Eve follows. "Can you just hold this for a second? I need to grab an extension cord," she says.

Eve grabs the cord and says, "Where are you even going to plug this in?" Silver Dancer heads for the door to the staircase and points to the plug, recessed in a pillar at the corner of the porch.

"Oh, right," Eve says, the cord taut in her hand. Dancer laughs and enters the building, using her newly recoded mag-key. She arrives at the living space. Devlin is still crafting the ward, admittedly not one of his specialties. Still, any ward is better than no ward. Eric is watching, he looks up and smiles as she enters.

"Need to grab an extension cord," she says as she walks past into the lounge.

Eric stutters then says, "Okay." She enters the room. Xan is checking his weapons. Kane's voice erupts from his palm.

"Oh sweet sexiness, if I knew any poetry I would totally spout some right about now." She shakes her head. Xan gives her an apologetic look. She doesn't understand that choice, a spectral parasite. He does benefit in a number of interesting ways. Still, she'd never agree to that arrangement. Xan's going through his gear. He's dangerous enough with his fists and feet. Today he brought a fully modified TT9X assault rifle, complete with a forty millimetre under-barrel grenade launcher. She looks at her bag. The cord is there, with her equipment. She grabs it and heads back into the living room.

"So, what does the sensor turret do?" Eric asks as she approaches. She considers for a second.

"It's a sort of combination scanner assembly including a long and short wave radar, a sonic detector and a particulate scanner. It will be able to create a detailed three dimensional map of the area within a one thousand foot radius. The scanner also gives all sorts of useful information, like material composition or the molecular construction of the air." She says. Eric sits quietly for a moment.

"Cool, I'd like to see the map when it's done." She smiles.

"Sure, I'll connect the cord and we can power it up, it only takes a few seconds to scan the area." He nods, obviously excited. She looks him up and down. She's never dated anyone younger than herself before, only older. Sometimes they're quite a bit older. It might be an interesting change of pace.

The porch door opens once again and she ascends the stairs then exits onto the porch. She takes the cord from Eve and connects the extension, which is in turn connected to the outlet. She hears the faint hum of electricity flowing to the turret. "There we go, thanks Eve," she says. Eve nods and walks back to the church. Silver Dancer stands for a few seconds. Misty grey clouds float through the tiny sliver of visible sky. Black specks wheel and dive in the distance. She turns and walks from the porch. Eric is there to meet her. "Mission accomplished, come on. I'll show you the system," she says as she walks past the kneeling Devlin, his hands putting together some unseen puzzle. Eric follows her closely.

"Is the turret up?" Xan asks as they enter the lounge. Eve is sitting cross-legged on the bed, meditating.

"Yeah, I was going to show Eric then get right to work."

Xan nods and says, "Good, co-opt all the potential cameras in the area then make contact with Cassandra before you start your research." She nods, grabs her porta-comp and sits on her folding bed. She pats the spot beside her and looks at Eric. He blinks wildly and sits, he's breathing hard. *That's funny,* she thinks, *he's naive.* She activates the porta-comp and calls up the turret program. The software is activated, and before long, a spherical, three-dimensional map is created of the surrounding area. The map includes a readout featuring everything from exact molecular compositions, to the number of cockroaches in the general vicinity, which ends up being fairly disturbing to say the least. Eric stares at the reams of data for a moment then says, in an uncertain voice.

"Do you think that you could you put up a translation in Human, northern dialect. Please?"

She laughs and says, "You learn quickly, yeah sure." She adjusts the display to show the translation as well. Eric begins to read. He nods slowly and smiles.

"Cool, it even says what the windows and desks are made of and what is that, a paperweight?" She smiles.

"Particulate scanners are pretty thorough; they tend to have a limited range though." He nods and looks back to the readout. *He's not a bad guy,* she thinks, *just a bad situation.* She knows what that's like. She was on the street early on, lost her arm young, but she kept going. Xan saw her talent. He saw her as more than just a piece of meat.

Another minute passes as Eric looks at the display. "Alright, I should start," she says as she collapses the display. She then adds, "If you want to look at the scanner again, Xan has a porta-comp with the same program, I'm sure that he'd let you use it." Eric looks around; Xan is in the living room.

He then says, "Okay, cool. I'll leave you to do your thing or work or whatever you do." She laughs, he lights up.

"Yeah, it shouldn't take long," she says. He grins and stands, then walks to the doorframe and pauses before looking back. Xan's voice prompts him forward again.

"Hey Eric, Devlin's done with the ward, he wanted to show you some things about magic." Silver Dancer hauls her legs up and lies down on the folding bed. She places the porta-comp beside her on the bed and unfurls the fiber optic cable. She searches for the port at her temple then closes her eyes.

When she opens them again she's the Silver Dancer. A buxom ballerina wrought out of living chrome. She sends out a scanning pulse. The weave here is sparse. The chrome dancer then throws a silvery ball into the air, a custom made smart-frame that rapidly grabs hold of her weave line. The program then begins to hop her digital trail through weave hubs at random, making her virtually untraceable. She enters the address of her public camera node of choice. The dancer blurs, and is soon standing across from the simple spherical node. She activates her forged I.D. program. A large list of I.D. icons appears in a window, floating in her field of vision. She selects the public camera system tag then applies it to her avatar. She then enters the node, as always, under the guise of "Ella Spencer", a falsified employee. The stone hall stretches out before her. *Those are new,* she thinks, *cyber nets, lots of them. They must have detected a recent intrusion.* She shrugs and flies through them to the central operating system. The chrome dancer activates her smart-frame template software. She'll infect the system with a series of "Watch dogs", same parameters as her military detection software, simple. She begins to create the programs. The coding piles together as she arranges its design. The task is soon complete, and she accesses the central system in order to quickly identify all of the possible cameras in the immediate vicinity, including the ones on the levels both above and below this one. She soon has twelve different cameras covered by the tenacious smart-frames. If they detect anything they'll send a warning through twenty-five relays and then to her weave construct. The construct will then send a signal message to a disposable phone before it disintegrates. The message conveys the street that the target is on, and the time that it was detected. The chrome dancer smiles and steps back out of the node.

She glides through her digital world for a little while. She'll have to start her research soon. That's one I.D. that she doesn't have yet, Raavel's College. They'd never just let her look at their ancient texts and manuscripts. She'd have to be some level of the circle, or an initiate of the stinky bummed weasels, or whatever. She doesn't pay attention when it comes to magic, as long as the spells work she doesn't care about the particulars. She'll have to create a new I.D.—that will take a little time, time and money. She'll do that before calling Cassandra, it might take her contact a while to acquire an I.D. template. Good thing she knows just where to go. She hovers for a few seconds more then, at a thought, the chrome dancer flashes into the digital sky.

Rudeboy's shack is misleading. She knows the amount of money and time that he spends on security. The bamboo shack is festooned with paraphernalia, bones, drums, jars and snake skins. It is exquisitely detailed. The shack itself is on a small floating island, complete with a tiny marsh. The island represents free construct space, using the internal excesses of digital landscapes to create moving virtual domains. They can normally only be found by those who have the address, like her. Though there are other ways to infiltrate these illicit constructs, hence the defenses. The chrome dancer approaches the shack. A Human skull dangling from a thick twine turns towards her. The deep voice of Rudeboy comes through the skull's open mouth.

"Dancer, well, well. I'd thought that you'd reached the limits of what my services could provide?" The skulls jaw snaps shut. The chrome dancer laughs and spins a series of perfect pirouettes.

"It would seem that there is always a need for a new I.D." The skull's mouth snaps open.

"Now you're speaking my language. Won't you enter my humble abode?" The shacks door opens and she glides through the threshhold. The inside is expansive; it's styled after a rough bar. There are animal heads mounted on the walls, while bones and skulls of all types decorate the various surfaces. A skeletal figure stands behind the bar. He's wearing a long tattered coat ending in split tails. His dress pants are ragged and torn. Two ruby lights glow in his eyes sockets. The chrome dancer crosses to the bar. Small groups of freakish dolls track her movement, they're clutching daggers. They're modeled after a Witch Doctors "Slasher Spirit" doll. She's only ever seen a real one once. It was the single creepiest thing she'd ever seen. That is until it leapt ten feet and stabbed a man in the chest with a butcher knife. Then *that* was the creepiest thing that she'd ever seen. She looks back towards the bar.

"I like what you've done with the place," she says, a covert scan revealing a cluster of new counter measures, including the dolls.

"I like to keep ahead of the curve, it's important in this business. So what type of template are you looking for today? I'll tell you if I have it, if not I may be able to acquire it, for an additional fee of course." He clasps his hands on the bar top after that final statement. She smirks.

"I need a top level research I.D. template for Raavel College." Rudeboy sucks air through his virtual teeth into his non-existent lungs.

"That is a template that I do not have, but, one that I can acquire, it would take a couple of hours to meet my contact. It will also cost an additional five K." Silver Dancer ponders for a second. Xan will reimburse her, or at least he damn well better. If not him maybe Cassandra, she's super rich, it'll be considered research costs.

The chrome dancer nods and says, "Make it sooner rather than later." She then accesses her digital funds and transfers the fifteen K, glaring at her remaining balance. There better be some recompense, or she may just have to re-consider the whole 'bank skimming smart-frame' route to financial gain.

Rudeboy flashes a skeletal grin and says, "I'm on it then, check back in two hours." She nods and floats from the building. *It's good I guess*, she thinks, *it'll help Eric too; he must be so freaked out right now.* She lingers for a second before calling up her encrypted phone software. She connects to Cassandra's line. It immediately goes dead. She pauses for a second, then hits connect again. It immediately goes dead again. She begins to get worried. The mansions weave address appears in her field of vision. The chrome dancer soars and a second later she's standing in front of the weave construct counterpart to the mansion. The platinum building is her piece of programming, her design. She approaches the building and peers into the coding. It's foreign, and there's an encryption that isn't hers, it's extremely advanced. She scans the area, nothing. She looks at the encryption again. The style seems familiar somehow. She doesn't quite understand the pattern though. A few minutes pass as she analyzes the encryption. Slowly, it begins to make sense as she unravels the style. Then it strikes her, she has seen this coding before, just once. She was paid to restore a ganger's node to its original state after they had been hacked. The job happened after an assassin by the name of Grimmfang had killed a large swath of the gang, apparently just after their computers went haywire, leaving them exposed. She gets a slow sinking sensation in the pit of her stomach. Fhaligun "The Wonderful One", that's what he calls himself. That's who pulled the job, he even bragged about it afterwards. That can only mean one thing. Her heart begins to race. Grimmfang was at the mansion. Fhaligun wouldn't dare to cross Cassandra, unless that freak was in his corner. And if Grimmfang was there, it must mean that he's after Eric. She begins breathing quickly, withdraws through the weave and returns to her entrance point before cancelling the integration. She stands, her heart pounding in her chest. *We can't let that monster get to Eric*, she thinks, *we have to protect him, but then, who's going to protect us?* She composes herself and looks at the doorway, the sound of laughter filters in. She swallows and closes her eyes. *Xan has to know*, she thinks.

Rex

Impetuous creatures, these mortals, they lack such awareness. Writhing about and battling the changes that they dance to. There are times that this discord may manifest in purity of function and subliminal intent. They enliven these moments, they animate themselves. The rest becomes a fall into repetitious patterns of reliving old glories and recapturing impossibilities. A series of fragmented justifications for time lost. The middle path always seems just outside of their realization, a balance in life, if such a thing exists.

Illusion of control shall ruin us as the hounds pick up the trail. I know Xan feels that we are safe, but no one can hide. I know the hound's intent. In knowing it I know the course that it shall produce, there is but one outcome. Chaos shall have its say, as it always does. Our path may alter the nature of the outcome; however its form shall remain. Not only shall its form remain, its function shall as well, a function which has proven to be more ruthless by far.

Curious one, this Eric Gibson, he's such a baby in so many ways. A fool mired in the strife produced by his own yearnings, not an uncommon state. He does adapt well however, speaking with nightmare beasts and unimaginable figures. A lesser mind would recoil, snap back through dementia, and never be found again. Dancer has taken a bit of an interest in him. He stares at her as though lust was a commodity, flashing his passion as some sacred lucre. Her desires are less than fathomable. Still, the gleam of that prize may yet attract her attention. We all like something different, every now and then. Only time shall tell, just as it always does, the blabbermouth in the theatre of life. I must now go for a stroll. I must now imbibe these new surroundings and hear the voice of the earth again, lest I am mired in perilous stagnation.

A slothful curtain of steam caresses the fortress balcony. Rex stretches lazily, dragging hard claws across the stone deck. The dim perimeter lights catch the whorls of his scales as he arcs and twists his back. His vibrant mane of red fur seems to gleam with its own inner glow, pouring ever upward as if caught in a reversed waterfall. The large animalistic Asura tastes the air. His vibrant eyes radiate power as he peers through the gloom. He moves slowly and confidently across the fortress's pitched roof. The chosen route leads past the sensor turret, and Silver Dancer's silent observation. Ambling briskly to the edge, he looks over briefly before leaping

223

easily to the neighboring building's roof. An explosion of pigeons burst angrily from the shadows as he lands. He glances sharply in their direction, deciding whether a snack on the wing would hit the spot. He decides against it for the moment. Constructions of steel, brick and glass slink by as he creeps over the roof. Tonight's chosen fortress sits near this level's edge, an expanse of open air that can be seen no more than two blocks away. The scene rests uneasily in the Asura's mind; it looms as a great yawning chasm that invites chaos in doses which soon become unhealthy. He moves on. Leaping from roof to roof, feeling each new building, each new texture, each new history. The earth has no voice here. The scream of the city drowns it out completely.

Ancient manufacturing concerns cluster in the grimy corners of this level's vast support pillars. Urban caves for nocturnal terrors and homes for urban hunters. Hopping gracefully to the guard rail's support bracket, Rex pauses at the level's precipice. Focusing keen eyes, he takes in the evening and the sprawling city below. A vast carpet of life, here a vendor serves roasted rat to gleeful Orcish teens. There, a nefarious deal occurs as credits shift to one and product to the other. Here, a group of corpies exit their limo for a night of slumming it, while there a lone enforcement officer sits in the midst of a forest of corruption. Roof-top gatherings and giant snarls of traffic locked in a perpetual dance. The pattern of chaos is as palpable as the myriad scents that drift on the breeze.

Axiomatic addiction pervades. One is never satisfied with the now. In dearth of consequence the tenants of chaos sharpen. The new comfort of their dwellings encourages them to greater depths. However, the malleable nature of chaos sees it in the opposing role as well. As Cable would say: "luck and chaos are your only savior". But there is no saviour here. None of these creatures shall depart from their chosen course, their consequences are set. You can't change the nature of a man. Sharpened blades, naked lust and bullets fired out of wrath, or worse, duty. You can't charge the nature of a man either. The costs are as uniquely variable as their aspect.

I deplore the very prospect of corporate intrigue. These well-funded armies, drones, soldiers and wage mages. They won't forget, they won't cease in their depravity, as long as profits are nigh. I have less to worry about than the others, of course. It's difficult to kill that which is only partially here. Still, magic is a concern. Never underestimate your foes. Praise wise "Origal of Nammurath", learn well his lessons or be consumed utterly by your own folly. You're not indestructible as others might believe, and there is something else out there. Trust this feeling now, chaos tainted with evil. Rank insanity writhing about in a mutated circus of faith. I smell the stink of old Thraligothrossolithoshrithox, nameless one, one of many names, perverter and corruptor. Chaos, as expressed through annihilation and delusion. It is as I feared. The stench of madness cannot be concealed. Rather, it congeals in the mind as stagnant puss. The Abyssal cult has staked its claim. I see them now. Small groups here and there, with sigils of dementia fitted into their flesh and clothes. The spirit realm stains with their passing, and long eddies of dark mist now suffuse the spectral sky. I must warn Xan. This variable shall be fatal if left unchecked. Madness has a way of becoming implacable in the face of hardship, unwavering in its crash course until the bitter end. They shall sink us all. And just as vultures bring other scavengers, the warp taint shall draw jackals, jackals of darkness and jackals of light. They shall all come to feed upon the carrion of the deranged, and they shall trample all who protest in their wake.

Rex turns from the steaming city scene and vaults back to the factory, gripping the pitched roof with his forepaws and strong leg talons. The return course unfolds naturally before him as he aligns his body with the axis of chaos. Leaping, stalking and sprinting in kind, he returns swiftly to the fortress. The dark brick of the converted church reveals itself to him as he approaches. The building was first turned into a barracks for the local enforcement center back when this district was booming. The church's sturdy stone walls and thick steel doors provide a great deal of protection against any assault. Rex enters through the bell tower balcony. Reaching the reinforced steel door he hits the intercom button with a long black claw, Silver Dancer's digital voice chimes in.

"Way ahead of you honey." Rex opens the door without saying a word. He enters the staircase leading to the church's second level as the door locks behind him. A convection oven is running in the adjacent kitchen, smells like instant food slabs. Rex would prefer to eat a live pigeon while it was shitting down his throat, but that's just him. Xan appears agitated.

"Rex, we need to talk, we've had news." Xan turns to address the large Asura as he plods up, claws and talons clicking against the

225

floor tiles. Eric turns to look, eyes wide with wonder. Rex flashes him a smile and bobs his head in the approximation of a bow. Eric just seems mesmerized, staring with intense fascination.

"Yes of course, we shall retire to my chambers and discourse."

Rex nods at the others then turns and heads for the storeroom at the far end of the modified second level. He peers down through the staircase to the church's first level as he passes. Xan slowly stands and follows, entering the Asura's temporary chambers and closing the door behind him.

Xan looks at Rex, breathes deeply then says, "We tried to make contact with Cassandra, there's no response from the mansion. Silver Dancer saw traces of Fhaligun's programming signature, which can mean only one thing."

"Grimmfang?" Rex asks.

"That's what we're afraid of, the Gnome is rabidly anti-corp and he works exclusively for a handful of clients. Grimmfang's the only one who's capable of taking out the mansion's defenses before Cassandra could send out an alert," Xan responds.

"What shall we do?" Rex asks.

"You have to stay here, guarding Eric is imperative, but I need to check it out, there's still a chance that she's alive," Xan responds immediately, a swell of emotion coming through his voice. Rex considers for a second.

"She may yet live, insanity gives no reason. He may have done any number of things, but be careful Xanshudan. The cyborg is a savant. A natural born killer built into a monstrosity. He has become an augmented servant of the true death. There is manifest destiny in his path, the likes of which I have not seen as yet."

"Yeah, I know Rex; I've read the stories just like everyone else. I have no intention of confronting him. I'll just put on another face, grab a cab somewhere near One Hundred and Seventh Street, then transfer to a monorail for the last leg of the trip," Xan says. He then thinks for a moment and asks, "Did you see anything on your walk?" Rex frowns.

"It would appear that the tendrils of the Abyss are out in force. If they come to us they shall draw the attention of many others, the likes of which you may well imagine."

"Oh that's just great! Those smelly freaks, that's all we need!" Kane opines loudly.

"Shit, that's not good. Do you know if they are aware of our location?" Xan asks, ignoring Kane's whining.

"It is uncertain at this time, but the time of its occurrence is a certainty. A day, a week, we must begin to seek answers or we shall drown yet in a tide of mutated flesh." Rex turns to the corner of his room and the large redwood chest therein. Richly carved spectral steel covers the chest's edges and corners. Its ornate lock is wrought in the face of a fierce, fiery Asura, with the keyhole located in its fanged mouth.

"We may have lost Elindriss but we have several other channels active, not to mention Silver Dancer. We need more time," Xan exclaims, he then adds, "If we can just hide out for a while we might get our answers."

"You know my opinion on hiding. But there may yet be another way, we spoke of it before." Rex inserts a single claw into the chest's keyhole and turns it precisely to the right. The lid opens smoothly to reveal a small collection of arcane esotery. Xan crosses over to the chest and looks inside. Rex motions towards the back wall of the chest where three small drawers are recessed in the thick wood of the chest's interior.

"The middle one," Rex suggests. Xan leans down and opens the drawer. A small crystal bead filled with swirling colors rolls to the front of the drawer and stops with a sharp click.

"A portal gem?" Xan exclaims.

"Ooo feed it to me would you Xan, they're one of the only things that I can actually taste." Kane moans and makes rude slavering noises.

"That's a six thousand dollar meal spirit, and it's not for eating," Rex answers.

"Come on Xan, lend us six k will you? Or are you actually thinking of using that thing?" The small face on Xan's palm looks genuinely concerned. Rex makes a note of that.

"Worry not vulgar spectral parasite, it does not head to where you may think." Rex smiles at Xan and raises his bushy red eyebrows.

"You're thinking about going to 'The Flux' again?" Xan asks while thoughtfully touching his chin. His eyes flash back and forth. Rex has seen that look before, the thinking pose.

"Feeling homesick?" Kane taunts. Rex laughs. It's been thirty-five years since he last felt the soft loam of the earth that bore him. A mere blink of an eye in the life of an Asura, he could spend a thousand years roving and still that place would never leave his mind. He sees the sky of churning life, the ground alive with change, revelling in the dance of discord. He soaks in the vistas of his mind for a moment more before reasserting his presence.

"If we must hide as the hounds close in, there is no better land than that which never rests. The trail becomes obscured and impossible to follow for those who cannot see the truth of it,"Rex suggests.

"It's also exhausting and dangerous to non-Asura. What about the council? Can we seek asylum?" Xan asks, still deep in thought.

"It's best not to interfere with Asura politics; it may incite the clans, and force them to make representations," Rex retorts.

"I thought you had disavowed your oath?" Xan remarks.

"The concern is not over my situation. There shall always be tension there, Asura have long memories. The concern is that other clans shall not want to appear uninformed. Information is power, and power craves wealth." Rex sits on his haunches and lets Xan think for a moment.

"You're saying they would sell us out if we approached the council?" Xan asks.

"Not the council per se. They have honour and even the proponents of chaos are bound by their own strictures, others are far less scrupulous however."

"You mean the fire clans?" Xan asks.

"Fire, air, water, earth, each has its black sheep. Their dark wool attracts flies that are darker still, and rather than swatting the vermin they shall receive their proffered filth, so long as it shines like gold." Rex lets the thought sink in for a moment.

"They deal with Infernals then?" Xan's gaze wanders back to the multi-colored bead.

"Any and all, their origin is of no consequence," Rex responds.

"Just like good little extra-dimensional whores," remarks Kane. Rex glares at the small spectral emanation, wondering briefly what it would taste like.

"We all whore ourselves for one price or another, and for one cause or another," Rex replies, somewhat agitated by the spirit's lack of respect.

"But you think that we can simply avoid them?" Xan asks, a disbelieving tone filtering through his voice.

"By ourselves? No. But the Flux branches off into mountains and valleys, rivers and trees, great deserts and small fuming grottos, and amidst them all the great sculptor Arguss plies his trade, unseen and uninvolved. We were friends once and we shall be again, the cycle has come," Rex says prophetically.

"Arguss? You've spoken of him before. You believe that he could shelter us?" Xan asks.

"If any could it would be him, he also may know a seer," Rex replies, glancing down at the crystal bead of whirling color.

Xan stands for a moment, right hand clutched under his chin, his eyes moving from side to side as if reading an invisible script.

"I'll run it past the others and see what they think. In the meantime I was wondering if you could check out the old line-tunnel that we passed on the way in here. I don't like its proximity to this place. We should see where it leads and plug it or trap it if we need to." Xan places the portal gem back in the drawer and closes it.

"It shall be done. Shall I announce myself or should this be a clandestine affair?" Rex asks.

"Keep it quiet for now. If you come across any critters maybe try to scare them off using your natural charms?" Xan offers.

"Surely, but if anything tasty appears I won't hesitate to dine. I'm getting hungry and the smell of that food slab is beginning to create disturbing cravings in my gut," Rex retorts. Kane laughs while Xan nods his assent.

Xan then adds, "I'll speak with the others quickly and head for Cassandra's. It shouldn't take long for me to return."

"I truly hope for the best Xanshudan, but do not get your hopes up." Xan looks at the ground and then to Rex, he nods and turns to open the door. He exits briskly, leaving Rex to ponder his next task.

Entropic paragons of greed and rancor know no bounds. Acquisition through social ataxia, bleed the desperate with influence fueled effluence, as it has ever been. The enemies stink shall always belie their presence. Recall your senses. Your kin are both worse and better than these mortal things. Intrinsic being propels them, but passion guides them. And paragons of passion will gamble in ways that drive one to distraction. Disarray existing as the only pattern within their experience. And experience does not connote wisdom, only change, only the recollections of transpirations. To interpret is to rise above. Remember always the teachings of wise "Origal of Nammurath". Reflect but do not become a reflection. Remain present in this place and your blood shall not darken the sewers of their industriousness. Those who would seek to sell you are only paragons of self-destruction. Remember the teachings! Greed can be guided and rancor can be sent screaming off of a high cliff. One just has to remain patient.

Xan is in grief now, I see the pain in him. The cyborg is the nemesis of life, he rarely leaves survivors. He may even be lying in wait, using the one soft point that Xanshudan has, a broken heart that has never healed. Should an ambush unfold I fear that I shall lose a close friend. Xan is a warrior of the highest caliber but the cyborg has foreordination. I have seen his kind before. Always taking the path less traveled. He moves at different angles, in thought and deed. A murderous creature made legend. We shall have to repel him using all of our guile and might. I shall break this body against him if I must, for some strange compulsion slowly grips my imagination. There's an incalculable sensation that beckons me to stand with this "dreamer", and guard him. It feels like an instinct born aeons ago, and designed for some unknown purpose that cannot be denied.

Rex exits into the still night air. Not wanting to attract attention, he cloaks himself in the arcane power that brings invisibility. Simple enough to do, Rex reaches internally and touches his chaotic core for a moment and instantly he vanishes from sight. Only the soft click of his claws against the pavement remains to gainsay his presence. The tunnel that Xan spoke of is three short blocks to the north, in towards the city's core. Rex moves with slow purpose, passing through streets all but devoid of life. Empty facades and rusted-out cars frame his progress through the city streets. The hum of traffic can be heard overhead at some distance. He takes a slight detour through the carcass of an old building. Leaping through the empty window pane he lands on a dirty, hard-wood floor. His paws send up a dust cloud that briefly outlines his form, as the echo of his landing bounces up through the rafters. Ghostly paw prints appear as he makes his way across the building's floor. He exits the building and steps onto the street running parallel to the tunnel. There's a rundown station sitting just outside of the tunnel's entrance. He focuses for a moment, scanning the scene with his wondrous sight. There's a strip mall across the way, as well as a diner, pawn shop and some other small sign-less stores, all long since closed. Parts of the tracks, guard rails and most of the street lights are missing, sold for scrap no doubt.

Rex proceeds up to the mouth of the stone and concrete tunnel. All of the other streets and alleys leading to the fortress have cameras which are being monitored by Silver Dancer's smart-frames. This tunnel has no camera coverage, or electricity for that matter. He draws in the murky breeze coming from the tunnel, dozens of scents filter in. *Not much air travel here*, he thinks. Still, something familiar strikes him. Cautiously he enters the tunnel while slowing his pace, so as to make less noise. The tunnel curves slowly to the right. He progresses further and further into its crumbling construction. He's travelled for no more than two minutes when he begins to hear sounds coming from up ahead. Stopping, and instinctively crouching low, he begins to listen more closely. Voices, he hears voices and the sound of movement. Rex proceeds up the tunnel, even more slowly this time. Upon rounding the next bend he spots the source of the noise. Koshikawa scouts,

Xan was right. He takes the measure of the situation. Five soldiers, light armor, silenced assault rifles, grenades and side arms. He doesn't see any magical support. He laughs inwardly, they don't stand a chance. For a moment Rex considers going back. But chaos and instinct take over, and without any further hesitation he springs forward, closing the distance in five short bounds. The soldiers twist their heads toward the sound of sudden movement. They raise their weapons and are shouting calls of alarm when, without warning, the first target is decapitated by a swift blow from an invisible paw. The four remaining soldiers panic and point their weapons randomly in an attempt to track the unseen threat. Meanwhile Rex wheels around and pounces on the closest soldier, a large Orc sporting a Mohawk. He slams his heavy body into the soldier while gouging great tattered lines through armor and flesh. The Orc crumples into a broken heap and Rex tears his head off, just to be sure. Then a Human soldier finally manages to see Rex's form, outlined in the dust cloud. He lets loose a stream of silenced bullets. The projectiles strike Rex's flank and are instantly repulsed and absorbed by his scales. Common soldiers won't have runes fused into their firearms, Rex knows this and laughs, the action coming out as an eerie roar. He then eviscerates the Human firing the "paper bullets" and turns his attention on the last two soldiers. The skinny Elven soldier is fleeing back up the tunnel, while the other Human is firing wildly at anything and everything. Rex reaches internally and touches his core of chaos. Instantly, a small distortion appears above the fleeing soldier and from it issues a flaring line of lightning which immediately incinerates half of his body. The soldier's charred remains twitch grotesquely in the grey light as Rex targets the sole survivor. The Human screams and fires a torrent of impotent bullets as Rex mauls him completely, removing his head and all but one limb in the process. Satisfied that none of the soldiers will be getting up, Rex begins to sift through their blood-soaked gear. He doesn't find any radios, cellphones or other communications devices, meaning that the soldiers more than likely have cybernetic augmentations for such purposes. He growls inwardly. He then stops and listens for a moment. There are more voices, movement, vehicles and drones. Then it dawns on him. The scouts have already found them. They've already called for reinforcements. This was simply the vanguard. He clenches his jaw, blood blending into the red fur of his short beard. *So,* he thinks, *you've done it again, chaos, old friend, you've surprised me yet again.*

Xanshudan and Kane

The melancholy streets blur. Dirty grey planes of awareness. Xan meditates in an effort to assuage the turmoil. He breathes rhythmically, unfurling thought and fear. If she has been killed there are measures that can be taken, rituals of great cost. The outcome can be uncertain however. Kane's voice fills his mind.

"So what's the plan? Run in guns blazing?"

"More like stumble up, drunk and smelly," Xan responds.

"Not the homeless man walkby scout routine, that's so played out," Xan rolls his eyes and replies.

"Well I was thinking Orc, even less approachable, but if you have a better idea I'm all ears," Kane moans.

"I had a better idea this morning, we'd be rich by now and who knows what else would've happened... or not happened."

"Stop Kane, there's no point now, what's done is done," Xan responds tersely.

"Alright, but it's not done. That's my point. If you die for this kid I might not bail you out this time." The taxi angles steeply as they enter a ramp. Xan laughs inwardly.

"Well as tragic as that seems, I suppose that it would make me just like everybody else." Kane snorts and remains quiet. Xan's first brush with death was at twelve, two bullets. The projectiles missed his heart by an inch. He still managed to finish the job before he passed out. That's the only reason that the "Venom Lords" saved him. That's the only reason that he's alive today. He peers out the window. They're on the seventh level, the entertainment district. The area is made up of thousands of studios and production companies, all situated around the TES main studio, virtually a city unto itself. The entire level produces an appalling amount of Holo-vid, VR, SIM and music products. Most of it is passable, with a few gems here and there. The rest of their stuff is garbage, serving as gruel for the sensation hungry masses. The taxi driver is a Dwarf, Sarkoff Visivich, he's dividing his attention between driving and watching the "Torus" match on the holo-vid. Rhiley Executioners vs. Tirileth City Reavers, fourth game of the series, tied 2-2.

"Are you seeing this? Give it to Stalislav! Morons!" The driver exclaims to himself. Xan peers back out the window. A holo-drone advertises "Sidney Fellows" as the next candidate for the Gold Party. A TTT corporate logo betrays his allegiance. Xan doesn't get involved in politics, corrupt and corporate- controlled, virtually down to a man. He pushes the intercom button.

"You can let me out in that parking lot." A "Greasy Guts" sits adjacent to the lot. A sign in the window advertises "2 for 1 cheeseburgers". Vat grown meat, not unlike eating a clone. He shudders. The taxi pulls into the lot and he shoves a fifty credit note through the slot. "Keep the change."

The Dwarf grins and says, "Cheers." Xan steps out of the car and adjusts the pistol under his left arm. He glances around briefly. A commercial zone, there are a number of shops and restaurants. He's on the eighth level, right near a monorail station. That track leads up to the ninth level, then there's a stop that's just two miles from the mansion.

"Seriously Xan if you're hungry go find some earth, you don't want to eat there."

Xan laughs and begins walking. "I'd sooner eat my left hand."

"Oh, har, har," Kane replies then sinks back into Xan's palm. The monorail will require a credstick, that's fine. He'll use the one identity that he hasn't used before. Fortunately he brought the perfect disguise. He walks on and it isn't long before he finds a secluded spot. He focuses inwardly.

"Alright, take the form of Darla, if you don't mind?"

Kane laughs and retorts, "Why? You want to grab your own boobs?" Xan shakes his head.

"That's what you would do Kane, and no I'm not going to let you do that either, now if you please? It's the one identity that I haven't used before, we're losing time." Xan begins to feel a swell of emotion. He breathes deeply and recenters. Kane's voice fills his mind, an uncharacteristic solemnity in his tone.

"Alright Xan, I can see that this is important to you." He then switches tones completely and adds "I told you that you still had a thing for Cassandra but you're like 'shut-up Kane you don't know anything'. But then I was sure that I caught you jerking it to her, I get glimpses of your thoughts you know buddy and sometimes I got to tell ya ..."

Xan interrupts his rant, "Kane! If you please?"

"Oh, yeah, right," Kane replies. Xan immediately transforms into a portly old Human woman. He then produces a plain dress, sweater and handbag. He retrieves the forged credstick and puts it in the handbag along with his pistol. His coat and the rest of his gear is stowed in his backpack which he then slings over his shoulders. A geriatric stroll proceeds. "You could've made her a young, hot Elf chick, like Silver Dancer's sister or something, but no, you had to go for inconspicuous, or whatever." Kane's whining fills his mind as they gradually make their way to the monorail station.

"What would you actually be like if you possessed genitalia, I'm just wondering?" Xan internalizes as he slowly mounts the platform's staircase.

Kane laughs in his head and replies, "I think we both know that I would redefine how mammals think about sex, perhaps forever. I would perform such acts of ridiculous perversion as to completely ..."

Xan interrupts, "I'm sorry I asked, let's just forget about it and be grateful." Kane scoffs telepathically. The credstick grants them access to the main platform. It's choked with commuters at this time. Several holo-displays show routes as well as departure and arrival times. After a short time the number of his train becomes apparent. "So when we get close, I need you to give me full control, just in case."

"Fine, sure, sigh, always the submissive never the dominant one," Kane responds dryly. Xan grins. A monorail glides past just behind a rush of air, the wait stretches on. Xan blends completely, remaining unnoticed by nearly everyone.

Soon, the monorail arrives, number eighteen cross-level express. He slots his credstick, and enters without a problem. Holo-display advertisements appear on every available surface. He finds a seat, as the train accelerates and quickly reaches top speed. Scenery blurs past in layers, seeming to move slower and slower as he peers into the distance. Dark sky creates a dour backdrop. He'll have to fight Grimmfang if the cyborg is holding Cassandra, even if it is suicide. He's heard tales of the assassin's combat ability. He can only hope that they're greatly exaggerated. The train glides to a halt, and passengers step on or off. Two more stops, then two more miles. He begins the mantra as he controls his breath, "Breathe in power, breathe out fear," the repetition fills his mind. Gradually the spark grows into a fire, the warrior's fire.

The old woman slowly shuffles off the train when it reaches the ninth level platform. The mansion is two miles towards the core, near to "The Warrens" but not actually located in them. The estate is surrounded on all sides by a block or more of abandoned factories and warehouses. The location's ideal for Cassandra's regular dealings, it also isolates her however. He moves into a position of concealment once again and focuses internally.

"We're close now, can I have control Kane?"

"Alright, but the safety word is 'Kumquat'." Xan laughs, and a second later he feels a flood of arcane power. The old training comes back to him, and he immediately transforms into an Orc of similar dimensions to his natural form. He changes clothes, stows the disguise and puts his pistol back in its holster. He retrieves a flask of "Viska" and takes a few sips. The clear liquid lights a fire down to his stomach. "Geez, check out the method actor over here,"Kane comments, Xan snorts.

"If Grimmfang is there, I'll bet you a million credits that he has a particulate scanner as part of his cybereye configuration. We have to *be* the part or he'll see right through the ruse." He takes another sip. The strong alcohol begins to take effect, he's getting buzzed. The alley sinks behind him as he progresses to the street, wavering slightly as he walks. "Kay, good, now if I need to do some shit, you have to puke out the alcohol right quick alright?"

Kane laughs and responds, "No problem, just be sure to hold up a lighter when I do, it will be funnier." Xan laughs. He lumbers up the sidewalk as the Orc, most seek to avoid him. The body and alcohol work in tandem to create a sort of social scarecrow effect. His mind lurches about in an alcohol haze, he doesn't usually drink. The sidewalk tilts at odd angles as he continues. Eventually he begins to blend into the crowd as the neighborhood degrades. He sees other Orcs and Goblins, some hard-looking Humans and even an Automaton. Exposed pistons and wires wrapped into a humanoid frame, its solitary lens tracks his progression. He waves and it awkwardly returns the gesture, as if it's unsure of the significance. He laughs to himself. *Nano-bots approximating life, they don't know why they're here either, just like the rest of us,* he thinks. The Orc stumbles on.

Soon he begins to see the landmarks that line the edge of Cassandra's property. He plans his route, just walk past, then up several blocks and loop around if it seems like a trap. If everything seems alright then just go straight in. Dirty brick surrounds him as he treads the chosen course. Cassandra owns a number of the outlying buildings. She had said something about developing them at some point. That obviously hasn't happened yet, unless the interiors are completely overhauled. He slows his breathing and opens his arcane senses. It takes slightly longer than usual due to alcohol's imposition. A grey haze slowly surrounds him, punctuated by small swirls of color marking animals or vermin. He arrives at the cross-street and gazes towards the mansion, trudging past as he does. No sign of an aura on the outside, she's never without gate guards. *Something's definitely wrong,* he thinks. The mansions ward is still up, he can't see past it, the latticed colors of the magical barrier bar his vision completely. He relaxes his focus and the world reshapes into its usual state. He has to assume that it's a trap. A sense of doom slowly sinks in as he walks past the mansion and up the street. A particulate scanner has a one thousand foot range, give or take. He'll have to run in from just beyond that point. He'll be attacked immediately if Grimmfang's there, the cyborg won't want to let him get away. He'll want to *question* Xan. He steels himself as he shifts back into his natural form. "Alcohol extraction if you please?" he internalizes.

"What, no lighter? Spoil sport," Kane retorts. A second later and a spray of clear fluid flows from his tiny mouth. Xan sobers instantly. He shakes his head.

"Thanks, that's better." He checks his equipment. Flash bangs, Grimmfang will have flash compensation built into his cybereyes. TTM4 with HEI rounds, it could make a dent if he's able to hit the bastard with it. The cyborg's notoriously fast. He leafs through a pile of surgeon's patches, a must, though he might not get a chance to use them. He grimaces and sighs, there's nothing else to be done. He closes his eyes and concentrates, stoking the warrior's fire. Then, two cords of arcane power stretch down through his legs, and he takes off like a shot. His legs blur as he charges forward, footfalls blend into a thunderous reverberation. Window panes rattle as he sprints past at a tremendous speed. The mansion appears as a glittering prize, locked behind a tall fence. The internal turrets might still be active. They aren't a threat until the gate has been breached though. He speeds towards the front guard house and stops with a great burst of dust. In an instant, he smoothly draws his pistol and takes cover at the edge of the guard house. If Grimmfang's here, he's aware. Xan's heart quickens as he waits, the area is calm, no signs of a struggle. He peers into the guard house window. There's blood inside, lots of blood. He aims his pistol across the front of the fence then quickly looks behind him. Kane's voice fills his mind, causing him to jump slightly.

"I don't know Xan; I don't think that you would've made it this far without something happening if he was still here."

He exhales and looks around again as he internalizes, "Yeah, you're probably right; he might be trying to lure us into the mansion though."

"I can't see past the ward, it's pretty strong."

Kane responds, "Yeah, I know." Another tense minute passes. He doesn't see anything, the mansion is completely obscured this close to the fence. He slowly edges into the guard house. Three bodies are inside, blood stains the floor. He swallows and looks them over. Two guards have their heads on backwards, the dull white of their spines showing through torn flesh. He looks to the third guard. The corpse is missing its face, a ragged hole shows where a fist destroyed the skull. He exhales sharply and glances around. No shots fired, not even a sign of a fight. They might have been killed elsewhere then moved afterwards. Xan looks at the security computer, it's locked, unresponsive. He thinks for a second. The turrets line the main driveway, they also frame the door. He steps out of the guard house. "I think you're right Kane, I don't think that he's here anymore, he might have left booby traps though."

Kane snickers, "Booby."

Xan groans. "Would you please focus?" Kane laughs as Xan continues "Now Cassandra mentioned something about significant defenses at the levels' precipice. I think there are claymores planted there or worse, we might be better off with the direct route. Jump in, leap to the roof and then hit the balcony on the other side."

"It's simple, I'll give you that."

Xan snorts and focuses on calming himself. He charges his arcane core and unleashes two pulses of energy. The ground rushes away from him as the mansion plummets through his field of vision. The main doors are blasted open. He lands in the courtyard, rolls forward and then dives through the air. Nothing happens. The forward roll is fluid and he's up and running instantly. He alters his course and reaches the door, still nothing. Kane's unimpressed voice fills his mind, "Well that was anti-climactic." Xan grins and glances around, the turrets aren't responding, they're still physically there though. He enters the lobby and checks the corners. A nervous energy washes through him as he surveys the scene. A pile of bodies, mutilated. Somebody did this intentionally. Blood pools thick beneath them. It looks like they were the guards and house staff. He breathes deeply and gazes at the pile carefully. A decapitated body stands out. Marcus, that's his coat, but his head is nowhere to be seen. He looks elsewhere. That sweet girl Katie, she's been butchered. There are more, many more. There are guards that he doesn't recognize, and others that he can't recognize anymore. He turns away, a queasy knot forming in his stomach as he looks to the office. The doors have been blasted off of their hinges. He focuses on his breathing and slowly shifts his perception. His heart skips a beat as he looks to the balcony. Cassandra's aura! It's turbulent. She's been hurt in some way. He sprints towards her. "Careful Xan, stop, it could be a trap!" Kane's warning drifts through his awareness, an ignored afterthought. He charges into the living room, it's spattered in blood and marred by bullet holes. The spectral aquarium is cracked, the spirit fish leaked back into their native realm. There, on the balcony. He sprints through the broken doors and sweeps the deck with his pistol. Cassandra's sitting on a chair, she's not moving. A row of heads sits in front of her.

"Cassandra!" He exclaims as he takes a step closer. The pieces of two guards are strewn across the balcony. She slowly looks over. Her eyes are glassy, far away.

"Xan, I wasn't expecting you." She goes to stand but instead she lurches sideways, off-balance. He moves to her instantly and catches her before she falls. "Oops, that was clumsy of me. Here let me call Katie, get you a drink?" She tries to walk but he holds her close. The heads, he swallows back his grief. Marcus and Elindriss, he doesn't recognize the others.

"Cass, are you hurt?" She looks at him and begins to shake.

She then stares off the balcony and says, "Do we have business? I'm sorry, I don't remember, you can speak with Marcus, he'll make sure that you're taken care of." Her voice is weak, distant. Xan holds her and moves slowly to the living room. White leather, flecked in red, the sculpture is no longer moving. She recoils at the sight of blood. He puts his hands on her shoulders and looks at her.

"Cass, I'm so sorry, I can't imagine ..." She begins to heave and then weep. He holds her close and shields her as they move to the front of the mansion. He makes sure that she doesn't see the pile, if she hasn't already.

Kane's voice enters Xan's thoughts. "I'm sorry Xan. I really am. I can't stand to see a beautiful woman cry."

Xan nods and internalizes. "Thanks Kane, keep an eye out would you?"

"Of course, no problem," Kane responds. Cassandra seems to drift out of a trance.

"Xan? Oh Xan! They're gone. They're all gone! They were butchered, it was horrible!" She clutches his coat and buries her face in his chest. A fresh well of tears streams down her cheeks as her body is racked by sobs. They embrace for a long time. Slowly he focuses on his arcane core and brings a blanket of power out and over her. The subtle waves wrap tight around her and serve to filter away the horror and the shock, leaving only the unavoidable grief. Her tears slow after a while and she composes herself.

"It was Grimmfang, he's after Eric. I don't know who hired him; I didn't even know what was happening, until it was too late." Xan nods solemnly.

"Silver Dancer was the one who saw that something was amiss, your system was hacked by Fhaligun." He then shakes his head. "I'm sorry Cass, about Elindriss and Marcus, the others." She smiles sadly, tears filling her eyes.

"I've known El my entire life; she never wanted any rez magic." She wipes away a tear and continues, "I don't have enough to perform rituals for the others, they might not even come back, it doesn't always work," she says desperately. Xan nods, he's familiar with necromantic magic, volatile at the best of times, there's never any guarantee. Some obsessed magicians have wasted their entire lives trying to raise a loved one from the dead.

"I know Cass and I'm sorry, but we'll have to think about that later. What does Grimmfang know?" She swallows and nods curtly.

"I'm sorry Xan. I didn't know that he'd killed everyone already." She stops and chokes back some tears before proceeding, "He knows Eric's name and he knows that your team is guarding him, but that's it, that's all that I knew."

Xan nods slowly and says, "It's not your fault Cass. He would have killed you too." She grimaces and replies angrily.

"You know why that psycho didn't kill me? You know what he said? Some fucked up rhyme about how I'm a part of his storyline, because I shopped out some jobs to him twenty years back, sick fucker." She kicks the pillar and seethes. Xan clenches his jaw.

"The team is in danger then. It will only be a matter of time before he finds them." She takes a sharp breath in and nods her agreement.

"I'm coming with you Xan; I want this bastard to pay." Xan shakes his head.

"It's too dangerous, he let you live once, he may not be so generous the next time." She snorts and wipes her eyes.

"Well I can't stay here." She motions towards the mansion. Xan's expression softens. She continues, "and I'm not about to sit around in some safe house waiting to hear if I'm fucked or not. And I still have some resources, plus 'Sharkey' owes me a favor and it's time that I collect." Xan crosses his arms.

"Alright, I guess, I just wanted you to be safe that's all." She nods glumly.

"No real chance of that, we can't let that murderer get to Eric, there's already been too much innocent blood spilt."

"You're right; we need to get back, soon," Xan replies. She looks back towards the wrecked doors.

"Sharkey can help us there." She then drifts off for a moment, lost in thought, before adding "I need to get some things from the vault, but I can't ..." Xan nods and holds up his hand.

"Don't worry, I'll grab whatever you need, hold on, stay here." He then heads into the lobby and searches around quickly. An assault rifle, not damaged or blood stained, and some extra magazines as well. Cassandra's hugging herself as he returns. She nods as he passes her the weapon and the magazines. She absentmindedly checks the weapon and loaded magazine, five rounds down, the guard got off five shots. "Is there a key or a code or both?" She nods and takes off the ring from her left middle finger. Xan palms the ring. "Code?" She shakes her head.

"You don't need it with that ring. Please get the two metal brief cases; they'll be on a set of shelves just to the left once you're inside the vault."

Xan nods and says, "I'll be right back."

The vault is in the basement, towards the front of the mansion. He glances at the bodies before turning to the left, walking a short distance and turning left again. The basement door is unscathed. Grimmfang wasn't here for the vault; he could've stolen everything if he had wanted. Xan opens the door and descends into the basement. He's only been here once before. The space is far more simple and straightforward than the rest of the mansion. A storage room branches off to the right while the left side of the hall is occupied by the armory. She doesn't own anything too serious: rifles, pistols and Smgs mostly, with a selection of ammunition as well. The end of the hall is primarily covered by the large vault doors. He walks up the hall, a light blinks green above him as he approaches the vault door. The ring grants him entrance, and the vault door swings open with a soft groan of hydraulics. The vault has a series of lockboxes embedded in the far wall. Several cases and crates are placed on the ground. He looks to the left. Sure enough, two large metallic brief cases sit on a steel shelving unit there. The one case is much wider but other than that they're identical. Xan retrieves the cases and exits, relocking the vault before he leaves the basement. He soon joins Cassandra in the front yard. She's staring at the ground, assault rifle slung. She looks up as he approaches.

"Thanks Xan, for everything, it means a lot that you're here for me." He smiles.

"I was worried Cass, I'm glad that you're safe." She nods and looks at the cases.

"Thanks, now I have to make some calls." She opens the small case revealing a selection of electronic devices and credsticks. "Then we're going to find that murdering bastard and grind him into little pieces, along with any other stupid bastard that gets in our fucking way." Xan grins. *That's the Cassandra that I know and love,* he thinks.

Cassandra

The pit of sorrow unfurls within her core. A writhing serpent buried in her guts, inescapable. Wretched memories take hold and she sobs. Gaping wounds and exposed bone, all that remains of her love. Grot couldn't have known. *I can't blame him, he was just protecting another child,* she thinks, *just as he did with me, just as he couldn't do for his own children.* The memories return. Villainous shadows that slash at her with cruel blades. The serpent coils around her heart, fangs biting deep. Venom burns through to her spine. The grief is a physical thing now, worse than a bullet wound. She clutches her chest and heaves, there's no stopping it, and tears flow again to stain the dusty floor of the warehouse. The serpent wraps tightly around her chest, crushing her with sadness.

The ruin of her home gleams just outside the checkered window. Images of twisted corpses pass through her mind, quickening her pulse. She wipes her eyes and looks toward the guardhouse. Xan is there, waiting for Sharkey and acting as bait for other monsters. A wave of anxiety hits her. He's the only one left now, him and Grot. *I need you now Grot,* she thinks, *where are you?* The serpent sinks back into her stomach, lurking as a coiled knot that threatens to lash out at any second. She thinks to the earlier phone conversation. Sharkey shared her outrage. He'll bring his "A" game, meaning some serious firepower. A tremor of rage passes through her as she smashes her hands against the desk. *We'll get him El,* she thinks, *we'll get that fucker.* Crossing to the window, she picks up the assault rifle leaning casually against the wall. She places the rifle on the desk and removes the magazine. The serpent lashes out and her breath catches in her chest. After a moment the toxin loses its edge. She clenches her jaw and anger returns, the war mask of grief. Rage seethes in her mind, while in the depths of her spirit the internal violence of tragedy slithers on, threatening to overwhelm her with its venom.

She opens the wide metal case to reveal her personal assortment of vengeance devices. Two spyder grenades, the dangerous automatons are coiled into metal balls at the moment.

Their telescoping blades carry a lethal neuro-toxin. Six boxes of custom, high-grade seven millimeter HEI rounds, each bullet like a miniature grenade. Nestled in the center is her pride and joy. She studies the smooth lines of the GII M-20 plasma pistol, a rare find, one of less than a thousand of its kind. The pistol fires an electromagnetically agitated mass of superheated ions. It can put an eight inch wide hole through three feet of rolled homogenous armor. This model featured the slogan "The tank killing sidearm of choice", providing that you have a million credits to blow. She hefts the heavy ultra-tech weapon. *Just give me one clean shot*, she thinks. A memory of Elindriss laughing jumps out at her. The serpent thrashes and her face contorts, vision blurring. She places the pistol on the desk and inhales sharply. She then retrieves three boxes of ammo and one of the spyder grenades before closing the case. A tear streams down her cheek and she wipes it away with the back of her hand. She loads two empty magazines with the HEI rounds then slides one of them into the assault rifle with a soft click. She removes her long coat and wraps the plasma pistol's holster belt around her waist, cinching it tight. A memory of Marcus creeps up on her, his lips, impaling herself on him during the nights of lust and passion. The serpent strikes. Venom seeps into her heart and she heaves again. The others, there are so many and it's so expensive to try to bring them back, it might not even work. She fills the holster and crosses to the window. The serpent hisses and she breathes out in ragged bursts. The guard house was soaked in blood; she couldn't even look at them. Another wave of anxiety washes over her. *I can't stay here*, she thinks, *I can't let him stand there alone, no matter what he said*. She slips on the jacket and slings the rifle, extra magazine in her left front pocket, the spyder grenade in the right one.

The mag-lock seals the steel door as she exits into the back parking lot. She shoulders the rifle and looks around. The streets are as deserted as ever. The path to the front of the building heads through a scaffolding tunnel, the temporary construction slowly becoming a permanent fixture as layer after layer of grime accumulates. The mansion's front drive slowly creeps into her field of vision as she edges down the sidewalk.

"Going somewhere?" Xan's voice erupts from behind her, causing her to leap around, heart racing.

"Bastard! You scared the shit out of me," she exclaims.

He looks at the ground and says, "Sorry, I thought that something was wrong, I didn't want to give myself away, if you were in trouble." She sighs.

"No, it's fine, I was just surprised." She pauses for a second. "I can't just sit there."He looks her in the eyes, perfect white orbs.

"Cass, we've been over this ..." She shakes her head and cuts him off.

"I know, I know, but I don't care! I won't just sit there while you're fighting for your life ..." The serpent lunges, her core burns with venom and she heaves. He smiles and grabs her by the shoulders.

"Alright Cass, come on, we'll go to the flower garden." She nods and they turn towards the mansion. "I'm serious though Cassandra, if something goes wrong, you will get inside and lock yourself in the vault; it doubles as a safe room doesn't it?" She nods and responds resolutely.

"Yeah, but I won't leave you Xan, if it comes to that we'll die together." He looks at her, concern overtaking his features. He seems to want to speak but instead they continue on in silence.

Soon they pass through the gates and enter the front yard. The fragrance of the garden causes the serpent to stir, a wellspring of memories, edged in fangs. She sees strolls with Elindriss and meetings with Marcus. She can imagine Katie and Crystal pulling weeds, and the thrill of late-night romances with Xan and others. Her mind snaps to the sight of Katie, cut to pieces, too many to count. She pushes back a fresh flood of tears and looks to Xan, sitting beside her on the stone bench. "I have to scan you as a friendly," she says as she produces the spyder grenade. He looks at it and nods. A band of blue light passes over his face, and the grenade registers the new ally with a soft beep. "Now just don't change your face."

Kane interjects, "But he's so ugly; can't I just make him a little prettier?"

She grins and says, "Oh he's not so bad; some girls go for that type of thing."

Xan laughs and retorts, "Hey, I'm sitting right here." Kane responds immediately.

"Yeah, just sitting there, ugly as ever." Xan laughs and she smiles for a second, before a quick memory of Elindriss and Xan laughing together sobers her. The serpent threatens to strike and she breathes out slowly. Xan looks at her tenderly.

"There's nothing else to be done right now Cass, I'm sorry." She nods.

"I know." She looks towards the remains of the front doors. *I'm going to have to move,* she thinks. *The third tragedy; the Arnoch was right, but maybe I can defy it yet.* She looks back to Xan, leans in close and kisses him on the mouth. The serpent recoils and slithers away, blocked by old passions and harried by desire. They kiss as they used to, rhythms of passion reconnecting. It feels like an eternity of comfort. Then Kane interjects, awkward as usual.

"I don't mean to interrupt, honestly this really pains me as it seems like you guy's were about to get it on, and I really dig that, but, someone is walking towards the mansion!" Her heart begins racing. Xan is standing in an instant, pistol drawn. She wheels towards the gate and shoulders the assault rifle.

Xan's gaze catches her eye and they stand for a moment, he blinks a few times then holds up a hand and says, "Move up to the switch, when I jump the fence, open the gate and stay under cover." She nods and moves with him to the gate. Whoever it is, they're not supposed to be here. She sent out an emergency broadcast to all of her regular contacts, they should be staying away until she contacts them again. He stops and peers intently at the stone wall. She's seen this kind of behavior before. He's using his arcane sight. Then he turns towards her, he looks confused. A smile creeps across his lips and he shrugs then points upwards. She nods and moves near the gate controls. A subsonic tremor radiates through the ground as Xan leaps thirty feet into the air and arcs over the wall. She hits the gate switch, heart racing. The gates open and she can hear the sound of a woman struggling. Then Xan's voice, "It's alright Cass, I got her." She turns the corner to see a pistol sitting on the drive, just in front of a Human female. Xan has her arms behind her back, plastic ziptie binding her wrists. Cassandra relaxes the assault rifle and moves forward. The Human is young, early twenties. She has purple cybereyes and spiky purple hair. She's wearing a stout vest, t-shirt and cargo pants, she's slim, small breasts. A data-port gleams silver in her temple.

"Who are you? Why are you here?" she asks. The Human seems frightened, she's breathing heavily.

"My name's Rebecca Arliss. I work for 'The Tirileth City Chronicler', I'll have you know that my cybereyes are broadcasting to a remote node located in 'The Tower'. If you do anything to me, everyone will see it."

Cassandra tilts her head and responds, "Our countermeasures are autonomous of the mansion's main systems, meaning that you are not broadcasting a thing. Now why are you here?" The Human swallows and looks around.

"Oh, shit, I thought that was worth a try," she says sheepishly, then adds "I'm here following a lead, I'm just trying to find a Goblin named Grot, I understand that you know him?" Cassandra furrows her brow.

"Grot died many years ago."

The Human shakes her head and replies, "That's not true, he's alive and well. He's also dismantling Koshikawa black ops teams for one reason or another. He was travelling with a Human teen and they ended up walking here. I have images." Cassandra snorts in surprise. Grot had told her all about the attack, he didn't know who they were though. Xan looks at her with concern. Cassandra looks at him then points at Rebecca.

"Could you bring me the image viewer please?"Xan nods.

"Where is it?" he asks.

"Left cargo pocket," she responds. Xan bends down and quickly retrieves the small palm display. "I've made copies," Rebecca adds. Cassandra nods.

"I don't doubt it." She holds her hand out. Xan crosses to her and gives her the display. She activates it, and sure enough an image collage of Grot is followed by a few images of Eric. She swallows and looks over to Xan. "Who else knows about these images?" Rebecca looks to Cassandra.

"My boss and like half of the news room, as I said I made copies, plus ..." Kane's voice rudely cuts her off.

"You liar! Don't insult me kid, you're not even good at it." The Human seems stunned, like she's never seen a manifer spirit before. Which could make sense; they're extremely rare, thankfully.

"Look, okay, so nobody knows, but you can't kill me. Please! I've been having the worst day ..." Cassandra laughs bitterly.

"You've been having the worst day?" The serpent strikes, venomous fangs burrowing deep into her core. Her composure crumbles and she turns back towards the gate. The serpent bites, again and again, and her face cracks with sadness. She hears Xan's voice.

"No one is going to kill you, just stay there." She walks quickly into the mansion's yard before breaking down into tears. Xan is there a moment later, his embrace is warm, it ushers away some of the toxin. Slowly, the serpent coils into a ball again. She sniffs and looks to him.

"What are we going to do?"

Xan considers for a while before he finally says, "We can't let her go, for her protection and ours." Cassandra nods slowly, he continues "If she runs a story the interested parties instantly multiply and if Grimmfang hasn't found our fortress yet, who do you think he'll be visiting next?"

She tilts her head. "So what are you thinking? Kidnap her?"

Xan grimaces. "It would be preferable if she came willingly. It might take some time to get answers. There's no telling how long we'll have to stay there." Cassandra nods.

"What if she doesn't want to come?"

Xan sighs. "I can't see another choice. They might not even run the story but it's not like we could trust her to keep her word, seeing as she's trying to run away right this very second, excuse me for a moment won't you?" Cassandra blinks a few times, surprised by the sudden shift in the conversation. A great cushion of pressure causes her to take a step back as Xan takes off running. She's seen him run down a sports car before; the Human doesn't stand a chance. She nods to herself; they could pay a psychic to wipe the reporter's memory when it's all over, there isn't enough time just now, but afterwards. There's still a slim chance that she'd recall meeting them but that's fine, the rest would be gone.

Jostled whining signifies Xan's return. The Human is tossed unceremoniously over his left shoulder. He enters the yard and deposits her on the grass. Cassandra closes the gate.

She looks at Rebecca and says, "We'll have no more of that." Rebecca pants and sits upright, cross-legged.

"Well, you can't blame a girl for trying can you?" Cassandra grins. The Human continues "Say, what happened to your doors?" Cassandra looks back towards the fractured, blackened portal. The serpent looms. She steels herself and speaks quietly.

"You're not the only one having a bad day."

Rebecca nods slowly and says, "So what happens now? I see that I can't make a phone call." Cassandra nods.

"Part of our countermeasures, you don't have access. I'll have to outfit you with a mobile signal blocker," she says as she looks towards Xan.

"Why? Where are we going?" Rebecca asks as she looks back and forth between Xan and Cassandra.

Xan looks down and replies, "I'm aware that in your line of work you've undoubtedly heard this many times before, but, you are currently in grave danger Miss Arliss."

Rebecca laughs and says, "Yeah, I've heard that once or twice before, but corpies don't off reporters, press is like their one and only deity." Xan smiles coldly.

"Yes, I'm aware that corporate interests would not want to be caught performing certain acts, which doesn't necessarily prevent them from doing so, *accidents* and so forth. But unfortunately I'm not referring to those interests." Rebecca snorts and replies with an edge of incredulity.

"What *interests* are you referring to?" Xan looks to Cassandra, she nods and he continues.

"Perhaps you are familiar with an operative who goes by the street name of Grimmfang?" Rebecca's smile disappears and she looks back to the doors before responding in a meek voice.

"But, I wasn't supposed to be covering that story," Xan furrows his brow.

"What does that mean?" Rebecca shakes her head.

"Nothing, never mind, umm so what are you saying? That he's after *me*?" Panic seeps into her voice with the final statement.

"We don't know, but it's not unlikely, he'll be searching every avenue," Xan replies. Cassandra nods. Fhaligun's insane, but he's also one of the most skilled hackers who ever lived. Grimmfang might be employing magical detection methods as well. There are countless Wizards and Shamans who will hire out their services in that field. "We would strongly suggest that you come with us when Sharkey arrives."

"Sharkey? Wait, what happens if I say no?" Rebecca replies.

Xan crosses his arms across his chest and says, "It's your life. But are you really going to give up this type of opportunity? You are a reporter after all." He flashes Cassandra a quick smile. She grins and then winks at him.

"Right, like you're just going to let me go," Xan shrugs.

"If you stay with us until the job's done, it wouldn't matter what you report on, we just can't have it happening beforehand."

"What job? How long are we talking here? I'll have to check in with somebody or they'll call the Marshalls you know, I have family, friends, co-workers." Xan laughs and transforms into an exact physical copy of Rebecca, just wearing his clothes instead of hers.

"Don't worry; I've got you covered there," he says in her voice.

Rebecca blinks in confusion then says, "Great, that's just great, very reassuring."

Kane interjects, "Quick Xan, find a mirror and show us her boobs!" Rebecca scoffs.

"Charming, well, it appears that I don't really have much of a choice now do I?"

Xan laughs, shifts back into his natural form and says, "We wanted to make it seem like you did, that has to count for something."

Cassandra smiles and Rebecca rolls her eyes then asks, "So where are we going?" Xan is about to respond when the roar of an engine overtakes the yard. A heavily armored helicopter crests the roof-line a second later. It hovers for a tense moment, tracking the group with a murderous looking thirty millimeter cannon. Then a gruff voice erupts from the helicopter's loudspeaker.

"Hoi Cass, I'm just going to bring this big bitch down on the drive there, her ass is too wide to park it anywhere else." The voice then laughs heartily and the helicopter banks out of sight. Xan raises his eyebrows and looks over to Cassandra.

She looks at Rebecca and says, "It looks like we'll both be finding out soon enough."

Eve

She's a ghost now, more than that, an undying specter. The notion of her has become an imprint in the back of their minds, no more. As inconsequential as the walls and floor, swimming the deep waters of their awareness. There are a dozen soldiers setting up, plus a mage, the real problem. Thermal weave blocks her heat signature, her ring wards her, but magic is always a concern, unpredictable.

"Cable's about to engage, Devlin's ready, are you set?" Dancer's voice comes through the demon mask, a short range tactical headset, not blocked by conventional methods. She clicks once for yes. Specters cannot speak; they do not exist as such. "Go on the boom," is Dancers reply.

Focus on life now, the warehouse greys. The mage nearly disappears, warded. The specter must reclaim the building. This is the flank, taken by snipers and heavy weapons. A stylized "B" marks the property. Soldiers walk the internal expanses. They cover the roof as well, the point of attack. Her core of power fulminates and she readies. The leap is not far. "Specter's Claw" flashes blue, a true mono-edge. She crouches low. In the distance two small missiles launch. The echo of their engines reaches her as she pushes from the stone. The specter soars, a black dot against the sky. Two quick detonations bring sudden orange light and a helicopter folds in on itself then plummets. The soldiers yell and move in an attempt to reciprocate. The specter dives. She lands on a prone sniper, heel at the back of his neck, death in an instant. The spotter yelps before a line is drawn through his throat. The specter blurs, and shadow becomes her. Shouts of vengeance are followed by bullets, three soldiers. They see the death but not the source. She moves swiftly, the wind cracks. A measured kick sends the first soldier toppling from the roof, bait for the others on the ground. A large Human swings at her with sharp blades that arc from his forearm. She parries smoothly and sends the soldier off balance, teetering on the roof edge. A fluid motion with both of her arms simultaneously sends a blade whistling through the air as she stabs the last soldier through the eye. The flying blade strikes its mark and the off balance soldier falls, a faint thump sounding a moment later. Specter's Claw is withdrawn from the lifeless skull, and she sinks back into nothingness, no thought.

The specter moves briskly. Peripheral awareness of conflict seeps in, she identifies weapons' fire and magic. She enters the warehouse, moving effortlessly and perching overhead. The bait worked. There are four soldiers proceeding to the roof. Three remain, plus the mage. He does not see the specter. She drifts across the span, not even a shadow on the wall. She waits, they seem unsure. The battle rages elsewhere. Amplified sounds of combat seem to come from everywhere. The soldiers reach the doors to the roof, and the mage signals them forward. The specter looms. She hears a helicopter engine, it's close. She recenters and peers through the ceiling. Bright whirling auras beneath a grey flying behemoth, she counts eight in total. Now's her chance, the specter plummets. The mage moves at the last instant. She readjusts, lands on top of a Human, and snaps his spine. An Elven soldier reacts quickly, spraying an arc of bullets towards her as she dives towards the wall. A line of impacts smash into the brick behind her, as she rebounds off the wall and corkscrews towards the soldier. Just to his left another soldier is raising his weapon, the mage is behind them. His hands are moving. She lands in a forward roll, springs up immediately, kicks the Elf in the throat then turns and stabs the other soldier neatly through the heart. A loud archaic word catches her attention and she instantly leaps backwards, a second too late. A searing cone of flame radiates out from the mage's hand, bathing her in heat for an instant before she sails out of the fire's reach. Her instincts take over and her arcane core channels away the pain, it will be dealt with later. She lands on the concrete and leaps to the right.

The imprint of her landing rushes forward as the specter sinks into the background. The mage snaps his fingers and an orb of swirling colors appears. The specter flickers and charges forward. The mage does not see, but the spirit turns towards her, not fooled by the imprint. Channels of energy well within the spirit and a searing bolt of pure mana rockets from its core. She barely manages to get out of the way. The bolt disintegrates a giant hole in the warehouse wall. The mage turns towards her, surprised, his hands move in a quick pattern. A lethal charge builds within the spirit's core. She leaps and flings a blade propelled by focused power. Steel sings through the air and digs deep into the mage's forehead. He drops, like a puppet with cut strings. The spirit crackles with energy for a second before it implodes.

She hears running feet, echoing in a staircase. The door crashes open and a soldier fires, indiscriminately. She surges back into the gloom as bullets snap and whizz past her. The warehouse is empty, just a few tall metal racks. More soldiers pour into the room. She is not a specter here, not now. There are calls of recognition, she sprints, they fire. A jackhammer punches her side but she keeps moving. There's a window, it's twenty feet off of the ground. She fires off two lines of arcane power and soars through the air, a torrent of bullets impact the wall as she shatters through the window and lands on the street. She quickly takes in the scene. An attack helicopter is overhead. There's an APC with a heavy turret far up the street. She glances down, her armor is intact.

"Eve, I'm tracking additional forces converging on your position. They're trying to grab that warehouse so that they can flank Cable and set up anti-air defenses, try to terrorize them but watch yourself!" She gives a single click. The specter must be clever now. She sinks into shadow and silently leaps back into the warehouse. The soldiers reacted quickly; all but two of them are heading outside already. There are still a half dozen soldiers on the roof. They must be dealt with. They are the real threat to Cable.

The two soldiers in the warehouse are looking over the bodies of their cohorts. The specter drifts to them. Their deaths are quick. She leaps to the overhead spans then moves nimbly outside and to the edge of the roof. There are six soldiers, two more sniper teams along with two other soldiers who are setting up a mobile SAM platform. The specter builds her focus, a tide of agitated energy bubbles within her. She waits for her chance. Distant detonations warp the air. The opportunity presents itself, and she explodes. The roof rumbles and she is upon them. The first two die instantly, broken beneath the velocity of her approach. The second sniper team draw side arms. She kicks one in the head, nearly decapitating him, as she throws the other from the roof with a precise hip toss. The remaining soldiers fire but she isn't there anymore, one hand holds her off of the roof's edge, a sixty foot drop to the street below. She glances down just as bullets smack the wall around her, soldiers on the street, a dozen or more. She instantly flings herself back onto the roof, snapping out one blade in the process. The steel sprouts from the Orcish soldier's throat as his comrade looses a volley of projectiles. She rolls and dives to the right before lunging at him quickly, his weapon tracks just behind her as she reaches him and frees his head from his body. The corpse falls and twitches. She takes a moment to assess their gear. Nothing of note except, one grenade each, standard issue fragmentation. She grins and gathers up the explosives.

The sound of shouting is overtaken by the roar of the helicopter returning. She pulls the pins on three grenades and throws them off of the roof as she's illuminated by a spotlight. Pulses of wind assail her, then explosions and screams. Her arcane core flares and she streaks across the roof just as a line of detonations shred the material behind her. She launches from the roof's edge and drops onto the neighboring building, a smaller more dilapidated warehouse. The helicopter banks to follow. Bullets spark off of the edge of the roof, fired from the soldiers in the street. She flings another grenade down at them and crosses the roof. A trio of detonations rock the factory across the way, thirty millimeter HEI shells missing their intended mark, her. She skids to the roof edge and rolls over the side, landing softly on the concrete of the parking lot some forty feet below. A cascade of explosions resounds overhead as bits of the roof are sent hurtling across the pavement. She sinks back against the wall and calms her mind.

The helicopter approaches, soldiers are surrounding the building. The specter quietly enters the warehouse, a broken loading door allowing easy access. The sounds of gunfire and explosions continue in the background. Cable's mini-gun is making a terrible racket. The specter looks for a sign of life. Auras surround the building, soldiers. The helicopter's still overhead. The APC is in front of the "B" warehouse, they both must be dealt with. The specter waits. The timing must be just right. Soldiers pile around the corners while others begin to converge at the entrances. A group of four are near the broken loading door, four more are at the front door. She stills her mind and throws the grenade. It arcs through the air, "cooked" for just long enough. The studded metal casing bursts apart as it reaches the loading door. She can see a slow spread of shrapnel fan out from the grenade, as a geyser of power spreads through her core. She moves, screams are drowned out as the windows burst with a sudden gust of sonic power. She kicks the front door from its hinges, ravaging two of the soldiers standing just beyond. A slow motion ballet unfolds before her eyes. The steel door cartwheels up the street, soldiers move as though under water, bullets and debris streak everywhere. She releases the last grenade and dashes through the street. A storm of projectiles follow her progression, then another explosion and more screams. She moves from the APC's line of sight and jumps with all of her power.

A wave of exhaustion hits her as she hurtles upwards more than sixty feet to the "B" warehouse's roof. She lands with a forward roll and she is up and running. The helicopter tracks and fires its cannon, fresh detonations blossom, carving the roof apart and leaving large holes. A shell strikes the SAM and she swears. The pilot guessed her plan. She darts a zigzag path across the roof, the cannon drums and fresh explosions burst to life around her. Soldiers spring from the roof's doorwell, they begin to fire and she dives off the roof. The landing is rough. A roll lessens the damage but her leg burns, a sprain at the least. She wicks away the pain and searches around for cover. The APC is on the other side of the building. The helicopter angles overhead. "Eve! Something's coming your way; it's not showing up on the scanner, I don't know what it is, be careful!" The cannon tracks her as she runs across the street to a squat building, an old guard shack. *I'm moving too slowly,* she thinks, *I need time to heal a bit and recenter.* Then, the street is suddenly alive with a high-pitched laugh, unhinged, full of madness. Without warning the helicopter explodes and is thrown violently towards the warehouse, a second detonation shakes the walls, fire plumes and the building begins to crumble. She crouches in cover and listens. Distant screaming and gunfire drift to her, and that laugh, always that laugh. She refocuses. The power swells and her injuries are forgotten. A loud explosion sends a tremor through the street, the building collapses further. She can still hear the distant battle, then, a voice, it's just behind her.

"Eve of the night, you run and you fight, your body is sexy, sexier still is your might. But now we're alone, with our keen blade's hone and so you should atone as you run away home, else I knock you down prone and then cause you to moan."

She flinches and turns. The nightmare awaits, Grimmfang, blades in his skeletal hands. She doesn't hesitate. The specter fades and she stokes the dragon's fire. The power floods and she roars. The nightmare laughs, his face a mocking white skull. She throws a blade and surges forward, faster than sight. He splits the blade in half and calmly begins to strike. Two swords moving in perfect balance, he's nearly as fast as her. A wall of slashing metal materializes, attacks from all angles. She parries and dodges, ripostes and counters. The two figures blur and flash, dark swirls shifting across the pavement. A sudden change in tempo and the dragon assails with "Tooth", "Claw" and "Tail", the cyborg retreats. He springs upwards suddenly, left hand firing out, trailing a steel cable. He swings an overhead pendulum arc then detaches and soars out of sight, laughing. She turns to pursue only to be struck from behind, a freight train smashing into her back. He laughs again. She rebounds off of the concrete. Her chest is a wall of fire. A red pin of light streams from his left eye, instantly she rolls and dives to the side as a line melts through the pavement where she was just lying. He springs forward, a different attacking pattern this time. But the dragon strikes back, she elbows him in the jaw, kicks him in the chest and slashes through his coat. He changes his timing again and lashes back, a perfect sidekick. The block is sloppy, and she flies backwards thirty feet. He pursues immediately, even before she lands. She flicks out a throwing knife, performs a backwards roll then slides to a stop. He catches the blade in his teeth and chortles. She swallows hard, as a lance of pain escapes the numbing effect of her arcane core. A barrage of attacks follow, she dodges and blocks then kicks him in the face. He rolls into the kick, grabs her and throws her, hard. A serene few seconds follow as she flies through the air. She attempts to recenter. The nightmare is still coming, unrelenting. *I need some help*, she thinks, as she rolls to a sliding stop, left arm broken.

"Dancer, I got Grimmfang here, I'm going to take him on a little run," she pants into the mask. A high-pitched laugh drowns out the response.

Cable

A wave of force hammers the building. *Fuck*, he thinks, *that's the sentry.* The explosion resounds from the west factory floor. He's considering an approach, when the hard skitter of Spyder drone legs calls his attention. He moves the gyroscope precisely, "Gerty" turns, six barrels of menace. Up the hall, three drones threaten, tiny bodies and long, lethal legs. Their cores are filled with explosives. "Gerty" whirls and roars. The sound of a grotesquely magnified zipper sends a cable of light arcing into the hall. Horrid explosions follow. Dozens of detonations materialize in a matter of seconds. The drones fracture into pieces, while the hall is instantly peppered in grapefruit-sized holes. He glances at the optical readout, 226 rounds remaining, down from 1 000. The ruin of the factory attests. There are corpse's strewn everywhere, torn to shreds. The remains of drones and helicopters litter the street. He recoils back into the stairwell, panting. Six bullet wounds so far, five stopped by the armor, one more that wasn't. The foil peels back and he quickly slaps a surgeon's patch on his leg, outer thigh. Silver Dancer's voice filters into his cyberears.

"Look alive sugar, Eve's in trouble. Grimmfang's here! he's not showing up on the scanner though. She's going to try and lure him past you guys, can you provide some help?" Cable grimaces. He worked with Grimmfang once, just once, years back. The cyborg's unnaturally good and extremely dangerous, top of the line cybernetics, and a mind built for murder. The flank's retaken, meaning he can return to the roof and leave a present for the assholes coming from the factory. He sighs and looks down. The hole in his leg is gone, just tattered armor and a blood stain remaining.

"No problem, tell her to try to get him onto Tabbard Avenue, I'll head to the roof," he responds, as he unhooks a claymore from his belt.

"Thanks sugar, watch yourself now." Cable laughs and attaches a tripwire to the stairwell's door handle. He places the claymore on the stairs across from the door, anchoring it with self-burrowing screws. He then pulls the tripwire taut and removes the pin, setting the double action trigger in the process. The trigger allows the mine to detonate if the wire is pulled, or if it goes slack. He moves up the stairwell, punctuated by bodies and marred by combat. The telltale signs of an earlier ambush. He knows all the standard corporate military tactics; it's easy to exploit them if the commander is going by the book. Only after the initial engagement does everything devolve into luck and chaos, tempered by experience of course.

The door to the roof is destroyed, along with the surrounding walls. The end result of a rocket launched by a now defunct helicopter. He pauses at the top of the stairwell and produces a satchel, five pounds of military grade plastic explosive. Its detonator is linked to his head computer, remote trigger at a thought. The satchel is concealed near the top of the staircase. He covers it in bricks and rubble then waits. He focuses and glances around the roof, cycling between thermal optics and light-amplified sight. The glow of firelight illuminates the warehouse at the flank, no signs of life there. Devlin is still in combat to the south, a large ground force was building up there. He seems to have it under control though. *Valkyr knows where Rex is or Xan, they'd better be bringing some good news*, he thinks. Cable plods across the damaged roof, last backpack of ammunition in tow, combat shotgun slung. A distorted crack of electricity sounds from the south followed by weapons' fire. He focuses on his cyberear's comm device.

"Dancer, there are still two missiles in the van. I'm giving you direct control. You won't be able to lock onto Grimmfang so see if you can help Devlin out."

"Sure thing sugar," responds Silver Dancer. Cable moves to the roof edge and peers over, rangefinder reads fifty-five feet to the pavement. He looks farther up the street, there, two dark blurs. One is chasing after the other. They're moving erratically, jumping and diving, running and fighting. Then a hand snaps out followed by a steel cord. He grins and wheels "Gerty" around. Implanted software localizes and tracks the target. An aiming reticle superimposes over his sight based on the mini-guns relative position, beside it a list of ballistic data cycles past. "Gerty" spins and tears the air, a twisted lance of projectiles lights up the street. The figure instantly rebounds off a wall and dives away from the stream of doom. A chaotic pattern of explosions follows, cratering the street and guttering within the building. He readjusts, the barrels spin, but now he unleashes short bursts, six or twelve rounds at a time. The figure jumps and moves, one burst catches his flank but he continues, barely scathed. Cable shakes his head. *The fucker should be dead*, he thinks. Eve, he's back at her and they're fighting again. They're moving too fast to see. He waits for a chance, when, an explosion shakes him. He quickly regains his balance. It must have been the claymore. A quick few steps put him in cover relative to the stairwell. The smell of smoke is accompanied by quiet groans of pain. "Gerty" tracks towards the top of the stairs. He waits tensely when the shriek of missiles launching comes from the direction of the van, a moment later and a pair of detonations rumble in the south. He nods and peers back towards the stairwell. A quick change on the audio receptors amplifies the sounds from the staircase. Maybe a half dozen, they're moving slowly, wary of other trip-wires no doubt. Sounds of combat drift up from the street below and he quickly moves to the edge, keeping his new-found cover squarely in front of the stairwell entrance. He looks over the edge, swinging "Gerty" around in the process. Eve is still fighting Grimmfang, she looks hurt, tired. He notices that she's not using her left arm. He quickly patches into her headset.

"Eve, I'm above you, jump up here and I'll give that bastard something to think about." She whirls and throws a series of aggressive attacks before rocketing straight towards the factory roof and landing a short ways from Cable. Without a moment's hesitation he lets fly the full fury of "Gertrude the Terrible". A rain of explosions assaults the ground. Grimmfang recoils, rounds slamming into his armor and body. Then he's gone, the detonations patter the ground for a second longer before the barrels whir empty. He swears and unhooks the mini-gun rig, dumping the empty ammo pack in the process. Eve steps close, wounded in more than one spot. "Get down here," he says, pointing to the industrial fan unit serving as cover.

"Soldiers are coming from that door," she says as she sits back against the metal. He smiles and winks. Then he crouches low and mentally triggers the remote detonator. A deafening shockwave pulses across the roof, followed by the sound of collapsing concrete. Eve laughs then winces in pain.

"Here," he says, producing a surgeon's patch. She grins and nods. His combat shotgun comes to hand as Eve applies the patch to her left arm, instantly the silvery clouds of nano-bots begin to reform the flesh and bone.

"Thanks, I think he's just messing with me. That fucker is...Watch out!" Eve yells. A searing pain passes through his left shoulder. He dives forward and twists around. A second of shock follows. His left arm, it's on the roof over there. It's not attached anymore. A dark hooded figure stands beyond the severed limb, skeleton face and hands. His swords are edged in a shimmering red light. Eve roars and attacks, blades streak and clash. Cable stumbles back and looks to his other arm, the shotgun, it's still there. He shakes his head. A pall of sweat instantly forms on his forehead. Eve falls back and his aiming reticle snaps up immediately, muscle memory doing the rest. He adjusts to absorb the recoil one-handed as the shotgun hammers with mechanical precision. Explosive shells strike home, blasting holes in armor and rending the cyborg's chest open. Grimmfang leaps, sheaths his blades and laughs. His right palm produces a barrel. The palm gun barks and Cable dives back as Grimmfang's own explosive shells strike the roof, spraying him with shrapnel. The cyborg then disappears.

"You see him?" he asks, tracking the roof with his shotgun. Eve bounds over.

"Shit! Cable, do you have any more patches?" He nods and motions to his belt, a short dizzy spell overtakes him. She retrieves the patch and quickly puts it over the stump. The bleeding stops and the wound closes. A shot of narcotics eases the pain a bit.

"Thanks. Well shit, I don't know if we should take my arm or not," he says, somewhat delirious. Eve smirks and shakes her head. Then a voice, it's just across the roof.

"Alas poor Cable, now he's unable, to tie his own shoes or act as a table ..." The rest is cut off as Cable turns and fires, explosive shells wrecking an air conditioning unit where the cyborg just stood. Eve rockets to the side and the clang of metal on metal causes him to turn in that direction. Grimmfang is laughing. To Cable's horror the cyborg's chest is reassembling. The damage is mending itself. He must have a core of self-replicating nano-bots, an appallingly expensive cybernetic augmentation known as the "Reconstruction Protocol". Cable grimaces, a wave of nausea washing over him. The two bodies in front of him clash with deadly speed. He waits for his chance to attack, when the faint click of metal on stone causes him to spin around, just in time. Two Spyder drones, either Grimmfang's or the corp's. His targeting reticle adjusts as the shotgun sways. The eight limbed drones rush forward and the shotgun thumps. A row of explosions walk up to first drone before it detonates in a spray of flame and metal. The second drone is faster. Cable waits for a half-second. The drone's first strike comes, predictable as ever. He steps quickly away from it then immediately launches forward and kicks it as hard as he can. His armored boot clangs against the oval body and the drone flies up and over the roof's edge, a muffled explosion follows a second later. A glance at the optical display reads seven rounds left in this drum magazine. Automatic weapons fire erupts in the background, farther away, not from the south either. He makes a mental note of the direction, before focusing on the battle again. Eve and Grimmfang are far across the roof, a savage engagement unfolding between them. He slings the shotgun and unholsters his machine pistol, crossing the roof as he does. Grimmfang launches a series of attacks, but Eve disappears. The cyborg isn't fooled however; he turns immediately and strikes out with a leg. The impact causes Eve to scream and sends her flying off of the roof. Cable swings his arm into place and fires, digital reticle at the cyborg's head. Armor piercing rounds impact and are deflected as they strike home. The cyborg dodges to the side then lunges forward, fast. Cable fires a line of bullets into Grimmfang's chest. Blades flash towards him, then, at the last second he concentrates on his emergency trigger. An orb springs from his belt and detonates forward. A cone of shrapnel strikes the cyborg, sending the blades skittering from his hands; simultaneously a short-lived field of compressed ions buffer the explosion, leaving Cable unaffected. Grimmfang crashes to the side, rent and torn in many places.

"Nasty! Nasty, you were shamming! Now get ready for your ramming!" Cable fires off a burst from his machine pistol as the cyborg rolls to the side and disappears behind cover. He feels a presence and instantly kicks to the side, using all the power of his bioni-flex muscle clusters. Grimmfang laughs as the kick impacts and sends him flying twenty feet through the air, a pin of red light flashes from his eye and Cable feels a wedge of fire carve across his stomach. He looks down to see a smoldering line etched through his armor. He laughs, drops the pistol and hefts the shotgun. The cyborg dodges to the side but Cable predicts the movement and fires in front of him. Explosions tear into Grimmfang sending him sprawling across the roof, the drum magazine clicks empty. He ejects it and fumbles, one-handed, for a fresh drum. The cyborg's gone, he's retrieved his blades. Cable could see the damage repairing itself already. *Fuck*, he thinks, *it's no good; we have to concentrate our firepower, or take out the "Reconstruction Protocol".* A high-pitched laugh draws his attention to the left, close. He's almost loaded the shotgun when the cyborg attacks again, his wounds all but mended. Cable moves to defend when Grimmfang is struck by a figure flying sideways at him. He hurtles violently through the air, bounces off a brick wall then falls from the roof. Eve lands softly beside Cable.

"Sorry, had to wait for my chance," she says. He nods and grimaces, the laser cut deep. Eve is holding her side as well, she's breathing with difficulty. He motions to his head then accesses his cyberear's comm device.

"Dancer, is Devlin still fighting?" Dancer's voice instantly responds.

"Yeah, still a bunch of soldiers there. I took out the tank drone with the missiles. And it looks like he's keeping them off balance somehow. They're not attacking him with all of their force for some reason."

"Alright, we're going to head there. We need some help here." Silver Dancer's voice is full of concern.

"Are you alright? You sound hurt." Cable grins and responds.

"I've had worse." He breathes out raggedly then continues, "Do me a favor though, try to find Rex will you?" He can't hear the response however, a high-pitched laugh drowning it out completely. *Well shit,* he thinks, *I suppose it's time for round two.*

Devlin

The first squad is still rapt in the arcane throes. Their minds locked in a perpetual loop, staring at the design, unmoving. The deep report of rupturing mana energy comes from the hallway. Immoth's thoughts drift to him.

"Got one, there are six more this way." Devlin acknowledges the spirit briefly when his headset chimes, a single click connects.

"Hey hon, Cable and Eve are heading your way, Grimmfang is after them. I hope that you can do something to help." Devlin gets a sinking sensation in the pit of his stomach. He recalls the news stories and exposés that he's seen on the cyborg. He's rumored to be an unstoppable amalgam of cybernetics, technology, weapons and skill.

"Tell them to try to lure him onto the second floor if they can," he responds, a pool of anxiety slowly building at his center.

"Sure thing hon, be careful now."

"I shall certainly try," he says, then disconnects the microphone. He concentrates and breathes deeply then looks to the workspace, low half-walls create a sterile cubicle maze. The third floor is relatively unscathed, unlike the two lower floors. A necessary inferno engulfed most of the area, before it was extinguished. The sickly reek of smoke and burnt plastic perfumes the air, reminding him of the threat still festering beneath him. He focuses on Immoth's arcane link.

"Keep them busy, more are coming from the fire escape." He focuses on his arcane sight, the squad is moving quickly. They gave up on trying rouse their second floor compatriots. He relaxes his focus and looks back to the fire escape door, lifting the small silver snake medallion as he does. The intricately coiled serpent seems to move along on a continuous, winding path. Automatic weapons' fire reverberates in the hallway, followed by the deep drawl of a mana bolt being unleashed. He feels the spirit grow weaker. "What is it?"

"They have runes. This one took some shots," Immoth responds telepathically. He nods and looks back to the door.

"It was only a matter of time before they got their shit together, be careful," he responds through the arcane link.

He looks back just as the fire door slams open, and a young Human soldier bursts into the room. Devlin instantly sculpts the spell and mutters the words, snake medallion pointed at the soldier. A dazed expression overcomes the Human's features. Devlin concentrates. The soldier robotically grabs a grenade from his belt and turns towards the door. He pulls the pin and pops the hammer just before two other soldiers charge into the room. The sharp detonation reduces the three of them to bloody tatters. Devlin grimaces, and then takes cover. He quickly builds an unstable orb of mana, not one of his best, but it will do. A subsonic throb issues from the direction of Immoth, then a high-pitched shriek followed by gunfire. Devlin readies the searing mass of purple-red energy, when two more soldiers spring from the fire exit door. They fire immediately, bullets spread through the room, punching holes through a random collection of objects. Devlin launches the orb then flattens against the carpet. A loud wave of sonic power unleashes a brilliant flash of light. One rifle silences. Then, fresh bullets slam into the wall above him, spraying fragments of concrete everywhere. The gem comes quickly to hand. The threads of the spell are woven around the gemstone. He chants the words and the stone evaporates, leaving the faint trace of a bubble around him. He begins to ready another spell when a shock overcomes his mind and he's struck by a wave of exhaustion. He lurches about drunkenly for a second before he calms his mind and refocuses. *Immoth,* he thinks, *goodbye old friend.* Before he knows what's happening, the soldier is on top of him, assault rifle firing frantically. Bullets streak towards him just to be repelled at the last moment, flattened against an unseen wall of force. He unleashes a flood of power, through the exhaustion. It's a simple spell, yet effective. Long slivers of air turn into steel and are propelled forward faster than the speed of sound. The space in front of him distorts with a short flurry of movement and the soldier stumbles backwards, a half-dozen wounds bloom on his chest as the steel passes through him. He reels for a second and then falls.

Devlin pants and crouches down, his heart's pounding in his chest. The sound of movement comes from the hall. He shakes his head. *Immoth was a good little spirit, it's too bad,* he thinks, *though Emma hated him, maybe she'll like the next one better.* He lingers for a few seconds thinking about her, when the ear-splitting boom of a flash-bang draws the preference of his contemplation. Fortunately the grenade is too far away to have any impact on him. It does inspire him to change tactics however.

Slowly, he peels off a layer of his aura and binds it with a skin of arcane threads. The illusion resolves into a perfect double of him. His arcane core froths and he snaps his fingers, the double multiplies into four exact copies. He concentrates for a second and the doubles stand then begin to run, each along a different path, as a tiny spark of chaos enlivens each of their cores. Cries of alarm are quickly trumped by weapons' fire, multiple shooters. One illusion is struck and seems to "die". Devlin uses the distraction, pops up and focuses on the essence of lightning. He lifts his arm and yells the words of power. An erratic beam arcs instantly from his hand to a pair of soldiers. The static pop of electricity lights the room with utter clarity. Both of the soldiers ignite, and drop as blackened husks. Without warning, a flower pattern of bullets slams into his kinetic ward, causing it to flicker. He turns and points at the soldier firing on him, a single thread of power, directly to the eyes. The soldier's aim falters as he blinks rapidly in an attempt to regain his lost sight. Devlin hits the carpet again. Bullets zing through the enclosed space of the office, some following illusions and others flying blindly. He waits for a few seconds, sweat pouring down his face. A clear arcane burn is forming in his core, he's running dry. The earlier fight was draining. The squad of sixteen is still being held in a catatonic state, but it won't last much longer. He quickly shifts his perception, three soldiers remain. There's something else as well. A figure on the roof, it's Cable's aura but it only has one arm, something's wrong. A rifle discharges and the last illusion collapses.

"Sweep," says a quiet voice, corp common.

"Can't see shit," is the response just to his right. Devlin pulls out a small, clear circular bead with a tiny speck of rushing air at its center. He rolls the bead through a sprinkling of arcane power, places it in front of the office and then closes the door. The movement provokes a series of shots. Two of the three soldiers are covering the front and left side of the room. He crawls forward through the maze of half walls and positions himself behind a square concrete pillar near the room's center. The familiar thumping of Cable's auto-shotgun drifts through the ceiling. His arcane sight greys out the room and reveals three bright auras; two are converging on the office door, the third is slowly edging his way to the hallway. He whistles a single shrill note, the bead shatters and the room is blasted into turbulent pieces. A shockwave strikes him through the pillar; flying bits of shrapnel flatten against his ward. The bubble of energy flexes, then shatters, leaving him exposed. His breath comes in great wheezing gasps as he looks at the destruction. The two soldiers closest to the door are twisted and mangled beyond saving; the third is still blind but also still moving. Devlin grabs a handful of eleven millimetre rounds from his coat pocket and holds up his clenched fist. The remaining soldier bursts from the rubble and begins to fire at random with his rifle. Devlin utters one word and encapsulates the bullets in barrels of force, then fires them, six brass casings falling to the floor directly afterwards. Four of the six rounds strike the soldier in the chest, breaching his soft armor and dropping him. Devlin immediately begins to focus on his arcane sight. There, on the roof. He can also see a hint of Eve. Her ring wards her but he's familiar with the design. She's moving erratically, the auto shotgun thumps again. *Shit,* he thinks, *I can't see Grimmfang at all.*

Chunks of half-wall mingle with broken pieces of concrete; he quickly retrieves a jagged block of the latter. Claws of energy radiate from his finger tips into the block, and he begins to hum. The block oscillates with power, as he grabs it with both hands then points it at the ceiling. A stream of particles bridges the span between his hands and the newly exposed sub-structure. The concrete of the roof shifts. He parts the swirling mass of dust in his hands, opening the concrete of the roof in the process. An instant later and a large perfect hole appears, revealing the outside of the building.

"Down here!" he yells, a fluctuating arc of particles raging between his hands. There's the sound of metal on metal, then a high-pitched laugh. He flinches as Cable tumbles through the hole

271

and lands clumsily on his side; he rolls onto his back and aims at the hole immediately. A second later Eve drops gracefully through the hole. Devlin relaxes his arcane focus and the hole snaps shut. He frowns upon seeing Cable. "Damn it mate, are you okay?" Cable laughs, some measure of narcotics in his system no doubt.

"I've had worse. Fire escape is there, windows are in the offices?" Devlin nods. Eve limps over.

"Are you alright?" she asks, numerous cuts and bruises color the torn sections of her armor.

"Don't worry about me. Here," he says, producing a surgeon's patch, "my last one." She smiles and quickly peels the foil then slaps the patch on the right side of her chest, just below her breast. "What's the plan?" Cable looks over from behind his newly discovered cover, auto shotgun in his remaining arm.

"The plan is, hopefully Xan and Rex will be bringing the cavalry real soon. If they don't, we're fucked, that's the plan." He then pauses for a second before following up with "You're looking kind of peaked."

Devlin nods and smiles weakly then says, "You could say that, yeah. Well shit, I don't want to be the bearer of bad news, but, I got like sixteen soldiers in a trance downstairs, they're going to snap out of it any time now." Cable snorts and looks to the fire escape when a sudden explosion sends a spear of debris down through the ceiling. A chilling high-pitched laugh follows. Then a figure appears, wreathed in dust. Eve is on him in an instant but he twists and hurls her through the office door, splintering it with celerity. The smash of a window ensues as Eve shouts and plunges from the building. Cable yells something inaudible and begins to fire. Devlin fumbles for the small metallic bar in his pocket. Grimmfang closes with Cable. Small explosions impact on the cyborg's ruined armor and exposed cybernetics, he slashes at Cable who barely manages to roll away from the onslaught. Grimmfang leaps after him as Devlin produces the bar, three inches long and a half-inch wide, solid platinum. A rush of fury overcomes him and he screams the words of power. Lancing ribbons of pure mana lash out from his hand then blast into the cyborg. The great beam of energy sends Grimmfang through the concrete wall with a grinding arcane detonation. Devlin falls to his knees, too exhausted to stand. Cable slowly regains his feet and peers towards the smoldering hole, gun at the ready. Part of the wall collapses, strings of mana flowing across the surface. Devlin hears a presence behind him and he spins. Eve limps over, bits of glass embedded in the side of her face.

"By Tempus! I think that you got him," she says as she plucks a sliver of glass out of her cheek. Devlin moves closer to Cable and looks at the hole.

"We should make sure that he's dead," Cable warns. Devlin nods.

"We also need to deal with the soldiers downstairs," he says in a soft voice. Cable nods then produces a satchel, plastic explosives no doubt. Devlin turns back towards Eve. "How are you feeling now?" She laughs.

"I'm going to need to go on a serious vacation after this is all wrapped up." Devlin snorts and nods. *I should plan a trip too*, he thinks; *make up for all the time spent working recently.*

"I always wanted to see..." He never finishes the statement. An excruciating pain intrudes, the blade piercing his heart. Then, a faint laugh and screams of rage, his vision blacks out, sounds fade. A sense of loss overcomes him, then, a glimmering field edged by a dark forest. *Emma*, he thinks, *I'm sorry.*

Rex

Swim the earth now. Veins of transcendence arise. Juxtapose their folly in this tunnel of woe and terror, partner to the chase. This monster howls, a necessity born of the defacement of that which is just. You shall quake before this beast, cowards. An ugly end shall come for you. I shall become the unknown horror that haunts the dreams of the uncertain. I do not mind the grim feast. Salt and the splinters of bone make a meal fit for a king, beast king. Gnash deep into their psyche now. Chaos controls through their reticence. Move as the earth and they shall always fear. The floor of the hunt is their enemy, basted in rot. Personify ferocity in this place. The tunnel quivers at the thought. Create nothing but consternation in their awareness. Shock them with brutality and they shall crumble. Veins of malice arise, unbidden, from some dark place they come. Gift the earth with life and give it the reason to kill. The tunnel slavers at the thought, a maw of hopelessness.

But wait. I feel the sudden instinct of loss. One of our number has been taken. These pestilent villains! One of my new clan is killed. It feels like Devlin, the kind-hearted fool. Indignation flares and paroxysms of rage electrify the earth. Fear is my reward. Yes, fear the beast now, meager thugs. Your actions have undone you. This crafty tunnel transforms into a tomb, as nerve returns to them. Courage foisted upon the unworthy on account of circumstance. Creep close then, prey. Creep into your own clever graves. I shall act as your undertaker. I shall act as the docent of your urban barrows, soon. It is almost time. The earth and stone have rejuvenated me. The wounds of this body have mended and vengeance seethes. The earth shall fight first; it shall rise and punish them with fists of acerbity. Then I shall attack during the crush. Always at the flank, tear into their soft underbelly and bask in the steam of their entrails. Veins of chaos rise up from my core. The earth is transfused with life, and given a brutal shape. Come then prey. Let the terror of cognition propel you, for the hunt begins anew.

Signs of battle trail through the tunnel. Bullet casings litter the blood-soaked ground, sitting amidst the ruins of mechanization. The walls are cracked and scorched. A last desperate group remains, cowering in a circle around a rune marked machine gun. Orange light wafts from around the far corner, an earlier destruction which left a persistent blaze. Thick smoke clogs the upper reaches of the tunnel. A tense minute passes, the group twitching and flinching at each new sound. A faint rumbling begins, the soldiers shift nervously. The rumble builds and Rex laughs; a hideous sound that causes one soldier to yelp in surprise. The group becomes unnerved, their guns tracking invisible threats in every direction. Meanwhile, the real invisible threat moves silently and positions himself across from the rumble. The earth then heaves violently upwards and the soldiers spin. A massive figure overshadows the group. An elemental made of earth and stone. It juts directly up from the ground, and faint white orbs sulk within its sunken sockets. Soldiers scream. The tunnel reverberates with thunder, and muzzle flashes strobe the hulking figure. A huge stone fist flattens a fleeing soldier into fractured paste. Bullets tear into the elemental, sending chunks of stone and earth flying. Rex chooses his moment, and pounces. Shock briefly passes over the first soldier's face as the mangling begins. Squeals of dismay gush from the remaining soldiers. The machine gun turns towards the gored soldier and Rex sinks back into the ground, disappearing without a trace. Bullets hammer the dead soldier and the ground where he fell. The others are fanning out and firing on the earth elemental, slowly chipping away at its stony body. The elemental lashes out again. A soldier's reflexes are a heartbeat too slow and the heavy stone arm splatters him against the wall. Rex uses the diversion and lurches up from the earth, just below the machine gunner. The Human shrieks as half of his ribcage is torn from his body. More bullets patter the elemental and a deep groan shakes the tunnel as life leaves the earth. The elemental collapses into a mound of loose rocks and dust. Meanwhile, Rex vaults at the nearest soldier, a tall Elf female. She begins to turn as all four of his limbs slash into her. The fury of his movements afterwards tears her apart. Assault rifles speak and the tunnel lights up with flashing light. Rex feels a sting on his flank, runes gifting the bullets with a special impact. He roars, becomes visible and shakes his core of chaos ferociously. Four exact doubles spring from his body, a trick that he taught to Devlin. Confusion washes over the group and they begin to aim at the figments. He lunges at a stricken Human soldier. A short burst hits Rex as he breaks the Human. This time the bullets evaporate under the influence of his scales. The guardian's scales, capable of redirecting lethal forces into small extra-dimensional pockets, most don't know of their true quality. *Unfortunate that their influence is unpredictable,* he thinks, *as with all aspects of chaos.* A circle of illusions herd the remaining soldiers, bullets passing harmlessly through them. He sinks back into the earth again, only to rise amongst them a moment later. A hallucination made terrifyingly real. A furor grips him then. He aligns his core with the axis of violence and a massacre results. The soldiers are quickly reduced to indistinguishable piles of carnage, accented by a head or a single limb. He tears at the group for a while as the torment of loss rages, uncontrolled. Finally, he calms and looks back down the tunnel.

I must run now, as trans-location can only be attained so often. These bilious curs! They shall pay. An equal measure of terror and blood is their fee, I shall see to it. Devlin is a kind spirit. He may yet be found and enticed back. There is hope, if only a sliver. Xan shall have to try, should any of us survive. The sounds of a great conflict have ebbed. It can only mean one of three things, victory, defeat, or the cyborg.

Grimmfang does not know terror. He lives without blood. Still, he can be disassembled. He can be razed to the ground using the apparatus of duplicity. Hubris is his lover, intimately connected by the sex acts of his own infamy. His story, wanting to become history, legend, an addiction to the furthering of his own image, it shall be his downfall. He wishes to defeat us, in word or deed. To force quarter or to slay us is his goal. I have little doubt. He wishes to steal our notoriety, and add it to his own. Else he could simply scoop Eric up, and threaten violence as he retreats. Perhaps this also has occurred. Though it is implausible, insanities requiem is an unfathomable tune. The tunnel's end shall bring resolve, one way or the other. Chaos again shall have its say, and I shall see what remains.

Rex emerges to the sight of smoke pillaring up from a half dozen points. Distant rifle fire begins, then multiplies. He looks to the southeast, the sound's source. A quick run follows. Buildings race by as he charges down the street. He peers to the left at an intersection. The bones of combat litter the streets. A large warehouse is burning there. Pavement scrolls by as concrete flecks explode from his claws. The fortress passes to his right, it still appears intact. He can see the body heat of Eric and Silver Dancer. They are in the employee lounge, monitoring the scanner. More gunfire, concentrated, many shooters. He charges forward and the gunfire grows louder. There are screams as well. A large office building slithers into view. Rex looks to the left, up the street. A warzone surrounds the factory there. Vehicles and drones smoulder in the street. He then looks towards the office building and narrows his eyes. Swirls of body heat flow in the second floor, one is split in half and a fresh chorus of gunfire begins. He moves slowly to the wall. A charge travels through his chaotic core. The wall flexes like jelly as he steps through without breaching the material.

Foul smells stain the air of the large open room. A hole in the ceiling catches his attention. Just beyond, the sounds of combat comingle with flustered voices. Invisibility comes at a thought and he moves to the fire escape, riven door flat on the floor. A high-pitched laugh rings in the stairwell, issued from the second level. Rex bounds up the stairs. A handful of soldiers huddle on the second floor. They're panicking and firing their weapons recklessly. Then he sees him, cloaked in technology, the cyborg. The soldiers cannot see him. Grimmfang turns and looks at Rex, a smile creases his skull tattoo. *I must first find the others*, he thinks, *soon enough abomination, soon enough*. Rex springs up the stairs, a heat signature now evident on the roof. A half-second later and the second level explodes. A fiery dagger of force smashes into the stairwell and the building shakes as he leaps through the fabric of the roof door.

He wills himself visible and says, "Eve, Cable, come let us regroup, Devlin shall yet be avenged." Eve limps from the shadows as Cable relinquishes his cover and replies.

"Rex, it's good to see you." Rex looks him over.

"I see that there has been some difficulty here, forgive me, a force came from the tunnel. Dealing with it was of paramount import."

"Right, the tunnel, of course," Cable responds.

Eve nods and says, "Thanks for that, probably would be dead if a second force came from the flank there." Rex bows.

"You are both wounded, follow my lead, the cyborg shall not escape my notice." He looks across the roof then continues, "Has there been any word from Xan?" Cable shakes his head.

"Some kind of powerful transmission blocker is in play, short range comms are unaffected but Dancer can't get a line out." Rex nods and focuses on his senses, just in time. A hooded skeleton charges towards them. The instinct of battle takes hold, and the frenzy drives him. A brief look of bemusement crosses the cyborg's face as Rex pounces. Blades hurtle end over end as a brutal grapple unfolds. Rex snaps and rips at synthetic tissues. He twists chrome and batters titanium, rolling through a vicious and unforgiving assault. Grimmfang lashes back with primitive savagery, hammering with fist, elbow and knee. The pair crashes across the roof, each battling for position. Grimmfang unexpectedly leaps into the air, a red pin flashes from his eye, as a barrel in his palm cracks twice. A line of fire slashes into Rex's side causing him to howl, but the explosive shells evaporate an instant before striking home, shielded by his scales. Cable's auto shotgun cuts in, but Grimmfang changes direction in an instant as his hand swings him back across to the ruined factory. Rex reaches into his chaotic core and a small distortion appears above the cyborg. He lets out a yell of surprise as the lightning strikes him. Electricity surges through him, only to be buffeted away without having any effect. He kneels on his right knee and smiles broadly. His voice projects across the way as Cable moves to retaliate.

"Oh mighty Rex, your speech is complex and your flex makes me vex, powers perplex! And so I annex, leave this metroplex else ride the vortex!" As soon as he finishes, the front of his left shin snaps open and a small missile streaks towards the office building.

"Incoming!" Rex yells then sinks through the fabric of the roof, landing graciously on a pile of debris. A half-beat later Cable tumbles in through a jagged hole in the ceiling. Then an explosion jars the roof, raining dust down on the carpet. "Eve" Rex growls. Cable coughs and sits up, shotgun slung. He points to his head.

"Eve, are you there!" Cable stands and retrieves the dangling shotgun then aims it at the hole. Rex glances through the room, low-walls splintered to bits. There, in the office, Devlin's body. He bows his head for a second. Eve answers and Cable nods, "Alright, go around the south side, we'll try to draw him here." Rex moves quickly to the fire door.

"Come, we shall sight him from the roof." Cable nods and follows while watching behind them.

They quickly reach the roof again, a fuming pit marking where the missile detonated. He scans the surroundings. "Tell her to get to the roof, now!" Cable relates the message immediately. A strained few seconds pass before an exhausted Eve appears on the southern edge of the roof. A high-pitched laugh rises from the street where she just was. Rex searches for the swords, they're gone, undoubtedly retrieved by the cyborg. Then he notices the dark figure rising up behind Eve. He roars and charges as a skeletal horror materializes behind her. She reacts and tumbles forward with a sudden burst of energy, as blades cleave the air where she just stood. Rex finds his chance then. *One arm*, he thinks, *dismantle him*. He latches onto the cyborg's left arm and wrenches with the whole of his violence. The limb shears off and a blade drops. Cable lets out a single short laugh. Grimmfang reacts immediately, carving a deep line through Rex's hind leg. A spray of oily blood escapes from his leg as he hurls the limb from the roof and spins to the attack. The cyborg anticipates again and kicks out, stopping Rex dead in his tracks. Rex's instincts take over and he instantly swipes a paw into the cyborg's head, sending him cart-wheeling to the side. Grimmfang rolls with the force of the blow and stands smoothly. Rex narrows his gaze. The limb is re-forming, slowly but surely. He grits his teeth. *Speed is the key then*, he thinks. They circle for a second, then, Cable attacks. Grimmfang dodges and melts his auto shotgun in half with a line of laser light. Rex moves to the assault only to be cut deeply through the left flank. He adjusts and ravages the cyborg, rending his side open before being thrown off. Peripheral vision catches Eve trying to stand, her face slackens and she falls on her side, unconscious from arcane drain. Rex roars fiercely. A high-pitched laugh answers. They circle and are ready to engage again when the rhythmic thump of helicopter blades intervenes. Rex and the cyborg both look to the approaching rotorcraft.

Rex smiles and says, "Now monster, drown in the consequences of your barbarism." Grimmfang looks at him. Then, he quickly turns and kneels on his left leg, right shin snapping open in the process. Rex's warning is drowned out by the rush of a small missile launching, followed closely by an energetic, high-pitched laugh.

Xanshudan and Kane

The helicopter pitches sickeningly. An internal speaker crackles to life.

"Horse-fucking cocksucker! Hold on." An urgent sideways inertia unbalances him for a second. Cassandra and Rebecca are strapped into their harnesses. He rights himself with the hanging strap, rushing air fills the interior. The open side door displays a ruinous scene below as the helicopter rights itself. "Ass-eating goatsucker! Got a hole in the main engine, this bitch won't be airborne for long; I'll bring her down over in that lot," Sharkey announces. A cloud of acrid black smoke billows in to support his theory. Xan calms himself. He looks back at Cassandra, her face a mask of determination. He points at the Human reporter.

"Stay with her and Sharkey, I'll be back for you." She shakes her head and reaches out but he's gone, through the open door. The pavement rushes towards him. *Breathe in power, breathe out fear,* he thinks. The warrior fire ignites and quickly turns into a raging conflagration. He smashes into the ground, a tremor ripples out. Power radiates through the cloud of dust. Two lines of energy stretch down into his legs and the world blurs. A harsh helicopter landing draws his focus for a second, no explosion. His relief turns quickly to anger as the sounds of battle encroach. Kane's voice fills his mind.

"On the roof there!" Xan looks up and to the left, compelled by an indecipherable feeling. Rex and Grimmfang are fighting; the cyborg is missing an arm, it's growing back at an alarming rate however. He turns towards the building, hops onto a stone gatepost, and rockets straight towards the roof. The parking lot falls away, he focuses on his awareness as he arcs through the air. A snapshot of images filter in; an interior destroyed by combat, Rex is wounded, the roof ledge approaches. Cable, he's missing an arm as well, Eve is unconscious, no sign of Devlin, he lands and attacks on the half beat. Rex rolls away as Xan collides with the cyborg. A shower of bone-shattering strikes flows from him, a hundred blows in mere seconds. Pulsing waves of sonic power pour off of him. Grimmfang recoils, stunned, then blocks and dodges; he parries and counters with deadly arcs of steel, Xan slips, missing the blade by millimeters. The cyborg retreats. Xan pursues immediately with a flying sidekick. Grimmfang blocks and slashes. Xan catches the sword arm and throws him, instantly drawing his pistol directly afterwards. A dozen shots ring out and a series of explosions hammer the damaged cyborg. Right afterwards, a swarm of projectiles slam into Grimmfang, Cable's machine pistol blaring away on full-auto. Xan reloads and goes to press the attack only to be struck by a foot, he blocks. The pistol skitters from his hand and he rolls backwards. Grimmfang is at him in a heartbeat and they clash. The cyborg performs a series of diagonal cuts ending with a spinning sidekick. Meanwhile, Xan envelopes his arm in "The bands of Zixi" and he parries, sparks of red and purple springing from the impact points. He then rolls into the sidekick and delivers a perfect spinning back-elbow in the process. A wave of thunder impacts with the cyborg and sends him cartwheeling through the air. Before Grimmfang can land Rex is on him, shredding and gnashing with a frightening intensity. The two battle briefly before the cyborg disappears. Rex looks to the ruined factory across the street. Xan tracks his gaze, nothing. He retrieves his pistol.

"He fled in that direction," Rex says then looks at Xan, several deep wounds cover the Asura's body.

"Cass, shit! Cable, Rex, are you two alright, where's Devlin?" Rex nods then looks down at the roof. Cable walks over slowly while reloading his machine pistol.

"I've had worse, Eve's unconscious, Devlin's dead." Xan winces and looks down at the roof. He then looks back to Cable.

"I see, stay here and protect her, try to get back to the fortress. Rex can you still fight?" Rex smiles then charges towards the factory.

"Worry not Xanshudan, this day has brought an invigorating amount of chaos to my plate, a grand banquet that has not yet sated my appetite." Xan leaps after him. They plummet into the parking lot and run to the street. Rex pauses to look around and Xan follows suit, when a high-pitched laugh comes from overhead, then an amplified voice.

"Xan, Xan, he's our man, if he can't do it the bogeyman can. Does our little brannigan fit into your plan? Where's your courtesan? Man of the 'Venom clan'. You charlatan and authoritarian, Dark Elf and killer, you Hit man and Con man and spectral parasite willer ..."

Kane interjects, "Hey, fruitcake! How about you stop spewing nursery rhymes and let somebody else talk for a second huh?" Grimmfang frowns, then roars with anger and launches to the attack. Both of his arms are restored, a sword is in each of them. Rex instinctively backs away and covers his ears. Xan's left arm raises, hand open and palm facing forward. Kane grins then unleashes a flesh-rending scream. The air writhes with terrible waves of sonic power, metal twists, windows shatter. Grimmfang plows into the cone of energy and is instantly thrown backwards in an awkward spin. He smashes into the ground and stands at once. Kane laughs. The cyborg's left arm is gone again. "Easy come, easy go eh?" Kane yells. Grimmfang looks down, laughs insanely and leaps forward. Rex collides with him mid-air but the cyborg anticipates and rolls under him, the Asura careens past and lands hard on his side. Xan draws and fires, three rounds burst open Grimmfang's left thigh and his side but he keeps moving. The cyborg's mouth opens and a single mono-wire springs out and back in, faster than the Human eye can follow. Xan looks down to see a small hole in his jacket. He stumbles back. Grimmfang attacks. Xan just manages to slip under the first strike; however, the second strike carves an inch deep line through his left shoulder and chest. He recoils in pain then counters with a series of blindingly fast strikes. Grimmfang bounds backwards, giggling like a demented schoolgirl. Kane's voice fills his mind.

"Nasty little poison that he just shot into you, I'll spit that out then, shall I?" Xan snorts and fires at the cyborg, the rounds barely missing as Grimmfang darts quickly to his left, towards Rex. A short dizzy spell overtakes Xan for a second, just before a small stream of toxic fluid pours from Kane's mouth. He shakes his head and moves to Grimmfang's flank.

"Thanks," he internalizes. Grimmfang lunges. Rex disappears into the ground, a small patch of actual dirt and grass providing him with a refuge. The cyborg rolls around smoothly, a line of red light streams from his left eye. A scorching pain strikes Xan's side.

He flinches away from it and fires off a half-dozen rounds. Grimmfang immediately zigzags, still, one round detonates in his left knee and the cyborg stumbles. Xan closes the distance, a rush of air flowing over him. The collision is brutal. Grimmfang skitters violently up the street before he hits a curb and instantly rebounds at Xan. The blade stabs through Xan's left side. Grimmfang laughs and pulls the steel free, through the intervening flesh. Xan collapses. The cyborg raises his sword just as a roar shakes the ground and he's tackled by a shimmering blue monster. Rex rips and tears into him; the blade is jarred from his hand. Xan concentrates and tries to wick away the pain, but it's too great. He fumbles around in his pocket. The surgeon's patch comes quickly to hand. He's peeling the foil when a starburst of shrapnel erupts at his feet, explosive shells from the cyborg's palm shotgun. Instinct kicks in and he rolls to the side, the patch drops from his grasp. A claw of agony greets him as he lands, dark blood pours from his back. Grimmfang batters Rex and sends him sprawling. The cyborg turns back towards Xan, blade in hand, other arm nearly regrown, again. The skull smiles and he rushes forward. Xan prepares for the inevitable when a pulse of energy discharges from behind him. A great searing mass of heat flashes past Xan and hits the cyborg square in the chest. Grimmfang looks down, stunned. A glowing fist sized hole is directly where his heart should be. Cassandra's voice fills the street.

"Let's see you heal now you sick fucker!" Grimmfang roars with wordless rage, another bolt streaks towards him, melting his right arm off at the shoulder. He looks at Cassandra and smiles. Then he bows deeply, and disappears entirely. Xan convulses as shock sets in, blood pools beneath him. "Hold on Xan!" Cassandra yells as she runs to retrieve the surgeon's patch. His vision swirls. Rex bounds over looking around frantically. She returns bearing the surgeon's patch. The nano-bots soon stop the bleeding and a pleasant narcotic haze settles over him. Kane's face breaks the surface of his palm.

"Great, now he's stoned." He then pauses and adds, "Thanks though, that was kind of close." Rex looks over at Cassandra.

"See to him, I must verify that this is not a ploy enacted to capture Eric." Rex then turns and jogs slowly to the fortress. Cassandra hefts the plasma pistol and sits near Xan.

"Shit, where'd that fucker go? He regrows arms fast," Xan says as he tries to stand. His legs give out and she helps him sit again.

"Slowly, shit Xan, he almost cut you in half. That sick bastard is gone. I was aiming for his head with that second shot. I definitely hit his 'Reconstruction Protocol', that's the spot for sure, right in the heart." Xan laughs weakly.

"Ah Cass, I forgot that you knew so much helpful shit, so how long until he gets that fixed?" She shrugs.

"Take at least a week to synch up a new nano-cloud, plus you have to find the cybernetics to begin with, 'Reconstruction Protocols' are ultra rare, even in 'The Tier'. Still, he might just rebuild and wait for the protocol, in that case it could be a couple of days." Xan nods grimly. *Next time he won't play with us*, he thinks, *it'll be sniper rifles and bombs.* A haze of heat rises from the plasma pistol's barrel.

He motions towards it and says, "That's one hell of a toy, didn't know that you owned one of those." Cassandra laughs and peaks an eyebrow.

"A girl has to have some secrets, doesn't she?"

He laughs, then coughs in pain and says, "Help me up, we have to go back to the fortress. Where's Sharkey?" Cassandra nods up the street.

"With the helicopter and the reporter, he put it in sentry mode. I figured that we could try to herd Grimmfang towards him; I guess that doesn't matter now though. That fucker! I'll put a million credit bounty on his head." Xan leans on her and stumbles towards the fortress.

"I wouldn't do that Cass; he's killed anyone that's posted a bounty on him, except for the Marshalls of course, although he has murdered a fair number of them. Still, if his mission was to capture Eric, all we have to do is figure out how to extract the whatever the fuck it is that's in him and they'll be no reason for Grimmfang to go after us anymore." She snorts. Her voice cracks with emotion.

"What about Elindriss and Marcus and the others? He's not going to get away with that, besides, don't you think that he's going to want to get payback anyway?" They turn into the fortress' street, no signs of trouble.

"Not the way I've heard it, he bowed to you Cass. I think he respects an honest defeat. I don't know that I'd provoke him. If he comes back at us we'll have to try to deal with him." An urgency overcomes him and he adds, "But, if you provoke him he'll come after you when you least expect it. I can't protect you all the time, please Cassandra." A soft desperation accents his voice. She looks at him, eyes glistening.

"Alright Xan, but I'm going to have to look into his contract, if it involves killing your team ... I won't hesitate." Xan smiles as they approach the church's main door, it's still intact. The mag-lock buzzes open at their approach, part of Silver Dancer's control.

Xan moves to the door and says, "Thanks, by the way, for saving my life or whatever." She laughs softly as they enter the internal space. The main doors snap shut as Cassandra pulls them closed. She then opens the internal door and guides Xan inside. Eric is on the stairs to the second level, just past the sentry. The boy seems distressed; he looks at Xan and speaks.

"Silver Dancer said to say that Cable and Eve are on the way back, but, Devlin, he's ... he's still there, in that building." Eric looks down at the ground. "I'm sorry; I saw it on the scanner. Are you alright?" Xan nods and looks at Eric.

"It's not your fault Eric; Devlin knew the risks, as we all do. Besides, isn't Grot able to perform a resurrection ritual?" He looks at Cassandra with the last statement, she nods her head.

"He's going to have his work cut out for him, soon enough," she says softly. Eric swallows and looks at Xan.

"Silver Dancer also said that she figured out how they tracked us, some kind of transmitter? A bullet embedded in the car, the drone, she said." Xan shakes his head.

"Damn it, I thought that she had a scanner in her car, why didn't she catch it on the sensor tower?"

Eric shrugs and says, "I think she did, she said the car's security system fried it so it was harder to find." Xan sighs and sits at an empty desk, a flood of fatigue flowing through him. Cassandra closes the internal door and sits next to Xan. "We're going to have to relocate; they'll send the big guns next time. No more of this corporate training exercise bullshit. They're going to start sending power suits, war walkers and corporate cyborgs, we can't fight that." He pauses for a second then adds, "Not to mention that the racket must have attracted other attention, it's only a matter of time before the Marshalls come in force, maybe the military." Cassandra looks worried.

"If we head out now we could still lose them, in the core or underground." Xan looks at her pensively then nods. He looks at Eric just as Rex limps to the top of the stairs.

"Eric please tell Dancer to start getting ready to leave, we want to be gone in ten minutes tops." He nods and turns to go up the stairs, stopping as he sees Rex.

"Oh shit, are you okay?" Eric says. A note of honest concern in his voice, Rex smiles and bows.

"Worry not young one, it is difficult to kill that which is only partially here. The earth shall rejuvenate me when I am able to enfold myself within its embrace yet again." Eric seems to be confused but he nods happily when he realizes that Rex isn't concerned about the wounds. The front door buzzes open and all eyes turn towards a battered Cable and an exhausted Eve. Eric then turns and heads further into the second level.

"What happened?" Cable inquires as they pass through the internal door. Xan smiles wanly.

"Cassandra put him out of commission, though he's probably still alive."

"Good, but, fuck," Cable says. Eve winces then slumps in an old office chair.

"How long will he be down, do we know?" she says. Cassandra looks over.

"I should have shot him in the fucking head." She sighs and adds, "Maybe two or three weeks if we're lucky, two or three days if we're not." Eve tilts her head from side to side, a "That's alright" gesture that Cable nods to. Eve then groans and wheezes as she tries to stand. Xan looks up at the second level as Eric returns to stand near Rex.

"Eric, bring one of those surgeon's patches to Eve." Eric looks confused for a second before he registers what Xan said. He then quickly descends the stairs and offers one of the silvery pouches to Eve.

"Thanks, I feel like a punching bag that's been worked over by an Ogre heavyweight."

Eric giggles, then looks ashamed and says, "Sorry, I didn't mean to laugh, it probably hurts ..." Eve laughs, winces and peels open the surgeon's patch.

"Don't worry kid, its fine." She then applies the patch to the torn section of her armor on her left flank. Eric nods awkwardly then announces.

"Silver Dancer needs some help with the tower and the generator in the basement." Xan nods, Cassandra stands.

"I'll call Sharkey, he may have the helicopter up and running again. He said that he had a couple of custom made nano-resconstruction treatments." Eve stands and stretches, Xan slowly rises to his feet as Cassandra produces her secure-com.

"I'll retrieve the tower. I've taken it down before," Xan says as he crosses to the second level staircase. Rex peers down at him.

"I shall relocate Devlin's body to the church here and then bask within the earth womb near to where we fought with the monster." Xan nods.

"Thanks Rex, do you need help with Devlin's body?" Rex shakes his head.

"No, I shall drape him across my back and grip his leg with my jaws." Xan nods.

"Alright, we'll come by that spot just before we leave."

Rex nods then adds, "The portal gem is still an option." Xan stops in his tracks for a second. He'd forgotten about that. He slowly nods his head. Cassandra's conversation continues in the background, it sounds like Sharkey is almost ready to go.

"You might be right Rex, let me think on it." Rex nods, and then casually trots through the far wall as though it were made out of water. Eric stands transfixed.

"The flux?" Eve says, Cable looks over.

"Shit, I hate that place, what about the van?" Xan looks back from the second level landing.

"Put on the security system and hope for the best I guess." Cable snorts and sits in an empty chair. Xan rounds the corner as Cassandra's voice drifts into the staircase.

"I tell you what; I'll buy you a new van or a new arm if it comes down to it, your choice ..." The rest is drowned out as he crosses to the steel door and exits into the winding staircase. He moves to the porch. A handful of small fires still rage. *This area's fire sprinklers are obviously non-functional,* he thinks, *just like the rest of the plumbing.* He stands and focuses on his senses, listening intently. Distant traffic comingles with the faint shuffle of flames. He gazes through the level then quickly disassembles the turret and unplugs it. His strength slowly returns as his arcane core focuses on healing. The sky darkens, and a purple-black bruise smears across the horizon. Xan looks to the south as movement catches his eye. It's the body of Devlin, lying sideways and moving on an invisible Rex. He furrows his brow then jumps as the sound of automatic weapons' fire begins in the north, towards the downed helicopter. The sounds are followed by the deep thump of the thirty millimeter cannon. *Grimmfang,* he thinks, *no, it couldn't be, could it?* He's acutely aware of a presence and he turns to see Rex, Devlin's corpse is slumped on the porch. Xan points to the north.

"Grimmfang, he's back!" Rex shakes his head and looks at him gravely.

"No, it is far worse than that Xanshudan, far, far worse."

Delirium's Ode

Eternity spent herding the nameless
shepherd unto lonely ciphers of flesh
Tendrils vie, undone by sharp fang's caress
of marching mutants, pilgrimage made fresh

Marvel at the new infection, made old,
similarities produce the same result
of decay and ignorance, always told
as a tale ever the same, life's tumult

Transmutation enlivens savagery
in thought and deed, a thing of importance
Untrue morals turned to adultery,
sodomize all life in a zealous trance

Rape the decent here with ugly belief,
a complete debasement is what we seek
No end to the hideousness until relief
Joyous torture made chiefly for the meek

Mollify nothing with this bitterness
of presence that cannot but counteract
any trivial reasons standing witness
to the act, and the nothing left intact

Our actions scar the buildings, consecrate
the ground built red with constant offerings
Righteous path, risible blood shall sate
from the humourless, needed sufferings

Come now brothers, fellows of acid faith
Perversion the word for our vain wallow
Voices of fallacy haunt as a wraith,
prompting the abhorrent hordes who follow

Maddening cries of semblance instigate
a world of fear sold off at a market
Glory be to the public reprobate;
shark smile, hefting guns, hand in your pocket

Unbound power from unnamed vagabonds
Shadowy trail of forces left unseen
Proliferate agony, ire responds
Vengeful behemoth sires, as always been

Come swift combat, clawed deep through exalt
of sacred mutilation made country
Voided out in grand rivulets of salt
Blackened husks remain to rule as gentry

Marbled road, strife of pitted ruin upon
this havoc reeks within new dooms embrace
Nameless faith I bring stapled to jupon
A calling born, pathogen of grace

Pitiless one stampedes before the cause,
abominable giant who rules the streets
A sun encased sits as *reason* because,
when I sleep the same prophet vision greets

War machine on high, blades whirl with fire, death
Pool of derangement here now manifest
Undulation of nightmares with each breath,
from dark church a bleeding prize we shall wrest

Jubilant army, pawns of fervent conquest,
madness their gift through reams of life digest
Siege the spoiled ground at dark voice behest
The parlor of their minds vile light infest

Josh Berg

Horror loud, the chorus that is attained,
a fallow tune, the dirge a living thing
The cannibal's song in all keys gained;
consume the faithless new abyssal king

War machine baulks before the wretched tide
Warrior's fire from the church now explode
Courage against the darkening void, pride,
will or not endure, delirium's ode

Eric Gibson

It's all a dream, just a dream, no, a nightmare. It's a nightmare, that's it, or I fell into a coma. That must be it, like that old cheesy show. The kid was in a coma but to him it was like he'd been transported to some crazy fantasy world. That's it, that's why it all seems so real. Just wake up, wake up, wake up, wake up, wake up, wake up, WAKE UP! ... Silver Dancer's voice cuts in, bringing stark reality with it.

"Eric, to your right!" I spin to look. There, on the north end of the front room roof, one of those big worm things. It slithers forward, needle fangs in a gaping maw, it's trailing a spread of long tentacles. I shakily put the laser dot on it. A shock of adrenalin hits me as I squeeze the trigger, a quartet of detonations scattering the mutant worm across the roof. A severed tentacle rolls clumsily to the edge. My heart skips a few beats as the sound of that thing bellowing comes from the street, just past the roof. Some horrible giant, I couldn't even look at it without becoming sick. I still feel shitty, even after eating that thing that Rex gave me. He said some crazy shit about "not giving in to the foul delirium of the warp" or something. I don't know, it was supposed to help. Silver Dancer's assault rifle cracks twice and another worm thing splatters and falls from the roof's edge. I look around, an explosion thunders in the street, then gunfire. Still, that sound, that terrible sound, it's digging into my brain. I look at Silver Dancer.

"What the fuck is happening?"

She scans the roof and says, "Bad shit Eric, a Zealot of the cult of the Abyss. There's no time to explain, just kill anything that looks disgusting." An impact shakes the building and Xan lands on the roof's eastern edge. He immediately takes aim and launches a grenade from the under-barrel launcher. The explosion is close enough to rock the building again. An unnatural scream is followed by a long stream of bullets, as Xan unloads his rifle's magazine. Then the sound of Rex howling, far up the street, it's almost worse than the giant mutant. Xan looks over.

"Rex is trying to keep that giant off balance, Cable and Eve got some more ammo to "Gerty" on the factory roof, Sharkey's looping around with Cass, he said that there's some powerful mojo floating around down there so watch out, I'll be back." He then

293

runs to the northern edge of the roof and dives from sight. My heart's about to explode, calm down, just wake up. I stumble for a second and look down. Devlin's body, it's his leg. He was really nice. He tried to cheer me up a couple of times, poor bastard. I feel a tear and blink it away. A storm of weapons' fire cascades through the streets to the northeast. Silver Dancer puts a hand to her ear.

"Keep an eye out would you Eric? I'm going to talk to the others for a second." I nod and peer down into the streets. A sense of the movement of living things overcomes me. I can't seem to make my vision work. It's like some kind of snow blindness. I squint and wipe at my eyes. A few seconds pass before my brain accepts what my eyes are telling me. My mind recoils in horror. The whole area is crawling with hideous creatures of all shape and size. Nonsensical profusions of insect limbs, eyes and tendrils adorn the bizarre mutations. There are bulky snake things with wiry hair, and horrid humanoid things that shouldn't be able to live. I can see car-sized blobs of tentacles with snapping mouths and insane eyes. Fearsome, bloated abominations roll around with huge knots of mutated worms, each more than five feet long. I'm going to be sick. My stomach goes through a gymnastic routine, I retch. The stink is unbelievable. Like an open sewer mixed with the worst B.O. in history. I'm trying to adjust to what I'm seeing, when the mutant giant appears again. Twenty feet tall, with a disconcerting assortment of eyes, the claws of its right hand are the size of scimitars. The other arm bristles with sharp spines, it's moving on all fours, trying to run down Rex, who's staying just feet ahead. The Asura leaps through the substance of a brick wall. The giant follows by haphazardly destroying half of the building, then lumbering through the wreckage. They both disappear from sight, and my mind sobers a bit as I look back at the mutant horde again. As I watch, Cable's mini-gun roars to life, he's at the edge of the factory roof firing the mini-gun with his one remaining arm, thanks to the gyroscopic rig. A chaotic line of broken light bursts from the factory roof, the noise is overwhelming, the result is disgusting. I turn away as the street is transformed into a charnel house. The mini-gun pauses for a second, and a warbled roar fills the gap, making my flesh crawl. I'm not sure what that was, but I'm sure that it was terrible. I glance back towards Silver Dancer, oasis to the senses in a dry ugly desert. She nods to an invisible voice and says something. I can't quite hear. She called it sub-vocalizing. I quickly look around, paranoia taking root as the brutal sounds continue. Silver Dancer looks down into the street then back across the roof.

"Sharkey's going to drop off Cass and some Human; we're going to get some shit ready to go." She points at the stairwell. A collection of boxes containing the remaining gear sits there in the living room. I nod and glance around. Another shot of adrenalin slams into me as I look back past the belltower. It's impossible. Tentacles support a humanoid torso, but, the rest, it's all wrong. There's a crab pincer in place of its right arm, the left arm ends in rubbery, clawed fingers and its face. I freeze. My arms won't work, I force out a scream. Silver Dancer whirls in my peripheries. That face. I can't look away. Its features are moving, flowing like froth on the ocean shore. Then the sound of the assault rifle slaps me back to awareness and I fumble for my gun, too late. The thing lunges, but it comes apart under the scrutiny of Dancer's explosive rounds. A sickening husk slowly slides from the roof. My legs give out and I find myself sitting. Silver Dancer kneels beside me. "Eric! Are you alright? Are you injured?" I gradually look to her. She seems far away, but oh so beautiful. I can't really see her anymore. I'm having great difficulty recalling my surroundings. But, I remember my fifth grade trip to the zoo. I felt so bad for the animals; no one else seemed to care. I didn't want to leave though. I ended up getting in trouble when they couldn't find me at the end of the day. I was trying to figure out how to free the tiger. I couldn't stand its constant pacing, the agitation made me so sad. Finally they called my parents. My dad was furious. He had to take time off from work to get me. He yelled the whole way home. The car's motor sounded exactly like that big, frustrated cat.

The sound of gunfire filters into my awareness. There's someone in front of me. She's shooting at something. She's gorgeous, she seems familiar. Then a voice, it's very far away: *Wake up Eric, she needs you now.* I blink and look around quickly, my mind jumps. Dozens of those melted humanoid things cover the roof. Their faces are masks of anguish, no lower jaw. They have skeleton arms and their lower bodies are just blubbery sacks of pus and entrails, they stick to things like slugs. Silver Dancer reloads. They're closing in on the porch. I stand and grab my vest pocket. The grenade!

"Look away and cover your ears," I yell while producing the metal cylinder. She smiles and winks at me. I pull the pin and pop the hammer, then hurl it at the group moving through the V created by the two pitched roofs. I duck and cover my ears. A half-second later a blinding light flares, and a subsonic boom rattles my ribcage. Silver Dancer laughs and raises her rifle. I look back towards the group; a half-dozen fell from the roof as their senses were overwhelmed. The rest are all swaying about and clawing at the air. She fires and I follow suit, the combined impacts quickly demolish the small group. She picks off the stragglers with single shots. I begin to breathe again, hard, in rhythm to my beating heart. She looks over.

"Are you okay now?" I just nod slightly. She's about to say something when the sound of the helicopter quickly approaches. She points to the helicopter, I nod and head towards the staircase. She hesitates for a minute and I look back towards the helicopter. A thundering barrage from the thirty millimeter cannon stings my ears, and makes me duck reflexively. The helicopter then sways into position at the southern edge, the short pitched roof serving as a walkway. The huge vehicle moves precisely and lines up exactly flush with the edge. The pilot has phenomenal control. Apparently he's a Dwarf named Sharkey. Cassandra appears in the open doorway and then jumps onto the roof. She has really good balance. A Human woman is with her, she has short, spikey purple hair. The Human stumbles off of the helicopter, scrambles for the peak and then clings on for dear life.

Cassandra moves to the porch and says, "We can't stay here, the helicopter can't carry everyone at the same time, but we're going to bring groups, up a couple levels, hopefully we'll lose them. Sharkey's going to grab Eve, Xan, Rex and Cable while we get the gear." Silver Dancer nods. The helicopter banks towards the factory. I can see all sorts of things collecting around the building's base. There are giant worms, anomalous indescribable things and creepy bugs with Human faces. The mini-gun blends in with the thirty millimeter cannon and a portion of the horde is blasted into a quivering mess. Then I get a glimpse of something, far up the street to the north. It's like a tall humanoid figure, basked in a purplish mist. The figure is wearing a hooded robe and a half-dozen insect appendages stick from the bottom of the fabric. They're the thing's legs. A sharp pain strikes my head, an instant migraine of unparalleled proportions. I fall to the side and vomit. The small sun, I see it, twisting and rolling in a circle. Silver Dancer says something but an odd-sounding explosion drowns her out. Cassandra gasps and I follow her gaze. A grinding crash comes from the street a second later. The explosion was the helicopter, it's burning and surrounded by mutants. A second explosion erupts from the chassis. The blast lights up the entire area, bathing the group of mutations in a rolling wall of fire. Smoke chokes out my vision. My head throbs, and I feel sick again. I swallow and force it back then look over at Silver Dancer.

Cassandra sniffs, hefts her rifle and says, "Sharkey ... damn it, alright, all of you come. We have to help the others."

"You're right," Silver Dancer says. I nod and look at the Human woman. She's staring at me in a strange way. She doesn't have a weapon, and her right hand is bandaged.

"Don't you have a gun?" I ask. She tilts her head for a few seconds, as if considering something.

"I did have one; they didn't let me bring it though." I furrow my brow. What does that mean? Cassandra looks over and sighs.

"Things have changed now. Here, take it." She hands the woman an assault rifle, and a number of magazines. The Human handles the rifle awkwardly before transferring it to her left hand. Cassandra looks hard at her and adds, "If you double cross us you won't live to regret it." The woman looks afraid, she swallows and nods. Cassandra then unholsters a large, advanced looking pistol. She vaults over the handrail and runs around the belltower. The roof is pitched on both sides of the porch, there's a valley existing between the roof over the second level and the vaulted ceiling covering the main front space. I crawl over the left side railing and walk into the valley. There are gross bits of dead flesh pooling with dark fluids in the central channel. I gag and try not to look down as I move to the northern edge. Cassandra and Silver Dancer are in position; the Human woman is just behind us. I peer over the edge.

A revolting assembly litters the street. Stretching above them is some huge eel creature with four eyes and tentacles pouring from its face, some of the tentacles end in clawed hands. The monstrosity rears up and expels a repugnant cloud of tiny, tentacle faced eels that float then fly towards us like a school of fish swimming through the ocean. A deep thump comes from Cassandra's pistol; a fast streak of white light distorts the air. The bolt incinerates a hole through the cloud but it continues, a collection of slimy banners caught in the wind. I can see them more clearly now, each the size of my forearm with four mandibles surrounding a circular mouth. A ring of eyes line their conical bodies. They're horrible, I shudder and another shock of adrenalin hits me as I aim. Semi-auto, I can't waste bullets. The grotesque cloud rushes forward. I fire nearly at the same time as Silver Dancer and the Human woman. Two detonations rip into the cloud. The collective parts into individuals as a number of them drop, then the cloud reforms. The firing continues. Cassandra is aiming carefully at something below, in the street. Another series of explosions knock more of the horrid things out of the air. Then I see them, just behind, another cloud of these things and another behind that. They're heading this way, along with a bunch of the freaks on the ground. My heart starts racing, adrenalin turning sour in my veins. Another deep thump comes from Cassandra's pistol, a half-second later and a frightening screech responds. Then the flying things drop, like they all just had strokes or something. Silver Dancer laughs and says something. The sound of the mini-gun firing in steady bursts blocks my hearing. Cassandra then points across at the factory.

I look over. A horrid mass of live and dead things now surround the building, a great gnashing floor of claws, spines and tentacles. Xan and Cable are at the roof's edge, I can't see Eve or Rex. The Human woman begins to fire, Silver Dancer follows. I look down at where they're shooting. The street to the north of the church is alive with those dangerous worms. There are thousands upon thousands of them. I try to slow my breathing as I begin to fire. Round after round explodes in the advancing brood. A grenade detonates in their midst, fired from Xan's launcher. Tendrils, teeth and rubbery flesh discharges from the squirming carpet of bodies. But they keep advancing, no fear or thought of their own safety. The Human reloads, Silver Dancer isn't far behind. I look at my vest, even with the extra magazines Xan gave me I only have three left, plus three for the pistol. A sudden bolt of lightning arcs downward and a large bloated mutant ignites then runs down the street. I look back towards the factory as a half-dozen Rex's appear in the mass of mutations. The creatures seem confused, they're moving randomly. The real Rex is among the copies as well. I can see him tossing them around like rag-dolls. He's running right through them with those razor sharp claws or talons or both, I guess. Then I see him again. The figure in the hood, he's walking in the middle of the worms. That light is coming from him, it hurts my eyes. A dagger of agony stabs my brain. I can't help but scream and grab my head. A searing needle flashes through my temple. I can see the sun, it's fuming and boiling. Silver Dancer is at my side, she's saying something. I wince and cry out as a spasm wracks my brain. She reaches out to steady me, I feel something wet on my upper lip. I reach up, its blood. I look at her, she looks concerned. The gunfire rages.

I wave her off and say, "It's okay, I'm fine." She looks doubtful but after a second she turns back to the street, taking aim and firing immediately. My brain twitches and throbs. It feels like small demons are stabbing it with pitchforks. I look towards the street. The figure is gone. A sharp silence blocks my hearing, my ears pulse with pillars of anguish. Then a voice overtakes the pain, it's quiet. It sounds like Devlin.

"*Hey kid, jacket pocket, on the porch, the bar*". The searing spike in my head fades to a dull ache. My mind resigns itself to my consciousness again, and the terrible sounds of our predicament filter slowly back into my awareness.

I look towards the porch then say, "One sec, I'll be right back." Silver Dancer looks confused but I quickly turn and move to the porch. A series of shots ring out between the church and the factory. The mini-gun has gone quiet, no doubt out of ammo again. I reach the porch. It feels weird to go through Devlin's pockets, even if he was the one who told me to do it. I inadvertently stop for a second at that thought. A chill runs down my spine. Think about it later, if there is a later. The bar, there, it's shiny, it looks like silver only shinier. It feels warm to the touch.

I'm pondering the significance of my find, when the church shakes violently. A second of absolute silence follows. I move back towards the far edge, and am shocked as the Human woman shrieks and runs down into the roof valley. My heart turns into a speed-bag being worked by a pro-boxer and I move in slow motion as the giant crests the northwest edge of the roof. Like a colossal mutant gorilla, with one arm tipped in scimitars fingers. Two thick tendrils sprout from either side of its head, an eyeball at the tip of each. The thing has at least seven other eyes covering its face and head. I feel sick again, it stops and looks at me with all of its eyes, then grins with a wide mouth full of sharp fangs. A wave of nausea strikes me. I double over and vomit, only bile, there's nothing else left.

Then a cacophony begins. Silver Dancer is screaming and firing on full-auto, while the Human woman is peppering it with single shots. I look up to see the thing lurching towards me; its torn flesh is healing nearly as quickly as it's being damaged. I yelp, no mind left, no cogent thoughts. I fall back and crawl away from it, I think. My mind registers movement. Out of the corner of my eye, a bolt streaks through the air and punches a hole through its chest, then another and another. It roars and scoops up a giant chunk of the roof then throws it at Cassandra. Silver Dancer and the Human duck into the valley. Cassandra moves just in time, sliding dangerously close to the roof's edge in the process. The giant bounds forward. I freeze again. My gun is on the porch, out of reach. Silver Dancer screams, she's reloading, panic in her eyes. Wait, to her right. There's some creature on the other side of the pitch, she doesn't see it, no! It's some terrible thing, mostly mouth, it'll kill her! I can't let that happen. NO! A furious fire rolls through my core and I yell. My right hand rises up, not of my control. The bar sings. I can see it clearly now, a beautiful staff of luminescence.

I scream in fury and the staff bursts with a volatile beam of dreadful light. My mind shudders and the world strobes. I see the beam slash through the giant, utterly disintegrating everything except for its left arm and legs. The huge limbs fall from the edge. The beam then rages through a swath of the roof before striking the mutation cresting the pitch. Silver Dancer looks over, surprised. The horrible mouth creature flakes away as the stream of energy washes over it. I lower my arm and a crushing wave of fatigue hits me, it's like I just ran for miles, worse even. I fall to my knees, panting. I would vomit if I could. A humming bird's heart doesn't beat this quickly. Cassandra regains her position and fires a shot down towards the factory. Silver Dancer signals towards the porch, the Human begins to move back. Cassandra fires once more then turns back towards the porch as well. I pocket the bar and feebly reach for my fallen gun, checking the magazine as I pick it up. There are just over twenty rounds left, based on the tick marks. I prop my back up against the guardrail. Silver Dancer rushes up.

"Eric, that, well that was amazing, but are you alright?"

I do my best Fonzy impression, thumbs up and a casually elongated, "Eh." Of course the reference is completely lost on them, still she laughs. No better sound in the world, which is ominously counterpointed by what has to be one of the worst sounds in the world. Thousands of huge worms moving in time to that insidious noise, that "meat grinder full of mutant pigs" noise that fills the cracks between the other noises, and just won't leave me alone. A vicious pain stabs into my head, Cassandra approaches.

"They've reached the far side, you two watch the roof. I'll take the east side, Rebecca you watch the street down there." Cassandra points to the southeast corner of the porch and the small parking lot below. The Human nods, Rebecca, that's her name. Cassandra then looks down into the street for a moment before looking back towards the group, "Everybody look back this way for a second," she says as she produces two small metallic orbs. My head swims. I shrug and look back towards her, Dancer and Rebecca look as well. She clicks each orb and a wide band of light projects from each of them, scanning us all at head level.

Cassandra consults the results for a second, then nods to herself, pulls some type of pin on each of them and then rolls them onto the porch. A few seconds later each of the orbs unfolds into a small spider like robot. Two of their forelegs look sharp and dangerous. Cassandra looks back down into the street, aims and takes a shot. I look back across the ruined roof; a gaping hole now leads to the main offices. The spider robots shift and start pacing around the porch. I aim for a second when, as if on cue, a muffled series of rifle bursts comes from inside the church. The sentry is still downstairs, in the main room there. Silver Dancer looks to Cassandra, she shakes her head. The firing continues downstairs for some time before abruptly stopping, hopefully because there aren't any targets left down there.

Movement draws my attention. Tendrils and razor sharp teeth, a dozen or more climb over the northern edge of the roof. I kneel towards them and begin to fire, one shot at a time. A worm ruptures and falls from sight. Bits of the roof explode, I adjust, another three worms split open, all jelly and gore. A short dizzy spell grips me and my vision blurs. Silver Dancer fires rapidly and a handful of the creatures spray oily bits as they are torn apart. Then Rebecca fires, down into the parking lot. Something horrible screams, she fires again and it stops. I take a deep breath then spit over the rail, the taste of bile fills my mouth. Another wave of tentacles reaches up over the roof edge as Cassandra fires down into the street again, a deep static thump breaking the sound of gunfire. Weapons' fire continues from the factory, and that noise. That bugs in the brain noise that won't stop, it's getting worse. I shake my head. A quick image flashes through my mind. The sun is fuming at my center, bubbling with power. Then a nail drives into my temple. I flinch and I'm aware of that figure. It's standing on the burning factory roof, to the northwest. A curtain of smoke wraps around him. Then it hits me, he was Human once. That face, it was a man's face at one time. Now a dizzying number of corneas swirl in eyes that are far too big for the head, ropey forms slick about underneath his long robes. A hammer strikes the nail in my temple and I fall, retching and screaming at the same time. Cassandra looks over. She frowns and gazes at the burning factory.

A look of surprise crosses her face and she points. Silver Dancer says something then looks to where Cassandra is pointing. She's worried as she looks back to me. She then looks angry and aims at the figure as Cassandra moves into position. The figures robe opens revealing a disgusting arrangement of mutated limbs and tendrils. A terrible nausea grips me then, and the porch ripples like water. The light around him grows. His mutated arms move. In response, Cassandra drops to the porch and begins convulsing. Silver Dancer fires a shot before she lets go of the rifle and grabs her head with both of her hands, she then drops to her knees and screams in pain. Rebecca takes aim and fires; the figure stumbles back on a spread of insect legs then disappears from sight. I look down at Dancer and Cassandra. They're both freaking out. Some white froth is coming from Cassandra's mouth, while Silver Dancer is just screaming and grabbing her head. I start to panic.

"What the fuck are we supposed to do?" I ask Rebecca, she looks shocked, and just as lost as I feel.

Then my head throbs with a crown of needles, that voice, Devlin, *"Grot's gift, help them Eric, it's up to you now."* I reach around inside the vest pocket. The tails are there. They're still slowly moving, three wondrous tendrils of light. I look at them closely. White and green veins of power buzz within them. Then it hits me. That's what they're for, it's all so clear now. I kneel on the porch and begin to move my hands in a way that seems as natural as breathing.

Rex

What a glorious day for chaos. Fly high the banners of war and live not for the future. Praise the great Vox Imaritrox, annihilator, fire bringer, the eternal soldier. Align this core with the axis of enmity. Become as them and you shall see their pastor, debauched soothsayer of the deranged. Feel their rancor and he shall stand out like a shining beacon, to be mauled. A few more minutes and I shall continue. It is useless if I move too soon. This body must mend, if only to regain mobility. The repellent horde shall be driven into the oblivion they so crave. First the shepherd must be slain. His dog is dead already. Some mystifying feat of magic, it felt like Devlin, only far more powerful. Now the same power mends the wounded and their battle begins afresh.

The fruits of Ner'Itash have inoculated them against the madness of the warp, yet still, the infection seeps in. The foul radiation of psychosis bombards us. We cannot endure the mental onslaught indefinitely, and, these barbarous creatures' blunderings have no doubt solicited the attention of others. They are not subtle, this stinking parade of murderous insanity.

But what is this? Yes! The earth aids this body now. It is a small pool, but it is connected to the core. It wishes this infection to be eradicated. It wishes to aid my subconscious infatuation. This growing instinct to destroy all that may hinder our sacred pact. Yes! Grant me your blessings and I shall find the horrid priest. I shall destroy their repugnant emissary. Rise up, power of the dirt and stone. A potent charge of life fills me. I am renewed and given new strength. A chaos reactor froths at my core. Join with me now, war. Join with me, and I shall make a new name for violence. Join with me, and I shall show these things what a true monster can do.

Rex rises from the earth into the hecatombs of the streets. The factory is encased in abyssal forms. Short bouts of weapons' fire come from the church and factory roofs. A sickening mutation rushes towards him, wide hippopotamus mouth fringed with tentacles. Rex laughs and pounces. He ducks to the side, flays the creature's side open then tears right through its body with a sudden burst of strength. The bloated carcass slumps to the ground, humanoid limbs twitching on its desiccated back. Rex roars and stokes his core. A searing pillar of lightning streaks down and fries a huge blob of spine-covered tendrils, which promptly falls from the factory wall. He charges into the street. A mob of warp touched blunder towards him. *Poor wretches,* he thinks, *Humans who have wandered too close to a warp gate, I shall put them out of their misery.* His heavy body crashes into the group. Claws and talons slash into the mutated fray. The pitiful creatures attempt to grasp at him but they are too slow, too clumsy. He demolishes them, sending bones and entrails raining through the street. He laughs and roars again. Wild monstrosities pour forth from the factory, drawn by his contention. He looks to the roof. Xan is crouching near the edge. Cable is lying prone next to him. Single precise shots rhythmically fire from both of their assault rifles. He looks back to the street. A deluge of abyssal horrors pours towards him. Rabid tremors rock his body and he plunges into the group. He tosses Abyssal Worms like chew toys and gouges fatal holes in Abyssal Parasite hosts, writhing tendrils pouring from their broken skulls. He eviscerates groups of Warp Touched and ravages Nameless Wretches, making sure to avoid their dangerous pincer arms. The group is soon wrecked beyond repair and he pauses.

An awareness of unnatural movement invades, towards the church. There, concealed in magic. *You cannot hide from one who knows that trick,* he thinks. The creature is bizarre, unfamiliar to him. It's at least fifteen feet tall. A dozen long legs are surmounted by a being split into two. One torso is reptilian with a spread of tentacles for a left arm. The other torso is vaguely humanoid; a mottled tumor covers the right side of its head and body. The torsos are working independently. The humanoid side appears to be casting some sort of spell. He growls and focuses on space/time. A half-second later he appears behind the towering grotesquerie. The reptile torso twists, reflexively whipping tendrils down at him in the process. Rex dodges to the side and collides into the mutation's legs, snapping four of them like twigs. Both torsos bellow in pain, one wordlessly, the other in the foul diction of the warp. Rex laughs and hops backwards as he shakes his chaotic core. Five duplicates appear. The reptilian side lashes down at an illusion only to slap the concrete with a half-dozen strong tentacles. Meanwhile the humanoid side is moving its malformed arms, and speaking rotten words. Rex pounces, aiming for the humanoid torso when a flash of arcane power hits him in the chest. He yelps and rolls to the side, a black fire licking over his scales. Figments lunge in and out around him. He falls into rhythm and disappears in their number. The reptilian tentacles strike down again, it rages in frustration as it passes through an illusion. Rex waits for his chance, then attacks, from behind this time. Claws, talons and teeth snag the humanoid torso, it screams and the other torso turns, but it's far too late. Rex seizes with ultra-violence and completely sunders his target, goring it to pieces as he tears the body from its vile foundation. The reptile side reels and stumbles as stinking, dark blood geysers from the gaping wound. It tries to regain its balance but the broken legs give out and the creature topples. It begins to convulse. Rex glances upwards. A surprised Cassandra is staring at the creature, suddenly made visible by its state. She waves at him and Rex bows before turning back towards the factory.

It's all so clear to me now. I see with redoubled vigor. Billowing seams of bedlam originate nearby. There is a calamitous portal, a warp gate. The creator is no doubt the herdsman of this abyssal flock. A shepherd must have fertile lands with which to rear his chosen brood. I now see the light that shines from his twisted crook. I shall flock to him as well, a wolf in invisible clothing. I shall rend a path through his misshapen herd. And gorge myself on the sweet meats of insanity, if I must.

A fire still blazes nearby. You cannot hide from me anymore, void prophet. I see your twisted form and your twisted trail. I see your nameless faith living inside a shell of mephitic dementia. Now then, let us do battle, you and I. We shall accept the bloody outcome, whatever it might be. We shall see what you have been transformed into and whether chaos has chosen you as its champion or not.

Rex creeps low. Dancing orange light plays across the dark street. He tastes the air, and the route soon becomes clear. The Zealot's looping to the south in an attempt to gain a new angle of attack. He hurries up the street as an invisible hunter. Controlled gunfire continues from behind him. He trots into the parking lot of a warehouse. The trail leads to the building there. He focuses on his sight. The warehouse is an open space, once used for some kind of construction or repair. He glances up. A dark mist swirls amidst violet light. The path becomes clear as he aligns his core with the axis of movement. He leaps, climbs and leaps again only to come face to face with the Zealot.

The abyssal fanatic is not fooled by the invisibility. A vibrant tendril of energy uncoils from the mist surrounding him, arcing towards Rex. A line of distortion carves across Rex's flank, guardian scales absorbing the energy harmlessly. He growls and catapults towards the Zealot, one of its disfigured arms points and Rex lurches to the side as a powerful vertigo grips him. *Sneaky,* he thinks, *refocus, peel it away.* His core flares out and the magic power clinging to him is stripped off, like how a person would shed their clothes. He shakes his head, regains his balance and pounces. The tendril of energy cuts into him for a second before he collides with the Zealot. They crash to the roof, battering and tearing at each other. After a brief melee, the pair parts, wounds covering both of them. Rex spits out the end of a tendril. The priest is about to speak when Rex reaches internally and a stroke of lightning angles down at the mutation. It screams and bucks, a pungent smoke coils from its singed body. Rex laughs and jumps forward. The Zealot makes a series of gestures with four of its five arms. A ball of absolute blackness springs from the limbs and strikes Rex in the shoulder. A crippling pain wracks his body but he continues, a quick second leap closing the distance.

The flood gates of chaos open then, and he mauls the Zealot with a ferocity that cracks the building. He twists off limbs and shreds its warped face. He wrenches at its neck and pulls free its head as he claws through the Zealot's chest, revealing mutated organs shot through with root-like tendrils. The disgusting light fades as the cavernous ruin of the corpse quivers and gushes black blood. A piercing ensemble of screeches blocks all sound for a few seconds. He flinches then winces as the fresh wound on his shoulder announces itself. *The flock has lost their shepherd,* he thinks, *they are reeling without direction.* He focuses on the Zealot for a few moments, ensuring that some dark magic doesn't reconstitute the mutilated corpse. The gore is then collected in a pile and he reaches internally, striking the remains with bolt after bolt of searing lightning until exhaustion threatens. There's still gunfire coming from the north. He frowns and then returns quickly to the church. Four of the survivors are on the roof. A clutter of dead meat surrounds the base. Eric looks down and points at him, Silver Dancer looks down and waves. Rex nods and yells.

"Gather the gear inside, bring the redwood chest, I shall return." He then runs past and heads towards the factory. The roads are cracked and slick with abyssal blood, countless body parts are littered everywhere. Xan and Cable are at the roof's edge. "The Zealot is dead Xanshudan, but we must go, a warp gate is in the area and this place is now stained with their scent, it shall draw others." Xan scans the street. Rex looks north. There is movement there, far away. A glistening mass of tendrils, fangs and claws pulses in the darkness.

"Can you come get Eve, she's unconscious." Rex nods and runs to the buildings wall. His core of chaos flexes and he steps through the brickwork. He slides into the fire escape, choked with corpses of all description, then quickly bounds up the stairs. The upper reaches of the staircase are blocked, the result of some earlier disruption. He again sinks through the atoms of the intervening material, a slight misalignment from reality. The factory roof soon opens up before him. Xan and Cable crouch at the same edge. Eve is slumped near the ruined staircase. Signs of combat cover the roof, mutant corpses punctuate the area.

"Come, you shall have to affix her to my back," he says as Xan looks back over his shoulder.

Kane interjects, "Oo, bondage, I'm game." Rex snorts.

Xan rolls his eyes and says, "I've got some para-cord, you weren't kidding about the gate, another bunch of something is coming this way, they're acting kind of randomly though ..." Rex nods.

"Without their shepherd they shall simply seek to break, destroy and consume." As he finishes speaking Cable fires a shot from his assault rifle, braced against his remaining shoulder and resting on the lip of the roof, he looks over.

"Yeah, we've got to go! Van's toast, helicopter's toast, Dancer's ride is toast, so what? Walk?"

Rex laughs then says, "I can forgive your narcotics haze Cable, we discussed this earlier." Xan nods as he lifts Eve's unconscious body and slumps her over Rex's back.

"The flux, remember Cable?" Xan raises his eyebrows and produces the strong cord. Cable makes a sound of sudden recognition.

"Oh, right, yeah, so what, to the church?" he responds before looking down into the street. Xan begins to wrap the cord around Eve and Rex, creating a figure eight and then tying it tight.

"Yeah, how are you going to get down?" Xan asks while testing the makeshift harness. Cable nods to his side.

"I've got an Em-parachute, shit; we've got to go now. Xan can you grab 'Gerty'?" Xan nods and pats Rex on the shoulder. Cable slings his rifle and produces a small handle with a handguard and a thumb switch. He engages the switch as he jumps from the roof. The static buzz of the electromagnetic cushion employing comes from the street a second later. Then Cable's armored boots hitting the pavement as he runs to the church. Xan picks up the mini-gun and moves to the edge then looks back.

"Down towards the parking lot, there's an outlying building that you can jump from, it's low enough that it shouldn't hurt her," he says as he points to the far end of the factory roof. Rex looks to him and nods.

"Go, I shall be there momentarily." Xan slings his rifle, hefts the mini-gun and looks into the street. He then rolls over the short wall ringing the roof and disappears from sight. Rex crosses the roof with his minor burden. He then descends as safely as possible, keeping Eve relatively stable as they reach the pavement. An urgent bestial sound comes from the north. The new wave of monsters is getting close. He sprints smoothly to the church's main door, Cable is waiting for him, rifle braced against his hip.

"Hey man, come on, let's lock this bastard up." Rex nods and bounds through the open doors. The smell of abyssal decay fills the room. The sentry is surrounded by dead worms, it's not functioning anymore. Xan looks down from the second level.

"Bring her up here, I've got the chest." Rex picks his way through the wrecked office and quickly climbs the stairs. Xan points to the chest and Rex unlocks it with a single claw. Cassandra and Silver Dancer work to unfasten Eve.

"No, leave her, and add Devlin's body as well," Rex says, Cassandra nods and they move to retrieve his corpse. Rex glances around, a selection of metal crates, his red chest and the mini-gun. Eric appears unwell. There is an unfamiliar Human woman with him. Rex saw her earlier, short with purple hair, she has a weapon but Cassandra eyes her warily. Rex looks at Xan as he retrieves the gem. "You need only shatter the gem to release its power, beware; we shall have but a minute to pass through, so we shall need to carry all of our goods in one fell swoop."

"Alright, sounds good ..." Xan is interrupted by a heavy impact on the main door. Rex looks down. The metal of the door is bowed inwards. Shiny black claws pierce the steel.

"Quickly now, time is short." Xan nods as he stares down at the wall. A flowing stew of tainted auras are all moving to the door, Rex sees them as well. There are more moving to the ceiling, a jagged hole allowing access.

The preparations are made in haste. The steel and stone shall hold for long enough, a last gift from the earth here. Intuition is aligned with this new course. It feels as though causation is at play in a manner that defies regularity. There is a preponderance of factors which drive us fluxward. It is immaterial to guess the reasoning at this juncture. For now, we shall see what chaos has in store for us. For now, we shall see if we are not heading into a den filled with creatures far worse than these feckless abyssal things.

Grot Fastwhisker

"Rat is sure that we are on the list, check it again."

The large Human scowls, he then sighs and says, "I don't need to check the list again. The list and I share a special relationship. You see, every night we make sweet love, the list and I. On the weekends we go away to our cabin at the lake. I'm so intimately connected with the list that I can tell you immediately that there is not, and there has never been, 'small, smelly, insane, bird-cage wearing Goblin', anywhere on the list's sexy tanned body. Now, push off before you make someone who is important enough to be on the list, ill, due to your unfortunate ..." the Human motions towards Grot "...circumstance."

Grot blinks a few times. Voices begin to speak up from the line, "Get out of here!" "Smelly Gobbo wacko." "Check this thing out man ..."

Grot laughs, then nods and waves at the crowd, a number of them make lewd gestures in return. He moves a short distance from the nightclub. Circles of smoke drift lazily above the long line of patrons. Holographic platinum clouds paint the world chrome.

We could make him let us in, he thinks, *that would be simple enough, but, that would probably end badly, Marshalls take a dim view of enchantment magic.* The club has a surprisingly strong ward, they no doubt paid top dollar for it. A hushed murmur flows through the line, flashy clothes glitter. Young Humans and Elves jostle each other. Grot studies the group. Many seem to be corporate, too clean and trendy, several sport firearms that look as though they've never seen use. He breathes low and peels back the substance of the Material Realm. The club's ward flickers for a second, only to be replaced by a large, black mountain. The spectral sky churns with subtle hues. The ground is steaming with a grey mist. He looks at it closely, spectral forms trapped in a fine mesh, it travels down beneath the spectral soil. There are rat spirits, twenty of them. A quiet indignation seeps in, he growls. A group of young Humans move away from him.

One comments loudly, "Zool's sake, what a freak! Where's a Marshall when you need one?" Grot relaxes his focus. The world reconstructs into its usual state. He glances over his shoulder, a long street lined with store fronts and restaurants. He searches the fringes of the street, finding alleys, stairs and catwalks. Across the way, a small porch is encircled by a metal guard rail. Just past it, the fifth level can be seen, stretching out more than three hundred feet below. He looks back the other way, past the nightclub. A few tall apartment blocks, some offices, and, something else. An old construction is there. He begins to walk towards it. Pounding music continues from within the club, its wanton heartbeat. The blocky construction soon unfolds before him. It's an old subway entrance. A rusted iron gate covers the stairwell, it's broken though. It stands open. Once again he shifts his focus to the spirit realm. His vision clears and he inspects his surroundings. The dark mountain thrums with an odd oscillation. He peers at the sky and narrows his gaze. There's a black thread, different from the other one somehow, but made by the same hand. The pattern is unmistakable. The thread is close; it is anchored through the mesh of the trapped spirits. The thread travels down into the ground, it disappears there. He relaxes his focus and peers into the gloom of the staircase. A quick check of his pockets and belt follow: egg shells, marbles, nails, dead rat, garbage orb, a wooden top and the fork. *Rat help them if we need to use the fork*, he thinks.

The gate protests loudly as it swings inward. He quickly ducks inside and descends. The path takes a number of ninety degree turns, a concrete landing starting each new direction. The base of the stairs opens into the beginning of a platform. Another iron gate covers the span. This one is intact, but old and rusted. It appears to be able to fold in on itself like an accordion, or it did at one time. Now oxidization keeps it open permanently. He looks to the far edge; an ancient padlock connects the gate to the wall. He shrugs and pulls out a rusted nail. A minute later and half of the gate is reduced to a pile of red-brown dust. He passes through and walks into the pitch black of the disused platform, Goblin eyes carving out a black and grey pool of perception. Grot calls for his watcher. The ghostly rat appears a few seconds later.

"How may we serve master?"

"Rat must be wary of dangers." He internalizes the standard mantra.

"And this one will always watch for them master," replies the spirit. Grot points to the tunnel.

"Fly through the tunnels, tell us what you see," he commands the spirit, it nods and departs. He glances down the length of the platform. A series of iron benches are collected near a pair of open doorways, bathrooms. Wires stick out from the ceiling, old roots once connected to the electronics of a past age. A familiar smell strikes him then. *A spider,* he thinks, *a big spider hunts in this area.* He sits on the bench and checks his phone. No new calls from Grenda. Grot hisses, thinking about the reporter. *Hopefully friend Delrog can scare her off,* he thinks, *we don't want to hurt her and we don't want to have to disappear again, not now.* A deep silence pervades the area, the clamor of the city a distant vibration. He stands and moves towards the open doorways. A quick check of each bathroom reveals destroyed stalls and naked pipes in place of fixtures.

A patchwork of graffiti remains, he glances at one scrawled in a Goblin script, *"Here I sit, broken hearted, came to shit, instead catharted."*

He laughs and walks back to the rusted benches, placing his backpack down in front of him. A short rummage later and he's holding a small wooden box, faded with age. He unsnaps the metal clasp and carefully opens the hinged lid. Inside, a pair of ancient bone dice sit in their velvet depressions, the faces are covered with two different images in random groups of three, a rat and a skull. He palms the dice and puts the box down. Then he sits cross-legged on the platform and begins to hum as he slowly shakes the dice with both of his hands. The walls start to resonate with the sound. A rushing whisper of voices soon flows through the tunnel. He focuses internally as he hums. The question is posed: "Do you have that which we seek?" The dice are rolled, rat and skull, uncertain. He snatches them up, the humming continues. "Does magic attach itself to you?" The dice are rolled, rat and rat, yes. The dice are palmed again. The chant progresses, "Does a hunter live within you?" The dice are rolled, rat and skull, uncertain. He grabs the dice and ponders. The tune changes slightly. "Does Rat live within you?" The dice are rolled, skull and skull, no. He smiles and stops humming. An instant silence imposes itself and barges around the room. He returns the dice to the box and places it in his backpack, which he then slings. The smell of new rot wafts through the tunnel, pushed in on some artificial breeze. A few minutes pass as he stands in the gloom. A shoddy door lies on the tunnel floor, next to the antiquated subway track, above it a small service tunnel churns with shadow, just beyond his sight range. He peers up the subway line. A collapsed pile of debris clogs the entire passage. The other direction is obscured by a curve in the track. A green blur melts out of the far wall and approaches rapidly; it stops and resolves into the watcher.

"This one has found the thread master; it is not far from this place. This one can show you."

He nods and asks, "What of the darkness of life?"

The rat bobs and twirls then says, "This one could not see past the dark magic, it may be hiding there, you must be careful master." Grot nods and puts a finger to his mouth pensively. He then motions towards the tunnel.

"Show us."

The trail leads through the service tunnel, a narrow and short pathway, though still several feet above his head. He's travelled a short distance when he notices a small corpse, a rat that has been killed but not consumed. He looks closely at it. Beetles slowly eat the flesh, but it was killed by something else first. He bows his head then continues. Soon, another rat corpse appears in the same condition. Slain but not eaten, not by the killer. He seethes. *Rat has many purposes, food for others is one, but not sport for cruelty*, he thinks, *no creature should know that fate*. The watcher spirit leads on, through a confusing glut of tunnels, constructed by the city, amongst other things. After a while a sickly smell begins to filter into his nostrils, an unusual heat as well. The smell is similar to before, new decay. The watcher stops.

"Through there master, another part of the subway tunnel." He stops and shifts his perception. The spirit realm manifests as a great tangle of dark roots. Something beats in their midst, through the passage There is a pit of great arcane power. His vision shifts back and he moves towards the passage. He reaches into the large leather pouch on the right side of his belt and he produces a small wooden top. Each face of the top's square body has the image of a rat in a certain pose, when it spins the images blend creating the illusion of a running rat. He forms a beak with his right hand, twists his palm upwards and balances the top on the tips of his fingers. An arcane charge travels through his core into his lungs as he inhales deeply. He then exhales forcefully on the top. The wood zings and shoots from his fingers, tiny running rat flickering white in the sunless tunnel. The top strikes the ground and begins to move erratically across the uneven floor. Still, the arcane charge propels it. The top skips and jumps, lists to the left, hits a wall then corrects itself. It's surging forward across a short rough patch when, a searing flash of red light leaves the afterimage of a complex circle in his vision. The top ignites with intensity and is reduced to ash in seconds. Grot looks to the passage. A glimmering circle of fire lingers for a few seconds before it fades. He smiles. *A Mandela rune,* he thinks, *Rat is all too familiar with traps.*

The passage is warm as he moves into it and rounds a corner, dead rat in one hand, fork in the other. It looks as though this was the spider's den, husks and signs of silk webs line the far wall. A dull red glow pulses just to the left of the passage, flaring and fading in a constant rhythm. No signs of movement, no hint of a presence. He ventures further inside. The light is coming from a circle, carved in the ground around a small stone altar. He stops and gazes at the remains, almost two dozen rats. The twenty spirits, he growls and shakes his head, then concentrates on his watcher spirit's tether.

"Remain alert; we shall be here for a little while yet." The spirit responds telepathically.

"Of course master, this one shall watch the passage." Grot nods to himself then removes his backpack and produces Sneezeguts' wand. He looks it over. The chicken claw melds seamlessly with the bone, which, in turn, melds seamlessly with the ten writhing rat tails hanging from the handle's base, given willingly from ten different donators. A short slideshow of memories passes through his mind as he gazes at the wand: the massive spectral boot, psychedelic trips with the old Devilkin, all those creepy dolls. He forgot how to get back to the Witch Doctor's place years ago. If he ever knew how to get there in the first place that is. He flicks some fuzz and a bit of string from the wand's claws. He turns towards the circle. A single thrust snares the ritual's foundation. He smirks and begins to fence with the arcane threads. After a few thrusts, and more than a number of parries, he starts to feel the ritual's cadence. The power becomes manageable. He begins to make inroads, his attacks are getting through. A few more precise assaults snap the thread and the room goes dark. An oppressive heat lifts and Grot's watcher spirit rushes into the area.

He wipes the sweat from his forehead and looks to the spirit. "Is there something?"

The vaporous rat bobs and points a tiny paw towards one of the far walls. "This one can see, now that the darkness has lifted, an object is there, it stands out to this one." Grot stretches and puts the wand away. He then points towards the wall.

"Show us."

The hole is up high, a jagged opening in the concrete, more than ten feet off of the ground. It's too high to jump and there's nowhere to climb, the hole might be trapped as well. He holds his breath and listens. A low muttering surrounds him, old voices, now returning as the darkness clears. A small tricky voice is needed now, one carved from concrete, but not a warrior. He stands for a long while, scarcely breathing. Then, gradually, he begins to hear it in the background. A small voice blending in with the others, he addresses it.

"Rat greets you with all respect crafty one. Rat stands in awe of your cleverness. Rat begs to ask a boon of one who is so cunning?" Stillness follows.

Slowly, the grinding of concrete moving against concrete forms into a voice and speaks, "Rat may ask, this one shall respond."

"Rat gives you all of our thanks, rat is not worthy. Rat only needs a small favor, there is something that Rat wishes and we cannot reach it." He waits for a moment before, the tunnel floor begins to shake and a sprinkling of dust falls from the roof. Then a small part of the concrete floor rises up, as though it was made out of water. The concrete slowly shifts into a crude, two-foot tall humanoid torso jutting directly from the floor. Two dark pits serve as the eyes within its domed head; its arms are stubby with mitten-like hands. Grot bows to the city spirit and points up to the crack in the wall.

"Go up into that place and retrieve anything that our watcher points out," he commands the spirit, as an arcane tether snaps out and snares the small concrete body. The spirit bows and immediately disappears within the concrete floor. Grot waits. After a short while the city spirit reappears, framed in the jagged hole. It's hauling some kind of large bag, it descends the wall, swimming through the concrete and finally coming to a rest on the floor of the tunnel. "Rat is grateful for your service. You may relinquish this form now." The spirit bows.

"Rat is strong, this one shall obey." It finishes speaking and sinks down into the concrete, leaving no trace other than the foreign bag.

Grot stares at it for a few seconds. A sinister feeling takes hold of him. The bag is made out of Human flesh, old memories of savage gang rituals seep into his mind. Ogres and Orcs can be merciless. Goblins can be worse than both of them combined, an attempt to make up for their small stature. The bag looks like the old banners that used to fly in certain parts of the warrens. The same banners more than likely still fly there. He tugs open the drawstring and looks inside. A small selection of arcane reagents, he's familiar with some of them. He sifts through the contents. A red gem sticks out, it's unfamiliar. He looks past it. A large bar of spectral platinum sits in the bottom of the bag. He whistles low. *Giselle will pay a small fortune for that*, he thinks, *well, we are tired, and the den is close to her shop*. He gazes at the shining bar again. *Well, close enough*.

The subway tunnel proved to be near enough to the edge of the hive that Grot could just jump down to level two. A simple spell reduces his weight, allowing him to drift gently down the thousand feet, before landing on a patio umbrella, much to the dismay of the cafe's patrons. He grins. Shouts of surprise turn into calls for security. A woman screams as he jumps to the patio floor then runs to the low glass railing. He vaults the railing and begins to drift down again when a sudden roof intervenes. He stands and looks around, surprised. It's the top of a very tall apartment block, on the city's first level, just on the edge of the hive. He can see a catwalk spanning to the streets in towards the core, built high into the structure of the first level. The other direction reveals an exquisite morning sky. He soaks it in for a second.

"You there! Stop!" yells a voice from overhead. He peers upwards. There's a pair of security guards with pistols. He laughs and jumps towards the catwalk, crashing down on the metal grate that serves as a roof. A trio of Human teens flinch as he lands, one giggles and snaps a picture of him with her phone. Grot sticks out his tongue then runs in towards the core, the security guards shouting inaudibly above him. He soon reaches the street and darts into the closest alley that he can find. He sits still and feels the rhythm of concrete and steel. The deep thrum of electricity cocoons him. He closes his eyes as the garbage and clutter of the city flocks around him. Nobody can see him now. He is one with the city. He can feel the signs and newsletters. The pipes, wires and curbs, homes full of life and old grounds sodden with death. After feeling the mood of the city for several long minutes he knows that he is safe. He then steps from the alley's embrace and begins to head further into the city's core.

Getting back up to the second level ended up being easy enough. Another forty minutes pass before he reaches "Madame Mystra's". He approaches the door, the shop is closed. He checks his phone, 8:17 Solar, the shop opens at 9:00. He sighs and looks down at the pavement.

The sidewalk passes by beneath him. A short walk ends at the timeworn facade of the infamous second level eatery, "The Pot". He looks down then stares at the back booth for a long time. A tear threatens and he looks away. *Maybe not here after all*, he thinks. Another short walk ends at an open-air street diner. A collection of

Orcs and Goblins surround the long, U-shaped counter. Grot pulls up a stool and studies the menu as though he's going to order food, but instead just gets a coffee. He sips at it slowly while watching and listening, catching bits of conversations here and there. Everything from personal matters and sports trivia, to bullshit and inane blather filters in, until, a pair of Goblins mention something about an Abyssal warning. The warning is primarily for the city's fourth level, near the south edge. He considers for a moment. *That could explain the dark swirls of mist in the spectral sky,* he thinks, *but what then? They're after Eric?* He shakes his head. *No,* he thinks, *we've dealt with that purpose, this is our new purpose, this is important now.* He sits in thought for a few more minutes. When the clock reads 9:15 he pays the bill and starts out towards "Madame Mystra's".

The familiar sound of the bell accompanies the equally familiar scents of the arcane shop. Giselle peers up from the counter; a surprised look crosses her face.

"Greetings Rat Shaman, Grot 'The Timeless', grandmaster of the tenth circle, walker of the endless fields. Didn't I just see you here?"

Grot laughs and bows, then says, "Greetings Giselle Starshade, initiate of the old way, daughter of the Golden Light and singer of the truth." She returns the bow. He then puts his hand in his inside jacket pocket and continues "Rat was probably here a short while ago. We recall something like that, but our purpose is different this time. We have something that we think you will like very much." He then pauses for dramatic effect before producing the large bar of spectral platinum. Her eyebrows shoot up and she puts a hand to her mouth. She then motions towards the door and the lock turns, a faint glow surrounds the doorframe.

"Please, come this way." She sweeps her hand towards the back room. The small space is lined in bookshelves. In the center, an old desk supports an even older set of balance scales. She moves to the desk and holds out her hand. "May I?" Grot nods and hands over the heavy bar. She grabs it and places it on one side of the scale, the beam tilts and the opposing pan rises. She begins to add weights, the pans gradually even out and she raises her eyebrows

319

again. She turns to him. "Would you mind taking store credit?" He grins and considers for a moment while studying the weights.

"What do you say to twenty K cash and the rest in store credit?" She puts a hand to her chin, performs some quick internal math, then nods.

Her eyes slowly narrow and she says, "Say, where'd you get this? Steal it from some supplier?" Grot laughs and holds up his hands.

"Worry not; it is not stolen from anything with a proper claim to it." She nods, lies always ring false in the ears of the "Truth Singers". Grot adds, "We wish that we could remember how to get to the boot, we found something that we think Sneezeguts could help us with."

She looks confused then furrows her brow and says, "Why don't you check your lockbox?"

He frowns for a second then responds, "In our den? No, nothing there." She shakes her head.

"No, your lockbox here, I remember you saying something about 'needing to get back to the boot ...', it didn't make sense at the time." Now it's Grot's turn to look confused. She blinks a few times then continues, "Do you truly not remember?" He shakes his head. A sad look creeps into her eyes, "I'm sorry Grot, here let me get your cash and I'll fetch the lockbox as well." He grins and nods. *Good,* he thinks, *Sneezeguts will help us with the purpose, if he doesn't kill us, or worse, cook for us.*

The shop door jingles shut behind him, a smile is etched on his face. *The mirror! How could we forget about the mirror?* he thinks. *No time for sleep now, Sneezeguts can help get around that, one way or another.* Not far from "Madame Mystra's" he finds a large bridge spanning a concrete channel. A tent town gathers around the base of the tall pillars supporting the bridge. Homeless Goblins, Orcs and Humans swarm about. He sits a short distance from an oildrum fire and instantly blends in. The ornate hand mirror is soon retrieved from his backpack's reinforced interior pocket. A wooden sheath covers the mirror's face; a detailed carving of the boot covers its surface. The mirror's handle and frame are made from bone carved with tangled runes. He uncovers the mirror and stares into it, focusing on a point in the background of the reflection. As he hones in on the spot, he steadily strips away the Material Realm, but only in the reflection, a skill that took years of practice. His eyes begin to unfocus. The world in the reflection shifts and flows. His vision fades, then, slowly blurs back into focus.

The dreamlike miasma of the Spirit Realm meets his new sight. A turgid mound of earth rolls past. He peers to the left. A translucent herd of gazelles fly through the fields there. He looks down. The spongy ground shifts and shimmers beneath his feet, a flower waves up at him. He grins, waves back and then turns around. The earth sweeps up to a sharp cliff, and there, standing on a dangerous precipice, larger than a house, the boot. He walks closer. An office building soars by overhead. It's trailing a great banner of animated sidewalk. He breathes deeply, oxygen filtered in through the veil. He's getting close, when the boot suddenly turns from the cliff edge. It spins on its enormous heel then takes a single gigantic leap. The descent has the same effect as dropping a fair-sized apartment building from the sky. Grot stumbles under the impact. He then falls onto his backside. The great boot towers before him, forty feet to the top, more than twenty feet long. A single circular window sits halfway up the leg, while a simple red door is embedded underneath, just above the sole. He shakes his head and stands, fork at the ready. The door snaps open sharply and a rough voice drifts out.

"Grot! You old so and so, you old such and such, you old this and that, you old that and the other, you rancid yak welder, you saucy fur-slapper, you inedible coniferous plant, you ... additional thing, you, get in here!" Grot chuckles and walks towards the door.

"We forgot how to get here." A generous laugh originates from inside the boot. Grot surmounts the steps, and enters into the impossibly large interior.

The rough voice responds, "Well, we're going to have to forgive you then, aren't we?" A squat figure steps into view, elaborate tribal mask blocking his face. Two long horns stick out laterally from his head and a flea market of miscellany covers him.

He pulls off the mask. Bright red skin, broad nose, wide mouth full of sharp teeth and beady black eyes, set far apart. Grot grins.

"It is good to see you again friend Sneezeguts, we've been having many reunions lately ..." He's interrupted by small running feet. The tiny doll charges at him, unnaturally quick, oversized dagger raised.

Sneezeguts puts up his hand and yells, "Shanky no!" The two-foot tall doll grinds to a halt. Small bones clatter against a mismatching selection of fur and fabric, a crudely painted-on face turns towards the rotund Devilkin.

Sneezeguts looks embarrassed, then points at the doll and scolds it, "No more of that kind of behaviour or I'll put the leash on you! Do you understand?" The doll's head sinks and it seems as depressed as a creepy, nearly featureless doll can seem. Sneezeguts then smiles and pats his knees, "Come on then, come to daddy." The doll looks up and then runs to him like an elated puppy. He continues, "I didn't mean to scare you but Grot is a friend, we do not stab our friends with large knives." The doll kicks the ground with its tiny foot. Grot laughs. Sneezeguts looks over, "I'm sorry Grot, he is, energetic."

Grot holds up his hands and says, "Worry not friend Sneezeguts, it is not a terrible thing to be energetic in one's purpose." Sneezeguts smiles a broad smile and motions towards the expansive livingroom. The whole area shuffles and clacks with small, terrible dolls. Grot swallows and forces a grin. Mouthless baby-faced dolls sporting switchblades mull around with spear wielding snake-skull things formed of wood and canvass. In the background, he can see tall feathered curiosities bobbing and revolving around steely skeletal horrors. The group turns as one and stares at him. He shudders as he follows Sneezeguts into the space. The edges of the room are lined with bookshelves, display cases and peculiar decorations. A large curio cabinet sits near an even larger fireplace. A shrunken head turns towards him, bright animated eyes and a tiny stitch-covered mouth. A large polka-dot bowtie rests just underneath its miniature chin.

"We see that you've been busy. Did you catch the spirits for the dolls in the fields?" He motions towards the creepy crowd as he finishes the statement. Sneezeguts nods and rolls his hand towards the group.

He then motions to the fire place. "Tea?"

"Yes please, regular, if you don't mind." Sneezeguts laughs and claps his hands twice.

"You're no fun." He then shifts in his seat. A number of amulets settle against his large potbelly. "You have this look about you like someone's taped up yer ankles and stuck an ill-tempered weasel in your pants. There something up?" The sound of metal banging against wood signals the kettle bearer's arrival.

Grot snorts. "How could you tell?"

The old Devlikin laughs and slaps a knee. "It's pretty obvious, besides you ain't the only one who speaks with the spirits you know. There's only one that ever mentions you though." The doll puts the kettle on the rack in the fireplace. Sneezeguts snaps and a fire roars to life. Grot stares at him. Sneezeguts looks over, eyes flinty chips.

"What are you saying friend Sneezeguts?" The Witch Doctor sticks a long black claw in between his teeth and begins to worry away at an unseen morsel.

He then laughs and says, "You remember Norman Robertson?" Grot reflexively furrows his brow at the new line of questioning. He slowly nods. Sneezeguts frees something from his gums and promptly eats it. He then continues, "You remember how obsessed he was with Cass? I mean like even *way* more than all the others." Grot frowns and nods. He had to beat potential suitors away with a rabid wolverine tied to a stick. Norman was unique in a number of ways. He was the son of a rich corporate, early assignment to "Special Studies" for latent psionic traits. That's of course only part of the difficulty with sending a Dark Elf teen to an exclusive private school while she's under continuous magical disguise. Grot frowns and stares at the depraved old Witch Doctor, Sneezeguts meets his gaze then continues, "And what did you say to me then?" Grot grimaces and swallows. A soft cloud of steam begins to pour from the kettle.

"We said to scare him off, by any means." A wicked grin crosses Sneezegut's face.

"And we did try our very best, oh yes we did, nightmares for weeks, the dolls, spirits of all type. I even sent ol'stinky to wreck his car, the whole rigmarole. But, then what did you say when he wouldn't get scared off?" Grot casts a sharp glance at him.

"You saw the boy's aura; he was going to be a murderer ..." Sneezeguts makes a rolling motion with his hand.

Grot stares at the floor and responds, "We said that we did not want to know what happened, just to take care of it. We did not want to know how."

Sneezeguts points a finger briefly then waves it around the room. "He haunts me still you know? From time to time, he always finds a way in." He stares darkly at Grot and adds, "Keeps saying the same thing, over and over, again and again, you want to know what it is?" Grot looks intently at the dangerous old Devilkin and nods. The kettle begins to spout steam. The high pitched scream slowly escalates. "Ah, tea! Would you care for some biscuits, a soufflé? A praying mantis perhaps?" Grot shakes his head then unhooks his backpack and places it on the carpet. The faceless doll hefts a tray above its head while a second doll fills the cups, its hands are skeletal monkey paws.

"You were saying something about Norman?" Sneezeguts grabs a saucer from the tray. The doll then moves over to Grot, he grabs the saucer. A rich green tea swirls in the cup. Sneezeguts takes a sip then points at the backpack.

"What is it that you got in there then?" Grot blinks a few times.

He takes a sip of the tea then says, "The usual stuff, we did find a bag that we wanted to show you." Sneezeguts smiles.

"A gift? We love gifts, don't we Shanky?" The spirit-animated doll skips in an exuberant circle, stabbing the air. Grot laughs and shrugs.

"Yes, a gift, we'd like to know what you think of it." Sneezeguts takes a sip and motions to the backpack. Grot reaches in and pulls out the strange bag made of Human flesh. "You may keep what's inside as well, though we don't know what it all is." Sneezeguts laughs.

"Ooo, I like this present already." He looks at Grot's hands. "What a lovely bag, thank you Grot." Sneezeguts beams, a toothy smile stretching from horn to horn. Grot passes him the bag and he immediately begins rifling through it, oohing and awing at each item in turn. Then he removes the gem. He pinches it between two clawed fingers as though it was a fresh turd. Sneezeguts looks at Grot and frowns. "Well that just ruins it now doesn't it? An Ing'Tha Slaver's Gem and not a single free demon attached to it?"

Grot snorts. *Of course*, he thinks, *Infernals, the darkness of life*. He takes a sip and looks back towards Sneezeguts.

He then adopts a ruthlessly casual tone and says, "So, Sneezeguts. What was Norman saying the other day?"

The old Devilkin tosses the gem into the corner of the room and responds, "Oh just to 'Tell Grot that the darkness of life will be near to the one who's close to Cassandra in two ways', keeps saying it, whatever it means." He then continues to appraise the bag casually. Grot stops sipping his tea.

"Thank you very much Sneezeguts. We surely hope that you enjoy the gifts, but we're afraid that Rat has to go now, however, we will visit again soon, now that we've remembered the mirror. Our purpose ...." Sneezeguts laughs, interrupting him with a mocking tone.

"'Rat's purpose' is to be completely messed out of his gourd for the next twenty-four hours at a minimum, that's 'Rat's purpose'." Grot puts down his saucer and stares at the dark green fluid.

"Sneezeguts ... what did you put in Rat's tea?" The old Devilkin laughs heartily.

"Welcome back, old friend, welcome back."

Rebecca Arliss

A sudden river appears on the horizon. Trees shrink away at its approach, an urge to run screams at her. The Asura is standing still, he said to not move. The others are standing still as well. They've been wandering for hours and his path has worked so far. She adjusts her large backpack, hand aching with fire. *At least I could disinfect it,* she thinks, *I should have just sprung for a surgeon's patch.* The river surges forward, the forest to their left disappears, replaced by a cracked valley.

"It is not far now, soon his works may be apparent," Rex announces.

"Are you absolutely certain that this 'Arguss' will be pleased to see us?" asks Cassandra. Rebecca nods in agreement. She's seen a number of stories on Asura. They're freakish and powerful monsters for the most part, maybe even as bad as the abyssal horrors that they just escaped. She thinks back to the well-known fire Asura holo-vid. What was its name, Vox something or other. He created a one hundred megaton blast out of nothing, just by blinking. It destroyed most of a massive, rampaging Abyssal hoard outright, for an enormous price of course. She shudders at the recollection of the creature. Thirty feet of armored muscle, six arms, four sporting huge swords while the other two held that cannon, some multi-weapon amalgamation. Its head was little more than a raging fire pushed through a four-eyed steel mask surmounted by a crown. Rex looks around then bounds towards the new valley, the body wrapped to his back jostling slightly.

"Worry not Cassandra, Arguss was not of my clan. We are merely old friends." Cassandra shrugs and glances at the others. Xan smiles at her and takes her hand. Rebecca smirks and nods to herself. She looks around the group. The other man was named Cable. He's massive, nearly seven feet tall, and he's doing surprisingly well for someone who just lost an arm. The Sun Elf is named Eve, she woke up a little while ago, seems like a hard case. She looks at Silver Dancer and Eric. *There seems to be something going on there as well,* she thinks, *I can't believe that's the Silver Dancer, and she's younger than me.* Silver Dancer's exploits are legendary. Underground communities put her hacking on the same pedestal as Fhaligun and

Zero-One. Eric and Dancer follow the others into the valley, hefting their designated load between the two of them.

"Ugh, he licked my hand!" Cassandra exclaims, Kane laughs.

"Damn it Kane!" Xan says, staring at his left palm. Rebecca laughs and shakes her head.

Kane whines, "What? You promised me some action the other day and you still haven't delivered there buddy, so, you owe me. I'm just saying." Xan laughs and shakes his head.

"I said that *maybe* we'd go, and I only said it to shut you up." A tiny shocked sound comes from his palm.

"I ... I don't know what to say. I just .... I don't know who you are anymore Xanshudan!" Cassandra laughs and walks after the others, followed by Xan. Rebecca glances back for a second. There's some movement there, on a distant mountain. She zooms in with her cyber eyes, it's not quite clear. Then it's gone. She turns towards the group; Rex is standing at the valley lip. The river is unfolding before him, crossing the path on the other side of the valley. A pillar of earth hangs effortlessly above them, in the distance a pageant of small islands fly through an unknown pattern.

"Hurry now, we mustn't tarry. The river was prelude to a great lake."

Xan rolls his hand forward and says, "You heard him people, let's pick up the pace!" Kane interjects with a drill sergeant tone.

"Come on people, double time! Oh ... I don't know but I've been told: Dark Elf girls are naughty and bold! Sound off!" The rest is drowned out as Xan puts his left hand under his armpit. Cassandra laughs and nods. The river begins to widen.

Rex approaches the bank, he then smiles and says, "Follow, quickly." He steps into the fast flowing water. The river bed is only a foot deep here, that may not last long however. Cable and Eve plunge in after him; Silver Dancer and Eric are right behind them. Cassandra turns and points at Rebecca then points to the river. She swallows and nods then steps into the water. The current pulls, cold water flowing up to her knees. Xan and Cassandra follow, prompting her forward. The river is still widening before her eyes, it seems to be getting deeper as well. "Hurry," Rex calls back as he crests the far bank. They slog on as quickly as possible, pushing a wake before them. She steps to the bank but it drifts out another inch and she stumbles then falls. Cold water douses her to the shoulders. She quickly stands, Kane is laughing. This time she scrambles up on all fours, her large backpack waddling back and forth. Xan and Cassandra climb the bank after her. The river is growing quickly now, it's filling the cracked valley. Kane's objectionable voice intervenes.

"Hot! A wet T-shirt contest." Rebecca snorts and pulls her vest closed. Xan pinches the bridge of his nose with his thumb and forefinger then shakes his head.

"You see Kane; this is why nobody came to my birthday party." Cassandra laughs and continues up the hill just behind Xan.

"Here, this shall be far enough away from the lake's influence," Rex yells from a hilltop several hundred feet away. Crates and bags jangle against each other as the group hurries along. The backpack is starting to get heavy, at least it's waterproof. It has most of the field rations, meals ready to eat and the like. A quiet awe trills through the group as they reach the hill, each one stopping and staring in kind. Her brow creases on its own accord and she hurries forward. The peak of the hill falls away and she is struck by an incredible sight. Rex looks the group over then announces, "Behold, the mountain 'Abundance of Arguss'". She stands astonished. Her cybereyes quietly begin to record. The ridges and valleys, trees and cliffs, it all forms into a great sculpture of unimaginable complexity. A gust of wind sways the boughs of the forest and suddenly a massive herd of deer are wrought out of green foliage. She moves her head; other images begin to stand out. She begins to walk slowly along the hilltop. Each new perspective brings a new saturation of images. Complicated scenes, animals, Asura and even buildings, all shaped out of the structure of the living land. A tear brims her eye as the beauty of it takes hold.

"Wow!" exclaims Eric softly. She glances at him. *There's still more to his story, all of this is about him*, she thinks, *but why?*

"It's not changing into rivers and deserts and shit like the rest of this place, why's that?" Cable says, eyes glued to the spectacular mountain. Rex glances over.

"Arguss is a skilled artisan, he has great power. The earth here listens to him; it speaks with him as well. It shall not be long now." Xan glances over from the captivating landscape.

"So, where to?" Rex laughs. A chill runs down her spine. The Asura then looks over to Xan.

"We shall see, do not be alarmed, but Arguss approaches." Rebecca looks around in concert with the others.

A bizarre sound begins in the direction of the mountain, like hundreds or thousands of trees being uprooted. The field down below churns and buckles with countless small mounds. Then, as she watches the mounds burst upwards and a forest pours out. Eric gasps. Rebecca stumbles back a foot. The trees continue to sprout up until they're taller than the hill, the new forest's edge a mere ten feet from its base. Then a different sound begins to stalk through the forest, branches being grabbed and released quickly. Thirty feet away, a tree top sways vigorously. A pair of large hands quickly breaches the forest wall, then a third hand. She swallows hard and tries to calm down, Eric is fidgeting nervously. A great arboreal crash precedes the huge simian figure. She breathes in sharply. It must be twelve feet tall, with a profoundly abnormal physiology. Three long arms line either side of its body; its clothes are minimal and brightly patterned with blue and yellow. A thick grey beard stretches down from its face, its head is topped with mineral deposits shaped as a mass of hair, and two dark depressions serve as its eyes. Three of its limbs suspend it from the trees. The arms don't look right somehow, like they're all different lengths. Rex bows. The thing known as Arguss smiles, the gesture seems to brighten the forest. Flowers grow around the base of the trees. Then, impossibly, one of its limbs stretches to more than thirty feet in an instant, growing out as he reaches. It's reaching for her. She recoils but it's too late. The enormous fist completely encases her right hand and forearm in an irresistible grip, she squeals. The huge hand flashes with green light then it lets go. She falls backwards with the unexpected loss of resistance. A booming laugh comes from the branches, the trees sway and giggle. She looks at her hand, it feels better. She tugs off the bandage. The wound, it's completely healed. She flexes her hand, no pain, it's working properly again.

She laughs and looks up. The massive Asura turns towards Rex and speaks.

"Rex Mar'Ing'Erithix, the sharp of your claws have not dug these lands for eons. I am truly rapturous at your arrival, but I mourn your loss deeply. Please, you and your guests are of course welcome to my hospitality."

Rex tilts his head and replies, "Arguss Mar'Ir'Zashithrack, your works are breathtaking my old friend. I thank you for your words, the honored dead is known as Devlin, his spirit may yet persist. These are my new clan, Xan, Cable, Eve and Silver Dancer. The others are our friends, captives and charges in turn." Rex motions to Cassandra, Rebecca and then Eric as he completes the statement. Arguss laughs again, colorful vines stretch up from the roots of the nearby trees.

"I enjoy this tale already Rex." He then spreads two of his limbs towards Rebecca and bows slightly, "Forgive my abruptness, I could not let such a beautiful and vibrant creature suffer within my demesne, it would have saddened me so. " The flowers droop for a second, they perk up again as he speaks, "The great web of chaos has seen fit to snare you in its threads, I see there is something with you that is of great value, recall the nature of your truth now." He smiles, a limb stretches down, plucks a flower then stretches towards her at a right angle. She blushes and smiles. The flower is superb, multicolored veins shift and glow throughout the petals. The scent is exquisite, comforting. Arguss then motions towards the group, "Please, we shall retire to my home. There you can all seek respite. I feel that it is something that is needed."

Rex bows. "You are most gracious Arguss, there is a matter that I wish to discuss with you as well." The huge Asura turns towards him.

"I am an open book my friend, but not here." He then casts an eye through the party and adds "is this the entirety of your number?"

Rex looks back and forth then nods and says, "Yes and the goods." Arguss smiles, the trees shine with green and gold.

"Yes, of course, I'm glad to see you still have my gift," Arguss says as he motions to the redwood chest. Rex nods, Arguss continues, "Good then, everyone hold on." He motions briskly with several of his limbs. She doesn't even get a chance to be frightened as her vision fades, and for a split second she's greeted with nothing at all.

It's hard to tell which is more amazing: the outside or the inside of the mountain. The whole interior is hollowed out, moulded into a vast town complete with a waterfall/grotto, windows to allow in natural light and even an impressive garden near the internal summit. Arguss moves smoothly through the space, using his astounding physiology to great effect. The echo of murmurs travels through the cavern. A mural comes to life and begins to roll through a chaotic scene: earth moving, bestial figures fighting. They continue over a wide bridge to a circular building carved between the ceiling and the floor. There are doorways twenty feet below on the cavern floor. The bridge leads to an open access point. A small trickle of water pours around a channel carved near the top of the building. There are also a number of catwalks above them, branching out from a high balcony. Arguss proceeds inside. They follow. The hall has vaulted ceilings while large wooden doors line the circular interior. The peculiar Asura motions around.

"Welcome, these are the guest quarters; pick any room that you wish. There is a staircase over here." He motions with a large arm. Then he stretches it out and around the corner, extracting laughs from the group. He continues, "There are more rooms on the floor below, a kitchen and pantry rest in the basement, please help yourselves to whatever you wish. Upstairs there is a patio and the pathways that lead to other parts of the mountain. When you are all settled, please, come to the garden, we shall discuss the problem that you have, and see if chaos has not already given us the answer." The pits that serve as his eyes glitter mischievously. Argus bows to Rex, who returns the gesture. The others wave and he uses each of his hands to return each wave in kind, Eric laughs. The Asura then hooks two arms outside and pulls himself through the door then up and out of sight. Eric laughs again.

"Cool, that guy is crazy." Rex laughs. Her skin tries its very best to crawl off of her body, the rest of the group shifts uncomfortably.

Then Kane interjects. "Remind me to never see a stand-up comic with this guy." Rex laughs again, this time the others join in. Xan looks to each of them, then to Rebecca.

"Alright everyone, take thirty, no, let's call it an hour. Wash up, eat something, then we'll see if Arguss can help us at all." Eric appears nervous; Silver Dancer puts a hand on his shoulder. He looks over and beams at her.

"I'll take this room," Eve says, pointing at the door in front of the bridge entrance. Cable begins to walk around the corner, followed by Silver Dancer and Eric. Rebecca looks at Xan and Cassandra, they're standing near Rex. Cassandra looks over.

"Go, pick out a room, you won't be attending this meeting." Rebecca frowns.

"Just what is this all about? It has something to do with Eric, from what I've seen he's some kind of magical initiate or something but that doesn't explain everything." Cassandra frowns, Xan looks to her then back to Rebecca. A sharp edge fills his voice.

"We're here to protect the kid, that's all you need to know. Now get to your room, no more questions." She blinks and swallows then nods. The Dark Elf is very dangerous. She was watching during the attack. He jumped out of that helicopter as casually as she would hop down from a curb. Rex peers over.

"The mind of truth should be ever wary of those who armor themselves in lies." She frowns. *Is he trying to tell me something?* she thinks. Xan glances at the Asura and tilts his head in an exasperated manner. Rex flashes him a smile then raises his eyebrows as if to say, "Yes?" Cassandra motions towards Rebecca again.

"Go, we have things to discuss." Rebecca holds up her hands, turns, then continues around the corner. She grins to herself and activates her head computer then quickly accesses the button microphone's software. The diminutive circle is stuck in an unobtrusive spot on the assault rifle now being slung by Cassandra. A crackling audio filters in as she chooses a door and enters. The voice is Xan's.

"... matter, if we're just going to wipe her memory." She clenches her jaw. Cassandra's voice responds.

"I guess you're right, but, she doesn't need to be there either. It's not like she knows anything about Eric and his situation." The deep growl of Rex intercedes.

"We shall see, Arguss may yet require her presence for one reason or another." Rebecca frowns and presses up against the door, closing it with a click. *Damn it, assholes!* she thinks, *Get some psychic to mess with my head.*

Xan responds, "What if Arguss doesn't know how to help Eric?"

Rex replies, "He shall be able to send us to the great city of Kar'nach, known as the 'Changeless City' to non-Asura." She nods slowly. That place sounds familiar; there are ways to get back home from there.

Xan responds, "Then what?"

Rex answers, "We shall seek out an Arnoch at the 'Flying Jade Cave', with any luck they shall agree to see us and provide some useful insight."

Cassandra cuts in, "I could arrange to pay them, but, they normally don't care about gold."

Rex responds, "You are correct on that account. Unfortunately greed is not counted as one of their vices. We can only hope that the winds of chaos blow in our favour."

Xan's voice crackles in her ear. "Alright, we're going to head to a room downstairs, see you in the garden in a little while."

Rex answers. "Indeed, I shall go and speak with Arguss now, we shall reacquaint." Claws moving on stone scratch in her ear, then, the sound of boots walking. Cassandra's voice begins after a few seconds of walking.

"I could use a shower."

A door opens then closes again, Xan replies, "That sounds like fun."

Kane's voice interjects itself into the conversation. "Now you're talking."

Cassandra's voice responds, "Let's go, you can watch, Kane, but I better not see any part of you anywhere on Xan's palm or I swear that I'll cut off his hand then pay to have it regrown." Kane and Xan laugh, then the distant sound of kissing and breathing.

Kane replies, "Don't you worry about me, now, let's see that exemplary body of yours." She hears further sounds of making-out, then disrobing. She cuts the audio feed, face flushed. *Guess I was right about them,* she thinks, *I knew that something else was up as well.* Stories of psychics erasing a person's entire life stream through her mind. Some were left as barely conscious vegetables. She shakes her head and looks around the room. It's spacious and circular. A round half-wall rises up about eight feet; it conceals the shower and bathroom. Other than that there's a massive bed, a desk, a chair and a simple dresser. The backpack slops to the ground and she begins to strip off her wet clothes. Soon she's nude, spectral platinum medallion dangling between her breasts. The air is a perfect temperature, somehow. The wet clothes are draped over the top of the half-wall as she enters the bathroom. Fixtures and apertures are elegantly etched and arranged, all of the taps are shaped as flowers. She looks in the mirror, dirt and grime, a small amount of blood edges her scalp. She sighs then steps into the shower.

The bed is soft and warm against her back. She stares at the ceiling, a beautiful carving flows and shifts. Her legs cross at the ankles and she sighs, medallion flipping back and forth on her chest. The Ogre was right; she should've just left it all alone. There's still no sign of the Goblin, just the boy, Eric. He is the reason why the Goblin summoned the rats though, he must be. She looks up quickly as there's a soft knock at the door.

"Uh, just one minute." She says as she looks around, clothes still wet: the blanket. She wraps it around her body and moves to the door, opens it a crack with one free hand. Eric stands just beyond. She smiles, he glances down then away.

"Umm, we're having something to eat downstairs, if you want to come," he says, nervously.

"No thanks, I got all I need right here." She kicks the backpack then adds, "Do you have a minute to speak with me

Eric?" She opens the door wider and steps to the side, revealing her leg up to the hip. His eyes roll around wildly, trying not to stare.

"Umm, I'm sorry. Look, you seem nice and everything, it's just that Xan told me not to answer any of your questions." He seems somewhat afraid. She smiles sympathetically.

"It's alright Eric, just doing my job, you know?" He nods then turns to leave. He nears the bend in the hall when she calls out, adding, "I hope that everything works out for you." He looks back, fear lurking in his eyes. He then looks down and nods again before disappearing from sight. He looks ill, he might even be a kidnap victim as well. The door closes with a thud. She tosses the blanket onto the bed and stands with her hands on her hips. She switches the microphone's audio feed on. A hiss of sound is replaced by soft moans of pleasure. She quickly disconnects, a slight tremor of arousal causing her to shiver. She shakes her head and sits at the edge of the bed. Her eyes close and she breathes deeply. She then accesses her head computer and quickly compiles a file of all the recordings and information that she's gathered so far. She crosses to her cargo pants and pulls a thin fiber optic cable from the side pocket. One end of the cable is plugged in the port concealed in her left arm-pit; she then plugs the other end into the port in her temple. Three seconds later and the transfer is complete. She returns the cord to her pocket. She crosses to the bed and lies down on her back again. The ceiling is alive with dynamic graven images. She stares at them for a long time, her body and clothes slowly drying. She's drifting off, when she recalls the microphone and transfers her hearing over. The sound of walking boots fills her hearing. Then, a loud knock, it's at her door. She glances at her optical clock, more than an hour has passed.

She shakes her head then says, "Yeah, just one minute." She wraps the blanket around her body again, clamping it under her armpits and clasping it with one hand. The blanket slides along the floor as she crosses to the door and opens it a crack. As suspected Cassandra stands just beyond, she shoves the door towards Rebecca, who steps back quickly, nearly losing the blanket in the process.

"Come on, you're needed." Rebecca frowns then points to her drying vestments.

"My clothes are still wet, and needed for what?" Cassandra glances at the clothes then shrugs.

"Arguss wants you there, you can go like that, you can go naked or you can go in wet clothes, it doesn't matter to me." She then shifts and stands in a posture that says she's not leaving until the decision is made. Rebecca sighs.

"Fine, give me a minute." Cassandra raises an eyebrow then looks down at her body wrapped in the blanket.

"You have thirty seconds." She then turns and leaves the room, the door slamming shut behind her. *Bitch*, she thinks, *shit, that thing did heal my hand, but what does it want now?* She looks over at the flower, arcs of light and color play across the petals. She takes a deep breath then looks back at the dripping clothes.

A squelching comes from her shoes. Wet fabric clings and chills. The winding stone path dips and climbs, turning to stairs a few times and tall bridges during other times. The garden soon sticks out, an enormous pillar ringed in paths and doorways. The top of the pillar houses a space that looks like a small forest. A crown of light prevails over the area, let in by a ring of windows in the ceiling. They continue, entering a doorway in the pillar's side. The inside is belted in staircases, a mass of mineralized roots hang throughout the center, coming to rest a foot above the ground. A slow dribble of water runs down the roots, eventually collecting in a puddle, which in turn drains off to somewhere. She begins to record with her cybereyes video camera again. *If I escape, I'll be able to do an Eternal Flux exposé as well as reporting on that Abyssal mess,* she thinks, *Too bad I missed the action with Grimmfang, the chief would've loved that.* They enter a staircase and begin to scale the steps. They spiral up and eventually emerge into a carefully tended garden. They then step into a winding path of trees twined with bushes and flowers, vines meander up the walls and exotic ferns conspire in the dark corners.

"Through there." Cassandra points to a rough grass path. They move between the rows of vegetation and arrive at a small clearing marked by a bewildering statue, a sort of totem pole featuring four large heads. The faces seem to be shifting subtly; their eyes are following her movements. She looks around. The group is standing nearby. Arguss is sitting just to the left of the statue. He smiles and spreads his two topmost arms, a small bed of posies erupt around him.

"Ah, welcome Rebecca. I am sorry for your wet clothes; if you wish to remove them I can dry them in a flash," he says, oblivious to the obvious issue with that statement.

Kane interjects, "Woo, yeah, take it off baby." Arguss glances over, puzzled. She holds up a hand.

"Maybe later, thanks." He shrugs and motions for her to step closer. She obliges. Arguss looks to Rex who is casually gnawing at some small animal carcass. Rex looks up and stares at her intently. She shifts uncomfortably. The silence stretches on. Kane's voice breaks the stillness.

"We got laid, it was awesome." Xan slaps his forehead. Cassandra blushes and looks away. The rest of the group begins laughing. She grins and looks at the ground, recalling the sounds. Rex abruptly stands. He then looks at Arguss, surprised.

"Ah, now you see it, don't you? Chaos has drawn her into the web for a reason." Rex nods slowly, she looks between them.

"What are you talking about?" Arguss laughs, a booming sound that makes the flora jitter and dance. Rex then stares at her chest. She covers her breasts. He laughs and sits on his haunches, staring at her chest. She looks down, a silver glint flashes in her eye. She grabs the medallion.

"This? I just got this in 'Reacher's Hope' the other day; some Goblin was hawking it on the street." Rex laughs, she twitches. He looks at Arguss who in turn looks at her.

He smiles and says, "You have no idea what it is that you possess there. It is a rare token indeed, a ticket of sorts." She holds it up and looks at it. The serpent like demi-god is moving its short clawed limbs, the body is writhing erratically. She looks back towards Arguss.

"What do you mean a ticket? Granting access to what?" Arguss smiles, the posies shimmy.

"Not a what, a where, the cloud temple of the Ouroboros." She blinks a few times. A silence covers the group.

Then Xan says, "Please Rebecca, we've been speaking with Arguss, and the Ouroboros may be the only one powerful enough to help Eric. Give him the medallion and we'll offer you fair recompense."

She thinks for a second, then meets Xan's gaze and says, "Alright, we can talk about that. But first, we're going to discuss this whole psychic memory erasing thing." The group goes quiet again. Xan swallows and looks to Cassandra, she shifts her eyes back and forth as if to say, "What do you want from me?"

Then Kane laughs loudly and says, "Awkward !..."

Eric Gibson

I know that I should be paying attention. Xan and that Rebecca woman are arguing about the mind erasing thing, Arguss is mediating. I know that I should be listening, but I can't focus, the afterthought of the magic, her. I look over at Dancer. She's lounging on the grass, flippantly ravishing. The memory of our kiss invades. Damn that Cable and his timing, if we'd just been left alone ... Wait, Arguss is looking at me, something was said. Xan, Cassandra and Rebecca are looking too, Eve is reclining and Cable's smoking a cigar or something. I can't see Rex. Silver Dancer looks concerned, she smiles sadly.

"Sorry, what?" I mumble.

Xan grins, Kane speaks up, "He was daydreaming about boobs! Don't worry kid, it happens to me all the time." I shake my head and look at the grass. Arguss motions and hundreds of small white flowers bloom in front of me. They slowly grow into a pattern. It begins to look like clouds, all sculpted around a huge temple complex. As I watch the furthest reaches of the "cloud field" grow tall and fold over, creating a cave-like structure.

"This is your destination; none of us here can accompany you there. The token shall grant you access but chaos alone shall dictate the terms of your visit. The Ouroboros shall decide, based on its unfathomable nature." I swallow and look around, my heart begins to race. Silver Dancer smiles and grabs my hand, my heart begins to race in a different way.

"Don't worry Eric. We've worked out a way for you to get back here," she says. I smile at her, lost in the moment.

Xan holds up a small glass phial and says, "Once you're there, if you should need extraction, just snap this tube in half, it'll send a pulse to Dancer and we'll teleport you out. We'll also automatically teleport you out if three days pass and we haven't heard from you." Arguss nods then opens one of his large palms, producing a smooth black stone that features a single intricate rune. The arm stretches towards me and he places the stone on the bed of flowers. The thick stalks of the tiny temple support its weight.

Arguss then motions to the stone and says, "Make sure to keep this stone on your person, and I shall be able to transport you from any locale within this realm." I nod and grab the stone with my free hand. Dancer lets go of my other hand and leans back. Xan walks over and offers me the small glass phial, a tiny microchip runs through its core. I grab it carefully and put it in a top vest pouch. I clear my throat and pocket the stone.

"Umm, so what does this thing look like?" I ask, not being able to think of any other relevant questions. Xan tilts his head in a speechless gesture. Cassandra looks at him and shrugs. Then Rebecca walks closer. She knows about my situation now, Xan had to spill the beans. Arguss said something about making sure that he kept his promise to her, the large Asura seemed very serious on the matter, something about 'the sacred ground we now tread'. Rebecca holds out a chain, a small medallion dangles from the center. A silvery snake like thing is twisting around and shifting, it has four stubby limbs that are clawing the air. Rebecca motions to the medallion.

"It looks like that, only infinitely larger." I swallow, my pulse quickens again. She adds, "Take it, part of the deal." She then looks at Xan. As I pocket the medallion a sudden hammer of pain smashes into my head. I try to ride it out but it's too great. I scream and shudder. Voices come from all around, comforting hands on my back. Another lightning bolt splits my skull. My vision displaces to the right. A searing image of the sun roiling and flowing at my core replaces my sight. I'm on my back, I hear a voice. It's close now.

"... Eric! Eric! Speak to me ..." An angelic face hovers above me, silver eyes, silver hair. My head quivers with spasms of anguish. I open my mouth but nothing comes out. "Help him! Please, Arguss." My vision fades through reams of pain. I can only see the sun, irradiating an orb at my core. I try to move but I'm instead met by a memory. The old house comes to mind, my BMX and slingshot as constant accessories. We would charge through the "monkey trails" as fast as we could, Jordan was always way faster, better aim with the slingshot too. I remember when we shot at those birds near my neighbor's house. I missed and hit the window sill. The owner chased me for three blocks. She found me hiding under a car, Jordan got away of course. I thought I was being clever, hiding there. A warm cocoon wraps around me. I smell a garden and something even more striking. I open my eyes to the second best scenario that I could've imagined; Silver Dancer is gazing down at me. The very best of course would be exactly the same sans clothes and group of peculiar onlookers. I smile at her, she smiles back. "Eric, can you hear me?"

I grumble out a "Yeah" then slowly prop myself up on my elbows.

Arguss motions towards me, then, he suddenly looks upwards and says, "To the ready, a herald of war approaches." Everyone starts reacting, drawing weapons and moving to cover. Rex bursts from the ground and moves near the statue. Arguss ushers Rebecca behind him. Silver Dancer grabs my arm and pulls me, stumbling, over to a tree. A blur of movement comes from above us, then a gust of rushing air. I look to the center of the clearing. A man is standing in front of the totem, he's wearing strange armor. No, wait; he's not a man at all. The body is that of a man but the head is that of a large eagle. He's carrying a long staff with a banner attached to the end. The banner is flowing without the help of any wind. A picture of four complex circles arrayed around a cruel bird face adorns the red silk. The bird man looks around frenetically.

He raises the banner and says, "I, Grossuk Aether'Ar'Norru act as harbinger of the 'Blood Wind Talon' clan, I announce our intent of pillage or warfare. We have but one pillage request." He points a talon tipped finger at me. My heart begins to race. I grip my pistol, submachine gun out of ammunition. Dancer glares at the bird man, she looks scared. My heart's hammering away in my chest. A rage fills my stomach. That bastard! I'm not some piece of property. He can't go around scaring people like that.

My voice erupts on its own, "Why don't you pillage my balls you giant turkey!"

Kane laughs energetically, Rex lets out a single bark of a laugh then says, "You see Grossuk, do you see what true courage looks like?" The Asura known as Grossuk turns towards Rex, disdain etched across his prideful features.

"Do not presume to lecture me, oath-breaker, your notion of courage holds no interest for me." Rex laughs and paces to the left, Grossuk mirrors his movements.

Rex snorts then says, "Tell me Grossuk, do you eat the flesh of Humans now? As your brethren do, your precious clan." Grossuk laughs, then waves a hand at the group fanned out around the clearing.

"It's no different than eating deer or rabbit or quail, doomed things, so far beneath us that their sentience is nothing more than a small candle in a hurricane. The chaos of eternity rages on with or without them." He then looks around the clearing and adds, "Now, you have our terms, we shall give you one hour to reply." Rex growls, his body tenses.

"I shall give you my answer right now Grossuk." He's about to act when a thunderous voice shakes the mountain, flowers sink beneath the ground. The trees snarl.

"There shall be no violence in this place!" Arguss had been listening quietly. His loud interjection brings the sobering reality of the situation. I hadn't noticed before for some reason, maybe because he was so nice, but Arguss could tear off all of our limbs and play a little ditty on our skulls without much effort at all really. He has those crazy arms, plus his magic. Rex stops, looks to Arguss, then bows. Grossuk sheathes a small knife. Arguss then turns towards Grossuk.

"Go now, vulture of misery, tell your masters that their petition is folly. The boy shall soon be out of all of our grasps and all that they shall find here is a land alive with wrath, do not mistake me Grossuk. The artist is but one facet of my gem. I am not a part of your system of clans, but that does not mean that I do not have friends." Grossuk looks back and forth rapidly; he then stops on me, staring intently. A chill travels up my spine, his eyes are dead. Cable speaks from behind the cover of a large tree.

"Don't even think about it turkey boy, you better believe that I've got a rune fused in this sucker." He motions to the machine pistol aimed squarely at Grossuk's head. Arguss glares at Cable but he doesn't seem to notice. Grossuk steps back and hoists the banner.

"You'll regret this Arguss, we'll make a glorious feast of your 'friends' yet." The Asura then floats for a second before he flies up and out through a large window in the ceiling. Arguss watches him leave then looks around.

"Do not fret, they shall not attack, it was merely a bluff. They know that the land here is too strong for them. They would have to descend from their lofty perches in order to assail us, and they would be crushed." Rex nods then looks at me.

"I do not wish to put undue pressure upon you Eric but we must perform this task quickly now, Arguss is likely correct in his observation, but if not, it would behoove us to send you to a place where they couldn't possibly follow. It would also appear that the power is beginning to exert itself against the walls of your vessel." Arguss nods grimly. I look at both of them in turn, then nod and try to slow my breathing. I have to leave everybody again. I have to leave her. We walk back to the clearing as the others reassemble. Dancer grabs my hand then turns and hugs me. I want it to last forever; it's more like five seconds, which is still awesome.

She smiles and says, "Be careful Eric, I'll be listening, the very second you send that pulse I'll tell Arguss, so don't worry alright?" I nod.

"Thanks, you be careful too, that turkey actually looked kind of dangerous." She laughs. A trill of electricity travels through my spine. She then winks and motions to the group.

"I'll be fine, I'm in good company." I nod then look at Xan and the others.

"Thanks guys, I mean, if I don't see any of you again." They're quiet for a moment.

Then Kane says, "Well shit kid. Now I'm getting all misty, get out of here will you, before we change our minds." I smile. A shiver of sadness passes through my face. Arguss approaches, he points to my pocket.

"All you need to do is hold the medallion aloft and say: Accept the eternal circle as my fare." I nod and take the medallion out of my pocket; low waves of adrenalin assault me as I stare at the small circle. I cast a glance through the group, finally coming to a rest in Silver Dancer's eyes.

My heart does a flip-flop and I say, "I love you!" Then quickly add; "Accept the eternal circle as my fare!" A fleeting impression of her smiling face is instantly replaced with absolute nothingness.

The hall is enormous and opulent beyond belief. Dark blurs rush towards me, a dozen or more. I step back and keep my hand away from the gun. The medallion still dangles from my other hand. The blurs skid to a stop around me, talons scraping against decorated tile. A shot of adrenalin is followed immediately by a sinking sensation in the pit of my stomach. Bird men, just like that Grossuk guy. They're wearing fancy armor; it almost looks medieval but different in some alien way. There are a variety of colors of plumage amongst them. A few have noticeable scars on their faces and beaks. A large black-plumed Asura approaches and looks at the medallion, then to me. I try to calm myself, with little success. He stares at me, large eyes with dark corneas; they shine with a ruthless glint.

"Explain yourself Human, how is it that you came across one of the lost tokens of the eternal Ouroboros." He makes a complex circular sign with his clawed hand as he says the name, the others replicate the action. I swallow hard and muster all of my nerve. Just remember the magic. I still have that metal bar.

I straighten my back and look the Asura in the eyes, "Someone that I just met bought it from a Goblin who was hawking it on the street. She gave it to me as part of a deal so that a group of other people that I just met wouldn't erase her memory." I stop and take a breath. The black-plumed Asura blinks, tilts his head then lets out a long laugh. The others join in. It doesn't sound quite as hideous as Rex, but it's close.

He stops laughing then looks at the medallion again and says, "Ah, grand wheel of chaos, may it ever spin as such." He bows solemnly and the others follow suit. He then adds, "You may proceed at your own discretion, however, be forewarned, the Ouroboros does not suffer fools lightly." He then motions towards the far end of the hall where a massive set of white and silver gates stand. I swallow and nod.

"Thanks, do I give this to you?" I ask, holding out the medallion. He grins and shakes his head. He then points towards the gates.

"There is a statue, you can't miss it. Good fortune to you traveller, may the Ouroboros be in a *gentle* mood." He then bows and makes the circle gesture. The group drifts upwards. I follow their path with my eyes. There's a whole collection of open rooms and bridges, it goes up for a long ways, maybe a couple of hundred feet. I stand for a few seconds, staring in wonder. The low babble of hushed voices percolates all around. I glance at a pillar, it looks like it's sculpted out of intricately patterned clouds, it even seems to billow and move like a real cloud. I look back towards the gates and begin walking.

I wonder what mom and dad are up to, I miss them. But, now, I don't know. I can feel the magic, I think. It's not just the sun at my core. When I healed Silver Dancer and Cassandra it just seemed so natural. Like when a drawing comes together, no real effort, just a certain feeling, like it will all work out somehow. I don't want to give up the chance to learn more about it, even if it means never seeing my family or friends again. Then there's her, I do actually love her. I'd do anything for her. I know it hasn't been long, but still.

I'm jolted from my thoughts as a giant form lands on the floor in front of me, and my heart leaps into my throat. Fuck! Strange electricity fills the air. I stare at it, terror rising. It's way different than the other things here. It's like thirty feet tall, humanoid but it has the features of a dog and a lizard or something. It has white shining scales. Two short black horns decorate its brow and a topknot of coarse hair sprouts from its scalp. Long whiskers droop down past its chin and its tail is reptilian, clawed multi-jointed legs support its bulk. It's dressed in armor like the others and its eyes are like Rex's, only magnified and more intense. A flood of adrenalin hits me as it speaks, its voice could kill a frail poodle.

"Fear shall not armor you here small mortal, instead, cloak yourself in your desires. The notion of the loss of them shall act as the fuel for the furnace of your courage." I breathe deeply and think about Silver Dancer. My heart slows. A meaningful determination fills my stomach. I nod and look up at the Asura.

"Do you know the way to the Ouroboros' cave?"

He grins, mouthful of machetes, "An answer already given, brave one." He then tilts his massive head, topknot swaying slightly as he does. He reaches into the pouch on his belt. "The winds of entropy compel me, here, a gift given to mark our chance encounter." He motions and a small object floats towards me, a dagger in a sheath. It looks really intricate; a likeness of the massive Asura adorns the pommel. I unsheathe it, the blade swims, it looks kind of like Xan's sword. I smile and look up.

"Thanks." He nods.

"Chaos needs no thanks; it is merely the tune that we all dance to. Wear it on your belt and they shall not trifle with you." He then stands to the side, revealing the gate, and continues, "Know this, mortal; once you pass through the archway there is no coming back." He then winks and disappears utterly, like Rex. I look around, the strange electrical feeling lifts. I look at the dagger again. Even the sheath is badass. It's shaped like the Ouroboros formed into a cone. The blade slides into the open mouth. I smile and look at the door. I immediately frown. Right, I've got to go outside, shit. I quickly fasten the dagger to my vest's belt, displaying it prominently on my left hip.

I move forward, the gates rise up in front of me. An arrangement of runes runs down the center of each side, besides that they're totally seamless. I look to the right side. A coiled statue of the Ouroboros crouches next to the gates, its body formed into a circle and its mouth pointing up. The statue's tail rests just beneath the mouth. I approach. Its scales are sparkling white. I look closer. They're edged in diamonds. Holy shit, that statue is worth very many fortunes. It looks like it's made from the same metal as Devlin's bar. They told me it was platinum, if that's the case it's worth all of the fortunes in the world. I walk closer and gaze at it for a while. The open mouth is hollow, the throat is too. I retrieve the medallion then open the clasp on the chain. The circle slides out and I pocket the chain. Here goes nothing. I flip the medallion into the mouth. A series of metallic clicks come from the opening. The statue's mouth closes smoothly, much to my surprise. It then uncoils and moves mechanically to the gate. It climbs the center of the gate and positions itself between the sets of runes. I'm suddenly aware of a presence above me. I twist up and look around. A huge host is gathered, most of them are the bird-headed Asura, but there are others as well. I can see large crane-like humanoids dressed in fine robes, and cruel vulture faced giants, with large bushy wings and terrible claws. There are also Elf-looking creatures with upward flowing hair and long tapered ears. While a two-foot tall cat-faced Asura stands alone, dressed in a flashy pinstripe suit. Its eyes are made of lightning. I turn back in time to see the statue stretch out fully and clasp the door with its four short limbs. The statue then splits in half, lengthwise, down the middle. The gate splits with the statue and swings out, a blinding glare causes me to shade my eyes. A mantra begins to ripple through the crowd. They are chanting in unison now, acoustics transforming the sound into a deep drone. My eyes adjust and I blink a few times. Clouds, all I can see are clouds. They're stretching out from the temple steps. What am I supposed to do? The mantra continues. The doors begin to slowly shut again. Shit, it's now or never. I run forward, turning sideways to fit through the closing doors. The droning is cut off by the sinister clank of the gates slamming shut.

I look around at a world of clouds, white clouds mostly. I look back at the temple, it's gigantic. It's like a dozen of those huge megastores from back home all stacked on top of each other. The temple is totally surrounded by clouds, is it flying? It almost seems like the temple stairs lead to a path, and, something else. It's a wooden archway, built into the clouds? That must be what that giant Asura was talking about. I slowly move down the steps. The base of the staircase is framed in a pair of stone statues that look like Rex. I can see the clouds lapping at the steps, almost like water. I take the pendant chain from my pocket and toss it into the clouds. The links strike the cloud then settle in a fluffy chasm, only slightly buried. What is happening here? I put a leg out and arc my foot down, it feels like stepping on sand. I put more weight on the foot, the cloud shifts a small amount but it seems to support my weight. I take another step and laugh. I'm standing on clouds; they're all around too, like sand dunes. I continue up the path a short ways. The wooden archway impresses itself on the scene. It's massive as well, like a hundred feet tall. The pillars are covered in rings of writing, they're accented with shining metal and sculpted figures. I hold my breath and pass beneath the archway, then look back. A moment of shock greets me, there's nothing but clouds. No archway, no temple, just clouds. I walk back, still nothing, just more clouds. I swallow and look down. A pile of white cotton slowly drifts around my feet. I guess I'll just keep going down the path then. That giant dude was right, though that shouldn't be surprising. He seemed like he was on the ball, or like a god or something. I don't even know anymore. A short pang of pain strikes my head. I grab it with both hands, no, not now. I stop and close my eyes, trying to breathe through the sensation. A few short jabs poke into my brain but then it subsides. I open my eyes again to a vast desert of clouds. Miles above me an enormous arm of matter drifts lazily along. This whole place is crazy, always changing, it's light and dark at random times depending on if you're facing one of the suns or not. Silver Dancer said that instead of planets and solar systems they just have drifting land masses, everything's flying one way or another. Bouncing off each other, or ringing a sun for a time before moving on. Without Rex we probably would have been killed by the sudden appearance of a mountain or a river. Or died, trapped in an endless field of clouds. I tap my vest's pouch reassuringly.

I walk on for some time. My legs begin to ache with the strain, just like walking on sand. I round a bend in the clouds and stop. Just a few miles up the path sits an all-encompassing thunderhead, a black and purple mushroom flickering with arcs of lightning. I watch it for a second. The wind is blowing across the path; it looks like the huge cloud is gradually moving to my left. I wait, it seems like getting any closer would be very foolish. The cloud continues to move. A thunderclap makes me jump. My whole body shakes, it's insanely loud when it's this close. Another lightning strike brings more ear-splitting thunder. I start giggling

348

uncontrollably. I don't know why. The clouds are shocked ultra-white as another bolt lances out, thunder rattles my teeth and I laugh again. It's like a case of "the giggles" put through an amplifier. I can't stop my face from smiling, gales of laughter spilling from my mouth. I grab my sides and look towards the thunderhead, several hundred feet from the path now and still a few miles away. As I'm looking, a circle appears in the middle of the cloud, a white circle, it's casting off electricity. The cloud then comes alive, exploding with dozens of lightning bolts. A pressure wave of sound strikes me and takes my breath away, my head bounces around as my vision blurs. I find myself sitting down. I stop laughing. I can see the source of the explosion. It looks like something is fluttering in front of the dark cloud; almost like a sparkling white scarf caught in a breeze. Then it begins moving, purposefully. It's flying at me. I stand, then stumble back a few feet. It's getting bigger, so much bigger. It's fast too. It's *so* much faster than me. There's no way I can escape it. A sense of dread grips me and I stand, stalk still. Then, a scale covered skyscraper drops down in front of me, and I find myself airborne. The landing is relatively soft, like falling into a snow bank. I dig myself out. I get clear of the clouds and instinctively freeze, breathe low and stare with naked fear. Its head turns towards me, pearlescent scales shimmer. Long whiskers jut down from its upper lip and an animated mane of silver hair flows up from its head and neck. I can't look way, it's utterly captivating. It opens its mouth; tree-sized teeth gleam within. A creeping horror travels through my whole body. My limbs stop listening to my brain, I'm petrified. I can't do a thing. I stare into its eye, like that giant Asura's, only infinitely more complex somehow. It speaks, except the sound comes from the very molecules of the air.

"I have long awaited you, traveller
Since ages before seething tides of chaos
Since time was unbound by structure or name
An ever present vision of the sun
Encased and brought by one unseen to me
Assurance of the entropic garden
The fuel for the great wheel of chaos

Nourishment for the realm that you now see"

I blink a few times then pinch myself. I guess I'm awake, or something. I clear my throat.

"Right, so I don't know what any of that means, but, you did say something about the sun, does that mean that you can help me?" The Ouroboros laughs. I pass out.

I sit up through a muddled haze. Clouds, they're all around. Is this some renaissance painter's vision of heaven? Then I glance to my left, building-sized demi-god; check. I swallow and sit up. It smiles then says;

"Apologies, I did not mean to wound

My actions are not designed to aid you

But I shall acquire the sun from your core"

I slowly nod, my heart doing its best tap dance routine.

"What happens to me?" It tilts its head as if it were looking through me. The words come from everywhere.

"A rare thing, to be born outside my sight

You shall live once I extract the power

Beyond that, I cannot say for certain

You are in the tangle of a new web"

Memories of back home crash into my thoughts; fast food, T.V., no "crazy shit everywhere". Then I recall my folks, Jordan, Matt, Mike and Jenny.

"So I can't get back?" The colossal Asura flexes its whiskers and speaks.

"I do not see a path for you at all

But nothing is a certainty, is it?

You should know that all too well by this time

If you are ready, I shall proceed now."

I nod and look down at the cloud. The Ouroboros stands, scales shining with startling hues. It breathes out and bathes me in a sweet smelling gust of wind. Then, it inhales and I jerk forward slightly before steadying myself. Suddenly it feels like a thousand knives of fire are stabbing me in the heart. I collapse and gasp for breath, nothing comes, panic mounts. Dots and static appear before my eyes. My head feels numb, mortal terror grips me and I pass out again.

It's so comfortable. It feels like I'm sleeping on a cloud. I blink and look down. I laugh. Clouds, of course, I'm still here. Now I remember. I search around and find the same scene as before, minus one building-sized Asura. I breathe deeply and grab my stomach. I feel a hundred times better, like I just threw up after drinking too much. I stand and search through my pockets. Rock, check; I reach into the chest pouch. Phial, check; alright, let's do this. I put the rock in my pocket and snap the phial in half. It creates a tiny spark and I sit down to wait. My mind drifts back home again. I really hope that they get over my leaving, or, better still, maybe in their reality I never left. Maybe some version of me is still there, oblivious to all of this. That would be cool. Shit, I should've tried to remember what the Ouroboros said. They're probably going to be curious. Yeah, it's totally gone, like a dream. That's weird; I can barely remember what it looked like. It was really big, I remember that much. It was kind of like the pendant, I think. I glance around. Something catches my eye, then, nothingness, followed immediately by the sight of Silver Dancer in the garden. The others blend into the background as she runs to me and kisses me hard on the lips. It lasts for at least five seconds. I feel my face flush and a crooked smile covers my lips.

Then Kane's voice, "Aw man, are you kidding me? I've been barking up that tree for years and he goes and makes out with it? I hope you get splinters!"

Silver Dancer and I turn towards him and say, "Shut up Kane" nearly in unison. Xan laughs, the others join in. Arguss then speaks.

"I sense that a weight has lifted from you, I am overjoyed that he could help you Eric. I also see that chaos has chosen to gift you with a rare prize." I smile and look through the group then nod.

"It's true, scariest thing I've ever seen, I think ... but yeah, I'm feeling way better." Then I motion to my side and add, "Yeah, you mean this?" I turn and show the dagger to the group. Eve whistles and Xan gives an approving nod.

Rex grins and announces, "A wonderful turn, I had feared for the outcome but it feels as though a great deed has been accomplished here today." I nod then laugh. Silver Dancer joins in, the sound is musical. Arguss claps all three sets of hands together.

"A celebration then, I shall have the earth serve us, come, let us relax and be merry." He motions towards the center of the clearing. A stone table rises from the earth; stump chairs sprout up along either side. A ghostly orchestra drifts into the forest and begins to play. They're either spirits or illusions, it doesn't matter the music is wonderful. I grin and look around. A relaxed ease travels through the group. Even Rebecca seems happy. The music continues and eventually we're served drinks and aromatic foods. The waiters are small humanoid clumps of earth. They don't have legs instead they're sprouting directly from the ground and gliding through the grass. We eat and talk. I even tell a story from back home, about getting baked and falling into the pond. Silver Dancer and Cable laugh the hardest. I end up speaking with Rebecca for a long while. She asks all sorts of questions, mainly about back home.

A sudden darkness brings calming twilight, and the hours tick by. I guess that Grossuk guy never came back. Arguss said that the whole realm knows that the Ouroboros saw me, though I don't know what that means exactly, he said that they won't bother me now. Xan looks over the gathering at the table, Rex and Arguss are speaking quietly near the statue. He then stands on shaky legs. I only had a couple of drinks, still not sure how I'd react after everything.

Xan then announces, "Alright, we're heading to bed. Tomorrow we're going to the Changeless City bright and early, so, right, anyway. Good job everyone and good night, good night." Xan and Cassandra head towards the staircase as Kane's voice interjects.

"Hopefully a great night, if you know what I mean? Tell me if you want him sober..." The rest is lost as they move out of earshot. Rebecca is next to depart, waving at each of us in turn and saying goodnight. I stand and look at the group.

"I'm beat too, time for bed."

Cable raises a mug and Eve says, "Good night." Silver Dancer stands and moves with me to the grass trail. My temples throb with my pulse, among other places. She takes my hands and we kiss, for a long time, standing in the winding garden path.

We part and she steps back then says, "Good night Eric, sweet dreams." She then winks and turns back towards the table. My eyes follow that perfect ass for as long as she stays in view. I sigh, alright righty, let's go to sleep. Who knows what's going to happen tomorrow.

The ten foot tall frog-man frowns at Rex and croaks, "Asura gold only, now buzz, I have other customers." Rex sighs and turns the redwood chest strapped to his flank towards me. He then looks back over his shoulder, a giant flame covered lizard-man walks past behind him.

"Eric, if you please, it is unlocked. Give him twenty gold pieces then grab our lunch." I nod. The smell of smoked meat mingles with a cavalcade of other scents, most of which are wholly foreign. I count out twenty of the heavy coins then slap them up on the high counter. The large frog-man looks at the pile closely, then nods and unhooks a dozen of the smoked carcasses. They appear to be deboned rabbits or something. I hook six of them in each hand. Rex begins to walk back. I turn towards the crowd and inadvertently begin to dawdle. The initial shock wore off a little while ago. Now all I can do is stare with a quiet fascination. It's such a bizarre collection of creatures. I see massive crab-like things chattering with foot-tall toad creatures. A shaggy beast lumbers by, an actual bird's nest embedded in its fur, and mice swarming all over its huge body. I turn my head. A twelve foot tall giant with three melded faces spews fire as hair; each of its four limbs matches the sabers lining its belt. We stop as a pair of spectral horses pulls an elaborate chariot; its driver is a humanoid tortoise as tall as me.

We continue on through the city. Rex said that it's actually an island floating above a lake of magma that continually pushes out against a huge ocean. I can actually see small chunks of stone floating up in the distance, the cooling lava forming up and breaking off through some peculiar arcane process. The city itself is so wondrous it doesn't seem real. The architecture, sculptures and frescos are all appallingly beautiful. Fragrant gardens float above, attached to stone stairs which moor them to the ground. Rex pointed out a number of clan houses with unpronounceable names. Each house is a massive, multi-tiered castle-like structure featuring its own unique colors and configuration. I guess the clans have some kind of influence around here. Arguss sent us to some part of the city where Rex's old clan doesn't have a presence. He said it might be really bad if he got spotted by them. We finally arrive back at the floating park where the others are waiting. He climbs the steps and I follow, soon the green space surrounds us. A number of small trees create a semi-circle at the far side. The group is sitting around a sort of stone picnic table. Xan is peering over the edge towards the building, if you could call it that. I mean it's actually a tree, but it's grown into a building. Complete with round windows and a balcony high up in the huge branches. Rex looks to Xan as I present the bundles of meat.

"The messenger has not come yet?"

Xan shakes his head then looks over and says, "Shit. That smells good." Silver Dancer grins as I offer her the first choice. She grabs one of the spitted critters and dives in. She nods and closes her eyes.

"Mmm, damn, that *is* good." Rex laughs and snatches one of the spits from my hand. He mutters through clenched teeth.

"Oh yes, 'Rhanid' always have the very best smoked meats, pricey, but it's worth it." The rest of the group begins to eat and soon nods of approval are coming from all around. I take a bite and instantly concur; it's so tender that you could drink it with a straw. As I'm eating it dawns on me that I'm going to have check out a bunch of different restaurants when we get back to the city. I grin and look at Silver Dancer. I wonder if dating is the same as back home. We could check them out together.

The food is soon devoured and we return to the waiting. Apparently this "Magzar" is a very busy magician of some sort or another. We've been here for the better part of the day already. Rex moves and sits near the edge.

He looks back and says, "Ah, here we are. I can see that the messenger is on his way now." Sure enough a few seconds later a small humanoid made of earth rises up from the middle of the island garden; it places a single white stone on the ground then departs. "Come, we do not want to lose our place in line." The gear is gathered and we descend. The tree building isn't far, just up a side street. A group of humanoid creatures flies past, clothes flapping in the wind. As we approach the building it becomes apparent that it's made out of many trees all twisted and formed around each other. A tangle of roots sinks into the ground as Rex steps close. A small waiting room is revealed just beyond. Rex enters, followed by Xan, Cassandra and Cable, then Eve and Rebecca. I move into the area with Silver Dancer. It looks like a typical high-class waiting room, except everything is either made out of roots, or it's a small tree in and of itself. Come to think of it the receptionist is a tree too. I blink a few times, becoming less and less startled each time a new crazy thing occurs. The tree smiles at us, its voice sounds like the creaking of thick branches.

"Greetings again Rex, Magzar shall see you and your group now." Rex bows and looks towards the group.

"This way." He then walks past the reception "log" and begins to surmount a spiral staircase. The group follows, gear and weapons ported between the designated pairs. The stairs lead to a floor containing a large wooden table that sprouts from the ground like a tree stump. The edges of the room have a number of chests of drawers, there's a large box of sand taking up one corner. Rex stops near the table, turns to his right and bows low. "Magzar, it was good of you to see us. The payment has been made. Silver Dancer, if you could bring over the images of 'The Castle'?" I furrow my brow and look around. Who's he talking to? Silver Dancer walks to him, producing a small palm display as she does. Then I see him. I almost burst out laughing. I would if it weren't for the reverence that Rex is paying him. This Magzar looks like a living teddy bear, maybe two feet tall. He doesn't seem to have a nose, shaggy fur covers his mouth and he has tiny black eyes. He's wearing an ornate purple robe. The little figure looks at the display as Silver Dancer shows him a series of images of "The Castle". Rex

355

nods all of a sudden and looks at the tiny Asura. "Yes, that's right." Magzar nods then waddles over to the sandbox. He motions towards it and the contents empty, as though the sand were made out of fabric. The sand swirls and flows onto the table. It begins to take shape, almost like a pyramid. The sand then settles and an intricate replica of the city appears, "The Tier". Silver Dancer showed me the holographic map, it's identical. Magzar then motions towards the far side of the room. A circle is etched in the floor there. Rex nods then moves into the circle and says, "Alright everyone, in the circle." The group moves to the space in turn. Rex nods at the diminutive Asura. I can see it make a series of motions then a brief nothing greets me, followed immediately by the incessant rush of the city. I look around, it's "The Castle's" courtyard. I laugh. Cable sighs, waves his remaining hand at nothing in particular then walks to the garden gateway. Eve begins to help Xan remove Devlin's body from Rex's back. The redwood chest is released as the counterweight. I sigh and look at the body. I really hope Grot can help. Shit, I'd really like to see Grot again now. I wonder what happened to him? Xan and Eve then disappear into the garage, emerging directly afterwards without the body. The redwood chest is stored next. They finish and Eve crosses to the bathhouse, waving as she goes. I wave back then look towards Xan. He and Cassandra are speaking with Rebecca in hushed tones. Rebecca then nods; Xan and Cassandra repeat the gesture, reluctantly. Rebecca then walks over to me.

"Well, I'm glad everything worked out Eric. I might see you around yet, it's a big city, but anything can happen." She walks towards the gate; they begin to open as she approaches. She turns back and adds, "Check out the news in the next couple of days, you might be surprised by what you see." She then winks and walks up the alley. I look back towards the courtyard. Rex begins to walk to the garden.

"A jaunty little trip, we should do this again sometime." He then laughs and disappears through the garden's archway. Xan laughs. Cassandra smiles at him and raises an eyebrow.

Xan then looks to me and says, "We'll just leave the gear here for now, get some rest Eric, we'll figure out our next move in the morning. If there are still interested parties, the trip to the flux will have thrown them off the trail for the time being." He then puts a hand under his chin and adds "I remember you mentioning something about magical testing, maybe we can look into that?" He then grins and puts his arm around Cassandra, they walk towards the garage. A laugh bubbles out of me. I have a feeling that this place is going to be alright.

Silver Dancer steps close. She takes me by the hand and says, "Come on, I want to show you my bedroom." My heart jumps. I suddenly get the feeling that this place is going to be amazing.

Moag

We smell you, short-sighted blue-scaled beast. Random sluggish interloper, soon we shall watch and laugh as you burn. It was tricky of you to flee to where we could not follow. But it was very stupid of you to return to your "castle". We have been waiting here, after visiting the pretty carnage near the church. We have been waiting patiently, even after our dark heart was destroyed. We shall find the culprits, their death shall be slow. They may have stolen the gem but it no longer matters for soon we shall use the "Black Hand". Soon the Eric Gibson shall be rent and burned. His spirit shall be imprisoned and scourged until all that he knows is wretchedness. We must prepare, this building shall do. It is the same apartment that we slew the two corporate slaves in, the corpses disappeared but their parent corporation has not returned. They no longer seek our quarry, some policy, it matters not. We shall claim the prize. We saw him with our own eyes. He was speaking with the Xanshudan in the courtyard. The Eric Gibson stays here. He sleeps with the *pretty* Elf. It shall not be long now. We must wait for the right time. It can only be used at the devil's hour, 12:00 lunar. Then we shall call forth the dread army of Ing'Tha. They shall not be able to stand before us. A hoard of living nightmares: Wailing Devils, Defilers, Filth Demons, Xilic and Hell Reapers, oh my! The pitiful scum shall taste the very worst of our blood dwoemers. Razor chains and showers of blades, we shall lift their skin off their bodies as one would remove a shroud. Soon, the masters shall be pleased. We shall beg and whimper and they shall not imprison us. They may even gift us with a present. Perhaps an Imp or a Hell Hound thrall, either would be useful. We could find infants much faster then. We could use the Hell Hound for "The Announcement". We remember where four infants are, some are in this area. We shall need twenty, after we build our new heart. We shall have to find another nightclub to influence, the one we had chosen may be wary of us now. It does not matter, there are many in the city. We shall have time after the slaughtering of Eric Gibson and these "Decided". One of their number did not return, instead some Dark Elf woman is staying with them. We saw the Xanshudan and her fucking, their blood heat comingling in the top of a tall tower. It matters not. They shall perish soon, as we carve the Eric Gibson from this "castles" grasp. The master shall come personally. He shall cleave them all with his burning blade. They cannot hope to survive. We shall surprise them, even as they sleep. Only the Asura shall pose a challenge, but we shall have powerful Blood Weavers with us. Their dwoemer shall make short work of him, or the master and his great cleaving blade. We can hardly wait. The festivities shall be grand. We move to the window and look towards the "castle". It can just be seen down the hill, two long blocks away. We do not need to be any closer right now. The army shall move swiftly and shock their defenses. We are charged with elation. What fun! We shall perpetuate a wonderful slaughter. The master shall flee with his prize but perchance others shall stay and the bloodshed could continue, then spread. Like the old days, the Infernal Wars, torture and mutilation on a large scale, the best days of our life. During the bloodbath we could snatch up infants as well, our greater kin providing a marvelous distraction. We dance and flip to the ceiling. Blackened brain matter clings to the white plaster. We laugh and look to the two guns on the table. Perhaps we shall be able to shoot one or two of the group. We shall certainly try. The Eric Gibson looked very insignificant. He shall be easily cowed. The master has ways of disabling a thing without breaking it completely. We shall now head to the dark basement. Our kill waits there and we hunger.

We open the door and move through the hall, nothing more than a shadow. The grimy carpet is patterned with vines and leaves flowing through a repeating pattern. We wish them to be intestines and tripe. We wish the carpet to be made of Human scalps. The basement is not far, it has a storage room, one pathetic little apartment and an empty laundry room, empty except for our kill. We move into the space. There on the floor, the boy, not young enough for "The Announcement", maybe six. We could save his blood for the next dark heart. But no, we are famished and the boy is still fresh. We killed him earlier today as he dawdled away from his family, our venom took hold quickly. It was then easy to throttle him and drag him here. Now we dine. Cheeks and legs, then throw out the dregs. He is skinny but there is enough meat.

We consume and leave a mangled carcass for the vermin of this place. Our belly is full and we pat it happily. We then twist off the boy's head and begin to peel the flesh from it, we shall eat the brains in a small while, and we shall have a skull to play with, soon. We scrape off most of the remaining flesh then roast it in the flames of Ing'Tha. Boil and bubble, get hot brain-drink for your trouble. We are satisfied. We shall shine and polish the skull as we wait for the devil's hour. Perhaps we shall occupy this "castle" for a time, decorate it in the bones of its former tenants. We sit in the basement with our new toy. This room pleases us now, with its dark concrete and fresh putrefaction. We shall stay here until it is time. Here we are hidden. We can easily ambush any who come using the clinging shadows, they shall not see us. We begin to polish the small skull using part of the boy's shirt. We surely hope that his parents suffer. We hope that they never know what happened to their offspring.

The wonderful smell of burnt flesh surrounds us as we peel away more bits from the skull. We look at the stolen display; its clock reads 11:50 lunar. We shall head to the roof in five minutes. That is where we shall finally use "The Black Hand of Setterack". That is where the master shall begin his conquest. We laugh and chatter the skull's jaw. We shall make a small puppet from it, to commemorate the day. We continue to clean the skull. Perhaps we shall see Mellick, if he still serves the master. That could be fun, if we find a small Human that we could torture together. We think again about the heart and stew angrily, reflecting on our stolen treasures. It is likely that they are gone. But we shall still have to check, if they have been taken we shall make the thief pay. We shall retrieve the platinum. It is our wealth. We need it to trade for the materials that we shall use in "The Announcement". The skull begins to become smooth. We shake out some brains, but we shall have to boil it for a while yet in order to clean it completely. We grin then check the clock, 11:54 lunar. A wave of excitement hits us as we stand. Oh such fun, they shall all suffer so greatly. Wait, we get the feeling of eyes at our back. Now a voice, it is soft, thickly accented and full of wrath ...

"So, darkness of life, Rat feared that Norman was tricking us, for what we had done to him in the past. We see now that he was telling friend Sneezeguts the truth." We spin and snarl, he continues, "You murdered some friends of ours darkness of life, and we are not pleased." A small Goblin stands in the doorway, he is dressed oddly. He sees us, even while we are shadow. We threaten him, screaming about his death and ruin. He smiles in a way that we do not like. He speaks, "Live, die, it's all the same really. But first you really should meet Rat's friends, they would be ever so glad to meet you." We scream and try to run. We cannot, a powerful dwoemer grips us. We do not see its design. The Goblin transforms. He is the specter of a large green rat. We scream and fight. He chants and a horrible sound begins. We rage and struggle, dread builds within us. Then they come. They stream in from the door and the cracks in the walls. Rats, of every type, everywhere, RATS!